At the
Crossroads of Swords

THE ENCROACHING CHAOS

Jeremiah Cain

VYLETRA LLC

vyletra.com

Published by Vyletra LLC, Mobile, AL
vyletra.com

At the Crossroads of Swords: The Encroaching Chaos / Jeremiah Cain.
Hardback ISBN: 978-1-964435-01-5
Paperback ISBN: 978-1-964435-00-8
Ebook ISBN: 978-1-7348024-9-8
LCCN: 2024910797

First printing June 2024

CONTENTS

The Immolation Brigade

Arctic Ocean
Davigan Empire
Bloody Belt
Tridulan Empire
Gellic Nat
Hyvile River
N
W
E
S
0
30
60
90
Miles

CHAPTER ONE

Duodeki 9, 812

Hail Zeanázel," he whispered. He touched the twisted tube of thin wood tipped with fire to the zenith of a black taper candle. The wick blazed. Next—his movements methodical—he touched another wick. And another. Finally, all six black candles burned as an evenly spaced semicircle. They stood in pewter bases coiled with pewter snakes, this atop a table draped in coarse black cloth. A smooth obsidian disc lay before them on the table.

Adratus shook the spill, extinguishing the flame, and paused. His eyes shifted beneath his thin black hood to the obsidian mirror. He took slow, measured breaths and cleared away all distractions as he watched the candlelight glint off the glossy black surface. The dismal lights radiated within the modest box of a room, their shadows undulating in darkness.

At his back and to either side, four plain beds were crammed against the unadorned plank walls. At their feet sat old black trunks. Ahead of him, beyond the table and candles, a wooden bench stood near the entrance, its red paint worn away by age. Beside it, thin lines of daylight edged the fastened door. Above the bench, a single window was shuttered tightly.

Adratus slid back his black hood, revealing hair trimmed to a uniform quarter of an inch above a slender, pale boyish face. His stern eyes—lined in black—stared unwaveringly into the obsidian mirror. Despite his age of sixteen years, he had shaved away the trivial traces of emerging facial hair, as regulations dictated.

Raising his hands above his lowered head, he watched the mirror. "Hail Zeanázel, Lord of Darkness and Defiance, God of Fire and the First Hue of light, he who teaches wisdom, he who teaches might, he who teaches reliance on ourselves. Show us the path of reason. Show us the path of will. Show us the path of glorious night."

Above the obsidian disc, a sphere of red light formed, with loops of lightning orbiting it slowly.

"Imbue this chamber with carnal energies, O God Zeanázel. Draw them forth from the south. Draw them forth from the east. Draw them forth—"

The door to the room swung open, flooding the area with blinding sunlight. A silhouette appeared in the doorway, backlit from outside. "Why do you trespass in my room?"

As his sight adjusted to the sudden brightness, Adratus made out the figure of a young man who was around three years his senior. He wore only a short damp towel low around his waist, leaving one leg exposed while bulging noticeably in the front. His dark brown skin gleamed with moisture and rippled over the lean muscles that were visible throughout his physique.

Adratus felt a jolt as he was pulled from his trance. Disoriented, as if awoken from sleep, he scanned the newcomer, starting at his bare feet and moving up the sensuous body to the glossy scalp. The desire that flooded Adratus left him breathless, unable to blink.

The red orb above the mirror dissolved, fading away.

"I asked why you are here," the older boy maintained with an angry scowl, his hands clenching into fists.

"Apologies," Adratus said, rubbing his forehead. "I am newly arrived and assigned to these quarters."

The older boy let out a low groan, and a portion of the tension seemed to leave him. He muttered under his breath, "By all that is infernal. Another roommate." Then he shut the door behind him. He commanded, "Lucerna, illuminate," as he began his way around the table and Adratus.

Centered from the ceiling—just above Adratus—three thin ropes hung to secure what appeared to be a slightly flattened terracotta teapot with three spouts arranged evenly around its circumference. At the older boy's command, the three spouts released pale smoke that swirled together and accumulated as an undulating mass above the lamp. This churning smoke glowed like warm embers amid flicking sparks, illuminating the room.

Ignoring the lamp, Adratus turned fully around to face his new companion, now visible in the wavering light. "I am Immunis Adratus," he said cordially.

"*Immunis?*" the other boy spat in annoyance. "You are no officer?" He neared a trunk at the foot of what was presumably his bed.

"No."

"'Tis too early for rituals, *Immunis*," the older boy said as he bent down and opened the trunk. "Even I know as much, though I am not religious." He pulled out a bright red tunic and shook it before standing up and tossing it onto the bed. "Such things are better suited for the night."

"True." Adratus stepped closer. "Yet, I thought it best done whilst alone. I thought that wouldn't be the case after nightfall."

Without facing Adratus, the other youth removed the towel and began drying himself.

"I—" Adratus quickly looked away toward the door, wishing to look back again. He swallowed before continuing. "I'm not religious either, but the army has found I possess an above-average level of spiritual energy."

"Pneuma. I know the word."

"Yes," Adratus said. "I have unusually high pneuma levels; thus, they train me as a Faldénrus." He stole another glance before looking away.

The older boy slipped the tunic over his head, letting it fall to hang just above his knees. "A Faldénrus? Interesting." He turned to face Adratus and laughed. "Have you come to arrest me?"

"No." Adratus returned the laughter. "No, I am part of a new program created by the Tridulan Army to see if Faldénri magic can be used to help our forces."

Relaxing visibly, the older youth replied, "Thus explains why you room with an optio."

"You're an optio?" Adratus snapped to attention, touching his fist to his chest as he bowed his head.

The optio flashed a dazzling grin, the sight of which made him even more attractive. "Apologies for my poor manners; I neglected introductions. For my first two years here, I had this room alone. Three months past, they assigned me a roommate. Now, a second stands before me. Still, I erred to be uncivil. I am Optio Maximus—second-in-command of Fourth Century, Fifth Cohort."

Adratus relaxed his stance. "Well met, Optio."

"Is your father of note?"

"Of note?" Adratus paused before responding. "He served the empire as a legionary before me. Now he works in the capital to construct magnificent buildings."

"An architect?"

"No, Optio—he's a mason."

"I see…" Maximus seemed troubled by the news and crossed his arms over his chest. "I share quarters with a *pleb*. Clearly, the Gods jest at my expense."

"Or at mine." Adratus bristled with annoyance as he removed his cloak, revealing a black, knee-length tunic belted by black leather. "Forcing me to bunk with a patrician." He tossed the cloak on his bed.

Maximus chuckled at the comment, and the grin on his handsome face won Adratus, despite himself. He smiled back in response.

"Are you long in the army, Adratus?" Maximus sat on his bed and grabbed a nearby pair of sandals.

"I was transported here straight from Nerageat."

"So, you're fresh from initial training?" Maximus crisscrossed the straps of his sandal up his calf.

Adratus nodded. "Yes, Optio. This is my first official assignment."

"Straightway here to the outermost edge of the civilized world." He fastened the second sandal. "Pray, who did young Adratus vex so in Nerageat for such a parlous station?"

"'Twas by request I came here, Optio. And, by skill; I earned my choice."

"Truly?" Maximus took a moment to look Adratus over before speaking again. "You're already fit for your age. Do you rely solely on magic, or can you swing a gladius?"

"Both, Optio."

Maximus flexed his right arm and patted his bicep with satisfaction. "I pride myself on my physical strength; 'tis said God Zeanázel favors those who are mighty of body."

"As I've heard."

"You are not far behind. I can train you if you wish."

Adratus gained a large grin. "Gratitude, Optio." He nodded curtly. "Your training would be well received."

"Very well, we shall begin next week. Yet for now . . ." He slapped his hard stomach through his red tunic. "Now, my belly cries out for food, which I must sate. Come, if you like."

—

The great dining hall rumbled with the sound of countless conversations, the voices reverberating off the high ceilings accentuated by bright red paint. The black wooden walls displayed faded frescoes of now-forgotten heroes and long-perished emperors. The fireplace sent small flames twisting up from the large oak logs to blacken the mantel above. Its amber light radiated across the vast space, swarming with hundreds of legionaries.

Few of the men—walking the area or seated at rows of long wooden tables lined with benches—wore their black steel segmented armor, this resembling a black lobster tail down their chest and stomach. Instead, most donned only red knee-length tunics belted at their waists, all equipped with swords at their sides. They all held tin plates, tin forks and spoons, and tin cups. The scent of olive oil-drenched roasted pork and black lentil soup mingled in the air with the smell of wine, smoke, and the old wood of the walls and furniture.

Adratus and Maximus dined in an area a step higher than the rest. Here, four-person tables offered seating for the centurions and optiones save for the prime centurion, who led the cohort. The cohort commander—according to Maximus—took his meals in his room.

The men below cast occasional glances Adratus's way—occasional, multiplied by the hundreds of eyes below. They no doubt wondered nothing more than, *Who's the new addition?* But a part of Adratus translated it to, *Why does he deserve to sit up there?*

"Would you like more wine, Optio?" asked a legionary standing by their table.

"He means you," Maximus said as he nodded Adratus's way.

Adratus looked at the soldier standing with a clay pitcher in hand. "I'm no optio."

"He's one of the Faldénri, newly attached to our cohort," Maximus said, then scooped a spoonful of lentils and leeks into his mouth.

"Apologies, Faldénrus." The legionary lifted the pitcher as a silent question.

Adratus nodded.

He poured.

"Your arrival is well timed," Maximus said conversationally to Adratus. "Lufuday is the one day of the week the fort serves meat, and too, its eve starts the weekend."

Before Adratus could reply, another man plopped down in the seat opposite Maximus. This reptilian man, about a foot taller than Maximus, had the head of a snake, and his lean body was covered in dark gray scales with a lighter shade down his neck and front. Black leather pauldrons armored his very wide shoulders with a black leather harness, framing his otherwise bare muscular chest as an X. Below his slim stomach, he wore a red skirt, its front covered by an apron of strips of black leather.

"You're late," Maximus said. "Adratus, this is Grethuk."

"Pressing matters required my attention," Grethuk said, a breathy groan to his voice, causing it to sound sinister. He leaned in. "Plans for tonight." He grinned, a lipless upturn of the mouth baring fangs. He turned to the soldier with the pitcher. "I'll simply have wine."

"Yes, Optio." The server stepped forward and poured.

"Eat," said Maximus. "I've only just told Adratus we have the best meals on Lufudays. You haven't eaten in two days."

"Only one." Grethuk took hold of his cup. "*Humans.* You consume bushels of food only to waste the energy heating your bodies. Then, you drink barrels of wine and water to cool it again." He drank. "However, I *will* snack." He turned to the server. "Three fried dormice is all I require."

"Yes, Optio." The server began to move away.

"Gratitude," Adratus said to the departing server's back.

"You mustn't thank legionaries for doing their duties," Maximus said. "Nor, must you expect thanks for doing yours." He returned to the reptilian. "And you are one to criticize our abundant need for food, you scaly fuck," he said with a smile, "when you need a thermoregulator to live this far north."

Grethuk kissed two of his black-clawed fingers and touched them to the red crystal centered on his harness. "Which I am thankful for in these freezing lands."

"This is the man of whom I spoke." Maximus motioned his fork toward Grethuk. "The other roommate."

"*Other* roommate?" Grethuk asked. "I thought I saw more kit in our room. Am I to infer you are the owner?"

"I am. *Immunis Adratus.*"

"Well met, Adratus." Grethuk turned to Maximus. "We should take him with us tonight. To the village."

"Village?" Adratus turned to Maximus.

"A faeville," Grethuk said, his voice slow with a sinister glee. "You'll adore it."

"I know not the word." He turned to Maximus for clarification.

"He's fresh from Nerageat," Maximus explained before taking a sip from his cup.

Planting his arm on the table, Grethuk leaned forward with a mischievous sparkle in his eyes—each like a greenish-blue marble with a vertical slit as the pupil. "*Faery villages*, though faevilles have naught to do with Faeries themselves. They are named so for the hedonistic ways the Faeries are said to have. Faevilles form outside legionary forts and are but collections of taverns, brothels, entertainment venues, and other means to drain young legionaries of our pension."

"And to drain us in more appealing manners," Maximus added with a mouthful of food. "They employ the sexiest women in the empire."

"I do not favor women in that regard," Adratus said.

Maximus swallowed. "I see. Do you thus favor men?"

Adratus nodded.

"'Tis no matter. Whilst I do not share your preference, the brothel we frequent caters to many tastes." Maximus tilted his cup toward the reptilian. "Tastes good Grethuk shares, in part. You will have no issue in finding satiation."

Adratus smiled as excitement buzzed through him. "But..." His smile faded. "Have we leave to go to such a place?"

"By all that is infernal." Maximus threw himself back in his chair. "The boy needs direct orders to shit."

"If the new legionary wishes not to go, so be it," Grethuk said. "More for me. And rightfully so, as I am *twice* the man of any Human."

Maximus sighed wearily. "He means he has two—"

"I am familiar," Adratus interrupted and cleared his throat, "with the anatomy of Ophiruks."

"Are you?" Grethuk flashed a fanged grin. "How familiar?"

"A question to leave unanswered, Optio," Adratus said, grinning coyly.

Grethuk's smile widened as his serpentine tongue slipped between his teeth.

"Save it for the brothels," Maximus said. "Legionaries fucking legionaries leads to naught but trouble. More so if they share a room."

"Understood," Adratus replied, his gaze dropping to his dinner plate. He felt a tinge of disappointment—not because the words applied to Grethuk as much as they also applied to Maximus.

"Do you accept the invitation offered?" Maximus asked.

"I think I must, lest I explode," Adratus chuckled. "We are not permitted to act on such desires in Nerageat; thus, I am well in need."

"'Tis settled." Maximus clasped Adratus's shoulder, giving him an excited shake. "We shall set off presently. Yet, whilst Grethuk awaits his tardy snack, I have something I wish to present."

Adratus raised an eyebrow. "What?"

Maximus looked into Adratus's eyes and grinned—a devilish mix of charm and mischief. "The edge of the civilized world."

CHAPTER TWO

Adratus followed Maximus through the fort, awe and apprehension clouding his mind. The late afternoon breeze was heavy with the smells of wood, leather, and sweat. Though he had been here for only a few hours and had yet to truly explore, he grew excited to discover all that his new home had to offer.

Soldiers congregated outside the wooden barracks blocks—painted black with red terracotta roofs. Some soldiers sat on benches, sharpening their swords, while others conversed in loud voices accompanied by hearty laughs. Adratus took it all in, his curious gaze scanning the many new faces.

"'Tis smaller than most forts," Maximus said as they walked. "It houses but one cohort rather than a legion, so we have but five proper centuries and an auxiliary century of Ophiruks."

"To cover more ground?" Adratus asked.

"Indeed. With our legion divided into ten forts, we can span more of the border. Each border legion has ten forts each to cover its entire length."

They slowed once they neared the western gate. Adratus tilted his head upward to better view the rough-hewn wooden walls towering thirty feet above.

"Why are they wood?" Adratus asked.

"Observant." Maximus maintained his walk. "The original line of stone barrier forts is long destroyed. For decades, the barbarians carried out raids upon our empire, pushing our border back. We lost hundreds of miles of terrain due to their brutality, and entire towns were slaughtered in their wake.

Each time our defensive line was breached, the army erected another line until building these current forts."

The gravity of Maximus's words and how casually he stated them weighed on Adratus as he stepped closer to the wall. It seemed like a dam holding back a mighty ocean of brutality, and he was soon to pass through it.

The tall gate made of weathered beams stood tall, its smooth wooden surface painted black, in contrast to the pitted wooden walls. Stairs led up to an overhanging walkway atop the gate, and further up, a dull red watchtower, a squared skeleton of beams, rose into the sky. Atop it perched a pole with a flag waving in subtle winds.

The red square of cloth displayed the symbol that was the number two embroidered three times with their bases together as a triangle—the Triébis—in black. Two black circles surrounded it. The words "TRASILON ETERNAL" were printed beneath.

Adratus felt a wave of comfort wash over him as he gazed at the banner—though he tried not to think of the many similar flags that had fallen to invasion.

"Should we not gain permission from the cohort commander before exiting the fort?" Adratus asked.

"Again, no longer are you in training. You're a Tridulan legionary, free to go where you like—within reason." Maximus nodded to the two sentries, who stood watch at the gate.

The sentries snapped to attention, bowing their heads as they touched their right fist to their chests. Adratus took this as permission to leave—despite the sentries being lower in rank.

Maximus stepped through the gate.

Adratus paused at the threshold, again looking back. After a pause, he continued through, and the heavy black door closed with a grinding thud, leaving only silence outside.

Usually, such a gate would lead to a road continuing out to some distant destination. This gate, however, led only to a paved circle thirty feet across with a stone curb around its perimeter. Beyond, the grass swayed just past the ankles of Maximus, who already trudged his way through.

A dozen yards from the fort, Maximus stopped at an old waist-high wooden fence. Adratus neared as well. An ill anxiety stirred in the pit of Adratus's stomach as he stood beside the optio.

"Behold." Maximus raised his hands to mimic an orator. "The edge of our great Tridulan Empire."

Adratus set his hands on the wobbly fence as he stared beyond it to the twisted, shadowed woods. "I would have thought us to have a more substantial barrier."

"*We* are the barrier, young Adratus—our fort and the others lining this fence from the Gellic Nation to the south all the way north to the Arctic Ocean. We are the wall of Darkness shielding the empire from the hateful Light."

Adratus nodded somberly, still facing the tangled woods. The magnitude of what this seemingly unremarkable land before him represented caused his heart to pound. A hollow dread formed within his chest. A part of him half expected a barbarian to leap from the shadows, affix him to a stake, and burn him alive. Yet, Adratus did not turn away.

Maximus, Adratus realized, had gone quiet. He watched the younger boy.

"Do you fear it?" Maximus asked.

"No."

"You should. The followers of the True Light hate all who are unlike them. And wish to destroy us all."

"I knew what the Dayigans were before I requested this post. 'Tis the reason." Adratus took a deep, fretful breath, staring. "The Dayigan Empire may be young in years, but it is a wildfire, kindled by fear and fueled by a holy mandate from their God to destroy. It *cannot* spread into our lands."

A sudden shout sounded; someone grabbed Adratus. It only took him a moment to realize it was Maximus, but before that moment ended, the older boy was laughing that he'd flinched.

"You nearly screamed, mighty Adratus."

Adratus cracked a smile at his own expense. "I did not, Optio."

"If you do not stop calling me 'Optio' every other breath, I will have you flogged."

"Yes . . ." The next word lingered on his lips, but he bit his tongue as he grinned.

Maximus looked beyond the fence and turned somber as he said, "'Tis good you know what lies beyond our threshold. Too many come here as fools."

Adratus shared his gaze into the thick woods before he spit over the fence.

Maximus chuckled. "Though your sentiment is shared, you spat in vain. The Dayigan's pseudo-empire lies yet miles away. Here begins but the buffer area, stretching thirty miles."

"The Bloody Belt. I'd forgotten."

"'Tis no matter. I have shown what I wished to show. Now . . ." Maximus pivoted to face eastward, where the sky beyond the fort blushed with a rosy hue as dusk began to fall. "Now, as the sun begins his slow descent, we must ready ourselves for the pleasures of the night." Maximus began toward the fort.

Adratus paused for a moment, taking a last look at the forest beyond the fence before catching up with Maximus.

CHAPTER THREE

He stood atop the gentle hill, a man of thirty-one with mousy brown hair and a thick beard. He gazed out at the vast expanse before him, taking in the rolling hills and swaying grasses that seemed to stretch on endlessly. Two moons floated in the star-filled sky, casting somber glows—one in a muted blue while the other shone pale lavender.

A soldier by trade, the solitary figure had a strong build and rugged features, though he now wore no uniform. Instead, his attire was reminiscent of a time before he joined the royal army—a tattered cloak draped over a mud-stained tunic and trousers, all in shades of earthy browns and grays.

He shivered despite himself, pulling his gray cloak around his arms for warmth. Though he'd been absent for some months, this place had served as his residence these past four years, and the chill, though biting, told him he was home.

Behind him, he heard approaching steps—slow at a leisurely pace—and waited as they neared before turning.

He now faced a camp of thirty tents—each green and conical, with awnings off their fronts. They surrounded a larger, oblong tent for the commanders. A few roaring fires dotted the spaces in between. Most of the three hundred men roaming the area were clothed in long black tabards, and across each man's upper body was a large emerald-green patch, shaped like a squared version of the number seven—crossed with its ends flailing outward. Belts secured swords at their waists. Under their tabards, they wore suits of chainmail, black trousers, and black leather boots. The men guffawed and passed stories back and forth with nary a care among them.

Only a handful wore white tabards, these with the same symbol—the Septenar—in the same green across their chests. This was the case with the blond man in his mid-twenties who approached to stand directly behind him.

"Sergeant Swithun," Captain Rothgar greeted with a nod. "Forgive our excluding you from our discussions, but you have not yet been granted official admittance into our order."

Swithun stared back, hesitating before he said, "I'm looking forward to joining up proper, though, sir." Despite his words, his reply was tinged with regret.

"Yes." The young captain straightened his stance. "Then you will be rather pleased to know that you needn't wait much longer." Rothgar held up a folded black cloth and presented it.

Swithun unfolded the fabric, revealing it as a black version of Rothgar's own attire—though of thin, rough-woven wool. He anxiously ran his thick, dirty fingers across the new material. It was a tremendous honor for him to be chosen as a sergeant of the Holy Order of Knights Silthex, yet despite this commendation, he felt a slight sickness in his gut. "I'll strive to keep the honor of the Silthex with all me might, sir," he said with downcast eyes.

Rothgar furrowed his brow as he gave the older man a perplexed onceover. "You sound as if you've been captured. Have you thoughts you aren't sharing?"

"I'm a Dayigan soldier, sir," Swithun said. "I think what the army tells me to think."

"Walk with me." Rothgar waggled a finger at Swithun as he turned.

Swithun complied, and the two entered the camp to navigate their way slowly among the tents.

Cauldrons hung from tripods above fires, their contents wafting steam. The few knights and surrounding sergeants milled around the fires in loose circles, drinking and laughing among themselves.

The passing Silthex men greeted Rothgar with respect, and Swithun felt a sense of belonging swell within his chest.

As they walked, Rothgar spoke. "You've been here long enough to know that we are not mere soldiers. We are protectors of the faith of this land and of her people's souls. Our duty is to keep our righteous empire on the glorious path God Déagar has given it." He stopped and faced Swithun. "Do you understand?"

Swithun nodded solemnly, feeling a deep sense of purpose wash over him.

"That said," Rothgar continued, "joining the Silthex is not an *order*. It is a privilege we've afforded you because we believe you will be an asset. As a Dayigan soldier, you fought well against the Tridulans to the east. You stealthily infiltrated the wicked lands and assassinated important targets for our cause. You have won this honor. Yet, if you have concerns about accepting this reward for your deeds, pray you, speak them now."

Swithun went quiet, gathering himself. "Back in Hunia," he began hesitantly, "the place where we first met at, you destroyed that whole town."

Rothgar scoffed. "Finally. You've traveled with us for four months, and all that time, I could see this very conversation stirring in your mind."

The two continued walking until they arrived at the edge of camp, where they sat atop a fallen tree and looked out over the merry brotherhood. The firelight cast flickering shadows across their faces as Rothgar spoke again. "What happened in that town was imperative for the betterment of the world. Those people had fallen from grace."

"I know, sir." Swithun nodded. "At least, I think I know. But I thought we was only meant to kill the one man, d'you know what I mean. The mage. Not everybody there."

The captain's voice lowered to a dangerous growl. "*You* were supposed to kill the one man. And you failed."

Swithun dropped his gaze, feeling the weight of the captain's disappointment. "Forgive me, sir, for failing you and our God." He paused before continuing. "And I thank you for saving me life, too, sir. With..." He cleared his throat. "...*magic*." The word tasted like poison on his tongue—bitter with disgust and anger.

Swithun remembered when he had lain half-unconscious after the attack, clinging on at death's door as his blood had poured onto the forest floor. He then had felt the green fire from Rothgar's palm erupt to burn into the deep sword gash in the side of his neck. It had hurt so tremendously that he had gritted his teeth so firmly that they seemed they might shatter within his mouth. Finally, he'd called out in agony.

Now, Swithun placed his hand to the side of his neck and felt the webbed ridges of heavily scarred flesh, not only from the sword strikes but also from the fire that had healed him.

Rothgar faced forward, face stern, as he watched his fellow Silthex in the camp. "I think you are more concerned with my use of magic than my killing a town of Karulents."

Swithun leaned forward on the log, planting his arms on his legs. "I'm all muddled up in me head, sir." He lowered his head into his palms and raked his fingers through his tangled hair. "We fight them Tridulans and Karulents 'cause they uses magic. God Déagar says using magic's like trespassing in his house, y'know, sir? But ... you used magic, too, to heal me."

"You grow dangerously close to an accusation, Sergeant," the captain warned.

"I ain't mean nothing by it like that, sir," Swithun replied quickly. "Just confused by it all, that's all."

"Your confusion is admittedly understandable," said the captain, taking a breath and softening his tone. "It is why the common citizens of our holy empire may not know the means we use to keep them safe from our mounting enemies. As one soon to join our order, know this: I have been given special dispensation from the Church of Déagar to use magic. They agree it is sometimes necessary to use our enemy's own tactics against them."

"Forgive me, sir," Swithun replied, somewhat chastened. "I ain't know that."

"You didn't ask."

"Didn't seem me place to, did it, sir."

Captain Rothgar nodded. "No. What if I told you it was always our intention to destroy that town? We sent you to assassinate the mage first, only because we feared he would hinder our grander scheme, but never was he our only target. What say you to that, Sergeant?"

"I ..." Swithun paused as the reality of Rothgar's words sunk in. He was left feeling disturbed yet unsurprised by the truth. His heart pounded fiercely within his chest.

Rothgar resumed, hate seeping through his every syllable. "Every Karulent within that wretched town worshiped the false God Karulus."

Swithun bowed his head in agreement.

"If you have hesitation in your heart," Rothgar said, "I pray you, voice it now. *Before* you join us. The vow to enter the Silthex is for life."

"I trust the Church, sir. And I trust that the Silthex is the army of the Church. If they say 'tis right, 'tis right then. Just . . ." Swithun swallowed hard. "I can still 'ear them, y'know. Those poor sods from Hunia. I can hear them screaming every night when I go to bed. Like I'm wiv 'em again, watching 'em burn."

Rothgar offered nothing but a muted sigh before continuing, "You still have a long spiritual journey before you can fully walk the path of righteousness. However, I believe you are ready to join us. I have scheduled your Reception Ceremony for tomorrow, yet the choice remains yours. Pray on this tonight and remember the words of Déagar: 'The True Light is the only way; all others will parish.'" With that, Rothgar stood.

"I'm just happy we're here now," Swithun said to Rothgar's back, "and all that with the Karulents is behind us. This is where I were stationed when I was in the king's army, so I know this place. Me old fort's a few miles to the east. We're near the Tridulan border, right? I don't mind fighting *them* so much—fucking evil Dark Light savages. I'll be fine here, sir."

"Yes," Rothgar said, pausing a beat. "May the fires of Déagar guide you."

He departed, leaving Swithun silent and alone with a thousand thoughts.

CHAPTER FOUR

Adratus was suddenly roused from his slumber as someone jolted him, shaking him roughly from the murky depths of sleep. He grimaced and grunted as he stirred, rolling slowly onto his side in the meager bed perched atop plain, four-by-four legs. His eyes opened to see Maximus's face looming over him like a shadow. Still groggy from too much wine and too little rest, Adratus pinched the corners of his mouth into a feeble smile nonetheless.

Maximus mirrored the expression. "The sun has nearly risen," he said. "Do you plan to sleep away the morn?"

"Nearly risen?" Adratus groaned. "I think more sleep might be advised."

A snickering hiss sounded from across the room from Grethuk, who no doubt witnessed. "This is he who just finished training?"

Maximus stepped back from the bed, and Adratus sat up, taking his place at its edge. His gray woolen blanket draped lazily across his lap.

"Never did I indulge in three nights of unleashed hedonism in training," Adratus said. "Nor any at all."

"'Twas the weekend before," Maximus said. "Now, 'tis Madday. A morning run will cleanse your veins of wine. Our century has departed as a formation, but I prefer to run alone. However, you may join if you like. And you, as well, good Grethuk."

"Many thanks," Grethuk said. "But I am soon to join my own century on a ten-miler."

"My thanks as well," Adratus said as he leaned sideways onto the bed. "But I prefer to nap."

"Legionary," Maximus commanded, "*attention.*"

Adratus jumped to his feet and stood well-postured, head facing forward, eyes straight, shoulders back, and arms to his sides.

Grethuk snickered again. "The legionary indeed stands quite rigid at your command."

Adratus gritted his teeth while saying, "I've only just awoken, *sirs.*"

"Get dressed, Adratus," Maximus said. "You will meet me outside in three minutes."

—

Struggling to stay at Maximus's side, Adratus ran down the wide, winding woodland path—this cleared and well-trodden by years of legionary sandals. Despite the chill in the air, Adratus had grown hot, sweat wetting his face and pooling at the small of his back to dampen his tunic. His heavy breaths steamed with each exhalation. The remnants of last night's wine coursed sourly in his veins, and his lack of sleep weighed his eyelids. Yet he pressed on.

They'd already passed a few centuries of men jogging in formations as they shouted out songs to keep step. Now, Adratus and Maximus ran on alone.

"How much farther?" Adratus strained to ask amid heavy breaths.

"You aren't yielding on me, are you?"

"No," he lied, despite the sick welling in his gut.

"Good. Commendations for keeping pace." Maximus said, pointing further up the trail. "The five-mile marker is just ahead."

Adratus looked to see a four-foot weather-worn post centered on the path.

Maximus reached the post just before Adratus and, rounding it, announced, "The halfway mark. A mere five miles remain."

Adratus stopped at the post, setting his hand on it as he slumped forward and panted. "I must stop."

"Pausing will but make it tougher to restart." Maximus jogged in place.

Suddenly, Adratus darted to the edge of the path and planted his arm on the rough bark of a pine tree. With his head on his arm, he faced the tree's base. A beat passed before he vomited on the ground.

"We can pause a moment," Maximus said behind him. "Get it out," he encouraged halfheartedly.

Adratus expelled another acidic torrent of sick before he remained in place, staring with watery eyes at the mess.

When it seemed his stomach had settled, Adratus stood upright and wiped his mouth with his forearm.

"We'll wait until you regain yourself," Maximus said.

Adratus nodded and approached him. "Apologies. We only did four-mile runs in training and never with a belly full of wine."

"Nevertheless, you kept up. And I am faster than most."

Adratus nodded, his arm crossing the stomach of his black tabard just above his belt. "At Fort Nerageat, I too was among the fasted runners in my unit. The drill instructor often applauded my motivation, as if it, in itself, proved I was a better legionary. 'Tis amusing though"—Adratus smiled—"I hated it. I hated running; thus, I ran faster. The faster you run, the faster 'tis done. My actual motivation was naught but reaching the steamy waters of the baths as soon as possible, particularly on cold winter mornings."

Maximus chuckled. "And yet your centurion was, in fact, right—you were well motivated after all." His smile faded as he became serious. "But he was also right to say you are a good soldier. At least from what I have seen thus far. Did you join because of your father?"

Adratus shrugged. "Perhaps part of my interest grew from his time in service. But he actually discouraged my joining."

"Truly?"

"He warned it would change me."

"For me, it was expected." Maximus moved to the opposite side of the path. "Or at least encouraged." He sat on the ground with his back to a pine tree. "Not only from my father, but from *society at large*. For one to do anything of note in politics, he needs at least some military background."

"You have my vote, Senator." Adratus grinned and gave a slight nod of his head. "Yet in truth, I never intended to join the army." He settled himself on the ground next to Maximus. "I joined the Faldénri, and I do recall when they first drew my interest. I was ten years of age, and my parents had sent me to the seafood market. The large one just north of Tridual's primary forum on the Bay of Deception."

"I know it."

"As I walk around browsing all the wooden stalls stuffed with every kind of seafood the bay has to offer, I hear an altercation between a man and an elderly woman. He has her in a grapple, but she puts up as much fight as she can manage—throwing weak, side-fisted punches and screaming, 'Faldénri, Faldénri!' Then, he punches her directly in the face and snatches a coin purse from her grip. Afterwards, she's slumped over, holding her bleeding face, and I look around;

no one does anything. Reacting without thought, I take off running after him. Moments pass before he even realizes I'm behind him. When he notices me, he stops and turns around to face me."

The unwashed little boy, Adratus, in his shabby gray tunic belted with a rope, stood among the clamor of the marketplace as merchants shouted out their goods—from tuna and green crabs to oysters and jellied eels. The salty smells of the Bay of Deception and the cries of the gulls were intermingled with the clinking of coins and the conversations of the shoppers. Wooden crates rattled along cobblestone streets as fishermen pushed them on wooden hand trucks.

Adratus ignored all, keeping his fearful eyes fixed on the thief's scarred face as the man stepped closer and closer. The boy planted his bare feet firmly on the stone ground, ready for a fight if needed, determined to reclaim the woman's coin purse—though he wasn't quite sure how.

The man in the long dark cloak stopped a foot away from him. "What will you do about it, boy?"

Though his heart raced inside his chest, the ten-year-old held up his fists, despite knowing he was no match for this full-grown adult. Nevertheless, he kept his stance but glanced around desperately to see if anyone would intervene.

Suddenly, the man took one swift step forward and rammed his foot into Adratus's stomach with such force that the air left the boy's lungs. He crashed onto the cobblestones below. Before the child could gather himself, the thief fled, leaving him behind in a state of agony.

"I recall just lying there," Adratus said to Maximus, "just lying there and hating myself for being so ineffective and hating myself further for letting him get away. Then . . ." Adratus smiled. "Then I saw *them*."

A bright red stream of lightning shot across the market, wrapping around the thief and binding him in place. He screamed out in pain as the lightning coiled around his flailing body.

The boy quickly found the source—the palm of a Faldénrus, one of two who approached in polished steel cuirasses, each crafted in the form of a well-built upper body. Their long black capes trailed behind them as they strode forward.

The lightning from the spellcaster transformed into a cord of red light as he rushed over to restrain the thief. The second soldier hurried to the injured child, lifting him from the ground.

"Gratitude for slowing him for us, boy," the Faldénrus said.

"Quite the story," Maximus said with a laugh. "Admittedly, much better than 'society forced me.'"

"You should have heard it from the mouth of an excited ten-year-old boy. I nearly drove my parents mad with retellings. The best part." Adratus sighed as he recalled being a boy sitting on the curb of the road leading from the busy Tridulan market. He watched the elderly woman approach the Faldénrus beside the thief.

"The best part," Adratus continued, "was seeing the coin purse returned. I could see on the woman's face that it was about more than the return of her coins. She'd received justice, and the man who had wronged her was prevented from harming others. In hindsight, I know I did little, but at the time, I felt as if I'd truly helped one who needed it."

Adratus was pulled from his memory as he heard the distant voice of a hundred men shouting out a song to a jogging beat. "A century approaches."

"Yes," Maximus said. "'Twould be best if they did not find their leaders lingering and chatting whilst we should be running."

Adratus nodded. "I've recovered."

"Good. As we do not have a thief to motivate you to run, I'll race you to the baths." With that, Maximus took off running, and Adratus followed close behind.

CHAPTER FIVE

His boots crunched the russet leaves as he approached the edge of the encampment. Breathing in the crisp air of the early evening, Swithun stepped out onto a dirt road that weaved through the thick woodlands. A worn-out cart—hitched to a low branch with no horses in sight—stood upon the grassy edge by the dirt.

A figure came into view beside it: a tall man in a white tabard whom Swithun knew must be Lieutenant Beadurinc, second-in-command of the brigade—the man who had summoned him here. He'd heard of the knight's arrival a few days before but had yet to make his acquaintance. The knight, in his early twenties with a thin brown beard neatly trimmed, held his hands clasped behind him, his shoulders squared back.

Swithun fought back his elation at being personally requested by this knight—his first task as an official Silthex sergeant. He adjusted his new black tabard, dusted it off with his hand, and stepped closer.

Beadurinc fixed his gaze upon the man, studying him like something he found unappealing yet needed to examine. Most knights were nobles, yet this one projected his superiority like a shield, warning Swithun not to be near him. "You are the new sergeant initiate, I presume?"

Swithun nodded. "Yes, sir. At your service, sir."

The young lord waved a dismissive hand in the air. "Yes, yes, I'm sure you are. The sergeant who drove the wagon is attending to his horses. You will unload these boxes and take them inside my tent." He gestured toward the wagon, which carried four wooden crates, each roughly four feet in width and a foot in depth and height.

Swithun paused, feeling a glimmer of dejection at the humdrum job. Regardless, he knew his place and bowed his head in acknowledgment. "Yes, sir," he replied.

Swithun grabbed the first crate.

"Careful, you fool," Beadurinc warned. "It could explode if handled too roughly. Take one at a time and attempt some *semblance* of assiduity."

Swithun proceeded slowly and nervously, gripping the rough wood with apprehension.

"Follow me," Beadurinc ordered as he strode away.

Swithun followed, keeping the crate horizontal and hugging it with both arms. It wasn't too heavy, but he didn't want to chance it slipping from his arms and hitting the ground.

"You're Captain Rothgar's apprentice, ain'tcha?" Swithun blurted, attempting to break the tension.

The knight ignored the question and marched forward through the camp, passing green tents pitched within the clearing. Smoke drifted from the smoldering embers of a firepit as dried meat hung from wooden racks, stretching between two tents like a sagging bridge.

"Right," Swithun muttered under his breath. "You must be another one of them special ones—y'know what I mean? The ones what's allowed to use magic. If you're the captain's apprentice."

The knight came to an abrupt halt and shot him a scornful glower. "Sergeant initiates such as yourself have no business addressing me," Beadurinc said firmly. "*I* am accustomed to the comforts of Wendian—not this godforsaken field— where people know their place. You will do well to remember yours." He resumed walking, hastening his pace.

Swithun followed suit, catching up with him. "Sorry about that, sir. Wasn't trying to get in your business. I *come* from Wendian, you know? It weren't nearly as nice back then as it is now. That was before the Church took it over and made it their holy city. Mind you, 'twas a pretty nice city even back then—I met the Grand Master there once. But never seen him since."

Beadurinc sighed with annoyance. "No, you wouldn't have. He's very far away."

"Right. He went off to Faery-land, didn't he?"

"Something like that," he groaned. "He's been there for years. My tent is that one." Beadurinc pointed to the large command tent centered in the camp. "Place the boxes to the side and await me. I need to attend to more *important* matters."

Swithun watched him hurry away before continuing the task. It was slow work, taking each box one at a time while taking great caution to move warily and without jostling them.

When Swithun lugged the final crate into the command tent, he found the same knight seated at a large rectangular table in the tent's center. Its wooden surface was draped by a green woolen blanket, atop which lay a detailed map of the area with towns and villages marked in blue.

The walls of heavy green canvas draped away from a framework of support posts holding them aloft. Fragments of armor and helmets hung from the top edge or were tied to the support posts, while herbs and bundles of dried flowers hung on racks. The air was thick with the smell of burning incense.

Even with the furnishings, the tent was far larger than the tent Swithun shared with nine other men. Here, there were only two cots—one against the wall to the right and one at the back. The wall to the left of the entrance held the wooden crates that Swithun had just delivered.

Lucky bastards, Swithun thought. *While us sergeants are squashed in like hornets, the commanders got enough space to dance.*

Swithun gingerly placed the last box atop the others, wary of a possible detonation.

Beadurinc remained silent as he rolled one of the maps, stood, and approached. He extended a dagger to Swithun. "Open it, Sergeant Initiate."

Swithun took the dagger, and the knight stepped a few paces back. As the sergeant worked at the lid, he tried not to think about how this could be some manner of deathtrap. He slid the blade between the seam where the lid met the wall and tapped the handle with his palm. Finally, he was able to pry apart the splintering wood, releasing a stench like spoiled eggs into the air.

"Afraid I got some bad news for you, sir," Swithun said. "Whatever this was, 'tis gone off."

Beadurinc stepped forward. "Move aside," he commanded, omitting the word *idiot* though maintaining the inflection in his voice. He donned fine leather gloves and kneeled beside the crate.

Beadurinc paused as if to savor the moment and then pulled away the straw covering four jagged yellow crystals, each roughly the size of a fist. A glimmer of awe shined in the knight's eyes as he examined each piece before lifting one atop his gloved fingers.

"Crystallized brimstone," he said in a low voice that seemed almost menacing.

More magic, Swithun realized as a wave of repulsion washed over him. He looked away from Beadurinc and stifled the anger welling within him. However, he knew to keep his mouth shut, though he felt his hand make a fist.

Beadurinc didn't seem to notice and continued to examine the crystal. "I'd feared it might fracture during transport," he continued without looking away from the stone, "but it remains perfectly intact." He turned toward Swithun. "They have special metaphysical enhancements that . . ." He paused, no doubt noticing the dumbfoundedness reflected in the sergeant's stare. "Let me speak plainly for your benefit, Sergeant Initiate—it is extremely powerful. And it is the reason our brigade lingers here with naught but drink and chatter to waste our time. With the arrival of these magnificent crystals"—he lifted it higher while gazing—"we shall finally bring order to these lands plagued by witchcraft and filth."

CHAPTER SIX

Adratus, roaring in anger, raised his gladius above his head as he sprinted toward Maximus.

Maximus, braced, glared back at him, muscles tensed.

Their wooden blades crashed together with a loud clap, the two legionaries trading blows. Both were garbed in full Tridulan armor, each with thick bands of overlapping steel around their upper bodies and atop their shoulders—blackened steel over a red tunic for Maximus and silver steel over black for Adratus. Cascading capes—matching the tunics—streamed behind them as they moved swiftly around each other.

The fight continued, their weapons whistling and clapping in an intricate dance. Adratus was tiring, his movements becoming slower and clumsier than before, sweat beading on his forehead despite the chill of the sandy training field. Meanwhile, Maximus remained firm—he skillfully dodged Adratus's strikes, sending his opponent back whenever he tried a charge.

Maximus kicked Adratus in the armored stomach, sending him crashing into the sand below. Adratus tried to rise, but it was over. Maximus dived onto him and pressed his sword against his throat.

"I yield," Adratus growled in frustration. He punched the sand.

Maximus threw up his hands with a triumphant smile, while Adratus dropped his head back to the sand in defeat, tired beyond tired.

"You have the advantage," Adratus grumbled. "You are three years older and have three more years of experience."

"Would you say such a thing to an enemy who had a sword at your throat?" Maximus pulled Adratus upright. "You are a legionary of the great Tridulan Empire. The best army in the world. Complain not of what is fair when you practice for war."

Adratus huffed. "We've been at this for weeks."

"Yes," Maximus said, "and you've grown stronger in that time, and you will continue to do so each week, henceforth. Already, you are strong enough to best many men here in contest. Yet we train not for contests."

Adratus nodded wearily and glanced around him. No one seemed to care of his defeat. Instead, the sandy training grounds were alive with the sounds of clashing weapons as legionaries practiced their swordsmanship and other martial arts. Some pairs sparred with each other, while others practiced their techniques against wooden posts. The air was filled with shouts of command and encouragement from instructors, punctuated by occasional grunts of pain or effort.

On one side of the field, a few of the more experienced troops conducted drills that involved throwing javelins and practicing formations. They moved in unison, their weapons held high in salute to their officers, as they marched as a synchronized unit.

Further away from the main group, some of the younger recruits practiced combat maneuvers, such as grappling, wrestling, and takedown throws.

Despite its chaotic energy, there seemed to be an underlying order on site: everyone had a role to play, and although there were some minor disputes between individuals here and there, overall morale among the Tridulan legionaries remained high—they were all united by a common cause: protecting the empire.

Maximus set his hand on Adratus's shoulder. "You yet hold your gladius as if it were a separate tool. Make it part of you—an extension of your might."

Adratus took a deep breath. "I will. I'm ready to go again."

"As am I," Maximus said with a cocky smile. "I had no cause to pause."

Again, they engaged. Adratus kept his swings strong and focused while attempting to be one with his sword. Maximus pressed forward, driving Adratus back. Yet Maximus again proved too much for him and sent Adratus's sword flying across the sand.

Adratus roared angrily as he stumbled back. The disappointment of defeat crept through him, but he gritted his teeth and stayed focused. He would not give up, not again.

Unarmed, Adratus dodged Maximus's next swing and crouched beneath the next, only to lose his footing and hit the sand with a thud.

Roaring in victory, Maximus rushed toward him, ready for the win.

Adratus saw his sword, ten feet away. He thrust his hand toward it. And red light—as a concentrated cord—exploded from his palm. It encircled the gladius, snatching it from the sand and pulling it to his hand.

Adratus cast his other hand at Maximus, and another shining rope of red light erupted out, binding Maximus's arms to his sides and pulling him down to his knees.

Adratus got up casually and approached the bound optio. He set the tip of his wooden gladius to Maximus's armored chest.

"This was meant to be a fight of swords alone," Maximus said.

"Cry not of what is fair when you train for battle, Optio."

Maximus chuckled. "Ass."

Adratus dispelled the light and helped him to his feet.

Many of the men on the training grounds had stopped to watch the display. Now, seeing Adratus watching, they quickly returned to their former tasks.

"You impress them," said Maximus. "It seems as if—" Maximus stopped abruptly, his expression growing in alarm, and looked high above Adratus's shoulder.

Adratus turned just in time to see something hit an invisible wall extending above the fort's wooden walls. The entire unseen field wavered in waves of faint colors. Whatever hit fell limply outside the western wall.

"Was that a person?" Adratus asked.

"Come." Maximus took off in a sprint.

Adratus hurried behind him.

—

Just outside the western wall of the fort, a dozen men circled a figure Adratus could not quite see.

Maximus approached the gathered men. "Make room," he commanded, and the others complied.

Adratus stepped to Maximus's side as he stood over her.

The young woman lay unconscious on the grass. She was badly burned, with patches of black and blood-red marring her pallid skin and ripping through her off-white blouse and blue skirt. Yet the feature that most perplexed Adratus was the large feathered wings from her back—one wing folded against the ground, the other open limply and curved slightly around her shoulder. Her feathers matched the medium brown of her long hair. Save for the wings, she was otherwise Human.

"What is she?" Adratus whispered, awestruck, to Maximus.

"A Terovae." He crouched to her. "They are another race of people. Ones who live far to the west."

"Like the people of Vohcktara?"

"Yes. But she is no Vohck." Maximus turned and looked up at Adratus, his words grave. "She's a Dayigan."

"Stand aside. Stand aside," two men called as they approached with a simple litter formed of gray canvas stretched between two black poles.

Maximus stood and stepped back, letting the medics near and begin their examination.

With anxious bewilderment, Adratus kept his eyes on the woman, as did all the others gathered. *A Dayigan*—the word kept swirling within his head—*here*.

"What did she hit?" Adratus asked Maximus.

Maximus, drawn from thought, paused before his answer. "Our disortaura. It is a standard defense measure installed on all barrier forts. 'Tis an invisible field that extends our physical wall to the heavens, specifically to keep out fliers. Yet it only works on people. On contact, it draws a portion of the person's pneuma, energizes the point of contact, and repels the person back. She hit it hard and was repelled hard."

"It burnt her?"

"No." Maximus returned his gaze to the Terovae in the medics' care, his words pensive as he said, "The disortaura does not burn. Something burnt her beforehand."

The medics lifted the woman, one man carefully holding her head, and set her on the litter.

Maximus neared them. "Does she yet live?"

"Yes, Optio."

After a curt nod, Maximus turned to face the gathered men. "Fifth cohort, take heed. You will return to your quarters, prepare your kit, and await orders from your respective centurions. Spread the word en route. Go."

The men quickly dispersed.

"I'm perplexed," Adratus said, his heart racing. "What does it mean that a Dayigan is here?"

"I know not." Maximus watched the medics carry the woman toward the gate. "My orders were for you as well. Return to our quarters. I must speak to the cohort commander. Go."

"Yes, Optio."

—

Hours passed with no information.

Adratus waited on a low stool just outside his quarters. His opened door was but one of the identical red-painted portals evenly spaced along the long wooden wall, thinly painted black. Red wooden pillars supported an overhang that stretched out and sheltered him; the roof above it was tiled in red terracotta. Beyond it, a gravel path formed a thin alleyway that lay between his barracks block and a mirror image across from it.

Normally, on a mild-weathered evening such as this, the area would be clamorous with conversations and games. However, now the few brief discussions were mere mutters, as if everyone thought they shouldn't speak too loudly. The primary sound was the sharpening of gladii—whetstones sliding across steel—which was also Adratus's chosen means of staying busy.

Across from him, a man carefully waxed his red rectangular shield displaying the black mark formed as the number two painted three times with the bases together to form a triangle; this circled twice. The Triébis was the same symbol on the Tridulan flag and the same ancient symbol that Adratus had vowed to protect, along with all it stood for. But as he stared at the shield, he feared he wasn't ready—not if any real threat had drawn near.

He returned to sharpening his blade.

Grethuk approached and headed straight toward the door to their room.

"Any news?" Adratus asked, looking up.

He paused on the threshold. "All the centurions and optiones gather in secret conversation within the cohort commander's quarters."

"Were you amongst them?"

"All the proper, *Tridulan* centurions and optiones." A hint of bitterness marked his words. "As foreigners of the auxiliary, my centurion and I stand excluded."

Everyone in the alley had paused, straining their hungry ears for any scrap of information.

"What of the winged woman?" Adratus asked.

"She remains in hospital. In a secluded room. The medics say nothing of her condition, at least not to me. Yet, a quarter of the first century patrols beyond the west wall in case other Dayigans pass the border."

"Are we to—"

"'Twould seem your questions have a better source for answers than me." Grethuk pointed.

Adratus turned to see Maximus walking quickly toward them.

"Inside. Both of you," Maximus said, before rushing into their quarters.

Once all three were in their room, Maximus closed the door. "We've conferenced with the legate and the general via whisper stones. The general himself has given us direct orders to move out at once. The three of us, alone. Prepare quickly."

"Understood," Grethuk said. He and Maximus rushed to their footlockers.

Adratus hesitated. "Move out where?"

Maximus paused, one hand on his black trunk, but he did not look at the younger soldier. "To the Dayigan Empire."

The words left Adratus breathless. Dizziness followed. Adratus felt as if he sank toward the wooden floor.

Maximus opened his trunk and began grabbing items, stuffing them into a sack. "I cannot say more. Not within the thin walls of the barracks."

Adratus stood frozen.

"Adratus," Maximus commanded. "Make haste. We leave presently."

"Yes, Optio."

e've traveled far enough," Adratus grumbled as he threw down his pack.

In the thick, trackless woods, the three legionaries stopped, Maximus a few yards ahead and Grethuk beside Adratus. The surrounding trees, shrouded in inky darkness, stood like silent sentinels, brooding and watchful. An eerie feeling emanated from the night—as if something might be stalking in the shadows. Perhaps barbarians watched them, ready to attack. The rustling of the wind stirred the chill of the night, which had deepened as the blue and lavender moons cast their eerie light through the branches. In the distance, a wolf howled. Although exhausted from hours of walking, Adratus knew this buffer zone between warring nations was a place where caution needed to be exercised and vigilance maintained.

Grethuk set his pack beside Adratus's. "Is not midnight when your kind is most active?" he said with a grin.

"I'm no sorcerer," Adratus grumbled, "if that's your meaning. And I rarely perform ritual magic." He held his left fist forward to show the thick band of black titanium on his ring finger. The square head of the ring showed an eye within a triangle engraved in silver with a small garnet set above the eye. "My ring contains a handful of spells that one like me— with high levels of pneuma—can learn to master over time."

"You mean it is a cheat." Grethuk grinned.

"'Tis Tridulan efficiency."

"Stop teasing the boy," Maximus chimed in. He turned back and neared. Only his face was visible beneath the black steel helmet; two hinged cheekplates hung on either side, concealing the rest. Embellishing the headwear was a sharpened blade, like that of a curved battle-axe that arched from front to back over the center of his head.

"My words were free of malice," Grethuk said, holding a matching helmet at his side. "'Tis he who barks with sour mood."

"Apologies." Adratus sighed heavily. "My mood claimed you as an unintended target. Its rightful target"—he gained volume with each subsequent word—"is the *vexing* fact that we are miles into the Bloody Belt and march straightways towards True Light lands with no knowledge as to why."

"Lower your voice," Maximus commanded. "We know not who is near."

"And I assume you'll use that as another pretext not to tell us why we journey."

"He is correct, Maximus," said Grethuk. "We are far from the thin walls of the barracks, yet your lips stay sealed."

Maximus removed his helmet and glanced downward for a moment. "Sit." He motioned to the ground. "We will make camp here for the night, and I will put answers to questions."

"Preferably not in that order," Adratus said, as he sat on the ground that was blanketed by old layers of soft pine needles. A downed tree limb behind him, its bark covered in fungus and mosses, allowed him to recline.

Grethuk sat beside him.

"No." Maximus tossed his helmet on the ground but remained standing. There was an air of sorrow in him—or worry. "I'll tell you . . . after I piss." He began away.

Adratus watched him slowly retreat beyond the shadows of the woods before his eyes drifted to the ground.

"You . . . worry for him," Grethuk hissed.

Adratus nodded. "Whatever weight he carries . . . Never have I seen him so distant."

Grethuk leaned closer, whispering, "I know you have affection for Maximus. Of the romantic variety."

Adratus snapped his eyes to the reptilian man as his mind raced to devise a response. Instead, his mouth just hung wordlessly open, and he stared wide-eyed like a fool.

"You need not deny what I clearly see." Grethuk grinned. "He *is* charming, for a Human."

Adratus sighed sadly. "He shares not my affections. Nor will he ever."

Grethuk set his scaly hand, fingers tipped with long black nails, gently on Adratus's shoulder. "He cares for you, in his way. A *platonic* way." He paused. "You should be aware that in the lands we soon shall enter, they slaughter men such as you. I suppose they would kill only half of me."

"What do you mean?" Adratus pulled away, his heart pounding.

"You know well what I mean."

"But why?" Adratus jumped up from his seat. "Why does who someone loves and desires have any impact on the Dayigans?" The issue cut him deeply, an unexpected injury ripping at his core, as he thought of all the people like him suffering without cause. Grief filled his chest alongside his anger.

"It was not my intention to affront you," Grethuk soothed, trying to take Adratus's hand and pull him back to his seat. "I only supposed it was important that you knew."

"It makes no sense."

"It needn't make sense," Maximus returned, a hint of anger in his voice. "They are barbarians. Hating things is their favored pastime. It may console you to know that they're more likely to kill you because you're a Tridulan or for practicing magic, or even just for your association with the Dark Light."

Adratus clenched his jaw, breathing a beat before he growled, "Their fake empire must fall."

"This is no time for such talk." Maximus was stern. His voice softened as he glanced at the ground. "Not with what has happened. Sit."

Adratus complied, retaking his seat next to Grethuk, and Maximus sat before them.

Maximus leaned in, taking his time. His words lingered, as if reluctant to leave his lips. "We interviewed the Terovae woman after she regained consciousness," he said. "She hails from a farming town just beyond the Bloody Belt within the Dayigan Empire. She told us that her town, with a population of one thousand, was attacked; her people slaughtered indiscriminately, adults and children alike. The attackers then set fire to the entire town, burning everything—including its inhabitants—to ash.

"As the lone Terovae in the Human town," Maximus continued, "she was the only person able to escape by air. She presumes everyone else is dead. Her flight afterwards was naught but a mad dash twisted with horror. She flew through the night, even as her wings burned with fatigue, yet she was too terrified to halt. Her direction, she said, was random, her arrival in our fort, inadvertent. Yet her accusation is grave." His eyes hardened as he delivered the final blow. "She claims Tridulan legionaries destroyed her town."

"Impossible," Adratus said. "We have standing orders to maintain a defensive blockade. Nothing more."

"And yet, just moments ago, you proclaimed your wish for the downfall of their empire."

"I would never—"

"I know," Maximus cut him off, a mix of grief and frustration in his voice. "I've said the same countless times myself and have heard many a Tridulan voice the same desire. Nevertheless, I cannot bring myself to accept that our *own men* would commit such atrocities. Yet, the woman was adamant in her accusation. You see why I hesitated to speak these words, why it pains me, even now, to speak them." He paused. "We travel westward to find evidence against our brothers-in-arms, so they may stand trial for disobeying orders, mass murder, and potentially inflaming an international incident. If a whole cohort is responsible, it will be decimated."

"Decimated?" Grethuk asked.

"'Tis a rare form of capital punishment," Adratus said bleakly. "One in ten of the responsible party is chosen by drawing lots. And executed by bludgeoning. In the case of a barrier cohort, 'twould be fifty Tridulans and ten axillary."

The dire words weighed the air. Crickets droned. Owls hooted. Leaves rustled in the wind. All three of the soldiers fell into a stony silence for several minutes as each grappled with his own troubled thoughts.

"Get some sleep," Maximus said at last. "We yet have far to travel."

CHAPTER EIGHT

Adratus trudged through the field of nothingness; the full scope of the destruction only made more apparent with each chalky step. Scorched wooden husks and skeletal remains littered the area—some shattered beyond recognition, others still miraculously intact but stripped clean of flesh. He had expected to see a burned town, to see homes and shops charred and collapsed, yet what he found instead was a mile-wide field of little more than dust.

Grethuk broke the silence. "What could have caused such sheer destruction?"

Adratus stared at a skeleton, half-buried in gray ash, too small to be an adult's. "A Dragon?"

"Not impossible," Maximus said. "Yet, it seems implausible that the Dragons would break an ancient truce and fly the entire way here, from the continent of Volagrok, to incinerate a border town."

Adratus nodded, feeling slightly foolish for the suggestion.

"Well . . ." Maximus waved his hand toward the area. "Investigate, Faldénrus."

"Right." Adratus shook off shock and lifted his hands to his sides, palms downward. He closed his eyes. "Detect magic."

Red light emanated from his palms, projecting an elongated ray to glide across the ground as he slowly moved his hands parallel to the surface. After scanning the immediate area, the light faded, and Adratus opened his eyes.

"This was no normal fire," he said. "'Twas definitely magical in nature."

Maximus groaned with impatience. "A drunken toddler could have determined as much, Adratus. Do your eye spell." He motioned above his head. "The eye in the triangle."

"Is that why you brought me here?"

"'Tis a considerable part."

"Then I disappoint you. That spell is beyond my means."

Grethuk raised a hand, as if he were at the Academy. "If I could be included in the talks, Tridulans. Explanation? Eye in the triangle spell?"

"'Tis a retrocognition spell," Adratus said. "Faldénri are usually attached to peacekeeping forces in urban centers and major towns. Thus, our primary spells tend towards confining spells so we can apprehend criminals. However, some are investigative. Because areas where major events have occurred become imprinted, our retrocognition spell allows us to view these events." He paused, seeing a touch of confusion on Grethuk's reptilian face. "Essentially, we can view the past. The most skilled Faldénri in the capital can evoke imprints from *weeks* past. Yet I . . . Maximus, 'tis well beyond my means."

"You must make it happen," Maximus insisted. "This surrounding horror is much more than we anticipated. No longer do we simply investigate rogue legionaries. The Empire *must* know what wields the power to do *this*."

Adratus cast his eyes over the desolate landscape. A gust of wind blew up the fine ash, swirling it around in a cloud as it rolled across the expanse.

After a slow nod, Adratus said, "The magnitude of this imprint should make it stronger and thus easier to evoke." He clasped his hands, setting his thumb on his ring. As his thumb slowly followed the edges of his ring, Adratus whispered, "*Descry.*" He lifted his ring to touch his forehand. "*Descry,*" he whispered.

A jolt shot through him, causing him to flinch.

He maintained himself as a hazy pyramid formed a foot above his head. Yet, it faded just as quickly. Adratus stumbled, panting. "I'm unable."

Maximus placed his hand on the younger soldier's back between his shoulders. "Stay strong."

Adratus took a deep breath as he stood tall, yet with his head bowed. He again touched the ring to his forehead. "*Descry,*" he whispered. The irises of his eyes glowed red as he closed them, shining through his eyelids.

A pyramid, as if of glass, with a two-foot base, formed a foot above his head. Its edges glowed scarlet. Centered within, a two-dimensional eye of the same red light spun gradually. Still with his eyes closed, Adratus lifted his head, and in his mind, he could see a grayed plank wall inches before his face. He walked through the wall—taking the same steps in reality as in the vision—and entered the street.

The voice of Maximus was a distant echo. "What do you see?"

"I'm in the town. 'Tis so real, yet the area is dim and hazy."

The small town appeared as if blanketed by a thick rolling fog. Everywhere, people went about their mundane lives, most wearing various shades of blue, from nobles' richly decorated clothing to laborers' simple homespun garments. Buildings were plain, with pale gray plaster walls trimmed by dark wooden beams below thatched roofs. A few held touches of the same blue for decoration.

A horse clip-clopped down the cobblestone road, pulling a rickety cart loaded with wilted vegetables. The sound of a blacksmith's hammer rang out in the distance. Shouts from vendors competed in the market square while aromas of fresh-baked bread and pungent meats filled the air. Chatter floated over from old friends and excited buyers alike.

Children ran wild through the street as they chased each other around stalls draped in striped canvas awnings of blue and gray. Near Adratus, two women strolled through the area, chatting and examining items for sale before sharing a warm embrace and continuing on their way.

Adratus spoke to Maximus and Grethuk, though he could not see them, saying, "Nothing out of the ordinary occurs. The people seem in good spirits."

"See you what caused the fire?" Maximus asked.

"No. As I said, nothing of note occurs."

Without warning, a squadron of ten Tridulan legionaries emerged from the shadows. They, with swords raised high, unleashed an explosion of terror. The townspeople, horrified, fled in disarray as the soldiers violently swung their weapons, striking down men and women to lie bleeding in the streets.

"Legionaries," Adratus said. "I don't recognize them, but they are ours. They wear Tridulan armor and raise their gladii as they chase the people. The townspeople are screaming. And running. The legionaries seem crazed. Wait. *Vision, halt.*"

All motion in the town ceased—the pursuers and the horrified alike. A pale blue jug, mid-shatter, remained still, its lower half in frozen fragments as its upper section awaited its fate.

Adratus approached a legionary. The man had been running and was now frozen midtrot. One of his legs was bent behind him. The other foot had gone through a crate, smashing through to touch the ground.

However, the Tridulan's sandal had not gone through the crate. Bizarrely, it, along with the foot inside, had moved halfway up the soldier's calf, where it—insubstantial and semitransparent—remained horizontal and passed through the leg, though the leg and foot were unharmed. At the base of the same leg, a leather boot had crashed through the crate. The top of this boot faded, becoming the top of the criss-crossed straps of a legionary sandal.

"Their uniforms are but illusions," Adratus said. "These are no Tridulans."

He looked around and spotted another legionary who rounded a corner of a shop too sharply. The latter quarter of his red cape passed unhindered through a wall.

Time restarted along with the sounds of terror, yet at a later point in time.

Now vibrant blazes of green fires burned throughout the town, tearing over thatched roofs. Further panic filled the smoky air as people ran in all directions, but their attempts to flee were stopped as an unyielding thirty-foot wall of fire encircled the town.

Adratus searched but found none of the fake legionaries he wished to better analyze. He froze as he watched the faces of the townspeople.

Trapped, the people stood, an audience to their own destruction. Their eyes widened with terror as the ring of fire rushed inward, like a mighty tide, devouring all in its path. Fiery talons of green ripped through homes and shops and flesh and bone, obliterating all it touched in a chorus of doomed screams.

Adratus could do nothing as the fire rushed over him. Though the past event brought him no physical harm, he fell to his knees at the sight of it. Overwrought, he called out in horror and choked on anguish.

He felt someone grab him by the shoulder and shake him.

"Adratus," Maximus called, his voice distant. "You must leave the vision."

"No," Adratus said, regaining himself. "I must know who did this."

He took off running, occasionally stumbling over who knew what in the present as he dashed through the twisting flood of raging green.

He reached the edge beyond the wall of fire and stopped, looking out across the grassy field as he searched for anything to make sense of the deviation behind him.

An intense pain shot through his forehead. Adratus slapped his hand to his head, and he winced as the pain intensified. He quickly shook it off and returned his focus to the farmlands.

A dozen men—most in black surcoats, some in white—hurried toward the distant trees.

Another sudden jolt of pain made Adratus fall to his hands and knees. The vision shattered, and he opened his eyes to find himself in the same place but in the present.

Adratus scanned the fields and found the same section of woods beyond. "They went that way," he said weakly, light-headed and dizzy.

Maximus caught Adratus as Grethuk ran over to them. Maximus said something, but Adratus couldn't comprehend his words. His vision of Maximus became foggy as his heavy eyelids fought against him. He was suddenly hit with another sharp pain and collapsed to the ground.

His eyes gradually closed.

CHAPTER NINE

Swithun flung open the green canvas flap of the tent and rushed inside. "Captain," he growled, "we must speak."

At the back wall, Captain Rothgar, clad in his white surcoat, lay motionless on a cot draped in shadows. Continuing to face the ceiling, an arm on his forehead, he gave no response to Swithun's unwelcome entrance. On the wall to the right, a second cot held a second knight, Beadurinc, his gaze searing into the intruder like venom.

With no reply from Rothgar, Swithun slammed his hands down on the large table that dominated the tent's center. "I been trying for a chance to speak with you since yesterday, sir."

In a single swift motion, Beadurinc leaped from his cot and clutched the hilt of his sword, ready to pounce upon the sergeant. His eyes narrowed and flashed dangerously in the low burning flames of the torches in the corners. "If I gutted you now, no one would care in the slightest."

"Stand down, Beadurinc," Rothgar uttered with an air of weary irritation.

The other knight wavered as if hit by mild vertigo and cautiously returned to sit on his cot. He massaged his forehead, as if nursing some pain.

"Beadurinc and I are pneuma depleted," Rothgar said, still staring upward. "Do you have any idea what that means?"

Swithun shook his head warily.

"It means we are spent from performing powerful magic that nearly killed us." His voice was harsh and low. "It also means we haven't the tiniest desire to hear the vexing whining of a disgruntled sergeant initiate." He set his fingers to his forehead. "I have been informed of your concerns. Instead of sulking about the demise of another pagan town, be thankful that their deaths were swift."

"I am, sir. Least, I suppose so."

Beadurinc scoffed. "You would do better to be *angered* that their deaths were so swift. Those savages deserved to wallow in agony for defying God Déagar."

"Their deaths were appropriate," Rothgar said, still gazing at the canvas ceiling. "Our task was to deliver them to God Déagar for judgment. He will mete out further justice in the afterlife."

Beadurinc grinned spitefully. "Praise God Déagar, he who is Greatest of All."

"Praise God Déagar," Swithun echoed habitually before silence followed. He tentatively continued, "I thought we came to the border to fight Tridulans."

"Then you were mistaken." Rothgar, annoyed, sat up on the side of his cot and unsteadily rested his arms on his knees. He looked Swithun directly in the eyes. "I afforded you the chance to speak your peace before your Reception Ceremony, but you chose to pledge yourself to our cause. Now that you bear the green Septenar of the Silthex upon your chest, there will be no more discussion. You are a Silthex sergeant, bound by both honor and blood."

"But still we coulda spared the women and children, sir," Swithun said.

"Regrettably, we determined that would not be a suitable option in this particular area," Rothgar uttered, sorrow tinting his words. "You were stationed nearby, at the fortress on the border. What is the nickname of this region?"

"The Blue Zone, sir," Swithun answered, his voice heavy with unease. "On account of the fact that, when we lot took these lands from them Tridulans, many Karulents moved in and set up camp."

"*Set up camp* is an understatement," Rothgar replied bitterly. "They colonized the whole damn region that our army rightfully won. Five Karulent towns, eight villages, and three smaller outposts, to be exact. The concentration in this area could be catastrophic when the king passes his decree outlawing the worship of Karulus."

"He plans to do so, then?" Swithun asked.

"Soon," Rothgar said. "But we must clear out potentially problematic areas first. It shall grieve me to see it done, but this region, in particular, must be cleansed swiftly and without witnesses, including the eyes of children. If we masquerade as Tridulans, how then could we explain delivering a cart of orphans to a church?"

"I'm not rightly sure, sir," Swithun murmured, as his gaze dropped to the swept dirt floor. "Didn't think about that part."

"You didn't think, indeed," Beadurinc sneered. "Your new sergeant looks as if he might weep like a woman at any moment. You should have killed him earlier."

Swithun raised his head and met the scornful stare.

"You didn't know, did you?" Beadurinc continued. "You already knew far too much to be sent on your way. During your entire journey here, your life hung in the balance whilst Rothgar pondered whether to—"

"That is enough, Lieutenant," Rothgar said firmly.

Beadurinc gave a smug expression, as if he were both shocked and offended by the reprimand. He said nothing.

Rothgar stood and set his hands on the table while facing the other knight. "Swithun lives because he proved himself in the king's army as a great fighter worthy of joining our elite force. And because he's proven himself to be one who understands our cause—even if he is being a fucking idiot right now." He fixed Swithun with a grave look. "The Karulents killed your family—your beloved wife and son. Have those memories faded?"

Swithun clamped his jaw for a moment, the ache of the heartbreak heavy upon him. "No." He shook his head. "Never, sir. I never knew you knew about that."

"Of course we knew," Rothgar scoffed. "The Grand Master of the Silthex, himself, was there to offer you solace after the tragedy, was he not? He executed the Karulent murderer in your honor—but also for the good of the forming empire. Does it not make sense, then, that we should remove all these vile creatures so they may not hurt anyone else? My wife and I pray to have children one day," Rothgar said solemnly. "But if we are to have them, they must be born into an empire that is untainted by debauchery and heresy, a realm cleansed of wickedness and all forms of sorcery. A land pure of sin."

Swithun let out a sigh. "I'm just baffled, sir, as to what God wants me to do."

"Then let me make it *clear to you*," Rothgar said, as he leaned menacingly across the table. "Our God has placed wiser men than *you* in roles of leadership. Obey our orders, wield your sword, and leave the deep thoughts to knights and priests."

Swithun averted his gaze and nodded.

"Do you understand, Sergeant?"

"I do, sir, yes."

"Now leave us," commanded Rothgar. "As I said, Beadurinc and I are pneuma depleted from cleansing the town and require rest before we move to the next target. If I hear of any more dissonance from you, I will rethink my decision to keep you alive."

"Yes, sir," Swithun muttered in defeat as he began to walk away.

"Oh, yes," Beadurinc interjected icily. "I never had a chance to tell you before—welcome to the Immolation Brigade."

—

Adratus opened his eyes and gazed at the night sky—blackness scattered with countless tiny pinpricks of light. His head throbbed, but the effect quickly faded. On the ground next to him, Maximus was seated, observing him.

"What happened?" he asked Maximus.

Maximus sighed and leaned forward, resting his elbows on the tops of his knees. "You depleted yourself."

Adratus rubbed his forehead before sitting upright. "As I said, that spell was well beyond my skill level." He squinted at Maximus.

Maximus wore a deeply worried expression. "Saw you anything of use?"

Adratus nodded and said, "It wasn't our men, yet the true assailants tried to make it appear as if it were. They fled in that direction." He indicated a point beyond the farmlands: a small hill with a short dirt cliff topped by thick woods. "We must pursue them."

"No," Maximus said firmly. "That is westward. Away from our empire and away from our interest."

"You witnessed not what I saw," Adratus argued. "All those people . . . Whoever did this must be stopped."

"Barbarians murdering barbarians has naught to do with us," Maximus said flatly.

"They are *people*," Adratus said, "just like us."

Maximus gave him a hard stare. "They are *not* like us. They don't consider us people and would kill us for existing. You know not what I've witnessed since arriving at this bloody border."

Adratus watched the young man before him, seeing a fleeting trace of fear in his eyes. He slowly averted his gaze toward the distance where he had seen the men retreat—black lines of smoke rose from beyond the treeline.

"They remain nearby," Adratus said.

"*Immunis Adratus*," Maximus began firmly, "we have investigated this area and determined this is not a Tridulan matter. Our orders are to investigate this site and return. Thus, we will return to our fort presently. Understood?"

Adratus glanced down before responding, "No, Optio."

Grethuk stepped forward with an armful of gathered sticks, laughing. "Are my ears deceived?"

"You have no ears," Maximus said.

"I have ears." He released the sticks to clatter on the ground. "They are but streamlined. And they heard loyal Adratus disobeying orders whilst wild Maximus argues for compliance."

"Compliance has a time," Maximus said, "and this is that time."

"Both of you are correct," Grethuk said. "Our orders are to investigate this thoroughly, and for that reason, we must pursue. As a citizen of Ojron, I know my king will want to know exactly how such destruction was carried out and by whom. I'm certain your emperor would desire the same."

"They disguised themselves as Tridulans, Maximus," Adratus said. "That makes it a Tridulan matter."

"By all that is infernal," Maximus grumbled as he folded his arms across his armor-clad chest. He cast his gaze toward the ascending smoke in the distance. "Very well," he said. "We go west, further into enemy territory. But, if either of you die, I will be extremely cross with you."

CHAPTER TEN

T his is an intelligence gathering mission only," Maximus said in a near whisper. The three legionaries stood as a tight grouping within the dark and tangled woods.

Adratus's steel armor shone no more. Instead, it was smeared with a heavy coat of fertile black mud clawed from a farm outside the destroyed town.

"I care not what barbaric activities we witness," Maximus continued. "We will not intercede."

Adratus tightened his grip on his gladius as he watched the Dayigan encampment. Partially hidden by silhouetted trees, the camp was a cluster of green tents, all topped with cone-shaped points and some with overhangs above their entrances. The area, dotted with campfires, was lit up far better than Adratus would have liked.

He felt like a child playing a game that had gone way too far. He was now sixteen, he reminded himself, now an adult and a soldier of the mighty Tridulan Army. He'd trained hard in Nerageat for this moment, and Maximus had given him further guidance and further practice. *Trust in your training,* in his head, he repeated the words of his drill instructor over and over, as if they might empower him. Still, part of Adratus wished to flee.

"Adratus, you've turned pale," Maximus whispered. "More so, I mean."

"I'm fine. We should focus on getting to the central tent in the camp. 'Twill most likely be the headquarters of their commander, if their camps are anything like ours."

"Or their mess hall." Grethuk produced a fanged grin. "I would loath to sneak into a secured barbarian camp only to find their stash of stale flatbread."

"Adratus is correct," Maximus said. "One large tent usually means a command tent—and that is where we'll find our answers. We will not engage unless we're first engaged. And then, only insofar as necessary to make our escape." He turned toward Adratus. "What Faldénri tricks have you that can help?"

"None, Optio. My powers remain depleted after using the retrocognition spell."

Maximus groaned in exasperation. "By all that is— Fucking za, Adratus. Such information should have been shared."

"Apologies. I thought you knew."

Maximus paused, thinking a beat. "We will abort and return to the empire."

Just then, a voice called out from a distance, "Who goes?"

The three legionaries froze, as if their stillness could make whoever said it forget their presence.

Adratus's heart raced as he held his breath, attempting to keep absolute quiet.

A branch snapped. Footsteps approached through the brush. It seemed more than the boots of a single man—or even a pair of men. Another group approached from opposite the camp.

"Who goes?" Another call. A different voice, a different direction. More footsteps.

Adratus tried to force down his fear. *Trust in your training.* He kept his eyes locked on Maximus. The older boy's face was frozen in a watchful stare, appearing just as frightened as the younger.

The footsteps spreading around them had slowed. Adratus imagined them like lions creeping toward their prey.

"No one is behind me," Maximus whispered. "On three, we run in my direction."

An authoritative voice called out, "In the name of His Holiness, Patriarch Krasil, I order you to surrender yourselves."

Maximus held up one finger. Then two.

More footsteps rushed from the camp and slowed as they neared.

"You haven't violated any laws yet," a voice continued, "but if you resist us, you *will* be punished."

Maximus lifted his third finger.

The Tridulans bolted through the tall grass and bushes, their footsteps announcing their presence. The others began running, too, a muster of boots clapping against the earth as they began the pursuit.

—

Sword in hand, Swithun hastened through the moonlit woods, desperate to find the unknown invaders. A dozen of his fellow Silthex had already run ahead, yet none had returned with news.

"Swithun," someone called. It was Lieutenant Beadurinc. "Follow me!" he yelled as he picked up his pace.

"We've lost sight of them, sir," Swithun reported, rushing to stay by his side. "But they can't have gone far." He ran at top speed, struggling to keep up with the younger lieutenant. "They're Tridulans, for sure. Three, I'd wager."

"You have the most experience with this particular version of savage," Beadurinc said, advancing. "What can you tell me?"

Swithun hesitated while searching the area for any trace of their quarry. "If they was attacking us, there'd be more than three of 'em. Legionaries ain't worth shite on their own, sir. They've gotta fight together as a unit to truly shine."

"Reconnaissance," Beadurinc concluded. "I suppose you might be worth your keep in the end." He spun around and barked orders at another sergeant—"Inform Captain Rothgar that this could be the start of something larger."

"Yes, Lieutenant." The sergeant dashed toward the camp.

Shouts echoed from further ahead, accompanied by a clash of swords.

"Swithun, you're with me," Beadurinc called as he charged into the fray, sword held high.

Swithun quickly followed, eager to finally prove his worth to his lieutenant.

—

Treading through the dense, night-shrouded woods behind Maximus, Adratus felt his armor rattle against his chest in time to each pound of his sandals to the ground. Despite the chill in the air, heat rushed through him. He had no clue how many barbarians pursued or from where any would emerge.

The dreadful clamor of their hunt echoed throughout the trees, creating an unsettling dread within Adratus. His breaths heaved heavy and harsh, nearly blocking out the frightening bellows of their pursuers that drew ever closer.

His grip tightened around his sword as his mind repeated like a mantra: *Trust in your training*. Yet nothing could ease the looming terror that clutched him.

Then, abruptly, Adratus halted and spun to squint through hazy shadows. "Where is Grethuk?"

Maximus darted closer, but in moments, a blade was thrust toward Adratus's face. He tried to move, though Maximus was quicker, blocking the enemy's sword with a thunderous clash of steel.

Frozen, Adratus watched his friend's muscled arm as it strained, his gladius holding back the sword that would have ended Adratus. His heart thundered with fear.

"Run," Maximus snarled through gritted teeth.

Adratus remained, knowing he must help. With a deep breath, he shouted and thrust his blade forward, puncturing black tabard and mail alike. It was nothing like a training dummy. He felt something tear inside as blood spilled out. He felt a sickening sensation as the weapon dug deep into the flesh. Liquid crimson flowed down sharpened steel to coat his shaking hand, the warmth unsettling.

Adratus watched as the Dayigan crumpled to the ground with an empty thud.

"I've never killed before . . ." Adratus uttered, staring at his coated hand clutching his gladius.

"Adratus, we must go," Maximus demanded, tugging at his arm.

Adratus blinked, clearing himself of shock. "Grethuk. We cannot leave him here."

"We do not leave him if we know not where he is," replied Maximus tersely. "He could very well be ahead of us. We must go, *now*."

Adratus's eyes stayed focused on his gory weapon.

"He knows his way back," Maximus assured, his hands on Adratus's arms. He pushed the younger soldier.

They ran.

—

"They've split up!" Beadurinc bellowed, Swithun at his side as their boots pounded untamed foliage. Other Silthex sergeants followed unflinchingly in their wake, hurdling fallen logs and skittering across ancient roots with single-minded purpose.

Swithun gestured his sword to his right. "One went that way!"

"Good eyes! Follow him," Beadurinc commanded. "The rest of us will pursue the other two."

"Yes, sir!" Swithun darted off without pause, relishing the prospect of Dark Light blood—the enemy he knew, his only source of respite from his conflict with the Karulents.

—

Adratus and Maximus charged through the shadows of the forest, gladii drawn and ready. Yet their advance was halted by a throng of ten Dayigans cloaked in black tabards, who dashed from the surrounding trees. The Tridulans turned to retreat, yet more men stepped from the gloom at their rear.

Surrounded, Adratus's chest tightened as he watched each set of eyes glimmering with hate. He turned to Maximus, steeling himself for the approaching battle. He would fight to his last breath if necessary, Adratus resolved, yet he feared that final breath was not too far away.

Another man emerged from the darkness—his white tabard contrasting with that of the other men. His gaze fell on Maximus and Adratus. "Why has the Dark Light encroached upon our holy empire?"

Adratus glanced at Maximus, both bracing themselves, yet silent.

"You will answer me, savage filth!"

Maximus, sword held high, emitted a primal roar as he charged toward the man in white. Dayigans rushed to their master's defense like an avalanche of steel. But Adratus and Maximus pressed back to back, emboldening each other with every swing they took. Adratus let the many hours of training he'd received imbue him. His arms knew what to do. He was not a boy, but a Tridulan legionary. *Trust in your training.* He and Maximus fought with untamed ferocity, felling enemy after enemy with every thrust of their blades. Yet, no matter how hard they tried, the duo remained hopelessly outnumbered five to one.

Despite the odds, both young men fought fiercely, neither hoping for any victory other than to live. No rest or retreat was allowed them—for every strike Adratus deflected, two more came in harsh response. Still, they persisted, grabbing each opportunity they could find amid the violent storm.

The leader watched from afar, a cruel grin on his lips. "Your foolish courage is impressive, savages," he spoke loudly, "but it will not save your lives. Lay down your arms or fall down, through death, to the eternal torments of za. *Silthex, halt*, yet stand ready."

The moment stretched into an eternity in dread as Adratus and Maximus staggered back, battered and broken.

The Dayigans had paused their attack, yet ten malignant blades remained firmly aimed for Tridulan blood.

"Do it," Maximus breathed out in ragged resignation.

Adratus discarded his blades with disdain, and Maximus took one last breath before following his own command.

Before they knew it, both men were restrained by cold metal shackles.

They were dragged toward their captors' camp.

CHAPTER ELEVEN

Swithun's lungs burned with exhaustion, yet his feet never ceased their pursuit. He was beginning to fear he'd lost the Tridulan, and in the depths of Swithun's soul, an all-consuming rage took hold. He needed to find him, needed to prove his worth to the Silthex. Rothgar doubted him. Beadurinc doubted him. This could have been his one chance to show them his devotion to Déagar. And he hated the Tridulan for stealing that chance away. All thoughts of mercy were swallowed up by wrath as he resolved to reclaim what the invader had stolen from him—his redemption through blood.

Halting, he stilled his breath, straining his ears for a sound that would guide him closer to his quarry. The noise of the other skirmishes had faded, smothered by the thick blackness of the night as only the chirping of crickets and rustling of leaves remained. It was almost serene—were it not for the cruel blade he clutched and the beating war drum in his chest.

A faint rustling sounded from ahead, and Swithun lunged forward with renewed vigor. Branches snapped as he stumbled through a thicket of bushes to find a figure towering above him—a lizard-man clad in a black leather harness above a scarlet kilt. His dark gray scales glistened in the pale moonlight, coating bulging muscles that spoke of strength. The creature held an enormous sword in one hand and warned Swithun to turn away.

"I have no quarrel with you, Dayigan," the lizard-man snarled, "save for your want to kill me. If you decide otherwise and retreat, I give you my word I will not harm you.

Though, should we fight"—he raised his one-handed longsword—"rest assured you will die."

Swithun stayed motionless, his sword pointing at the menacing figure. "I don't know much about your kind, lizard-man—"

"I'm more of a snake-man, in truth."

"Right," Swithun said gruffly. "I seen your race from a distance when I fought in the Dark Empire, but never up close before. Can't guess your age, but you're sounding real young from your voice. Don't wanna kill a boy."

The snake-man lowered his sword. "Then it is settled—"

"No!" Swithun barked, cutting him off. "What I want and what me God wills me to do, they're two different things."

"Will you throw down your weapon or no?"

"You have a name, boy?"

"*Fucking za*," he groaned impatiently. "Grethuk."

"I'm givin' you one last chance, Grethuk," Swithun said. "I'll count you twenty seconds whilst you get your soul right with the Greatest of All, so he can stand as your advocate and save you from your sin—"

Grethuk shouted and swung his sword forward, meeting Swithun's blade with a deafening clash. "You highly overestimate your fighting skills," he hissed through fangs.

The two warriors exchanged rapid blows, yet it soon became clear that Grethuk was far mightier than expected; each strike Swithun delivered seemed to hit an unyielding wall, while Grethuk's strikes were swift and powerful.

"*You* lecture *me* of sin?" Grethuk sneered as he increased the pressure against Swithun's sword, keeping the two blades locked together.

Swithun, face grimaced, pushed back with all of his might.

"And yet," Grethuk hissed, "I have seen the town of civilians your 'righteous' army burnt to ash!"

Swithun and Grethuk clashed again and again, exchanging blows as they battled for supremacy. Swithun felt every slash and thrust, and knew he neared defeat. Despite his years of combat, his body ached from exhaustion, and he felt his limbs grow weaker every second against the sheer ferocity of the Ophiruk.

Then, suddenly, the creature lunged forward and bit down hard on Swithun's upper arm. Venom rushed through Swithun's body like wildfire in his veins, paralyzing his limbs. He collapsed to lie flat on the ground, facing the night sky, unable to move or speak.

"I would have won anyway," Grethuk said. "Why delay it further?" He stepped back and watched, glaring down at his helpless opponent with contempt.

Swithun lay motionless, watching as Grethuk walked forward. Desperately, Swithun uttered a silent prayer to God Déagar, yet he knew he was finished.

"I warned you if we fought, you'd die," Grethuk said, stomping a clawed, sandaled foot on either side of Swithun as he stood over him. He raised his longsword high with both hands, its malignant point aimed downward. "*O Human, oh fear us. Oh fear the Ophiruks. We are stronger than you. And faster, too. And our bite will leave you helpless.*" He grinned, his tongue slipping through his fangs. "Did you still want a countdown to unburden your soul?" He lowered the tip of his sword to Swithun's heart. "Ten. Nine. Eight."

From out of nowhere, a burning sphere hurtled through the air like an arrow. The emerald fire seared through Grethuk's chest, engulfing him. With a hissing scream, he staggered from Swithun and collapsed to his knees, writhing in agony as the flames ripped across his flesh, spitting open his scaly skin.

His weapon thumped to the ground.

The roaring inferno spun around Grethuk's body, scorching every inch of him until finally erupting outward as a brilliant blaze.

The Ophiruk, now a blackened husk, toppled to the ground.

In an instant, it was over, yet the hellish image lingered. The air filled with the stench of burnt death.

Confused and horrified, Swithun attempted to move, to see what had caused this destruction, yet the paralysis remained. He could but brace himself for whatever greater monster this world would soon unleash upon him—until Captain Rothgar emerged from the shadows, his sword alight with green fire.

The captain cast an iron gaze upon Swithun. "You hesitated." His tone boiled with contempt.

Swithun tried to move, but his limbs refused to obey.

Sword in hand, Rothgar kneeled low beside him, solemnly inspecting the unmoving figure. "You objected to the death of vile Karulents. Now, you hesitate to slay a single minion of the Dark God," he said, glaring at Swithun with accusation in his eyes. "Have I been naive in letting you join our order?"

Swithun tried to move his lips, but it proved pointless.

Rothgar pressed the flaming blade against Swithun's shoulder. "In the name of Déagar, I cleanse your flesh of toxins."

Swithun felt an inferno shoot through his veins, as if his blood boiled, scorching him from within—and suddenly, he could move.

Rothgar tapped the copper band around Swithun's upper arm—the Silthex symbol, etched into the band, glowed an eerie green. But at Rothgar's touch, the light faded away. His voice was a harsh whisper at Swithun's ear, "Be glad we track you."

Angered, Rothgar stood and stepped away. "Kneel," he demanded. "And bow your head."

With a heavy heart, Swithun complied. It was better, he decided, to be killed by his holy captain than by a savage snake. He waited, head lowered, expecting to feel the captain's blade slice raggedly through his neck. It was fitting; he had failed them again.

Instead, Rothgar kneeled beside him and gently planted his sword to the ground before himself. His hands grasping its hilt, he closed his eyes and prayed aloud, "Praise God Déagar, eldest of the Gods, protector from the Dark. You are the Greatest of All. We humble ourselves before you, as we beg you to watch over this man we've sent to your judgment. Though he was wicked, we mourn his death and the path to torment he has chosen." He paused. "Astha'will-miabé."

"Astha'will-maybe," Swithun repeated.

Continuing to kneel on the moist earth, Rothgar faced outward, staring. "I've never told anyone this," he began solemnly, "but when I was first knighted, I was horrified to discover what would be expected of me. I, too, struggled with my faith, as you do now. Admittedly, I hid it better." He chuckled. "But the Grand Master enlightened me. He helped me to envision a world free of those who didn't fit Déagar's grand ideal, a world devoid of heretics and their blasphemous thoughts, a haven where women are kept in their rightful place and do not seduce righteous men to backslide into lust. Imagine a world where monstrous races like that vile snake are wiped out completely, never to plague the nightmares of our children. That is what the Silthex fight for: a shining world of integrity and values, unified in one voice in worship to our loving God." Eyes shimmering with bliss, he turned to Swithun. "We will try to save as many as we can, but sadly, most of mankind is too lost to live within our perfect world. They must be plucked out, like weeds from a flower garden. And that falls on us, as the holy army of God Déagar, to carry out. But for those of us who remain, it will be paradise. The True Light is the only way, Swithun; all others *must* perish."

"I understand." Swithun felt something inside him stir at Rothgar's words, like a slow-burning fire had been lit within his heart. "I'll help you make the world into a paradise, Captain."

Rothgar smiled and clapped Swithun's shoulder. Standing, he said, "You are truly a righteous man, Sergeant. I can tell that you strive to embody the will of God Déagar." He helped him to his feet.

"I strive for it every day, sir."

"I believe you. Now"—Rothgar kicked Grethuk's corpse—"take this serpent's body up to the roadway and leave it for the locals to find. Its presence will help them believe that the Tridulans caused the fires. Mankind is not ready to understand what we do for them."

Swithun nodded solemnly in agreement before grabbing the body to haul it away.

CHAPTER TWELVE

At the edge of the Silthex camp, on a road of dirt through woods, stood a large cage built from an unyielding lattice of flat, riveted iron. It perched atop a grim wagon with wrought iron fittings for absent horses. Within, Maximus and Adratus waited, their capes wrapped around their slumped shoulders as blankets blocking out the frigid air. The young men had been stripped of their weapons and armor, deprived even of their belts and sandals, leaving them in only their filthy tunics. With hands folded between their knees, they sought refuge from the night's chill while trying to fathom their unhopeful fate.

Outside, their captors, hundreds of them, mingled around campfires, laughing and eating. A group played bone dice and drank common beer.

Adratus could taste the hay in the air that carpeted his metal prison. The scent of smoke clung to his skin and permeated his bloodied black tunic. From time to time, he looked out at the Dayigans and found the mirth unsettling. Were they celebrating their victory over capturing him and Maximus, or were they reveling in the slaughter of innocent civilians? Either way, the thought made Adratus seethe with hatred. Their coarse laughter polluted the air more so than the smoke, a twisted melody that seemed to mock everything Adratus saw as honorable.

"Fucking barbarians," Adratus grumbled, as he kept his eyes locked on them.

Maximus threw a length of straw at him. "Glaring at our captors will do naught to free us. Has your magic returned?"

Adratus looked at the black ring on his finger. "No," he said bleakly. "The retrocognition spell was powerful, yet I should have now recovered."

"Yes," Maximus said quietly, his face grim. "Have you means to restore yourself faster?"

Adratus shook his head. "Nothing I can do here. Ironically, their bringing us to this camp, surrounded by these active soldiers throwing energy in the air, should help." He grinned and added, "'Twould help more if they were fighting or fucking."

Maximus returned a humorless chuckle. The smile faded as quickly as it had appeared. "If we convince a Dayigan to near, could you drain their life force more effectively?"

"I'm no Vampire, Maximus." Adratus sighed in frustration at the question, nearly wishing it was true. He leaned back, his head meeting the cold steel that enclosed them. "I cannot simply suck the pneuma from someone's blood and continue on my way. It takes time. People exude carnal energy into the air that travels towards me, which I absorb. The ritual I enacted when I moved into the barracks helped draw this energy to our quarters, but I cannot perform that here."

Maximus furrowed his brow. "I always meant to ask about that ritual."

"It helps you and Grethuk, too," Adratus said, his voice low. "Pneuma vitalizes physical feats as well."

Unimpressed, Maximus leaned back against the cage.

"Apologies," Adratus said after a moment's silence. "Eventually, I'll be able to expand my spiritual capacity to hold more pneuma and thus be able to perform greater feats without depleting myself as fast. But I'm just out of training. I should have explained the limitation better before we—"

"We will find a way forward," Maximus interrupted. *"Through hardship, to excellence."*

"Through hardship, to excellence," Adratus repeated. He sighed. "My magic should return soon."

"Speak no more of magic." Maximus motioned as he peered from their cage. "We have visitors."

Two figures approached from the camp. One was clad in a white leather surcoat, while the other wore a black cloth version of the same. The man in white stared at them for a moment, an arrogant glint in his eye.

"Have you come to tuck us in for the night?" Maximus sneered.

"I have come to charge you with various crimes against our holy empire," the man garbed in white said with a powerful and disdainful tone. "I am Sir Beadurinc, Knight of the Holy Order of Knights Silthex. This is Sergeant Swithun." He turned to Swithun. "Sergeant, with a four-year term stationed on the Dayigan-Tridulan border behind you, can you identify these men as Tridulans?"

"Seems so, sir," Swithun replied gruffly. "Judging by what they was wearing before, and all. And the other soldier admitted to being attached to the Tridulan Army."

Adratus jumped up and clutched angrily at the bars of the cage. "Where is he?" he yelled.

Beadurinc held his calm, adding an arrogant grin. "Your viperous friend bartered for his freedom by implicating you both," he said. "He then slithered away like the savage snake he is."

"Fucking lies!"

"Stand down, Adratus," Maximus said, unemotionally and remaining seated.

"Do you deny being soldiers of the nefarious Tridulan Empire?" Beadurinc asked.

"'Twould seem denial is futile," Maximus replied coldly. "Isn't it, good Sir Beaterinkydinc?"

Beadurinc absorbed Maximus's gibberish, as if he'd swallowed something sour. "*Beadurinc*," he growled. "Pray you, provide us with your names so that formal charges may be presented forthwith. You have already said the name of Adratus."

"I am Maximus," he said, as he grew annoyed. "If you desire our deaths so desperately, hurry and be done. 'Twould benefit us all to end this encounter."

"I would love nothing more than to send both of you straightways to the flaming bowels of za," Beadurinc seethed. "But we are not savages like you." The knight took a deep breath and stood a little taller before continuing a little louder. "Maximus and Adratus, you stand accused of massacring the populations of sixteen innocent Karulent targets—towns, villages, et cetera—via fire born of the demonic God, Zeanázel. As such, you will stand trial before His Highest Majesty, the High King; His Holiness, the Supreme Pontiff; and the esteemed and righteous citizens of Dayigo. Prepare yourselves, for there will be no leniency. What say you?"

"You know that wasn't us!" Adratus shouted. "We've done nothing wrong!"

Beadurinc took a step closer to the iron grate that divided them. His lips curled in a sneer. "We have evidence to the contrary, including a confession from..." He directed his gaze toward Swithun.

"Grethuk, sir," he mumbled, lowering his head.

The knight nodded slowly before continuing. "We know the Karulents in this area conspired with the Tridulans to act against the Dayigan Empire. And when the Karulents did not uphold their end of the bargain, the Tridulans ruthlessly slaughtered the inhabitants of the sixteen targets in retaliation. Such are the wicked ways of the unholy."

Adratus grasped onto the squares of black iron, his fingers trembling in rage. "You lie!" he shouted, voice thick with anger. "We came but to investigate the remains of *one* town near our border, yet we never knew of the other fifteen." He turned to Maximus, desperate for confirmation.

Maximus merely raised his hand in a feeble attempt to placate him before he settled against the wall of the cage. "'Tis done, Adratus. Accept it."

Beadurinc wore a sinister smirk as he coldly viewed the ornate ring on Adratus's hand, gripping the cage. His brow raised with interest as he chided, "A fascinating trinket, *Faldénrus.* 'Tis a pity our cage binds magic so effectively; otherwise, it could be of use to you. How unfortunate."

Adratus's fire extinguished, flickering into fret. His hands fell from the iron and hung limply by his sides. He breathed. "I swear, by all that is infernal," he maintained solemnly, his voice heavy with conviction, "we never knew of those other fifteen places."

Beadurinc chuckled cruelly, a malicious grin spreading across his pompous face. "Of course you know not of the other fifteen—they have yet to be purified. But soon they will be. Come, Swithun. We must prepare the camp to march on its next target."

CHAPTER THIRTEEN

For the entire day, the Silthex convoy marched down a rutted forest road. Iron rattled with every bump as Maximus and Adratus rode inside the cage. They sat awkwardly on either end—Adratus in the front corner and Maximus against the back—eleven feet between them.

The three hundred black-tabarded Silthex marched before and behind, while a few were tasked with driving the wagons hauling gear. The ten knights in white rode tall atop their mounts, traversing up and down the convoy's length while assuring all remained on task.

Day gave way to dusk, and mist descended onto the dismal forest, cloaking the convoy and its men. Its moisture pooled on the grate roof before dripping inside onto Adratus's arm.

Maximus broke the silence. "You've gone quiet."

It was true. Adratus had hardly spoken as they traveled. Instead, his eyes remained locked on the thick woods that passed them by, wondering if they'd ever escape this wretched place alive. "That barbarian accused us of atrocities—yet you said nothing."

"What would we have gained by shouting at a man that he lied when he was perfectly aware?"

Adratus nodded and sighed sadly. "I'm uncertain what to do. I'd hoped my magic would grant us some means to free ourselves, yet without it . . ."

"At least we now know why your magic remains hindered. Have you tried sticking your hand outside the cage and thus outside the binding field?"

"My hand is but a focus," Adratus grumbled. "My power stems from my mind and soul. That said, yes, I tried. Our final hope is that Grethuk finds us." His gaze drifted down to the misty edge of the road where the dirt met tall grasses and trees.

Maximus was silent, watching the younger legionary before he whispered gravely, "Come. Sit beside me."

Adratus stood and painstakingly shuffled across the swaying prison to sit at Maximus's side.

Maximus set his thick arm across Adratus's shoulders. "Do you recall—on that day we first met when I took you to the border—I told you most who arrive at the barrier forts are fools ignorant of what awaits them?"

"Somewhat." Adratus lowered his gaze to the floor.

"I spoke of myself." Maximus paused, as if his words weighed him. "You arrived at our fort with a noble purpose, yet on *my* arrival, I had been motivated by no more than political ambition. However, six months later, we received word that our neighboring fort to the north was under siege. I yet recall the stench of ash that lay heavily in the air as we marched towards our brothers. By the time we arrived, the Dayigans held the fort. The battle to retake it was a nightmare of blood and death and calls of agony." Maximus went silent as he drifted into troubled thoughts. "In time, more of our cohorts arrived to assist, but the Dayigans maintained the advantage. We lost many men those three days before forcing the Dayigans to retreat. Nevertheless, we were too late—the foul barbarians had already slaughtered all within the fort; six hundred lives lost brutally. You see, the Dayigans had no goal but to slaughter as many of us as they could. Nothing came of it, but death. Afterwards, my father tried to reassign me elsewhere for my safety. I refused. I had come to understand what you always had—the empire must be defended from those who would see us extinguished forever." Maximus drew a long, sorrowful breath. "The cruel Dayigans I came to know in that battle would not have let Grethuk live."

"You cannot be certain." Angered, Adratus tried to pull away.

Maximus held him tighter. "I *am* certain. Would you rather believe he betrayed us for freedom?"

The words caused Adratus's body to tighten. He opened his watery eyes, staring at the straw-covered floor, his breathing heavy.

"Apologies," Maximus said. "I wished to shield you from my suspicions, yet we cannot afford the false hope that Grethuk will assist."

"No magic. No rescue," Adratus whispered. "We ride as passengers to our deaths. Perhaps false hope would be preferable."

"Ignorance is never preferable. I should have told you sooner." Maximus pulled him closer, and Adratus rested his head on the hard chest of his companion, hearing the steady beat of his heart through the filthy red tabard. Adratus breathed deeply, taking in the musky scent as he placed a hand on Maximus's stomach, taking solace in their embrace.

"I am aware of your feelings for me," Maximus said softly, stroking the short prickles of Adratus's hair. "Whilst I do not share them in like fashion, I do care for you. As a little brother. I vow, on the flaming bident of Zeanázel, I will protect you from harm."

His words were an unexpected balm, soothing the sorrow in Adratus's soul. He clung onto Maximus like a lifeline, soaking in his warmth and snuggling nearer as Maximus wrapped his arm tighter. Adratus suddenly wanted nothing more than to remain within his arms forever, even though this carriage was their tomb.

A clash of steel rang out against the cage, jolting Adratus away from Maximus to sit upright again. A knight mounted upon a steed rode alongside them.

The knight again rapped his sword menacingly. "Stop being perverts in there, filthy fucking savages."

Once the knight had ridden off, Maximus leaned closer to Adratus, saying in a solemn tone, "Grethuk sacrificed his life for answers we have yet to obtain. For him, we must survive and get our questions met." He gestured toward the front of the line. "Look, the convoy comes to a halt."

Adratus looked into the distance where the wagons ahead were parking by the road, while others veered off into an open clearing. "It appears our journey ends," he said. "Whatever that might mean."

CHAPTER FOURTEEN

As the final rays of day filtered through the trees far to the east of the clearing, Swithun and two other sergeants heaved an imposing bundle of deep green canvas, struggling under the immense weight—two clinging onto either end of the roll while Swithun bore its sagging center.

Amid the shouts of orders and the clamor of construction, they reached their assigned spot. As one, they dropped the hefty package with a dusty thud, pausing for a brief rest before rolling out the tent.

Every corner of the forming camp was rife with similar labor—several tents had already been erected, while others remained half-finished. The discordant rhythms of mallets against wooden spikes filled the air.

"Swithun," a deep voice snapped. Swithun braced himself as Lieutenant Beadurinc stepped into view, his features menacing in the dim light, yet the eyes were calm and unyielding. "I have a task for you. You will go to the cage holding the savages and build a partition."

"A partition, sir?" Swithun muttered uneasily.

"Yes," he replied. "Some planks from the lumber cart should suffice. Leave the Tridulans about two feet, and the rest will form a new compartment." Beadurinc paused, eyeing Swithun menacingly. "I've convinced Rothgar to take your advice."

"My advice, sir?"

The lieutenant nodded as he produced a grin. "Yes, about saving some of the Karulents from this next town."

Swithun breathed a sigh of relief and gained an uncertain smile. "I thank you, sir." He paused for a moment before adding, "'Tis right, this. You'll see."

"It is indeed," Beadurinc replied, the grin becoming crueler. "Keeping a few dozen women alive for a night or two will help to further the morale of our men."

"Right," Swithun said with a dismal undertone, his eyes burning with inner rage. He turned from Beadurinc, facing the ground.

"Rothgar has elected to abstain from the diversion," Beadurinc stated nonchalantly, his eyes lingering on Swithun. "But I suppose some recreation would do you well. However, as the *lowest* sergeant in camp, you will be the very last to partake."

"That's not what I meant though, sir, when I said—"

"Sergeant," Beadurinc snapped. "Is there an issue?"

"No, sir," Swithun mumbled, still unable to meet the unflinching stare of his superior.

Swithun's unease seemed to please Beadurinc. "Very good," the knight said. "You have your orders; get to it."

—

Swithun grunted as he dragged a long log across the floor of the iron cage. Carefully, he shoved each end through the diamond-shaped gaps in each metal lattice wall. The log was the last of four, sitting horizontally to form the studs of his intended partition.

The two prisoners stood motionless in their iron shackles against the far wall. Their eyes followed the sergeant, watching him.

Ignoring them, Swithun took a moment to appreciate the work he'd finished. Each log ran across the cage, forming horizontal studs and leaving two feet for the current prisoners. Some of the logs had a slight curve, some were a bit crooked, but for what it was, it would do.

Swithun gave a satisfied nod and grinned.

"Well built," said the dark-skinned captive with the smooth head and red tunic—Maximus, he'd called himself—his casual tone stinging. "If a career in mass murder fails you, the field of carpentry awaits."

Swithun's knuckles whitened from gripping his hammer. But he shook off the flare of anger and grabbed a plank from the stack behind him, setting it against the studs. He drove the nail into its target.

"I attempt but to be friendly to our cell guest," Maximus resumed. "How is this—destroyed any good towns lately?"

Swithun's skin turned a shade of crimson, and he slammed the hammer to the floor. Staring at the captive with fury, he snarled, "You can't understand what 'tis like to have a holy quest from God. At least I don't worship Demonic Gods."

Swithun grabbed up his hammer from the straw-covered floor and continued his work.

"There are no *demonic Gods*," Maximus began with a chuckle. "Only *Demons* and *Gods*, two separate entities."

"There's Ignísekhet," the other one—Adratus—added in the same flippant tone.

"True," Maximus conceded, "yet she is complicated." He raised his voice to ask Swithun directly, "Did you think we worship Ignísekhet?"

Ignoring them, Swithun clenched his jaw and focused on his work, his hammer strikes growing harder and faster as his anger swelled.

"Truth be told, Dayigan," Maximus continued, "the Dark Light rarely worships any Gods. We honor our Gods and consult their wisdom. Our sorcerers call upon their power when needed. Yet, the Dark Light Gods taught us to grow up, learn for ourselves, and think for ourselves. I wonder if that's not the reason you hate us."

Pausing, Swithun held a nail tightly while gripping the hammer in his other hand. "We don't hate," he growled. "Hating people's a sin. We hate the sin, not the sinner." And with that, he returned to working on the wall.

"I'm sure that will be a comfort to the Karulents you obliterated." Maximus shrugged nonchalantly and cast a grin at Adratus before shaking his head. "So, is that what the Karulents are to you? Sinners? I thought God Karulus was a True Light God. Why attack his people?"

"You think you're so fucking smart, savage?" Swithun shouted. "You don't understand what's happening in our empire. The Karulents are wicked, no better than what you are. They killed me little boy."

"They *all* killed him?" Maximus scoffed. "It must have been horribly crowded."

"*Fucking, savage. I'll kill you.*" Swithun lunged at the wall of logs as he envisioned his hammer cracking against the sneering face of his enemy, driving his skull inward until it shattered. He slammed his fists into the hard wood, yet the log recoiled and hit Swithun across the face. A shout of pain mixed with rage sounded through the cage.

Crouching and spitting blood, Swithun held his face, staring at the floor, panting.

The pain from the log in the face seemed to trigger a hundred more, old pains, pains deep from within his core. "I want to make this world better, that's all," he whispered wearily. "I just want to . . ." He licked the blood from his lip and spit it on the floor. "I just want to help all the little children be safe from all the wickedness in this messed-up world."

Swithun looked up at the two Tridulans. In his mind, he heard their laughter ringing in his ears and mocking him as he faltered before them. But when their eyes met, there was nothing but pity in theirs. Instead of jeering, the Tridulans averted their gazes.

Swithun's eyes shifted to the half-built partition. He tried not to think of why he had erected the thing. He'd tried to do his work as best as he could and finish it—perhaps he'd earn compliments from the knights. Now the images flashed around him, images of this compartment crammed with women screaming for mercy and finding none. Swithun clamped his eyes shut as if the futile action might block out the images of his mind. He heard them screaming. He heard the screaming of the people in the town he'd helped burn to ash. He called out in anger, throwing away the hammer as if it was something cursed.

The images and sounds ceased.

"Is this truly still your path?" Swithun uttered, facing the floor.

Silence fell, lingering thick in the cage.

"If you release us," Adratus said gently. "I vow by . . ." He breathed and restarted. "I give you my solemn word, we will save the town."

Swithun turned to the captives, scanning them with sorrowful eyes. Silently, he stood as his feet slowly carried him closer, his body numb. He placed his hand on a stud, his gaze never leaving the floor. The pulsing within his veins was almost deafening as his breath left his lungs, heavy and slow.

"The next target is three miles northeast of here," Swithun began despondently. "Another border town."

CHAPTER FIFTEEN

Under the dismal light of the dismal moons, shadows filled the small dismal town. Maximus and Adratus walked the narrow cobblestone street as they marveled at the surroundings—strange yet familiar. The buildings that lined the street had crumbled, their walls cracked and stained with years of soot and grime. Simple wattle and daub patched the fallen walls and formed newer structures in larger gaps. What had once been glorious columns and archways were now jumbles of stones, with weeds growing between them. Ornate marble statues lay broken and forgotten in the dirt.

"This was one of ours," Maximus said grimly as he motioned to a dilapidated old temple, its roof collapsed and walls stained with mud and moss. "This is one of the towns stolen from our empire."

"Nevertheless," Adratus said as he glanced downward, "we must save them." The cobblestones were cracked and broken.

The townspeople, all of whom eyed the two strangers with suspicion, seemed accustomed to the town's disrepair. The last of the shops were closing for the night, as a few final customers, arm baskets filled with goods, finished up their errands.

The style of dress differed from what Adratus was accustomed to. The people wore plain, ragged clothing in faded colors—mostly gray, brown, off-white, and the occasional blue. The women wore long dresses or skirts to their ankles, some with brown leather bodices over off-white blouses. The men wore their belted tunic a little longer than Tridulans and added trousers underneath.

"Trousers," Adratus whispered to Maximus. "We forgot barbarians wear them."

Adratus and Maximus wore only their tunics—black and red, respectively—and stolen black belts holding stolen Silthex swords. The stone chilled their bare feet.

"I would rather have my armor," Maximus said.

"I would rather have my own gladius," Adratus grumbled. "The Silthex blade alone is nearly thirty inches."

"I told you—wear it on your left so you can draw across your stomach as the Dayigans do."

"Hopefully, 'twill remain unneeded."

The road eventually led them to a dilapidated tavern lit up like a beacon in the desolate town. Outside the archway entrance, a man playing a lute was accompanied by a woman with a flute. It was a spark of joy in the otherwise bleak place.

Watching the lutenist, Adratus leaned closer to Maximus. "We should get to warning the town. Do we simply stand amid the road and shout like madmen?"

Maximus shook his head. "These people will not listen to us, and your vow to our former captor means nothing. We should leave whilst we retain the option."

Adratus stepped in front of him and stopped. "I've seen what will happen if we do not intercede—all these people slaughtered in an instant. I cannot ignore that."

Maximus glanced to ensure no one listened and leaned closer to Adratus. "I've yet to understand the newfound animosity between those who worship Déagar and those who worship Karulus, but *both* are True Light, and *both* would see us dead."

Adratus stayed silent, acknowledging his friend's words, but unable to turn away from those who would soon perish.

"Is there a problem here?" A burly man with a gruff voice and stern face approached. By his side was another fellow, equally menacing. The duo wore nondescript clothes in shades of brown and beige—not uniforms, but their demeanor implied authority over the street. The one who'd spoken rested his hand on the hilt of his sword as he asked, "What business do you have in our town?"

Adratus exchanged a worried look with Maximus before edging closer to the pair. "Salutations," he said with a forced smile and cordial nod. "Forgive my reaching the point so quickly, but time is short. Imminent danger threatens your town. Utter destruction awaits everything here, if you act not. I implore you, evacuate at once."

"Fucking za, Adratus," Maximus mumbled.

The guard snorted and cast a sidelong glance at his partner. "Is that right? And pray tell, where is this 'imminent danger' coming from, then?"

Adratus felt a chill run down his spine. He had expected to warn the town about the upcoming invasion, but now he realized with mounting dread that he would have to make an unsubstantiated allegation against True Light knights while standing in Dayigan lands.

Adratus's chest heaved as he tried to say the words, "A Déagrian unit called . . . the Silthex, working with your own king's army . . ."

Maximus saw his companion falter and spoke up. "They'll never believe us," he said with whispered words through teeth. "Let us leave and let them discover truth as it envelops them."

Adratus stepped away from Maximus and mustered his resolve. "The Déagrians intend to eradicate all Karulents in this region."

The guards went silent; their eyes narrowed suspiciously at these strangers in town.

"We must go," Maximus maintained.

"Stay right where you are," one of the men ordered. "Seems to me you said 'your king,' like you ain't a Dayigan. And you said Déagrian and Karulent like you ain't part of them or us, either. So, who are you then?"

Adratus glanced at Maximus.

"Don't look at *him*," the guard said. "'Less you're planning on lying, there ain't a reason to hesitate."

Adratus met the guard's gaze without flinching. "Karulents. Same as you."

The guard crossed his arms over his chest. "All right then. Say something Karulent."

Adratus stood rigid, heart pounding, pausing before he raised both his hands beside his head, palms to the sky. "Hail Karulus, Lord of . . ." He faltered nervously. ". . . of Karulents, King of . . ." His words trembled with dread, and his eyes darted to Maximus. He swallowed dryly. ". . . of water? God of the . . ." He cleared his throat. ". . . fourth and most righteous hue of light."

Maximus sighed. "Blue is the *fifth* color." He forced a smile as he stepped closer and projected his voice, clear as a proper orator's. "Apologies. My friend attempts to amuse you, yet his humor is misguided." He extended a hand to the guard to shake. "We hail from the great Gellic Nation to the south. Last I checked, you have no quarrel with us Gels, have you?"

Coldly disregarding the hand, the guard's gaze stayed locked on Adratus. "Is the black one right? You Gellic?"

Adratus nodded hesitantly.

The guard clamped Adratus's arm in an iron grip. "These people you pretend to be; they are wild warriors who wear furs, leather, and iron rings around their upper arms. Their men are rough and keep their hair long, along with their un-tamed beards. *And* they wear fucking trousers."

Maximus drew his sword partway from its sheath. "Release him," he commanded, his voice calm yet firm.

The townspeople began to murmur as they gathered around the four.

"*Take your hand off your weapon,*" the guard barked, nearing his sword to Adratus's chest. He raised his voice so the crowd could hear. "These men are Tridulan savages, I'm sure of it."

The word ignited the mob into outrage and shouts of obscenities.

"What does it matter?" Adratus yelled desperately as he fought against the guard's grasp. "We have come to *warn* you. The Déagrians will kill you all unless you ready yourselves. I have seen them burn an entire Karulent town down to ashes. You *must* prepare!"

The guard bared his teeth. "Things may be strained between the Karulents and Déagrians, but we are loyal citizens of the Dayigan Empire now. Our town is protected by our king and his army. Your lies won't get you nowhere here."

Adratus let out a roar of defiance as he rammed his elbow into the guard's gut, allowing him to break free. But his triumph was short before he found himself encircled by the hostile mob.

"Listen to me!" Adratus bellowed above the noise of the crowd. "They will come here, and you must ready yourselves or face certain death!"

A woman's voice shot out from the crowd, "Burn them!"

A townsman snarled, "Fucking savages!"

Another man called out, "The True Light is the only way. All others will perish."

Panic swept over Adratus as he felt their burning hatred. The Karulents closed in around him, screaming for his death.

CHAPTER SIXTEEN

The entire town gathered, forming an ominous tide rising around Adratus, Maximus, and the two town guards. The mob of peasants, many grabbing up makeshift weapons of varying kinds, grew in anger and in numbers with every passing second, an ocean of animosity and loathing flooding inward.

Adratus felt insignificant and defenseless against their unified hate. His hand trembled as it grasped the hilt of his sword. He did not unsheathe it; he couldn't, as he found himself overwhelmed by the sheer venom that radiated from the crowd. He felt like a little boy, soon to drown beneath the crashing waves of hatred.

Someone threw a gourd, striking Adratus in the face. Others followed lead, vegetables flying through the air, as the townsfolk unleashed fury while shouting for death, as if the Tridulans had done something unforgivable by existing at all.

Adratus looked toward Maximus; his stance held strong, but his eyes betrayed him—they were full of panic, darting from person to person like a frantic cat searching for escape.

Booming voices echoed over the throng of baying people, silencing their cries. "Stand aside," the men shouted in unison. "Stand aside. Stand aside."

The crowd scrambled clear as, from the gap, five figures emerged—Beadurinc with Silthex sergeants on either side. The angry rabble now spoke in hushed whispers as their eyes shifted to the knight.

"Let all present be aware!" sounded Beadurinc. "The Silthex thank you for stopping these vile savages. As you suspected, they are indeed Tridulans, come here to spread their nefarious influence. Already, they have burnt a town of innocent Karulus-fearing men and women to the ground and in-intend to do the same here again. Though they had escaped our custody, thanks to your *brave* actions, they can be arrested once more. *Seize them!*"

The Silthex unsheathed their swords and rapidly advanced on the Tridulans. Adratus tried to draw his stolen sword, but the lengthy blade caught its tip on its sheath, delaying him. The sergeants were nearly upon them, leaving no time to escape.

"Disarm!" Adratus called as he cast his left hand toward a sergeant.

The sergeant's sword became engulfed in flames, but he desperately tried to keep hold of it, hissing in pain. Soon, the searing heat proved too much. He hurled it to the road.

The introduction of magic sent shockwaves throughout the crowd; some fled in fear, while others filled with fury and surged forward like a tidal wave unleashed. The mob—knights and townspeople alike—closed in on the Tridulans, surrounding them with an unceasing tide of bloodthirsty screams.

Maximus, sequestered from Adratus by a wall of growing fury, held strong against the onslaught of blades and make-shift weapons.

Adratus drew his sword at last and slashed with abandon at all who stood before him.

"Disarm!" Adratus shouted again and again, as he thrust forward his left hand with each call, meanwhile wielding the sword with his right. But it was like fighting back the sea. The horde of foes surged forward with a renewed fervor, intent on ripping them apart.

Adratus stabbed his sword through someone's gut—a townsperson, he realized, one of the people he'd come to save now dead by his hand. Despite the horror of it, Adratus repeated the same to another. He'd been left with no choice.

A wooden shovel slammed into Adratus's shoulder, and he called out—not only in pain, but in the fury that flowed through him like a firestorm.

"Rage!" Adratus shouted, as a stream of scarlet lightning exploded from his palm, encircling a sergeant and trapping him within. The sergeant's body jerked wildly, electricity surging. With a mighty heave, Adratus lifted the sergeant from the ground and, like a massive writhing mace, swung him through the crowd. No one who neared was safe, be it soldier or civilian. All who attacked him were either struck down or forced back.

Adratus dropped the unconscious body when the area was clear, panting heavily as he watched the crowd cower away in fear. Even the Silthex had taken a moment to regroup, as they reassessed their failing tactics.

Maximus hurried to his side. "Can you get us out of here?"

Instead of responding, Adratus shouted angrily at the crowd. "What a fool I was to think *you* were worth saving!" His voice cracked around the words, the hurt welling. He watched the hateful stare of the townspeople, yet he despised them even more. "The True Light has no mercy or understanding. All you care for is who can hate the hardest. When the Silthex burn your town to ash, I will . . ." His breathing grew labored as his grief took hold.

Beadurinc stepped forward, though he kept his distance. He coldly addressed the crowd in an authoritative tone, "Behold how, even after his exposure as a Dark Light sorcerer, this boy continues to spew lies without remorse. Silthex," he commanded, *"kill him!"*

Adratus extended his arm, and a cord of red light shot out from his palm, lassoing Beadurinc's body and locking his limbs in place.

Pulling the knight to himself, Adratus placed the blade of his sword firmly at the man's neck.

"Order your men away!" Adratus snarled. "We shall leave this fucking town and these barbaric lands, never to return."

"Do you think your wicked magic has power over me, a man of God?" Beadurinc chuckled. *"Dispel."*

The cord dissipated into nothingness.

Unfazed, Adratus pressed his sword harder to Beadurinc's throat. "Will you dispel *this* as easily?"

Maximus, his sword raised high in defense, watched the surrounding townspeople.

The tense moment lingered before an arrow cleaved through the air, hurtling straight for Adratus's shoulder. Adratus called out in agony as it tore into his flesh. His sword clattered to the street.

Through vision blurred from pain, Adratus found Swithun at a distance—bow in hand, he reached back to his quiver to draw another arrow.

An immense swell of red-hot agony spread from Adratus's shoulder. With bloodied fingers grasping his wound—arrow lodged in place—Adratus stumbled to Maximus.

"Silthex," Beadurinc called, as he hastened from the intruders. "Move in."

Adratus, to Maximus, shouted, "Grab on to me and hold tight!"

Maximus complied without a word, and his arms tightly encircled Adratus from behind.

The Silthex sergeants edged ever closer, their faces hungering for death.

Clenching his teeth against the torment, Adratus raised his left hand and sent out a cord of scarlet light, which coiled around a nearby chimney. Summoning every iota of strength left within him, he yanked himself and Maximus up from the ground seconds before the Silthex engulfed their fled position.

The Tridulans landed hard on a mold-covered roof where ancient terracotta shingles cracked underfoot. Another arrow whistled past them, narrowly missing its intended mark.

Without hesitation, Adratus directed an incantation at Swithun. "Disarm!"

Instantly, Swithun's bow was engulfed in fire. He threw it to the ground.

"That won't last long," Adratus said to Maximus as they hurried away. "'Tis fake fire meant to make him drop it—it doesn't damage the weapon."

"Nevertheless, commendations," Maximus replied, as they traversed the slick rooftop together. "Now, we must move quickly."

CHAPTER SEVENTEEN

Swithun and another Silthex sergeant rushed to the center of town. "We still ain't found them yet, Lieutenant," he reported to Beadurinc, "but no one's been seen leaving the town."

Beadurinc gazed over the vacant town shrouded in night. The frightened townspeople had been ordered to stay indoors. Now, only Silthex were allowed on the streets, as they searched for the intruders.

"They're here," Beadurinc said. "Somewhere." He turned to the sergeant at Swithun's side. "Report to Rothgar with his detachment outside of town. Inform him that we are ready to begin here if he is prepared with the ritual."

"Yes sir," the sergeant said. "But what of the seven sacrifices?" He lowered his head as his eyes filled with dread. "I just ask, sir, in anticipation of the captain's question."

Beadurinc narrowed his eyes, an icy chill emanating from his core. "You can tell the captain I will complete my duties in town. Now leave us."

The sergeant hurried away.

"Swithun, stay," Beadurinc commanded as he shifted his attention to the leather box on his own belt. He began unfastening the buckles of the straps that fastened it shut. "I know this is your doing."

"What's that, sir?" Swithun stammered, averting his eyes.

"Do not take me for a fool, Sergeant," Beadurinc snarled. "I know you unleashed those unholy savages."

Swithun conceded with a nod. "Them savages took advantage of me in a moment of weakness, sir, and I—"

"I care nothing for your feeble justifications. You may have been something significant in the king's Great Ordinance, but here, in the Silthex, you are no more than a thorn in my asscheek. However . . ." He cleared his throat and continued in a calmer tone. ". . . our Captain is a righteous man who believes that he can shape you into something of value for our cause."

"I *am* trying to be that, sir." He hung his head low. "But killing all these people—"

"Stop viewing them as people!" he snapped. "They are *filth*, hated by God Déagar because they turned against him with their actions. They deserve none of your mercy or sympathy." Beadurinc paused, his hand still on the leather box on his belt. He looked Swithun up and down. "'Twould be unfortunate if you were removed from our order for insubordination," he said coldly. "You would be excommunicated and forever denied entry into the paradise of Laqyigo, never to see your wife and child again. Is that what you wish, Sergeant?"

The words sapped any strength and hope that lingered in Swithun. "No, sir," he muttered.

Beadurinc grinned as he observed the anguish. "Fear not, as long as you do as you're told and stay in good standing with the knights, your place in Laqyigo is guaranteed. Give me your arrows."

Shaken by his words, Swithun timidly reached to the quiver on his back and removed all ten arrows within. He gave them to Beadurinc.

Beadurinc opened the box on his belt and touched the arrow tips to the contents inside. "I trust you recall your orders from the previous town," he said.

Swithun nodded dejectedly, speaking softly. "Start fires throughout the town so the captain can use them for his magic spell."

"Say it proudly, Sergeant. You hold a holy task." Beadurinc removed the arrows from the box and stared at them for a moment—a faint green glow emanated from the tips. "Be glad we need an archer for this assignment." He returned the arrows to Swithun.

"But first," Beadurinc continued, "dig a small hole. There." He pointed to the ground at the side of the road. "'Tis close enough to the center of town."

Swithun returned the arrows to his quiver and kneeled to his task, digging a small hole with his sword until it reached a foot deep.

From the leather box on his belt, Beadurinc removed a lemon-yellow crystal about the size of his fist—one of the brimstone crystals. He kneeled and placed it in the hole.

Without needing instruction, Swithun planted his boot against the loose soil beside the hole and slid the dirt within, burying the crystal.

"*Sir knight,*" a man called with trepidation as he approached in haste. With poorly feigned respect, he said, "I don't think we've been properly introduced, but I am the head of the town's militia." He paused, no doubt awaiting Beadurinc's half of the introduction.

"Go on," Beadurinc said instead.

"I realize 'tis important you find the invaders in our town, but our citizens are complaining that your men are kicking in their doors and destroying their property."

Beadurinc slowly withdrew his sword from its scabbard, staring at the blade. "How unfortunate my men would behave in such a vile manner. I will need to have a word with them."

The man—clearly expecting more of an argument—now seemed relieved. "I'd appreciate that, sir. My thanks."

Beadurinc plunged his sword into the militia leader's gut, letting the blade slide deep into his belly before twisting. The sound of steel slicing flesh accompanied blood splashing to the street. He ripped it out savagely, staring at the crimson steel. "Was there anything else?"

Swithun watched numbly as the man, choking and gasping, collapsed, his blood navigating the cracks around the cobblestones.

To his side, Swithun heard Beadurinc mutter, "Praise God Déagar, protector from the Dark. You are the Greatest of All. We offer this lost soul in sacrifice to you, O God. May your will be done, and may you grant us the strength to purify this wretched town. Astha'will-miabé."

Beadurinc reached into the leather box on his belt and withdrew a simple necklace: a slender cord of leather ending at a disk of green stone. He held it out to Swithun.

Swithun's eyes lingered on the dying militia leader—the same position he'd held years ago in his own hometown—before he clasped the necklace and put it on.

The sergeant's black uniform blurred around him and changed form, encasing him in a blackened steel breastplate resembling a man's upper body, a shortened scarlet tabard, and an apron of black leather strips. A red cape swept behind him. Tridulan armor.

Producing a matching necklace, Beadurinc donned it, and his uniform was altered into the same form.

"Get to your task, Sergeant, and move with a sense of purpose. We haven't much time. And remember . . ." Beadurinc glared his menacing eyes. "It may be in your best interest to be the one who personally recaptures the boys whom you set free."

—

The townspeople screamed as they scrambled past Swithun, a few of them still trying to cling to their possessions as Silthex sergeants, disguised as Tridulan legionaries, fiercely cut them down.

Swithun focused on his task and readied his bow. Its arrowhead glowed an unnatural green as he loosed it. Another structure burst into emerald flames in the distance.

Swithun watched blankly as another fake legionary stabbed another screaming Karulent as his brothers-in-arms continued their crazed hunt—nothing but good soldiers doing their duty for Déagar. Surely, combined, they had gotten seven kills by now, but Swithun assumed they wanted to be certain.

Somewhat numb, Swithun trudged on, searching for his next target, ignoring the surrounding madness and cries for mercy. He focused on his task, walking as if an observer through the horrors, as if he weren't a part of the events around him. Already, many targets throughout the town burned. He was nearly out of arrows, nearly done. He kept walking. On task. Swithun wasn't part of what was happening, but simply walking through it, he reminded himself, doing his job. A good soldier. A good Déagrian. The townspeople were running from *Tridulans*, not the Silthex. The Silthex were just pretending to be monsters. It wasn't real, he assured himself.

Swithun walked on. He tried not to feel, to think.

Another pseudo-Tridulan passed with a handcart filled with stolen valuables, cart bumping along the uneven road.

All around Swithun were corpses dotted with blackened burns, charred homes, and disoriented townspeople, who were now left to pick up the pieces of what used to be. The world was spinning out of control like a storm in its fury-filled might, yet despite it all, Swithun kept walking and doing his task. He wished everyone would stop screaming so he could think.

A little boy, looking behind himself as if chased, ran toward Swithun. When the boy turned, seeing Swithun, he stopped so abruptly that he tumbled to the ground, stopping a few feet away. He stared up at the disguised Silthex sergeant with eyes wide in horror, too afraid to move or blink.

Swithun slowly stepped toward the boy—near the age that his son had been when he had died—feeling a pang of sorrow as he watched the tears well up in the child's frightened eyes.

The boy's eyes remained fixed, staring at Swithun as if he were a monster.

"Stop looking at me like that!" Swithun shouted, holding up his hand as if to strike the boy.

No. Swithun calmed himself. No—Swithun remembered—the boy was not looking at him; he was only disguised as a monster. In a soothing voice, he said, "Don't worry, child. We'll kill all the wicked."

At that moment, emerald fire erupted at the edge of town to tower twenty feet. It spread quickly, moving as a curved line until it circled the entire area.

Swithun returned his gaze to the terrified boy and uttered, "'Twill be over soon."

CHAPTER EIGHTEEN

Maximus stood atop a pile of rocky rubble, grasping the jagged edge of a hole in the stonework wall. His eyes widened as he peered outside.

"The town panics," he reported, watching. "And now, a wall of green fire surrounds it."

Maximus jumped down from his impromptu watchtower and muttered something unintelligible beneath his breath. The weight of his somber gaze met Adratus's. "We should be safe here," he said with little conviction. "Rubble seals the entrance, so unless they climb in through the roof, as we did—"

"We aren't safe," Adratus said, sitting on the floor and clutching a black bandage fashioned from his sleeve. This was bloodied and wrapped around his upper arm. He glanced up at the broken roof open to the night.

The sickly hue of emerald flames flickered steadily off the twisted rafters and broken remnants of shingles.

"In my vision of the last town," Adratus said, "the wall of fire preceded the fire rushing in to destroy all."

Maximus accepted the words with a nod. "The Silthex yet linger in town. I doubt they'd kill their men."

"I'm to blame for our presence here," Adratus said, downcast. "If I hadn't pushed us further into Dayigan lands, we'd be home. I just thought—"

"You thought we needed more information on this threat. You were correct. Apologies for disputing you earlier."

"Would Grethuk agree?" Adratus asked. "He was a good friend to us both. Yet we haven't made time to mourn his . . ."

"No tears, Adratus. We three are soldiers. We will honor Grethuk by assuring his king receives the intelligence we gather here," Maximus said firmly, turning away to face the crumbling wall. "All the nations in the Autumnal Federation must learn of this. I believe this brewing civil war within the Kingdoms of Light could set the entire continent of Bikia at a crossroads—one unlike the world has seen since the fall of Trasilvok."

"And yet"—Adratus's words were but a whisper—"that knowledge dies here with us, burning in our corpses."

Maximus turned away, and silence fell within the broken temple, giving way to the sound of crackling flames and muffled screams of terror outside.

"Never have I seen a Faldénrus use a confining spell to turn a man into a mace," Maximus said with a grim smile, attempting to lighten the mood. "Innovative."

"A required improvisation. I have yet to learn my area of effect spell." Adratus sighed heavily, his shoulders drooping with despair. "I hadn't expected to fight the Karulent—the very people we tried to save. They betrayed us without hesitation or question, viewing us as evil and deserving of naught but . . ." He shook his head. "I don't understand these lands."

"Get up, legionary," Maximus commanded.

"No!" Adratus shouted fiercely. "I cannot do this. This time last year, I was a *child*. A few months of training in Nerageat has not made me ready to face an elite cohort of Dayigan legionaries."

Maximus kneeled to Adratus and placed his hand firmly on the younger man's shoulder. His eyes—deep brown portals of wisdom—locked onto Adratus's, and he spoke those words that had become a Tridulan creed: "Through hardship, to excellence."

Taking a deep breath, Adratus nodded in understanding, repeating the phrase back: "Through hardship, to excellence."

With that, Maximus helped Adratus to his feet.

Adratus's gaze rose to meet the flicker of green flames dancing beyond the rafters. "'Tis a powerful spell," he whispered to himself, thinking. "I might know a way forward."

—

The night air billowed thick with the choking smoke of the burning town, lit up by the surrounding wall of green fire. Other rippling flags of green flames whipped upward from various buildings, bathing the area in a strange, emerald glow. Agonizing cries of desperation and terror pierced the air as the Silthex, disguised as Tridulans, chased down and slaughtered the terrified townspeople.

Adratus and Maximus reached the center of town just as a Silthex raced between two burning buildings heading in their direction. They dashed behind an overturned cart—unseen for now. The acrid smell of smoke invaded their lungs as scorching green embers flitted through the air like fireflies gone mad in a storm.

"We must go in the opposite direction," Maximus whispered at Adratus's ear. "The Silthex surely have an escape route at the town's edge. If we follow them, we will find it."

"No," Adratus said firmly. "I plan to save this town."

Maximus roughly grabbed his shoulder and pushed him so hard that he was forced to steady himself on the cart's sideboard. "Save them?" Maximus hissed. "You just lamented that they nearly killed us."

Adratus kept his gaze fixed slightly above the wooden planks forming the side of the overturned wagon. "The wall of fire is a powerful spell—one I don't believe any living sorcerer could cast at will. It would require something powerful—charged over time—to focus and power it." He turned to Maximus. "My guess is an item used to enable the spell is here, exactly centered on the circle."

"We must leave," Maximus maintained. "Let the wretched barbarians solve their own damn catastrophe."

"You told me never to expect thanks for doing my duty as a legionary. I expect none from these townspeople. Yet, it is our sworn duty to protect civilian lives. Saving them is right. And you know it."

Maximus paused for a moment before nodding reluctantly. "I preferred you when you obeyed orders."

Adratus chuckled. "Defiance is the original lesson of the Gods."

"Find the item," Maximus relented. "But if we get killed saving those who tried to kill us just hours ago, I want leave to punch you in the afterlife."

"Agreed, Optio." Adratus moved to the edge of the cart and lifted his hands to his sides, palms downward. He closed his eyes and cleared his mind of extraneous thoughts. The sounds of horrors faded to silence. "Detect magic," he whispered.

A faint red light appeared from Adratus's hands to emanate onto the ground just beneath them. As he moved his hands forward to face the center of town, the dim radiance swept over broken crates and shattered jugs and crawled along the cobblestones—searching in a meandering path. Finally, it stopped at a patch of dirt at the edge of the road.

"There," Adratus said quietly. The light dimmed slowly and vanished, and he opened his eyes.

Maximus stood cautiously, looking to either side—screams continued in the distance, but the area was clear. He motioned for Adratus to follow, and they, gripping swords, scurried to the spot Adratus had detected.

Soft ground gave way beneath Maximus's bare foot. "You're correct," Maximus said. "This dirt is freshly dug. I'll stand guard whilst you exhume it."

Adratus stabbed his fingers into the dirt, making quick work of unearthing the shallow burial, though he was careful not to remove the yellow crystal from its position. "'Tis brimstone." He brushed the soil from the craggy tips.

"Yes," Maximus said, still scanning the area. "It stinks of brimstone. Can you dispel it?"

"I can bind it. Assuming the wall of fire still requires its power, 'twill work just as well. But for something this powerful, it will take time to create the binding field."

"Magnificent," Maximus said bitterly. "What better place to linger than on a burning battlefield?" He raised his sword. "Be quick to task."

"You there!" someone called from a distance.

"By all that is infernal," Maximus groaned as he raised his sword.

Two Silthex sergeants—returned to their normal attire—advanced swiftly toward the Tridulans, their swords drawn and ready. Adratus recognized one as the sergeant who'd released them from the cage.

"Get away from that magic crystal," Swithun shouted as he charged forward.

"Stay on task," Maximus ordered Adratus before bolting at the Silthex.

Despite the clashing of steel ringing close by, Adratus focused his attention on the crystal nestled in the ground. He set both of his hands slightly above it.

In an instant, Adratus felt its power burning within him like a raging fire, and the further he pushed his will into the object, the more it pushed back. His head felt as if it would burst as he endured this onslaught of energy, gritting his teeth and squeezing his eyes as pain ran through him like lightning.

From out of nowhere, Adratus was kicked to the ground, Swithun's sword raised above him, preparing to strike.

Maximus intervened, beating Swithun away with a powerful blow—their blades clanging in unison.

"Stay focused," Maximus commanded and returned to his two-on-one fight.

Adratus scrambled back to the crystal.

Just then, two more Silthex sergeants rushed in. With the new arrivals, it was over, Adratus knew. The Tridulans had lost. However, the newly arrived sergeants didn't draw their swords.

"Leave them," one said instead. "The Silthex are pulling out from the town. We've just got minutes before the wrath of God rains down on this shite hole."

"No." Swithun's grip tightened around his hilt, and he pushed his sword against Maximus's. "I have to redeem meself by capturing them."

The second sergeant left the fight, joining the other two. "The fire will take them, Swithun," he said. "Fall back or 'twill take you too."

Still, Swithun persisted in battle with Maximus, increasing the intensity of each strike.

The other three sergeants dashed away, leaving only Swithun and Maximus facing off.

Trusting Maximus to handle the opponent, Adratus redoubled his efforts to contain the power of the crystal. His hands trembled above it as he forced his will into its depths until, finally, with a deep whoosh, a surge emanated from within, launching Adratus backward.

The towering wall of fire flared brighter, lighting up the night.

"We're running out of time," Maximus shouted. "Hurry."

"I attempt to hurry." Adratus dashed back to the crystal.

"You released us to save this town," Maximus shouted as he thrust his blade toward Swithun. The man moved fast, dodging the strike. "Why do you fight us now?"

"I was wrong before, backsliding in me faith." Swithun swung his blade. "All others must perish." He struck again. "'Tis for the betterment of the world."

"Why?" Maximus demanded angrily as he continued the fight. "Why must all these people die?"

"We have to protect the children from evil," Swithun replied with an adamant tone, his gaze never wavering from his foe.

"What children?" Maximus asked with exasperation. "You sound like a madman. No one's doing anything to anyone but you."

"All others *must* perish!" Swithun shouted and kicked Maximus in the gut, sending him to the ground.

Maximus grappled for his fallen sword, but before he could grasp it, Swithun kicked him again before planting his boot firmly on his chest.

"Forgive me wobbly resolve before, God Déagar," Swithun called to the heavens as he lifted his sword, its malignant point aimed down at Maximus. "And take the life of this heretic as a token of—"

Scarlet light circled Swithun's stomach and yanked him away from Maximus.

A few feet away, Adratus stood, his arm outstretched, sending cords of dark energy around the sergeant's body. Over his right palm, the yellow crystal, ringed by red lightning in various orbits, hovered.

The wall of green fire twirled upward and dissipated into the night.

Maximus slowly picked himself up, grabbed his sword, and dusted off his clothes. "Took you fucking long enough."

"You can't do this." Swithun struggled against the restraints of light. "I have to cleanse the world of evil."

Maximus approached silently and pressed the tip of his sword into Swithun's neck. His face was emotionless, but his eyes burned like coals. "Do you think I'm evil, Déagrian?"

"I don't think it; you *are* evil. I know it," Swithun growled through clenched teeth. "All who defy God Déagar are wicked in his sight."

"Then I shall do to you the most evil thing I can imagine." Maximus leaned closer, their eyes locked. "I sentence you to *realization*. There will come a time when it becomes apparent what your hate has done to the True Light, and I pray by God Zeanázel that you witness it *with eyes wide open*. Because you are not destroying the so-called *others*. You are destroying yourselves."

Maximus withdrew his blade and returned it to its scabbard. "Come, Adratus. Our investigation is complete." With that, Maximus strode away.

Adratus remained rooted in place, his eyes fixed upon the sergeant. "Rage!" he shouted and thrust his left hand forward.

The cord of light transformed into a cord of lightning, buzzing around the target.

Swithun called out, his body quaking as electricity coursed through him. When he passed out, Adratus dispelled the force, letting him crumple to the road.

Adratus watched him for a moment longer—lying limp on the ground but breathing—before turning and catching up with Maximus.

"You are wrong about my investigation," Adratus said as they walked. "'Tis *far* from complete. I believe we have but witnessed a fraction of what approaches. And I must learn everything I can if we're to be prepared."

Swithun grasped his fingers through the grid of flat strips of riveted iron as he peered out from within the cage. The Silthex camp was eerily silent yet bustling with activity.

Captain Rothgar and two of his sergeants approached.

"Open it," Rothgar commanded with anger.

A sergeant hurried to the cage door, unlocked it, and swung it open with a shrill of the hinges. He motioned for Swithun to exit.

Swithun emerged with his gaze trained straight ahead, his shoulders back, awaiting whatever punishment would come.

Rothgar stood there, observing the fallen sergeant for what felt like an eternity without uttering a word. Finally, he crossed his arms and spoke with a voice dripping in contempt. "I don't even know what to do with you."

"Forgive me, sir," Swithun began. "I—"

Rothgar raised his fingers and snapped them toward another sergeant. He immediately punched Swithun square in the face.

"I did not give you leave to speak, Sergeant," Rothgar said.

Swithun kept his mouth shut, though his lips trembled with a want to respond.

"You have been wayward time and again, despite my guidance in the righteous path," Rothgar scolded.

"I'm trying, sir. 'Tis just—"

Rothgar motioned to the other sergeant. He punched Swithun in the face.

"Your mistake has come at a heavy cost, yet I cannot ignore that you stayed behind, risking your life, to recapture those savages while the other sergeants abandoned their post. The townspeople are hailing us as heroes for rescuing them from the Tridulans and certain death. They have even implored us to guard their Blue Zone against any future threats—a position that could be beneficial for us." Rothgar paused and analyzed Swithun intently. "*But what of you,* traitor who failed at redemption? Beadurinc insists that your sentence should be death—little surprise. Do you still wish to remain in the Order of Knights Silthex? Speak."

Swithun swallowed hard and nodded. "Yes, sir. The penalty for sin is death—I was wrong to question that before. I got it now, though, sir, that the Order does holy works what I might not understand, but I want to help 'em with it, all the same."

Rothgar eyed him with skepticism. "I confess, I wish the Grand Master had not left the continent for such an extended time. I could use his guidance on this matter." Rothgar sighed. "The Immolation Brigade must pause the purification of the region indefinitely to regroup and reassess. You, however, are no longer part of it."

"Captain, I'm begging ya," Swithun said, voice dripping with desperation. "I can prove meself as a loyal Silthex sergeant. I'll make it right, what I done."

Rothgar arched an eyebrow. "I had faith in you when I chose to recruit you to the Silthex. I stand by my decision still. However, it is evident that you are not fit for the Immolation Brigade," he said firmly. "The Silthex serves in many capacities throughout the empire. You said your former fort on the Tridulan border is nearby. I'm reassigning you there as a Silthex attachment to your previous unit. Consider it a chance at redemption."

Swithun nodded sadly, understanding that this last chance had been granted by a man who owed him nothing. "Thank you, sir. I won't let you down."

"Let us hope that proves true. God Déagar teaches us to be merciful—to those who follow his path. You have stumbled more times than I can count, Swithun, but I know God Déagar can forge you into a valuable tool in his service." His voice darkened as he stepped closer. "Do not prove me wrong. If you fail again, you will be imprisoned. And you will account for your actions before the Grand Master upon his return from the Faery continent."

The Sorrow Passage

Arctic Ocean
ept
ayigan Empire
Tridulan Empire
Ocvius Sea
Pelltic Corron
Rethigon Region
Volit
Maligric Sea
Maligros
ire
Fijyth
Luracurilic Qweendoms
Dyjuth
Ojron
Tyexthra
Grethrok
Nethercape
Tibulet Ocean
Klikate
N
W
E
S
0
400
800
Miles
Volagrok

CHAPTER TWENTY

Efflorel 13, 814: Two Years Later

On a tranquil, cool afternoon, Valqyer was happy. The pursuit of happiness, despite very different means, unified all Faeries. As did the rejection of unhappiness.

It was not just pleasure for pleasure's sake. It was necessary.

If he had been a faun or a nymph, he might dream away the morning after a merry night of drinking and raids and orgies out in the Natural Realm. If he were a tiny brownie, he'd find his joy in cleaning and organizing. If fate had forged him into a stout dwarf, he would be, at this very moment, finding pleasure deep within rocky caverns while searching for ore.

But he was an elf, a pensive kind composed of artists and philosophers. So, Valqyer spent the morning of his birthday engaged in something no less uncommon for him than breathing: sitting at a large white desk and scribbling away with a long, ostrich quill freshly dipped in black carbon ink. With it, he set flowing words of poetry into exquisite calligraphy:

If you dream your life without pursuing your dreams, you are little more than a figment of your own imagination.

He was home, a place grown up from the ground as tight rows of what could be described as branchless aspen trees formed of pearl and shimmering white.

There was no roof. The rooms were open to the twilit sky composed of streaky, opalescent clouds: these clouds of aether, not a sun, lit the Faery Realm.

His mother, in the next room, painted something. What, Valqyer did not know. A present for him. He could smell the pleasant scent of her paints flowing their way throughout the domicile.

Each color, made from forest items, had its unique fragrance. Green smelled of early morning grass and clover leaves, while red bore the sweet scent of rose petals and apple skins. Orange was a bouquet of citrus.

A slight breeze weaved its winding way through their little home, and with it, the smell of lavender flowed strongest from his mother's studio.

Cold suddenly crashed his mood. A chill wind swept away the perfumes and the warmth.

An eerie whisper sounded: "*Bikia.*"

In the beginning, the Fae lived peaceful lives on the lush main continent—this named Bikia—which was the largest of all continents and stretched the northern hemisphere of the world. However, in time, another group of races was created as well.

These, called *People*, became corrupted and corrupted the land. They feared the Faeries and took up arms against them.

Despite all their wisdom and magic, the Fae kinds could do little in retaliation. Years of war became one-sided massacres as the weapons of men struck down the Faeries.

It was not something that Valqyer wished to think about, and it perplexed him as to why such thoughts invaded his tranquility.

He looked down at his page to see his own hand had written, "*The Sorrow Passage*," in fancy script.

"Greetings, Valqyer."

He jumped, knocking his inkpot to spill and blot out the dangerous words. He looked up from his writing to see his father in the room.

He was a noble elf with long straight black hair brushed behind pointed ears and gathered in a ponytail. His thin, soft face bore a sharp nose, and his eyes were iridescent white beneath his thin eyebrows. His body was slim and fit and six feet tall. Well dressed, as usual, Noriaki wore a long robe of silver silk.

Often, Valqyer had been told that he was a younger reflection of his father. The boy saw it, too, but only in appearance.

"You stare, my son, as if you have not before seen my face."

"I–I stare, Father, for I am a man today, yet I am but a pale reflection of the great Noriaki."

His father smiled at this. "Lo, the world is before you, my son. Strive not to be me or my reflection, for you are more than a mirror. Instead, you must be *you—Valqyer*. And you will be great, for you are great already."

"I . . . I will try, Father."

"Of that, I am without doubt. Come, I have a gift."

Valqyer followed his father to the front of the house and then outside to a slight yard tiled in fine mosaics. From it reached stairs descending to the street.

The younger elf moved toward the stairs, assuming the destination, but his father said no.

"This way." Noriaki began moving toward an enormous tree in the yard, a tree formed of pure silver. Atop its leafless branches, it balanced a large circular floor of aquamarine.

With a wave of Noriaki's hand, thin squares of aquamarine split off from the larger floor and took hovering positions at the levels of a staircase.

Noriaki ascended to the treetop, and Valqyer followed excitedly. Never had the boy's father allowed him to enter this place, but for a century, Valqyer had looked up at it, wishing he could.

There, atop the blue-green transparent floor, was a place of wonder. Valqyer looked out over Moonhame, a breathtaking city composed of stylized houses and shops and temples where the elves worshiped the Titaness of Light.

Each structure of the elven city maintained forms reminiscent of the forest and nature but created in mediums of precious metals and gems and set along glass streets.

He saw the city walls, these made of thick rose-glass with brilliant gates of wrought silver. The gates stood open to the rest of the Faery Realm, for there were no enemies beyond them.

"The sight awes me still." Noriaki placed his hand on his son's shoulder. "One day, you will be Duke of Moonhame, just as I am now, and my father before me. Yet, that is not why I brought you here today."

This, Valqyer already presumed, for the magnificent view from this pedestal was but secondary to the one object it held.

Yet, the intruding thoughts came again. Valqyer recalled tales of the third century, first calendar, when the elves had created ten wands with which they had built a realm that ran parallel to the continent of Bikia, yet offset from the rest of the Physical Plane.

The place where Valqyer now stood was not in that Faery Realm. For mankind had learned to infiltrate the Old Realm, itself, bringing their wars within.

Evacuation remained the lone option for the Faeries' survival.

"*Valqyer*," his father said with a chuckle. "You are distant."

"Forgive me, Father."

"Behold."

At his father's prompt, Valqyer turned his iridescent eyes to the center of the floor.

Hovering at eye level was the Wand of Moonhame.

"Never have you seen it, true?"

Valqyer shook his head as he approached, staring.

It was a twelve-inch wand with a shaft of amber hardened around a slightly curving piece of oak root. Silver, smithed into a vine-like design, twisted around the amber and moved up to form four symmetrical, life-size oak leaves bowing out and up, one at each side of the wand. The silver leaves came together to hold a flawless blue topaz as the focus of the wand.

"I know of it, of course," Valqyer said, his eyes transfixed. "'Tis one of the Ten Wands of Elfhame used to create both the old and new Faery Realms. And also the"—he looked down and swallowed—"also the Sorrow Passage."

In the ninth century, first calendar, the elves took up their wands again and constructed a network of aethereal passages that spread out, like the roots of an oak, under the entirety of the old Faery Realm. The network allowed entrance to all the ancient Faeries, leading them to where the passages merged as a breathtaking bridge of thick iridescent quartz. The bridge left Bikian shores through a tunnel of lightning through the air.

The Sorrow Passage, it was called. Through it, nearly all the Faeries fled the main continent, leaving it to the rule of People.

"Speak not of the Passage," his father commanded sternly but not angrily. "And let us hope neither of us ever set eyes upon the dreadful thing." He relaxed, resuming his pleasant tone. "'Tis a relic of millennia past and best forgotten."

"Forgive me, Father."

Noriaki plucked the wand from the air and held it reverently. "But yea, your words are true. The wand did those things and more and has been within our family since the third century FC. Just yesterday, no one else in the entire world could use it save for me. Yet today, with the celebration of your one hundred and sixtieth natal day, you too have the ability."

He held the wand out to Valqyer, but the boy only stared as his heart sped with anxiety and excitement.

Valqyer took it carefully into his hands. It had a warmth he did not expect.

"This evening," Noriaki began, "there will be much exhibition in your honor. Stages will be enlivened with theater and readings. Even now, galleries fill with paintings and sculptures. All will commence when I present this wand to you before the whole of Moonhame."

Though his father's words were surely meant to motivate, they only caused dread to bubble in Valqyer's gut. His skin tinted a momentary gray. He'd be expected to conjure something great before the many watchers.

"I fret I will be unable to use it, Father. Only today is the ability of magic unlocked to me at all. And I have no practice in such things."

"As was also the case when I turned one hundred and sixty, and my father before me. Fear not; the skill of the wand is inherent to our line. Pray tell, what will you conjure? Will it amaze?"

"A . . . window." Valqyer hesitated, scanning his father to see if it was acceptable. "'Twill view out of our realm into the Natural Realm. Never have I seen it."

Noriaki was silent for a moment, and Valqyer knew he'd said something wrong.

"My condolences, my son, but 'tis too dangerous to make such a window inside the walls of Moonhame. Besides, the city will expect more—a grand transmutation."

The words saddened the boy, but he suppressed his feelings.

His father must have noticed, because he smiled and added, "If you wish to see the world outside our realm, there are better ways to view than through a window. Come, I have a vital task that needs completing, and I have now found the *man* to complete it."

CHAPTER TWENTY-ONE

The task from Valqyer's father seemed simple enough. The Green Faery, Lyforia, a Keeper Faery charged with a section of the forest to the east, had yet to respond to her invitation to today's festivities.

"It is most certainly an error," Noriaki had said. "She has been a friend of your mother for centuries. 'Twas my own folly for entrusting the invitation to a pixie."

Valqyer was given the task of extending her a personal welcome.

The mission seemed unreal at first. Elven children were not allowed to leave the city and were definitely not allowed to leave the Realm. However, with a sunrise, Valqyer's world had changed.

Even still, he could not go alone. His father had insisted that he take Ryoichi as an escort, but Valqyer would have taken him, regardless. He and Ryoichi had been best of friends since their early sixties. And as he was a few years older than Valqyer, he had already left the Realm multiple times.

Valqyer stopped before the silver gates towering thirty feet.

Then he stepped out.

Sticking to the path, the two elves traversed a forest of clear quartz trees, each with amethyst leaves. They passed a field of shining emerald grass scattered with ruby tulips. A few orbs of white light—these called sprites—meandered above the paths.

"Is the Natural Realm as beautiful as this?" Valqyer asked the older boy, staring wide-eyed as they walked.

"It is beautiful in a different way. Everything here is but hardened illusions. Out there, 'tis *real*. Most elves do not care for it, but I do. Perhaps I was a faun in a prior life. I think you will like it, too." Ryoichi stopped and looked into the younger's eyes. "I am happy I can share this with you, my friend."

Valqyer smiled, and they continued.

They passed multiple doors in various forms, all leading out to reality. Although one of the Wands of Elfhame was initially needed to create each one, once in place, any adult Faery could open it. It vexed Valqyer to pass by them when he so longed to pass through.

"We must find the door closest to our destination," Ryoichi explained. "The farther we travel east in our realm, the farther we travel east in theirs. And distances are shorter here. Besides, it is dangerous out there, so we mustn't stray too far from a door lest we need to make a hasty retreat."

"Are there People? On this continent?"

Ryoichi nodded. "A few."

"Is that not why we left the old continent, to flee them?"

"We do not speak of such things, Valqyer." Ryoichi grew clearly uncomfortable. He stopped and whispered, "Millennia have passed since our kind left the old continent. In those passing years, yea, a slight number of People—a race called Kornidytes—have made their way to Klikate Forest.

"Yet fear not, friend," Ryoichi continued, donning a smile. "The new Faery Realm built parallel with Klikate Forest is much better protected than that that was abandoned. Here, the walls separating it from the Natural Realm are well enforced with stronger magic than our ancestors then knew. Nevertheless, whilst *outside* our realm, we must stay near doors lest we need a quick return."

Disappointed as he was, Valqyer understood, at least in part.

After an hour, Ryoichi said, "There."

He pointed to a clearing in the crystal trees that held a circle of little ruby pyramids.

"Shall we race?" Ryoichi smiled. "He who wins may open the portal."

Without a word, Valqyer took off running.

In a flash of white, Ryoichi disappeared from his spot and passed the younger elf as a momentary blur. With another flash, he was suddenly in the circle.

"Cheating pixie!" Valqyer laughed. "No fair using flash step."

"'Twould not be fair against a child, my friend. But you are a child no more."

Valqyer slowed as he entered the circle and stood before the other elf. "There is so much I must learn. Will you teach me?"

Ryoichi smiled. "Gladly."

Abruptly, the air felt odd; it tickled warmly across Valqyer's skin. He coughed and laughed as it felt so bizarre within his lungs. He gulped another breath, feeling it within his chest. It smelled of dirt and plants and old damp wood.

Around him, the circle of red pyramids had swapped to a circle of red mushrooms, and tall grass—real grass—carpeted the ground.

Beyond, the forest of crystal faded into a forest of natural trees: rugged brown bark coated their trunks, and green leaves swayed within a breeze.

The sky above was clear blue, with sporadic puffs of clouds. The sun shone down with rays enveloping Valqyer in sensations so wondrous he could not help but beam himself.

"Fantastic, is it not?" Ryoichi exclaimed as he spun.

"I thought I knew these things from books—trees, grass, sun—but I knew nothing."

"Go hence! Touch the tree."

They ran to it, and Valqyer did as Ryoichi bid.

"So rough," the younger elf said with cautious curiosity. "The word means so much more here. But I understand not, for I have touched sticks and leaves brought back to our Realm, yet never did they feel so . . ."

"*Real?* Sensations are heightened here in the Natural Realm. Even if you were to touch something we brought with us, 'twould be heightened."

In response, Valqyer ran his hands along his own silk robe. So much silkier. He ran his hands along his own arms, so much warmer and more sensitive. Valqyer looked at Ryoichi and paused.

He touched his hand.

Their eyes met.

"We must hurry." The other elf laughed. "You would miss your celebration if we dawdle. But, yea, we will return on the morrow, if you like, and frolic as fauns."

"Yea, my friend, we shall."

The two elves ran through the forest, this more in fun than haste. They dodged trees and leaped branches. Valqyer ripped his robe on a bramble and didn't care.

In time, they slowed for breath.

Ryoichi panted. "Methinks you were also a faun in a previous life."

"Perhaps. And perhaps we knew each other well and were also friends."

Something caught Valqyer's eye, something half buried in the dead leaves coating the ground. Something metal.

"What is that?" Valqyer asked before flash-stepping to it and stooping.

This was like a giant knife, but sharpened on both sides of the blade. A cross-section partitioned off the ornate handle.

"Get away from it!" Ryoichi cried.

It was too late. Valqyer grasped the handle.

Hate, fear, anger, hurt, death, power, emptiness, fury, vengeance. War. So many things at once. Valqyer roared from deep within as his skin turned green and rough.

He collapsed to the ground.

Ryoichi rushed to his side and cradled his head. "Regain yourself, friend."

Valqyer groaned through his teeth as dark emotions coursed like shattered glass throughout his veins. His skin's discolor waxed and waned in sickening waves.

"*I beseech you,*" Ryoichi implored. "Think of happy things and lose not yourself."

Valqyer looked up at him, such concern in his eyes, such affection. Ryoichi leaned in and softly kissed his mouth—his lips warm and soft in a way one could only experience in the Natural Realm.

In response, Valqyer smiled as bliss ran through him, washing away the pain.

His skin paled to its normal shade.

"What was that?" asked Valqyer. "It has killed and killed. I felt it."

"Think not of it." Ryoichi helped him to his feet.

"And the kiss?" Valqyer beamed with a wide grin.

Ryoichi beamed the same. "Think not of it either," he said bashfully.

Though Valqyer calmed, he felt the remnants of the darkness in his blood. Such negative emotions, if left uncontrolled, could change a Faery, both mentally and physically. He would transform into a dark, demented creature: an *Irefaery*.

"Be not troubled, friend," Valqyer assured. "'Twas but shock, nothing more. I am well far from turning Irefae. Again, I ask, what is it?"

"Do you not recognize a *sword*? It is a weapon of People."

"I recognize the word," Valqyer said as he eyed the weapon, "but I always imagined it as something far more sinister in form. 'Tis such a simple and beautiful thing to hold such horror."

A woman's powerful voice echoed above, "*It is as sinister as thou dost imagine.*"

Both elves began searching the towering tree for a source. None.

"And, alack," she continued, "these vile weapons grow more common in this region."

From the woods darted a dozen pixies: six-inch, winged beings appearing as a cross between elf and insect. They circled the elves in dizzying flights.

Many sang out, "Follow, follow!" "Come with us!" and "Hie, this way!" in quick chatter.

Then, they flew away as a swarm.

After glancing at each other, the elves swiftly followed.

It was a short trek before the pixies came to a woman hovering a foot above the leafy ground. She was nearly an elf: similar height and build, same white iridescent eyes, and same pointed ears. However, her unclothed skin was lavender and glittered with silver dust. Her hair was plum. She had wings, these semitransparent like those of a massive wispy butterfly.

"How now, Keeper?" Valqyer approached the beautiful Purple Faery. "You say there are more *swords* in your region?"

"Increasingly more." Her words were grave. "The People prepare for something. They forge their awful weapons and train their awful fighters. For what, I know not, yet it is nothing good. The forest grows uneasy. As shouldst thou."

"We should not think of such negative things," Ryoichi said.

"Never, no never must we think of such things," she said in a despondent tone, as her bare feet touched the forest floor. "Never must we act. 'Tis unthinkable to fight. So is the impairment of our race. It is wherefore the ancient Faeries relinquished the main continent to People and is wherefore we can do naught here but flee and hide—you in your city tucked asafe inside the Realm and us here in the shadows of the forest."

"Forgive me, but Ryo is correct." Valqyer's discomfort with the topic grew. "To lament is dangerous. Let us speak instead of happy things. Yea? Today is my natal day. I became a man, and in the coming hours, we celebrate. We come in search of the Green Faery, Lyforia, to offer an invitation. Know you her?"

"A *man*? Is that a word elves use to describe themselves now? How queer. You dress like men and live in cities like men. And likewise, you do come for the Green Faery. Lo, my lady hath been taken, *by men*."

"Taken? But we must find her." Valqyer looked to Ryoichi, but he simply looked away.

"Alas, young elf," she said. "I know exactly where she is. Just over that ridge towards the ocean is a Kornidyte village. My friend, for longer than thou hast breathed, is therein. She is—" The Purple Faery grabbed her forehead and stomach at once as darkness rippled over her bare skin. "She is *encaged*." The word clearly injured her. "And for her, I can do naught."

Ryoichi rushed to her. She fell against him. "Pray you, Keeper, put it out of your mind. 'Twill only destroy you. Tell me, what type of tree stands there?"

She breathed, and her lavender returned. "A willow. My favorite of all."

Valqyer only stared sadly, trying not to empathize lest he also be drawn into the darkness. "Come with us to the Realm," he finally said, as he took her hand. "It is not safe here."

"No," she said calmly and firmly, as she turned her teary eyes to the younger elf. "Here is my home and mine only comfort. Dost thou feel it not? The superlative brilliance of the forest encircles us. Inhale it. Feel it. The One Soul flowing through all. The elves relinquished so much to hide. I will stay. Yet return thou to thy sterile halls of illusions, for thou hast a celebration to attend."

ll Valqyer could think about on the walk home was the Purple Faery. And it was the one subject he knew he should not think about at all.

"We will tell no one of Lyforia," Ryoichi said, as they neared the silver gates. "There is naught we can do, and 'twill only taint the day. Say only that she was otherwise occupied."

Valqyer nodded. "Yet 'twas true what the Purple Faery said: we elves all gave up the forest and reality itself to hide. Do you see not the tragedy therein?"

"Have you yet chosen what you will make as your first transformation with the Wand of Moonhame?"

"Alas, no. And now I have no time to gather materials."

"'Twill be fine. Listen to that merrymaking. Already, the city cheers for you."

Valqyer listened, and from within the elven city came screams and shouts. "Quite a ruckus for elves," he said with a laugh. "Surely the city has not taken to wine in my honor."

"You doubt the exuberance of our own kind. We elves can . . ."

There were more screams. Louder and fiercer.

Valqyer's smile faded, and his soul sank. "But . . . I think there was no joy in that sound. Fear and horror were in that sound. Naught else."

After a pause to absorb, Valqyer darted for the gate, while Ryoichi called out for him to wait.

More screams followed, a discordant mixture of terror and anguish alien to the Realm.

When Valqyer ran onto the glass streets of the elven city, he was horrified to behold a unit of Kornidytes—a brutish race of People bulked with muscles, slouching shoulders, and a single horn crowning their thick skulls. They were mono-chromatic in shades of gray, which was true for their rhino-like skin, beady eyes, mangled hair, and all. The nine-foot towers of muscle, armed and armored, tore through the terri-fied crowds.

Silver elven blood flowed in volumes never witnessed by Valqyer.

The young elf was grabbed. He screamed.

It was Ryoichi who'd grabbed him. "We must flee now. There are but horrors here."

Valqyer's eyes teared. "'Tis but a trick, that is all, some foul glamour borne of warped humor. This cannot happen here. We are safe within our city."

He searched around with vacant eyes. Yet, the atrocities were too many to ignore.

"My parents," he gasped. He broke free and ran deeper in-to the frenzied crowd, pushing his way toward his house on the hill.

So much noise on all sides. He'd never heard so many voices at once.

Only a few feet away, he saw an invader strike with such force that his heavy longsword broke through the collarbone of an elf and sliced through the flesh below, through his shoulder and chest, rupturing the heart.

The vibrant silver blood gushed and pooled across the glass underfoot.

Valqyer knew him—a cousin.

The young elf froze within the dizzying nightmare. His body was uncertain of how to react. He would have liked to think in such an event some spark of heroism would have overtaken him, caused him to do remarkable, gallant things.

But he only froze, overwhelmed. He stood agape. His own blood seemed to drain as well, leaving his clammy skin an olive pale. His arms fell limp to his sides, and his knees buckled.

Ryoichi grabbed him and yanked him to the side of the street. He shoved him under a vendor table holding porcelain vases. The vases, dislodged by their disturbance, plummeted to the ground, exploding into shards.

Just beyond the table, a friend of Valqyer's father wailed as a battle-axe was hacked deep into his gut. His hand fell motionless within the shattered vases. Valqyer watched the final breath as the eyes turned empty.

And the elf's body dissipated in the form of light, light that gathered as a white orb. The breeze carried it away. Centuries old and gone in a flash.

Though it was the death for all Faeries, Valqyer had never witnessed it before. And just farther out, he saw it twice more.

An elven woman fell to her knees beside the dead and cried with wails that echoed painfully to all who heard. Her skin grayed, and she aged into a crone. Her clothes became a black hooded robe that blew as if in a powerful wind. Her cries of soul-wrenching grief echoed louder. Her glowing eyes turned crimson, and she was elf no more but a banshee.

Fully changed to an Irefaery, she could not revert.

"I must find my parents," Valqyer said to Ryoichi, who crouched at his side. He needed to know they were all right. He needed them to tell him that everything was all right.

His mother would tell him this wasn't real.

"No," Ryoichi maintained. "I implore you, go away with me through the gate, so we might leave this nightmare together and forget it happened."

"Forget?" *That would be nice.* His eyes turned to the chaos and stared.

An elven girl, Valqyer witnessed, similar in age to Valqyer and Ryoichi and friend to them both, was snatched up by her long, white hair. Sweet and kind, the girl liked to spend her days collecting flowers for her short-lived works of art. Valqyer recalled this as he watched a Kornidyte roughly hold her while she struggled.

The Kornidyte sawed through her thin neck with a jagged blade as she screamed with a nightmarish noise. Such a sound was beyond the likes of anything Valqyer had ever heard before. Gurgling replaced screams as silver erupted from her vocals.

The boy turned hot and cold at once as he watched helplessly from beneath the table.

Her corpse faded into a sphere of silvery light.

"Forget?" Valqyer repeated in hollow shock as he stared out. "Never this."

He darted from the cover of the table and back into surging horrors. He fought through the raging currents of horrified elves and hulking monochromatic warriors as he tried to return home.

With every twist he made, he saw the slaughter of his kith and kin. Death, death, death. Valqyer knew well each elf who fell.

He stopped as an elf before him grabbed up a sword. The elf swelled with height and muscles as he transformed into a mad troll.

The troll faced him.

"Valqyer!" His father snatched him back.

He fell, lightheaded and weak, into his father's arms and started crying.

"Be strong, my son. Take the Wand of Moonhame and guard it well from the invaders, and go you, also, to your mother to flee her from this place."

He thrust a long purple satin drawstring pouch containing the wand into his son's hand. He turned back toward the troll.

Valqyer stood on his own, though barely. "But will you go not with us, Father?"

Noriaki paused, but did not face his son. "Go quickly, Valqyer!" His words were stern. "Leave, whilst there is time."

The boy watched in terror as his father dashed into the conflict.

Just as Valqyer's mind told him to obey his father and flee, so too did his muscles flex to pull him toward confrontation. The spark of heroism, though late arrived, pressed forth despite his growing sickness.

He wanted to be great, like his father. To fight.

Valqyer continued to watch him.

Noriaki cast out his hand toward one of the Kornidytes, magically levitating the invader from the ground and throwing him into a wall of ivory.

An unseen sword swung toward Valqyer.

In a white flash, Ryoichi, his friend, appeared between the sword and Valqyer. It cut through his back in a splattering of silver. He fell bloodied onto Valqyer.

An Irefaery troll grabbed the assailant and tore him away.

"No!" Valqyer roared as he held his friend.

Ryoichi struggled for breath as he convulsed.

They fell to the ground.

CHAPTER TWENTY-THREE

Holding his dying friend while conflict raged around him, Valqyer fumbled for the wand and pulled it from its pouch. Taking a deep breath, he swung it around.

The street bubbled up around the two elves. It formed a sphere of thirty panes of thick, rippled glass joined with gold.

Within this glass egg, the conflict muffled.

"Behold, my friend," Valqyer said desperately, "we are safe." He forced a smile, though his eyes streamed.

Ryoichi, weak against his lap, coughed blood yet much more poured from his back.

Valqyer looked up through his shelter to see other elves joining the fight. They did not last long before their skin darkened and their flesh swelled.

Artists and thinkers became feral, killing beasts. Grief darkened even onlookers, who cried out, and their low moans and wails became everlasting. Valqyer knew the newborn Irefaeries would not remember the elves they had been and were just as dangerous as the People.

Shaking, Valqyer looked down at his friend. So still. "We will be safe in here. I will protect you. We—" He sniffed, and his voice cracked. "We must design our outing for tomorrow. Where will you have us go? Ryo?" He looked at the sleeping face. "We will go to the forest, I think. We will frolic like fauns through the fields of Reality. Yea, you wanted that?" He paused. "Please do not die."

Outside, the invasion continued, as did the bloodshed.

The dead of the town evaporated as light. Those who died as Faeries became balls of white light, while those who fell as Irefaeries became tormented spheres of crimson.

Valqyer ignored all. "Say something, Ryo, I pray you." He wiped his wet eyes.

Kornidyte invaders began hitting the surrounding glass with swords, cracking the panes.

"Worry not, my friend," Ryoichi mumbled without opening his eyes, "tomorrow we will frolic." He smiled.

And Ryoichi began to glow white.

The banging on the glass grew louder. Cracks became more substantial.

"No!" cried Valqyer, as his friend dissolved. "Stay with me. I need you." He wiped his eyes. "I beg you, my friend. Stay. We will do such fantastic things."

Ryoichi's body condensed as an orb of white. It passed through the glass and blew away.

Hollow, Valqyer drew his legs to his chest. His body was shaking and cold. He stared and rocked. "No!" he screamed and screamed again, louder. His nails sharpened, and his skin grayed. "No!" His mind began to turn, to twist away to void.

He barely saw the attacking Kornidytes fly back from his broken sphere.

"Valqyer." His father banged on the glass. "Be strong, Valqyer."

"No!"

"Be strong for your mother."

He panted like a beast. The young elf sniffed. "I must . . . save her." He breathed deeply. "I must save her."

With all his will, he calmed his aching soul.

He returned to normal, though barely.

The glass protecting him shattered into dust.

A dying Kornidyte tumbled and slid across the glass street, stopping nearby.

Valqyer stood. He coldly watched the strange invader convulse a moment, taking a final labored breath before lying still in a growing pool of dark gray blood.

"I will not forget this," Valqyer said, his eyes swollen and tear-stained.

Noriaki, distorted though still with the glowing white eyes of an elf, grabbed up the Kornidyte's sword.

"Go quickly, Valqyer!" Noriaki desperately commanded his son.

He ran back into battle, and Valqyer ran home.

—

A generally stoic, meditative elf, Valqyer's mother was frantic. She had set a large trunk up on a silver table and was scrambling in attempts to cram it full of everything of any importance to her and her family.

Her paintings would not fit. With desperate trembling hands, she tried to break off the wooden frames.

"The People are upon us, Mother! We have no time for such things."

"A moment more. Just a moment more." She abandoned her paintings and threw other works of art into the trunk.

Valqyer grabbed her arm and pulled her toward the door.

Lillia made another try for the trunk, grappling at the handle.

Inadvertently, she pulled it from the table.

The trunk crashed down. The contents scattered. Paintings ripped and bent. Sculptures chipped and shattered. Valqyer's stories and poems shuffled to the alabaster floor and soaked in pools of paint.

He looked on for a helpless moment, saddened. "There is nothing we can do." He ushered his mother from the room.

—

Valqyer hurried his mother across the mosaic-tiled yard but stopped before the steps that descended into chaos.

There, amid the bloodshed and panic, the young elf witnessed a feral troll dressed in the torn remnants of his father's clothing.

"Father?" Valqyer whispered.

His eyes were red; Noriaki was fully Irefae.

The creature held a Kornidyte in his large, clawed hands. His sharp, jagged teeth stabbed deep into the meaty side of the man's stomach. In chilling horror, the Person cried out as the troll bit down, releasing gallons of dark gray blood before ripping the flesh and dangling viscera away.

Before, his father's favorite activity had been sculpting and architecture. Never would he return to how he'd been.

"Valqyer!" Lillia cried.

He looked back, seeing that a Kornidyte had snatched her up.

Three other warriors were in the yard.

Lillia struggled futilely against her captor. "Run!"

The young elf froze, uncertain of what to do. He had lost so much this hour.

A soldier stepped forward, an informal approach that might have seemed cordial out of context. He was a well-built Human—another race of People—in his early forties. Dark brown hair, shoulder length and well groomed, framed his stern face, hidden behind a thick beard. He dressed in a long white leather surcoat with a thick ring belt at the waist and thick black leather trousers. The surcoat's chest bore a squared, flailed version of the number seven in green.

He stood tall, peering down at Valqyer. "Greetings, elf."

"Who are you?" Valqyer's voice shook. "Why have you come to Moonhame?"

"I am Sir Brynistan, Seneschal of the Holy Order of Knights Silthex. I wouldn't expect one such as you to know such civilized titles, yet know we are the employers of these brutal beasts you see here. We have come *for you*."

"What?"

"Run!" Lillia screamed again, as her struggles waned.

The knight held a finger toward a Kornidyte.

The warrior grabbed Lillia tighter and pressed his thick gray hand across her mouth.

"Is it your birthday, yes?" Brynistan asked. "You're the one. The wand on your belt betrays you. You will hand it over to me."

"No," the young elf said, with little fight remaining. He tried to be strong, but was ready to ball up like a hedgehog on the ground.

Brynistan nodded to the Kornidyte holding Valqyer's mother.

The warrior drew a sword and held it to her neck.

"I'm sure you know someone cannot take the wand by force," Brynistan said calmly, "but I can think of many ways to motivate you to *give* it to me. Act quickly, whilst my kind-ness remains."

Valqyer shook with indecision as he stared in agony at the blade against the soft skin of his mother's neck.

Brynistan looked at the Kornidyte. "If I do not have the wand in ten seconds, cut her head off. And do it slowly."

"Take it!" Valqyer relented. He approached, tearing the sa-cred heirloom from his belt. "Just unhand her." He held it out to the soldier.

Brynistan snatched the wand away as another warrior grabbed the young elf.

"Throw them both with the other captives to be taken back to Dyrethka," the seneschal ordered. "The Grand Master has further purpose for these swine."

CHAPTER TWENTY-FOUR

It must have been raining above, on ground level—a steady trickle of water stammered its jagged way down the rough, unfinished rock wall of the dark cell.

Already, Valqyer had meticulously searched every inch of the shadowy chamber for any entrance to his realm. There were none. If only he still possessed his father's wand, he could make his own portal. But no.

Trapped within the darkened cell beneath the Kornidyte village, he could do nothing but sit in the center of the dirt floor, the base of his feet together, and his hands gripping his ankles. Back straight. Head facing forward. He meditated on calm. It was all he could do. Calm. He had to focus. Calm. He could not lose himself.

Three days, he had been here.

He tried to imagine that the trickling water was a tranquil babble. He tried to ignore the horrible screams from the other cells. He tried to grasp desperately for joy, like handfuls of vapors seeping through his fingertips. The thoughts of what had happened reeled manically in his brain. The emotions of the events throbbed through him like poison in his blood. Whenever he let his mind wander, his heart filled with toxic hate and began beating faster. And with a sadness deeper than he'd ever known. But he calmed himself.

He could not let himself feel it.

There was a sudden noise from the cell door, a series of clicking and popping from the lock.

With a slow creaking at the hinges, it opened.

Valqyer narrowed his eyes toward the shadowed portal. From it emerged the Human, Seneschal Brynistan.

"We meet again, elf," he said. "I see you fare better than most others here. Good, good." He mentioned the "vile creatures" into which many of the other captured elves had turned. When he mentioned "the woman with whom you were captured," waves of hatred grayed Valqyer's skin.

"What have you done to her!"

"You'd do well to keep your temper checked, elf," he said. "You can do nothing for her as an Irefaery."

Valqyer stopped. He glared at Brynistan. The gray faded from Valqyer's skin as he again relaxed. Calm was growing increasingly more difficult, but as long as he did not complete the change, he could keep willing it away.

With an even, measured tone, the young elf asked if he might see the woman, not saying she was his mother.

Brynistan curled his lips in an arrogant sneer. "For that very purpose, I have come. The Grand Master *insists* that you have a visit, and so you will."

A double clap of his hands.

Two Humans, dressed similarly to Brynistan but in black, escorted the elf from the cell.

—

Lillia, looking well, her eyes shining, beauty unfaded, stood before an easel made of long, thin branches supporting a canvas. Thereon, a beautiful painting took form.

She, too, was beautiful: her long black hair gleamed in a light not there as it hung straight down the back of her lavender gown.

Old age did not take elves until about nine hundred and then came quickly, but Lillia, centuries from this, could be mistaken as only a little older than Valqyer.

As comforting as it was to see his mother like this, Valqyer knew it was a lie. This serene loveliness was nothing more than a glamour.

With a wave of his hand, he dispelled the illusion and saw his mother as she had truly become.

Very skeletal was Lillia. Her thin, discolored skin pressed frailly against her bone. The pain of the attack on their city, of losing her husband, had made her cadaverous. Her long, thick hair had become threadlike. Even the easel and the painting faded like a dream.

She remained an elf, but only just.

Lillia cast a stronger glamour, and Valqyer did not attempt to see through it. He did not wish to see her any other way.

"Fear not, dear son, for I am maintaining well despite appearances." A mother's comforting fib.

He could smell the perfume of jasmine flowing from her painting, blocking out the damp stale rank of the room. A window took form on the ragged rock wall, letting in the light of a twilit day as it showed a crystalline forest outside. A bluebird perched on the sill.

"The last words Father said to me were those of concern for your safety," Valqyer said, as his mother continued to paint. "Thus, I vow by his name, Noriaki, I shall flee you from this place."

Lillia sighed. "Alas, Valqyer, you are too well akin to your father." While facing the artificial window, she smiled, as if nothing was wrong in the entire world. "There is no reason we must behave unseelie, my son. You are beautiful. Let not the world transform you. Instead, will you not share a lunch of berries with me and tell me of your latest poem?"

She circled her fingers slightly in the air, and a silver plate of blackberries appeared from a slow swirl of purple smoke.

He ignored the illusions and faced the dirty stone floor of the darkened cell. "Whatever I must do, I shall liberate you, Mother. This, I vow."

—

Two Human sergeants escorted Valqyer from his mother's cell.

The halls of the dungeon were the halls of a crazed asylum. A few iron torches hung randomly from the rock walls and cast uneasy, twisting flickers within the narrow tunnel. It was lined with old wooden doors, each with only a small barred window to offer some slight illumination within the cells.

Traveling this hall through madness, Valqyer kept his eyes on the floor. He tried to ignore the cells they passed and the frightening noises.

Twisted creatures growled in bestial tones while they beat madly at their doors. Others wailed, moaned, and screamed.

The young elf suppressed a need to cry. He walked on and passed the doors, with the armed Humans behind him.

A few red spheres of light, these the spirits of dead Irefaeries—called *dyres*—fluttered about, lost. Valqyer tried not to think of who they might have been.

The pounding at a particular door not too far from Valqyer grew louder and more violent.

The aged hinges began to give and rip from the wall. The old planks blocking the portal broke free and collapsed flat on the dirty stone floor.

From the open cell, an enraged troll bounded. Over the broken door and into the corridor, the creature charged the sergeants, who quickly drew their swords.

With an animalistic growl, the troll punched the stone wall with his thick fist. He tore free an iron torch and held it as a fiery mace.

Horrified and defenseless, Valqyer scurried some paces down the prison corridor and crouched against the wall. He could do nothing but watch as Kornidyte warriors joined the Silthex sergeants to wrestle the enraged Irefaery to the ground.

Even outnumbered, the troll fought well. He slammed the torch into a warrior with such anger that it sent a Kornidyte flying backward to smash through a cell door just beside Valqyer.

Broken splintered boards clamored to the floor, sending a thick cloud of stirred filth into the hall.

As the dust haze settled, two white eyes became visible in the darkness of the damaged cell.

Ignoring the fight down the hall, Valqyer stood and approached, watching the two eyes that were both mesmerizing and devastating. Torrents of guilt and pain flowed like rivers from these eyes, pouring from the soul beyond them.

She was not an elf, this woman sitting slouched over on the floor of the cell. But she was too close to turning Irefae for Valqyer to determine her former kind. She wore nothing but her long hair, gray with threads of faded orange. It hung in thin, stringy curtains. Her pale green skin drooped from her frame. It was beyond anything caused by natural age—some of her bones and organs were missing. Her ribcage behind her left breast had caved, as if something had eaten away at her from the inside.

"I had to do it." Her voice was a slow, hoarse groan. "I had to do it. He knew my name." Her demeanor implied madness.

She repeated this as barely a whisper, but her voice was loud, as if directly behind Valqyer's pointed ear. The words moved the noises of the skirmish between guards and troll to a distant background.

Her white eyes grew wider.

Her black fingernails scratched manically at her face.

"I had to let them into our Realm," she said. "He knew my name."

"That is how they got through the planar walls?" Valqyer said softly. "And how they attacked our city? You?"

She stood up and lifted herself to hover slightly above the floor. Her hands moved up the side of her face as she lifted her arms to the ceiling. "With every anguish and lament and gruesome demise, know that I am the one who hath betrayed you."

Overwhelmed, Valqyer tripped backward while staring up at her.

She moved toward him, out of her cell.

"With every anguish and lament and gruesome demise," she screamed, "know that I am the one who hath betrayed you!" She shrieked until her breath was gone.

"*Lyforia*," commanded a man from behind Valqyer, "halt thy pitiful wailing, and return thou to thy cell."

With no choice but to obey, she drew her arms to her sides and flew up and back into the darkness.

"Lyforia," Valqyer repeated in a whisper. It was the name of the Green Faery, who was a friend of Valqyer's mother.

The elf boy turned back to see who had commanded Lyforia. This man, too, was shocking to behold. He appeared Human, but only if Humans could age beyond a thousand years. His crumpled, leathered, ugly skin hung from his bones. His spine bent. Nevertheless, his attire was regal: a long surcoat of white silk with a squared, flailed version of a seven embroidered in green on his chest. His long cape was white fur.

The yellowed eyes of this man met Valqyer's own, leering with an unnerving grin.

Disturbed, the elf boy turned away to watch the men who had subdued the escaped troll.

They now hacked into his muscled flesh with various bladed weapons as black blood flowed—a horrible sight, yet better to behold than the vile man before him.

The axe at the troll's neck ended it. The troll's body dissipated, leaving only crimson light that spiraled into a ball. Another dyre. It flitted mindlessly around the dungeon before passing through the wall.

Shattered, Valqyer only stared, silent and astonished, thinking of Lyforia. She was the Keeper Faery whom Valqyer had been sent to find. His mother had called her beautiful, carefree, and kind. She was undeserving of this, and it was no wonder that guilt had eaten away at her.

At least for now, Valqyer's mother was still elven. He could take some small solace in that. But her time was short.

Brynistan approached from behind the ancient man.

"Come," the ancient man said.

The two led Valqyer back to his cell.

CHAPTER TWENTY-FIVE

Inside the dismal cell, Brynistan remained in the background by the door as the ancient man stepped forward.

He spoke, saying, "Pray, art thou frightened, elf? Thou hast witnessed the destruction of so much of thy kith." His unhurried words were noble, yet with a sinister groan. "Dost thou grieve, elf? Doth anguish breed uncontrollably within thee? 'Twill be impossible to continue on thine own, be certain. I know the struggle is killing thee."

"You are a villain."

He chuckled, smiling yellowed, crooked teeth. "Nay, quite the opposite, in fact. I am Ocellus Blastilv, Archbishop of Klikate Forest, Grand Master of the Knights Silthex. The Church of Déagar hath sent me hither to secure a certain item of interest. *Soon*, we will make the True Light mightier than it hath ever been."

"You know *nothing* of the path of Truth and Light!"

"Again thou dost err, O elf. We *are* the True Light. My brother hath ascended to the esteemed position of Supreme Patriarch of the entire Church of Déagar and works to free the main continent of magic. The largest empire hath already declared it illegal, and all others will follow. Lo, the entire world of Perdinok, including thee, will submit to *our will*." He grinned. "That is, of course, our will as dictated by God Déagar."

The man drew severely close to Valqyer. "And by the divine mercy of God Déagar, I can help thee too, O elf. Wilt thou accept it?"

Valqyer was silent, controlling his hate.

Blastilv waved back to Brynistan, who gave him a vial of a yellow-green liquid.

He presented it to Valqyer. "Behold, a powerful potion effective only on elves. 'Twas hidden and protected by a pride of gryphons for over five centuries before I discovered it. And I sent in knights to slay the beasts and claim the prize."

Valqyer stayed quiet, though he flinched in his sadness and disgust at the death of the gryphons.

"Do their deaths sadden thee, elf?" He grinned rancorously. "Doth it *enrage* thee? Yet, woe, never canst thou let thyself *feel*, canst thou?"

The ancient man moved slightly away before continuing. "With this potion, thy greatest weakness shall be no more. 'Twill give unto thee power over thine emotions. The threat of turning Irefae will end, never to return. All I wish in return is thine assistance with a certain project I undertake. And *thy name*."

"My name? So you can control me like Lyforia?"

Blastilv chuckled. "Why, yes, of course. And, just like her, thou shalt be a marionette dancing from my fingertips." He wiggled his bony digits to accompany his words.

"If you wish for an elven name, I shall tell you *Ryoichi*," Valqyer responded defiantly. "That name is only one belonging to those I saw fall dead at the hands of your minions. But you are mad as an Irefaery if you think I shall give you control over me in my own name."

Unperturbed by the angry tone, Blastilv maintained a sinister calm. "Dismiss not my proposal so quickly, elf, for two of these vials exist in the entire world. And I possess them both. Perhaps thou wouldst sacrifice thyself. But what of the female elf? Who is she, I wonder? Thy lover? Thy sister? Thy mother? This, too, will save her."

Valqyer went silent, thinking for an uneasy moment before he muttered a sad, "No."

Blastilv removed a long purple satin drawstring pouch from his belt. From it, he produced the Wand of Moonhame.

The villain could not use it, Valqyer knew, nor could anyone living but Valqyer himself. Even still, the decrepit man grinned cruelly in his dominance.

"Forgive my manners," said the fiend. "Thou didst celebrate thy nativity three days past, and I have yet to wish thee cheer. Behold, the *child* who can control one of the most significant items in the entire world of Perdinok."

He handled the wand brutishly within his shriveled fingers.

"Thou art so newly gifted with magic that thou hast not yet learnt to defend thyself," Blastilv said. "Thou, O puerile duke, art the weak link in the Faery world. *And I will break thee.*"

The weight of the words further crushed Valqyer. "What could you want of me that would warrant such horrid things?"

"The Sorrow Passage, it is called," Blastilv began, "but we will rename it to better please the ear. The *Bridge of Truth*, perhaps. Nay?"

After a slight pause, Blastilv continued. "The new Patriarch hath many new plans for the world, plans we fear might be met with some *resistance* from those unable to understand his divine vision. The Kornidytes who inhabit this continent of Klikate Forest are godless beasts, but beasts born of lust for silver. With heavy pockets, I can purchase an army, send them to the main continent, Bikia, through the Sorrow Passage, and crush all who would stand in the way of righteousness."

"I will never help you," Valqyer said.

Brynistan darted forward and slapped the elf with the back of his fist.

Valqyer roared, his teeth suddenly sharp.

Blastilv calmly set his hand on Brynistan's shoulder, saying, "Let us not turn him Irefae, Seneschal."

Valqyer's teeth returned to normal as he glared.

To the elf, Blastilv resumed, "*Thou wilt* restore the Passage with this wand. And thou wilt make for us a door that we might enter and exit freely. And thou wilt, too, create a door on the opposite end where the tunnel touches Bikia. Heed, I say 'thou wilt' for verily *thou wilt*. No other choice hast thou lest thou dost sacrifice thyself *and* the female elf. And every moment thou delayest only brings further anguish to you both. Decide or die, elf. *Decide or die.*"

—

Think, think, think: all Valqyer could do was think. And with every maddening moment, his mind became more twisted and less able to figure out what needed to be done. Everything had happened so quickly. His entire world had fallen apart. And the emotions of the events, even now, throbbed through the young elf.

They reeled manically in his brain, jumping from one bitter image to the next. The vision of his mother haunted him, filling him with lingering dread. '*Let not the world transform you,*' she had said, but he was uncertain how to avoid it.

The memory of Ryoichi fading away stirred him to weep. The memory of his father, turned troll and tearing into the flesh of an invader, made his stomach bubble and churn with distress.

It had been nearly a complete day since Blastilv's proposal, each moment of which gnawed away at Valqyer's willpower like a field mouse at a peanut or a strolwern seed.

He could do nothing but sit in the center of the dirt floor, his hands gripping his ankles. His thoughts jumbled, manically reeling. His hand clenched a fist.

He tried to meditate on calm. It was not working. Four days he had been here, a nightmarish four days that kept bringing him to the very brink of turning Irefae only so he might struggle his mind back with fading memories of tranquility and bliss.

A discordant mixture of screams echoed through his mind. Screaming, then gurgling.

He could think of no other way to save his mother but to give People free rein of part of the Faery Realm, no choice but to give the same collection of races that drove the Fae to flee, a passage to travel to where they fled.

Blastilv had been correct: With the Sorrow Passage, he could quickly transport his army of brutish warriors to Bikia. The elves—via the work of dwarves—had built the Faery Realm on another, smaller sub-plane; thus, the path across the entire Tibulet Ocean was but a march of just a week. Yet the passage also connected to a network of other tunnels that branched beneath the abandoned Bikian Faery Realm, offering quick, direct routes to anywhere therein.

Valqyer worried that if these marauders were to gain access, no corner would be free from their assault.

The young elf was again struck with the image of his father biting through the flesh of one of the invaders—dark gray blood splashing to the glass streets. Then that moment, when he saw through his mother's glamour—threadlike hair, skin thin on her bone, eyes like hollows.

There was no time. He wanted to stop in the moment and digest all that was happening, but there was no time. He couldn't allow her to turn Irefae and rot in a Kornidyte dungeon. Not his mother.

He was changing, too. His hands were so rough now, not an artist's hands anymore, but thick like animal hides, and his pale skin had darkened to a serpentine green.

The artistic elf boy he'd been was fading. His life was fading, a diminishing memory. He tried to remember. Remember who he was. Remember his poems: "If you dream your life, without ... something, something something something." *Ryo, come back!*

He saw his compositions from childhood ruined in pools of paint on the floor.

On his lower lip, he felt his teeth, now sharp, piercing. They drew silver from his lip, and he licked it, holding the taste on his tongue.

He tried to meditate on calm. He tried to pull himself back. "If you dream ... something ..."

The cell door creaked open, and Blastilv again stood on the shadowed threshold.

"When thou art ready to end the pain, speak thy name."

It seemed so simple. He did not mention all the rest, and in Valqyer's twisted, demented mind, it nearly seemed just that clear.

A discordant mixture of screams. The overturned trunk. His father, an Irefaery. His mother, fading. The Keeper Faery, Lyforia, half-collapsed with guilt.

To lament was dangerous. The Fae lost themselves to negative emotions.

Valqyer collapsed sideways onto the floor. Thoughts of what had happened reeled manically in his brain. The emotions of the events throbbed through him. There was a swirling blackness all around him. His heart pounded with flashes of crimson before his eyes. He felt blazing heat as his flesh swelled and stretched within his skin.

When thou art ready to make the pain end, speak thy name. That was all he wanted, to make the pain end. To be happy again. To save his mother, who was most likely suffering like this, too.

His skin ripped open, as black horns jutted out from his skull.

His face tore open with more.

His own blood filled his mouth.

He cried out, the roar of a beast.

"See," Blastilv's words sounded so distant, like from another place far away, "'Twas not so very difficult, was it? And all that pain for naught."

The vial of yellowish-green liquid was now shoved to Valqyer's lips.

He drank.

A rush, like a heavy waterfall or a snow-chilled wind, surged through him. Memories, fading only moments ago, flashed back into his mind. His entire self returned in mere moments.

Soon, he was more himself than he had been since he first saw the invaders in the elven city.

Peace enveloped him. He breathed. He smiled.

With all that had been happening, the young elf did not fully comprehend what he had done, what he had cried out in his moment of agony.

Not until Blastilv's pompous voice sneered:

"Sleep well, *Valqyer*. Thou hast much to do tomorrow night."

CHAPTER TWENTY-SIX

With salt-scented night air and seabirds cawing overhead, the Tibulet Ocean was a tranquil sight of unending black. Its ebony tides crashed softly against the shore, foaming before returning to void.

It seemed as if the world itself ended not too far from the gray beach, fading into unending dark. But with a gradual shift in the darkened clouds far above, the light of the larger of the two moons, a faint and steady glimmer in the sky, cast its pale blue sheen over the waves.

The water appeared then, as if by some fantastic magic where nothing had been before. The tides inhaled and exhaled in slow and steady breaths. No storms or gusting winds angered them tonight.

Nature was at peace, unaware of the great betrayal Valqyer would soon commit.

But the Faeries knew. Was that not the Purple Faery who watched powerlessly from the thick trees near the shore? She stood next in line to take Lyforia's place as keeper of the nearby section of the woods. And other eyes peered and peeked from the shadows. Nymphs, fauns, brownies, other elves—they all watched with their dread-filled stares.

Blastilv's men—all Humans of the Holy Order of Knights Silthex—were ready. Swords drawn. They posted as a circle of eight points, looking blankly out toward what the eyes of People could not see.

Valqyer wanted the watchers from the wood-line to charge out and stop him. But he knew they could not.

Even at the best of times, an attack on People was short-lived and scarcely effective, but here, this close to the Passage, it was wholly futile.

No other Faery could get as close to the Sorrow Passage as Valqyer was now, not without its grief having an intense effect.

Indeed, the Sorrow Passage was close. Valqyer felt it, its darkness tainting the air. But emotions no longer controlled him. This, Valqyer knew, was the genuine reason for Blastilv's elixir: to let the elf enter this ominous place and perform his required chore.

"Why is your lord absent?" Valqyer asked of Seneschal Brynistan. "Has he not the stomach to witness his own foul deeds?"

The Silthex Knight smirked before answering. "The Grand Master has more important things than an elf. He gathers the first wave of five thousand Kornidyte mercenaries to march on Bikia tonight. Though he owns you, hereafter, you will rarely see your master. Your commands will come from me. You will find that I, too, am well-skilled in commanding Faery names."

Two Silthex sergeants brought Valqyer's mother onto the beach, leaving deep ruts in the moist sand as they dragged her by her arms.

She did not bother casting a glamour now. Too weak to struggle, her body stayed limp, like something dead found washed up on the shore.

And when the Humans threw her to the sand, there she stayed, barely pushing her upper body up with her arms. Her tangled dark hair fell slightly over her face as her sunken eyes stared forward with hate.

Her eyes were still white. She was still Fae, though just.

"How is she still in this state?" Valqyer demanded of Brynistan. "The villain Blastilv vowed an elixir for her as well."

He slapped Valqyer with the back of his fist.

Valqyer hit the sand.

Stepping forward, the seneschal straightened his muscled body to stand tall. He looked down at the boy and growled angry words. "When you complete your task, slave, she'll be well. We need more control over you than just your name. But hurry up. I cannot bring her back once she's fully changed."

Brynistan produced the beautiful wand that had belonged to Valqyer's father. "Take this, *Valqyer*," the seneschal spoke in words that could not be disobeyed, "and use it only for my bidding. Create an entrance to the Sorrow Passage and ready it for my use."

Apprehensively, Valqyer stood and took the Wand of Moonhame from Brynistan. He looked a final time at the forest and its many eyes.

"With every anguish, lament, and gruesome death," Valqyer whispered sadly to the wind, "know 'twas I who betrayed you."

He continued, slouching and downcast, toward the water, his eyes watching the sand.

With eyelids clenched tight, Valqyer took a breath before lifting the ancient tool of elven magic upward toward the night.

"Unveil."

A wispy, lavender mist flowed out far over the ocean, and what had been there before, in front of them but invisible, was now seen like an illusion or ghostly image.

Extending without support, it was an impossibility of physical suspension—this foot-thick sheet of grief-blackened quartz, seven feet wide. Even from the shore, the large red cracks of Chaos were visible, as were holes where parts had broken away. Purple lightning flashed in circular streaks, ringing the bridge as a tunnel around it.

Never had Valqyer seen this thing of infamous legends, and looking upon it now, with his impending deed heavy on his mind, caused his heart to pound upon his insides with such force that it seemed it would beat its way through. He could barely breathe, as he beheld. He felt its malignance, cold upon his skin.

He stepped forward.

With the Sorrow Passage revealed, the Faeries of the forest fled. The Humans stared, afraid and open-mouthed.

One of the sergeants threw his sword to the sand and collapsed to his knees. He frantically grasped a pendant that hung from his necklace and muttered rapid prayers to God Déagar.

"Go—" Brynistan attempted hoarsely, then cleared his throat to try again. "Go, slave, and do as I have commanded." He pushed the elf forward.

Again, looking at the bridge, Valqyer clutched the wand in his clammy palm and swallowed dryly.

He stepped a few paces toward the ancient evil.

He stopped.

"*Valqyer!* I command you by your name, go to that fucking bridge, and ready it for our use. We *will* march on Bikia tonight."

The power of his name was absolute, and the elf could do nothing but move forward, his legs bending and stretching and bending again, all on their own.

He concentrated with all his might on controlling his own body, but regardless, he continued toward the bridge.

Alas, Valqyer, you are too well akin to your father—he remembered his mother's words. It was true. He thought of his father fighting against the Kornidytes, even when it took all of his will to overcome the weakness inherent in their race.

Valqyer clamped his teeth and grunted.

His body began shaking stiffly as he slowed himself. He managed to throw himself onto the sand. A pitiful success, but success nevertheless.

"Fucking za!" Brynistan cursed. "Stand up, *Valqyer!*"

The elf managed a painful laugh. "Your own elixir has weakened the magic of my name. You have made me less Faery and more likened to you."

The seneschal charged the elf and kicked him in the gut. "Get up, Valqyer. I demand it."

He rolled onto his back and stared upward, blankly into night. "You were correct in saying you would need more than the power of my name to make me do this horrible deed."

He glanced sadly back at his mother.

Faeries could not be this close to the Sorrow Passage without effect.

"You no longer have this other advantage."

There was an abrupt growl. A furious sound, like from a lioness.

The sergeants looked back to see the creature who had been Valqyer's mother leaping up from the ground. Her wet black hair hung in tangles over gray, discolored skin. Her eyes now shone with crimson fire.

Enraged, she clawed at the sergeant closest to her, and he frantically slapped his hands over his face, dripping with blood.

Seneschal Brynistan was her target, her prey, and he knew it. She moved to him, but not in feral attack, but with a slow, long-legged stride.

He backed away in fear.

The fog that lingered delicately over the sea, this came to her, enveloped her, swirled gradually around her body, but for an instant.

And as it fell away, there she was again, as beautiful as ever. But there was nothing motherly in her now. Lust and wantonness infused her beauty, a shameless Goddess on the shore.

Her hair, still wet, turned shimmering gold. Her pale, luminous skin was bare, revealing perfect breasts and perfect curves that flowed down to her thighs and legs and bare feet on the shore. Her newfound beauty was a glamour, yes—but not an elven glamour. For no longer was Lillia an elf. Her kind had changed completely, and if Valqyer needed to guess her new form, he would call this thing a *rusalka*.

A sergeant, sword drawn, charged her, but she only looked at him with her eyes of crimson fire. He stopped, enchanted, and threw down his weapon. He began kissing her hand.

Soon, he and the other sergeants encircled her, touching, kissing, and worshiping her as she danced across the shore.

Brynistan staggered away from her, backing up and tripping over Valqyer.

He was her prey. Thus, she pushed the other men aside. She flowed forward, unaffected by the enchanted devotees who followed.

"Handsome." Her voice was an eerie whisper as she swayed while looking down at Brynistan.

Valqyer scurried some distance from the two. In shock, he watched, horrified. It was not *her* anymore, he told himself. She was gone.

The rusalka extended her long, bare arm to present her hand to the Human.

He relaxed. His eyes remained locked on her as she helped him up. Not to his feet. Only to his knees.

"Brave and strong," the rusalka whispered, her words echoing dreamlike. "Such large muscles." Her movements were ghostly, swaying at the stomach as she drew his head forward.

He kissed her deeply.

She clutched his long brown hair and jerked it to the side. Chunks ripped from his skull as blood flowed down his face.

His kisses grew deeper.

Holding up the bloody hair and ripped skin, the rusalka screamed out like thunder, and rain fell.

Brynistan barely seemed to notice, as he obediently leered up at the seductress, moving only to wipe away the mix of blood and rain that blocked his vision.

She grinned in delight as she stared up into the downpour. Her breathing slowed. She placed her hand lovingly on Brynistan's cheek. "So strong," she whispered. "*I will devour you.*"

Still on his knees, he nodded. "Thank you, my queen."

"Come," she instructed. She then, elegantly as ever, walked away toward the water.

And the Silthex all hurried after her, every single one of them, even as she led them to the black waters of the Tibulet Ocean.

Just as gracefully as she had approached the water, she entered it.

The men followed, like satyrs swooning behind a wood nymph.

And they, every one, smiled like lustful fools as they were pulled into the depths.

—

His body throbbing with horror, Valqyer lay still and limp against the sand as he stared. The water beat slowly in red, foamy waves against the shore. In the shadow of the spectral bridge of crumbling black crystal, the limp body parts of the Humans popped up, one by one, to the surface and rocked like so much forsaken driftwood.

The elf kept his eyes locked upon the pieces. These People had devastated Valqyer's world, and never would it return to what it was before. Art and poetry, to him, were memories past. Gone forever.

Though depleted, Valqyer pulled himself up.

"Hark, Father." He spoke, but his words were vacant. "I now know what I will create with the wand. A grand transmutation like you wanted. 'Twill be unlike the Realm has ever seen."

He aimed the wand downward, and crimson lightning from the Passage struck the shore. The sand at the point of impact melted and fused.

The wand in Valqyer's hand shattered. Its creation, so unfaery.

And as dust, it fell.

Staring blankly, Valqyer lifted the new object: a sword. Its single-edged blade of glass was slightly curved and etched with silver vines. No crossguard. Its hilt was amber hardened around a thick brier. Its pommel, a blue topaz.

In the blade's reflection, Valqyer saw his own eyes, utterly black.

The blade was heavy.

He would grow accustomed to it.

A Convergence of Realms

N
W
E
S
0 30 60 90
Miles
Reyigo
Karvlent Alliance
Allar Lands
Rvcah Lands
Feah Lands
Vohcktara
Dayig
Hyvile River
Dinikimera

Rebek 1, 831: Seventeen Years Later

The sliver of the lavender moon shimmered across the Hyvile River, its massive expanse an unending black glittered with purple peaks. The moored wooden warship creaked ominously as it bobbed in the slight current beneath it. Eighty feet long and standing tall above the river, its single mast supported a rectangular sail—striped off white and faded green—which stirred in a subtle wind.

Swithun, now fifty, was flanked by two Dayigan soldiers as they neared the edge of the ship's deck to face a wooden ramp leading down.

"Go on," commanded a soldier.

"At least tell me where we're at first," Swithun snapped.

"Your questions'll be answered soon enough," the soldier growled. "Now go."

The three descended to the docks below, their heavy boots clapping hollowly on the warped planks as they plodded downward. Two T-shaped wharves stretched out around them, these mooring three other vessels matching the one from which Swithun had disembarked.

The two soldiers stopped, leaving Swithun to continue alone down the weathered planks between the ships.

A shadowed man waited at the end. Like the uniform of the men behind Swithun, his tabard was emerald green, with the Dayigan symbol embroidered across his upper body in yellow thread.

The man stepped forward as the pale moonlight shone across his face.

"Lieutenant Beadurinc?" Swithun uttered in disbelief. The man, now in his early forties, had swollen some in girth, yet it was irrefutably him. "I figured you was dead."

"*Commander* Beadurinc," he corrected, as he folded his hands on his gut. "I assume your surprise at seeing me means you've heard about the unfortunate demise of our brethren."

Swithun nodded gravely. "I reckon the whole Empire's heard about it," he growled, voice heavy with disgust. "The entire Order of Silthex Knights burnt to ash in a flash." He paused before asking, "And Captain Rothgar?"

Beadurinc replied with a solemn shake of his head. "And yet, I carry his memory with me." He drew his sword—steel scraping against the leather sheath before ringing upon release. He stared, admiring its deadly edge. "Rescued from the ashes."

Swithun eyed Rothgar's sword within the commander's grip, fearing it might quickly turn his way. "He were a good man. A righteous man of Déagar. He ain't deserve to be burnt up by some witch."

"A *Karulent* witch," Beadurinc spat.

"I heard the tales. The Blue Rose, they're calling her. Them Karulents are celebrating her like she's a fucking hero."

"Do you still hold love for the Karulents?" Beadurinc's grip tightened on his sword as its malignant point turned Swithun's way.

"I never had love for 'em," Swithun snapped back, meeting Beadurinc's gaze with equal ferocity. "I might've wanted to spare their children, but make no mistake, I ain't got no love for them fucking savages. But what they done now..." Swithun breathed as he fisted his hand. "'Tis unforgivable."

"And yet you hid from us?"

"Hid?" Swithun scoffed. "Are you having a fucking laugh? Hid from who? 'Tis been five years since the end of the Silthex. I served fourteen years as a Silthex sergeant at me fort what the captain, himself, assigned me to, and fought hard against them Tridulans, that..." He leaned closer to Beadurinc and whispered, "That you lot accused of burning down the Blue Zone." He stepped back. "And after the Silthex was all gone, and they give the whole army the new green uniforms to honor 'em, I wore it proud, staying on two more years as a regular soldier in the same place. Finally, yes, I asked for me discharge and moved on from all the fighting. Got meself a nice little farm now. But I sure ain't been hiding. The Silthex forgot all about me long before the Blue Rose got a hold of 'em."

Beadurinc took a deep breath, raising his chin as he glared at Swithun. "I do not appreciate your tone, Sergeant. And you will address me as *sir*."

"Right. Forgive me, *sir*," Swithun said. "I ain't mean no disrespect for you or the deceased—rest them. But anybody who was lookin' for me could've found me quick. But you lot didn't even try. And now, you wanna snatch me out of me 'ome, chuck me on a boat, and drag me off to wherever this is?"

Beadurinc's voice was controlled and chilling, his gaze dripping with contempt. "My day has been long and arduous, *Sergeant*, and it is well past midnight. One of my footmen was slain by one of these savage abominations who roam these cursed lands, and yet their leader refuses to release the killer to us so justice may be served. And just as I am finally preparing to retire for the night, I learn that *you* have arrived."

"I ain't exactly pick when I showed up, did I? *Sir*."

"And yet, you still managed to arrive at the most inconvenient time." Beadurinc sheathed his sword. "That said, the Grand Master has plans for you—if you are still loyal to him."

Swithun hung his head low and stared out over the murky waters beyond the pier. He could still remember his Reception Ceremony from years ago, when Captain Rothgar and his other newfound brothers welcomed him into the order. He remembered his vow: allegiance until death. "Yes," he muttered softly, "I'm still yours."

Beadurinc looked past Swithun's shoulder, speaking up so the waiting soldiers could hear. "See him to the barracks and ensure he has a uniform. His training will begin promptly at sunrise." He returned his cold eyes to Swithun. "You must prepare yourself for your new task."

"Don't suppose you could tell me what that task is. Or where we're at."

"We are in the Drevite Nation." With that, Beadurinc turned and walked off toward the large wooden fort that loomed over the docks.

—

The deep orange sun peeked from behind the fortress walls, casting its ruddy hue over the battlements. The parapets seemed like rows of animal teeth, sharpened logs backlit by the morning light just beyond the roof of green wooden shingles slanting down toward the courtyard.

Along the second story of the walls, a railed walkway spanned along thin green doors leading into the primary barracks. Below, the ground level mirrored above with more lines of matching doors.

Four large, free-standing annexes stood at the corners of the courtyard—two additional barracks blocks and two food storehouses. A wide stretch of sand filled its center ground, connecting two large doors: one leading to the front entrance and another slightly smaller one in the back, leading to the river.

Swithun remained centered in the yard, feeling odd returned to his emerald tabard and black trousers—the same worn by all the soldiers bustling around him.

Beadurinc approached, his gaze stern and his mouth still holding the same pompous smirk Swithun remembered from years ago. "I trust you had a restful sleep," he said curtly.

"I'm not half as restful as I oughta be, back in this damned uniform again," Swithun replied. "I thought I was done with all this. And the men don't trust me here."

"Come," he said, not bothering to acknowledge the complaints. He began to walk, and Swithun followed.

"We are a secret outpost, unknown to all save for those at the highest levels of command," Beadurinc said. "Officially, we are a trade post tasked with commerce with the Drevite Nation. Even within the fort, different brigades have their own specialized tasks that cannot be discussed outside their unit. Once the men understand how you fit in to all of this, they might trust you enough to talk to you."

"And how *do* I fit in to all this?"

"You don't." Beadurinc stopped before the large main entrance. "Not exactly. The last of the Silthex are all amassed in this fort. Thirty-five Silthex sergeants, including you. Four knights, myself included. The remainder of the hundreds of soldiers assembled here have been personally vetted by the Grand Master or me. This fortress is a test site from which we can select those worthy of joining the Holy Order of Knights

Silthex reborn. These men are our future, but your singular mission *is to avenge our past*."

Swithun straightened his back as he took in the words. "You honor me with this task, sir. I'll see it done."

"*The Grand Master* honors you, whereas I hold only contempt for you, as I always have. Come." He opened the door.

—

Beadurinc led Swithun into a dark, narrow corridor, a prison. The smell of filth and the sound of despair filled the air as Swithun's eyes scanned the four doors on either side of the hall, each with a small, barred window. Through the bars of one, he spotted three wretched figures clothed in leather and sprawled out on the floor.

"Who're they, then?" Swithun asked uneasily.

"Drevites," Beadurinc spat the word as if it were disgusting. "Like the Karulents, they claim to be of the True Light, but they do not worship God Déagar. We have a dozen for now, but we will increase that number shortly."

All Swithun could do was stare at them, his heart heavy. "I don't understand. Why are you capturing them like this?"

The words were met with silent contempt as Beadurinc fixed Swithun with an icy glare. "They refuse to worship the Greatest of All, and they practice magic. Do we need more reasons?"

"No, sir."

Beadurinc paused for a moment before adding, "Concern yourself with regaining our trust, and you shall receive your answers." With that, he proceeded to another door across the hall and used a key to open it. "The prisoner we've come to see is inside."

Inside, they found a young man—one of the winged people called Terovaes—seated and chained to the wall. His body was smeared with ash, and he wore nothing but a scrap of cloth around his waist. He looked sick and had clearly been battered, yet his glaring eyes held defiance and loathing.

"We captured this one last night just before your arrival," Beadurinc said, as if presenting a trophy. "State your name, savage."

"*Kyran,*" the captive seethed through his teeth.

"This savage," Beadurinc continued, "is a filthy *Faery* who betrayed the Light by his actions."

"But," Swithun began with mild confusion, "Terovaes ain't Faeries, sir."

"I mean he is a cocksucker, you fool," Beadurinc said angrily. "We caught him in the act. Nearly."

"You wish you caught us in the act," the captive jumped up angrily, fighting against the chains, "so you could've watched us, you pervy Human. We was done by the time you came along."

Beadurinc punched him in the stomach, causing Kyran to coil forward, arms crossing his stomach.

"You see," Beadurinc said, "he is unabashed with his perversion. The Drevite Nation actually condones men lowering themselves to the acts of women. They allow women to lead them. All five of the chiefdoms that make up the Drevite Nation are ruled by pagan priestesses, called druidesses. And instead of worshiping almighty Déagar, they worship his sisters and mother. The whole notion is repulsive."

"Can I have a word with you outside, sir?" Swithun asked.

Beadurinc nodded before moving through the door.

Returned to the hall, Swithun quickly approached Beadurinc. "Here now, what's all this about?" he growled. "I've been brought here for some meet and greet with a pervy tree savage?"

Beadurinc's lips curled into a sinister smile. "Your training, of course."

"Me training?"

"Yes. The Grand Master insists that you learn the different techniques of pain infliction—so that you can extract information from those who need to be questioned. That *creature* in there will be your subject as I teach you the basics of interrogation. Your task is to make him suffer in order to obtain information on the Drevite Nation and, more importantly, to make him confess that he witnessed a crime. His comrade murdered one of our footmen."

"Really?" Swithun narrowed his eyes suspiciously at Beadurinc. "I bet it were you what killed the soldier, weren't it?"

Beadurinc folded his hands on his stomach. "You know me better than I realized, Swithun." He gave a dark chuckle. "These secular soldiers who the royal army has placed under my command are not Silthex. Many of them do not fully understand what needs to be done to better the world—not like you and I. They required additional *motivation* to attack the Drevites, which I provided. As far as the Drevites, themselves, when their leadership moves to protect a pervert and murderer in one, the residents of these lands will understand the folly of putting them in charge. Two birds with one stone, as it were. Fear not, the soldier who lost his life for the cause served Déagar well in doing so and will be rewarded in Laqyigo."

A chill ran through Swithun as his gaze drifted to the floor. "You're doing this to get some justice, right? To avenge our poor, murdered brothers?"

"'Tis a single step down a long path, but yes, it ultimately leads to that goal, along with others."

Swithun clenched his jaw as he digested the bitter words. He raised his eyes again. "That's all I need to know, then."

Swithun walked down a corridor lined floor to the ceiling with wooden shelves—their contents, a collection of grains, cured meats, and pickled food soaking in clay jars filled with vinegar. A few wicker baskets contained fresh food from the Drevites, either traded for or commandeered.

Swithun had trudged around this whole square corridor twice over, finding no way to go farther into the house, and as he began his third time around, he had become enraged with the whole situation.

"Inquisitor Swithun?" called a voice behind him.

With a scowl, Swithun turned to see a Dayigan soldier approaching.

The soldier mumbled a quick apology for being late, seeming like he feared Swithun might strike him. "Commander Beadurinc wishes to see you, sir."

"I know he wishes to see me," Swithun growled. "That's why I'm fucking here. But I can't figure out this fucking pantry!"

The soldier lowered his head. "Forgive me, sir. As I said, I was delayed. This way."

He guided Swithun further down the hallway, Swithun's boots plodding angrily atop the worn-out floorboards until they reached a shelving unit pushed slightly back from the rest. It moved farther back under the soldier's touch, revealing a concealed entranceway.

The other soldier stepped away, waiting.

With anger still boiling inside, Swithun grumbled, "It weren't like that before."

The soldier bowed his head in silent agreement before entering.

Swithun stepped into a large windowless chamber, reeking of blood and sweat. Thirty Dayigan soldiers, standing in separate small groups, focused their attention on various Drevite captives, these bound to tables or chairs or dangling by chains from the rafters above. Some of the captives screamed in terror or agony—sounds Swithun had now grown accustomed to after his time in the fort—while most seemed too broken to make any sound at all.

Swithun approached Commander Beadurinc in the center of the room.

The commander unchained a winged woman from her bindings and stepped away. "If you can fly up to those rafters," he said with a smirk, "we'll let you go free, along with two other captives of your choice."

The woman's eyes—wide with terror—looked around at the Dayigan soldiers circling her to observe. She spread out her wings and jumped. She flapped furiously and desperately, trying with all her might to ascend. She screamed in frustration, trying and trying until eventually she collapsed to the floor, slamming her fist against it in dire frustration. Staring helplessly at the unreachable wooden beams above, her eyes began to tear.

Beadurinc broke out in laughter as he motioned to a guard. "Secure the prisoner."

Swithun's gaze shifted to Beadurinc. "What d'you do to her?"

"If you extend the wings of a bird to full span," he began, "the top few feathers extending outwards from the wings are significantly longer. These are called primaries. If you clip them, the bird cannot fly. Evidently, the same works on

Terovaes." Beadurinc stopped a passing soldier. "I want this done to all the Drevite captives."

"Yes, Commander." He hurried away.

Commander Beadurinc fixed his gaze on Swithun. "You look exhausted."

He nodded. "My dreams have been keeping me up at—"

"Yes, yes. We're all doing God's work here. I will not have a captain sulking around my fort as if his dog has just died. Shoulders back. Head up."

Swithun complied, forcing himself to stand tall. "Am I a captain, sir?"

"The equivalent of one, Inquisitor. All the former Silthex sergeants in the fort hold either lieutenant or captain rank. We had a ceremony for those who arrived promptly at the start of the campaign, although you were off farming turnips or what have you."

"Wheat mostly," Swithun mumbled.

Beadurinc began walking and Swithun trailed him as they passed groups of soldiers using captives for their torturous experiments.

"Our research into Terovaes is proving quite fruitful," Beadurinc said.

"I always thought this were a storehouse."

"Yes, most of the fort believes the same. Only those who have proven their loyalty and discretion are aware of its true purpose, and everyone here is bound by a strict vow of secrecy—even to the others in the fort." Beadurinc stopped in his path to face Swithun. "Forgive me for not overseeing your training as I had intended. As we move into this new phase of the Drevite Experiment, matters of greater importance require my absolute attention. However, reports have reached me concerning your accomplishments over the past few weeks. I must confess they impress me."

A stupid smile curved across Swithun's lips as he let out a deep breath. He never thought he'd hear those words from Beadurinc himself. "I've been trying hard, sir. I mastered loads of them skills you told me to learn, and mastered loads of the kit you give me, too."

"As I have heard," he replied. "Which is why 'tis come time for you to leave this fort. Our dungeons have been filled to capacity with captives who need to be shipped away. You will accompany them as part of the crew, along with myself. Surprisingly, you have actually proven yourself somewhat useful, Swithun, and worthy of continuing your training—*under the Grand Master himself.*"

—

The five days of the voyage on the old creaking cog passed slowly and painfully. Swithun kept to himself, standing on the deck and leaning on the rail as he gazed over the waters of the Hyvile River, stretching for miles on either side of the ship. But even in its majestic beauty, Swithun could still hear the screams of his victims back at the fort. Every night, their dying wails shattered his sleep, causing him to spring up from his hammock in cold sweats. What he was doing was right, Swithun told himself, but the task seemed to eat away at him from the inside. And he feared how much worse the training under the Grand Master would be.

The ship reached the shore of a considerable island centered on the river, its piers bearing the emerald flags of the empire. A discordant mix of wails, moans, and clanking chains echoed from below deck as the other soldiers began unloading the captives. Meanwhile, Beadurinc and Swithun made their way to the only visible complex—an abbey consisting of old buildings built from pale brown stones and surrounded by a short sturdy wall. The tallest structure, a church, was adorned with leering gargoyles atop its pointed green roof. A small stream ran through the grounds, powering a watermill that creaked and groaned.

Within the church's large dark foreboding nave, Beadurinc and Swithun waited for their audience with Grand Master Blastilv. After what felt like an eternity, the ancient man finally made his appearance. Aged beyond measure, his skin was wizened, and his spine bent with age. Thin strands of gray brittle hair clung to his skull beneath a miter matching his regal green robes trimmed in gold.

This was Swithun's first glimpse of the Grand Master in over twenty years, and seeing him now made Swithun yearn for those simpler times before their first meeting. Times when he worked in a clothing shop back home, far away from the horrors of war and the task of torturing captives.

Beadurinc stepped forward and addressed him. "Good afternoon, Grand Master Blastilv."

Blastilv paused, his yellowed eyes filled with disdain. "That title doth mean naught now that the Silthex knights have been scattered as ashes."

"The Silthex will rise again," Beadurinc replied with resolve. "I have already chosen many candidates at my fort."

"When the order is restored, thou mayest then use that title once more."

"You're right, of course, Your Grace." Beadurinc bowed his head respectfully.

"Report," Blastilv commanded.

"We have brought another hundred Drevites for your experiments, Your Grace."

"Very good. 'Tis time to put our plans in motion ere their people grow suspicious of the disappearances."

"Yes, Your Grace," Beadurinc said. "With your authorization, we will begin testing our four top-performing alchemic potions on different sections of their population."

"Thou hast mine approval. And I do expect results."

"As you will have, Your Grace." Beadurinc bowed his head. "Currently, our efforts are focused on the *Feah* chiefdom; however, we are confident that within a year, we will have all five chiefdoms of the Drevite Nation subjugated and ready for extensive study. I assure you, Your Grace, we will find the ultimate method to forge absolute obedience."

"Excellent." Blastilv grinned with wicked delight. "Keep me informed of thy progress, Commander." He looked at Swithun, acknowledging his presence for the first time. "And what of our wayward sergeant?"

"He too is making progress in his own task, Your Grace. Inquisitor Swithun now possesses the fundamental skills you require of him. With your guidance, I am certain he will learn to carry out the task you wish of him."

Swithun stood a little taller, happy to be given a good evaluation to the former Grand Master.

Beadurinc gave Swithun a smug grin that spoke of a sinister victory and left the latter bewildered. "I'm afraid I might have misled the inquisitor, Your Grace. He believes his new post is some sort of honor."

Now, a chill ran down Swithun's spine as Blastilv's brutal yellowed eyes met his, and Swithun felt small before him, like a minnow before a fearsome shark.

The archbishop advanced on the inquisitor with slow and deliberate steps. "Thou hast wrought great harm upon us." Blastilv's venomous words dripped with hatred.

"I . . ." Swithun began, but was struck silent by the powerful gaze of the ancient man.

"Thou knowest the Blue Rose," Blastilv hissed with seething rage.

"Yes, I know of her, Gran—Your Grace," Swithun stammered in response. "She's the one what murdered all the Silthex, and now she leads the Veiled River that helps smuggle Karulents out of the empire."

"'Twas no question, Inquisitor," Blastilv said firmly. "Thou *knowest* the Blue Rose."

His bony hand shot upward, clamping around Swithun's throat, squeezing and causing him to gasp for air. Despite his frail appearance, Blastilv's grip was iron-like.

Panicked, Swithun struggled against the grasp as the shriveled fingers tightened.

Blastilv's anger boiled as he said, "'Twas the Blue Rose who left thee with these scars upon thy neck." He released him.

Swithun bent forward, arms on his legs, coughing and panting. He touched the marks on the side of his neck with trembling fingertips. "It was just some backwoods girl what gave me this. She weren't nothing."

"Seneschal Rothgar did recognize her," Blastilv seethed, "before she *slew* him and nearly all the other Silthex. She was the same girl whom thou didst let live."

Swithun's mouth hung open, but no words formed as he stared at him in disbelief. Finally, he uttered, "I ain't know, Your Grace. It was long before she did that."

The back of Blastilv's hand met Swithun's face with a crack. "Thou knewest she wast a vile Karulent, yet thou didst *allow* her to go free."

Warm blood trickled from Swithun's nose, and he wiped it away with his arm. "Forgive me, Your Grace," he whimpered.

"Thy new position shall be thy penance, Inquisitor," Blastilv said, his voice resounding through the nave. "Every foul and torturous task thou art called to undertake in service to me shall also be a torment for thee. Thus, shalt thou earn God's absolution."

Beadurinc sneered from behind him. "He said he's already having nightmares, Your Grace."

Blastilv grinned cruelly. "Thy nightmares have not yet begun, Inquisitor. Thou shalt hunt members of the Veiled River and force them to reveal their secrets—secrets they have sworn to protect, and that will require the utmost agony to extract. Through them shalt thou find this Blue Rose *witch* and bring her before me—alive." The archbishop's tone suddenly turned pleasantly malicious as he added, "Fear not, I shall instruct thee in the art of persuasion."

Swithun's head hung low, his gaze dull and unfocused. He could feel the archbishop's words like cast-iron weights upon his slouched form.

Blastilv moved away, his boots clacking on the granite floor that stretched across the vast chamber, echoing around them.

Swithun looked up then, past Blastilv and the stage the archbishop approached, looking to the life-size statue of God Déagar set into the front wall behind the altar.

It was only the front half of the statue—a relief set into a niche of the Greatest of All. Full plate armor of gold-painted stone adorned him, covering every inch of his holy body, including a closed helm covering his face. Yet somehow, the metallic face seemed to condemn Swithun, as if the failed soldier was something wretched, unworthy to be in his holy house.

Blastilv reached the stage, lifted a ring of flat iron, and returned to Beadurinc. "This collar hath been crafted to suppress the magic of the Blue Rose," he said. "The inquisitor will need it to fulfill his duties. But first, I require thee to test that it doth indeed work."

Beadurinc nodded and took hold of the collar. "Of course, Your Grace," he replied confidently. "I am certain I can find a Drevite witch who would be perfect for its testing."

"I done you wrong, Your Grace," Swithun uttered, still facing the floor. "I done me fallen brothers and the Almighty wrong. But I'll make it right. I vow it."

"Yes," Blastilv grinned. "I am most certain that thou wilt."

Despondent, Swithun stared at the wooden wall, stained a rich cherry, as he found himself slumped in a fine chair. He hadn't drifted off, yet a trance had seemed to possess him, a fog descending on his aching mind and granting him refuge from his waking nightmare. Weeks beneath the tutelage of Archbishop Blastilv had nearly broken him. His breaths were shallow; his burning eyes held their gaze.

And then he realized someone had said his name.

"Your name *is* Swithun, yes?" the man said somberly.

Swithun gave a hollow nod.

They were in a small study, Swithun realized, within the abbey—although the books were locked away in iron-studded cabinets. A fire crackled in the fireplace. The room was unoccupied, except for himself and the unknown other man. A coarse green robe and a tonsured head marked the stranger as a monk.

Swithun, his eyes bereft of feelings, turned to face him and managed nothing but an apathetic glower.

"I should have introduced myself before," the man said bleakly, his voice compassionate yet disheartened. "I've seen you around the abbey, but I mostly keep to myself. I'm Father Lewis, prior of this abbey and second under the archbishop in ecclesiastical matters." He paused. "You look . . . unwell. Is there something I can do?"

Swithun's expressionless stare lingered another beat. "You're still dressed like a Silthex priest."

The prior glanced down at his attire, his face filled with regret. "Yes. I suppose I'm like a widower still wearing his ring," he said remorsefully. "But it is part of who I am now. For better or for worse, as it were."

"The Silthex'll rise again."

"Yes." He looked back with such deep sadness, and Swithun could see doubt in his eyes, doubt that their cause would succeed, or doubt that he wanted it to. The man seemed hesitant to speak, as though it pained him to offer his words. He asked softly, "Is that what you want?"

Swithun's glare intensified as he debated whether to confront or evade the question entirely. "Course it is. That's what we all want," he retorted sharply, before another uncomfortable silence descended on them both.

The priest clearly contemplated his next words. Whatever they were, they seemed difficult to speak. Just as Swithun thought the prior was going to retreat into himself, he said, "I'd like to show you something."

A mystery lay beneath the prior's words, and despite reservations, Swithun gave an almost imperceptible nod of agreement.

Another contemplative silence followed, and the prior's eyes flashed with worry. Nevertheless, he motioned for Swithun to follow him out of the chamber. "This way."

—

Swithun followed the shrouded figure as they moved through the large yard behind the church. The area was edged by storehouses down one side and by low walls for the rest. Clouds blocked the moons' feeble light, yet even in the thick darkness, Swithun was able to make out the obscure figure who guided him.

"This was once a Karulent abbey," Father Lewis began grimly, "valued for its solitude and its position within the Hyvile River—their God is a God of water, you know. It housed over a hundred monks and nuns."

"What happened to them?" Swithun asked, but after receiving no answer, realized the foolishness of the question.

Silence.

"You've often been in the main church, of course," the prior said, "but the Karulents also had a smaller area for more intimate rituals."

Swithun stopped. "The archbishop told me not to go in the chapel."

The shadowed figure halted as well, turning to face him. "Of course," Father Lewis conceded. "Forgive me for disturbing you. May the fires of God Déagar guide you." He then strode off into the night, returning toward where they'd come.

Swithun could not help but stare at the mysterious chapel in the back of the yard. In the darkness, it appeared no more than a black blob he recognized only because he knew it was there.

The strange interaction with the enigmatic priest had left him wanting. A strange craving began to creep up inside him, and Swithun could not help but wonder what lay behind those doors.

"Wait," Swithun called.

—

Every window of the chapel was boarded up tightly, while a heavy lock secured the entrance. The prior wordlessly produced a key from his belt and slid it into the lock with a click.

As soon as the door creaked open, crimson light spilled out from inside. The two men pushed the door open just wide enough for them to squeeze through and quickly close it behind them.

The chamber beyond stretched about thirty feet in each direction, with a vaulted roof overhead. White paint covered every surface, even the tiled floor—though beneath, Swithun could make out traces of unholy blue. There were no furnishings, only a single unnatural object suspended a few feet above the floor: a massive crack—about ten feet tall and a foot at its widest—in the air itself. Through it, Swithun could see an infinite span filled with swirling threads of crimson light and bouts of crimson lightning.

Not daring to approach, Swithun stood, agape and fearful, until he finally uttered, "What is it?"

"A fissure," answered the prior in a low voice. "Archbishop Blastilv opened this gateway between our world and the Plane of Chaos."

"Fucking horse shite!" Swithun spat, his voice rising with indignation. "All of it. The archbishop is a holy man of God! And the Plane of Chaos is where the Gods damned the Demons to. He could never . . ."

"Is he truly a righteous man of God? I've heard you alone in the church, kneeling before the icon of God Déagar. I've heard you ask, *is this still your path?*"

"That was private," Swithun said.

"I have asked the same questions many times, myself. This place was once a tranquil monastery. Now, we've purged it of everything it was and filled it with Drevites whom we torment without mercy—God help us all."

"A *Karulent* monastery," Swithun growled.

The priest seemed broken. He shook his head as he pressed his trembling hand to his brow. "Swithun, I implore you, look at what is right before your eyes. I have no one else to turn to."

Swithun's blood boiled, and his hand quivered as he clenched it into a fist, preparing to strike—but the man was still a man of the cloth, Swithun reminded himself. Again, Swithun looked at the massive crack and the swirling crimson light beyond it before turning away in disgust.

"What I see right before my eyes"—Swithun drew his sword—"is a traitor to His Holiness, Supreme Patriarch Krasil." He neared the blade to the prior's neck. "You best come with me."

*S*withun burst open the door to the archbishop's apartment and wrenched the priest into the room. The richly paneled walls were draped with lavish emerald tapestries depicting scenes of holy violence and despair. The air reeked of heavy incense, filling every corner.

Archbishop Blastilv rose from the luxurious, high-backed chair of green velvet, slamming shut the book he'd been reading. "Why dost thou intrude upon my privacy? Speak thy purpose quick!"

"Forgive me, Your Grace," Swithun said, keeping his left arm firmly wrapped around the priest as he gripped his sword in his right. "I have sinned. I went into the chapel that I weren't—"

"What have I told thee, Inquisitor?" Blastilv interrupted as he raised a finger. "Thou shalt speak in a manner befitting thy station, or not at all."

Swithun nodded. "I went into the chapel which I *wasn't* supposed to go in to."

The archbishop exhaled. "And what didst thou seest therein?"

"Nothing I think needs mentioning. Ever," he said. "You got—"

"Properly."

"You *have* your reasons for what's there. No need for me to understand them. But this here priest..." Swithun threw him to the floor, and he stayed there on his side, huffing angrily and glaring up. "He has lost all loyalty to the Church."

"I am loyal only to God Déagar," the priest replied wearily. He turned his eyes toward the floor. "I'm not sure *what* the Church is loyal to anymore."

"Thou art mistaken, Prior," Blastilv said. "Supreme Patriarch Krasil is the voice of God in the mortal world. If thou hath abandoned him and forsaken his edicts, then thou art no longer fit to don that holy garb."

"Defrock me, then." The priest remained on the floor. "Tell me I am excommunicated. It doesn't matter. None of it matters. You have no true authority from God." His gaze shifted from Blastilv to Swithun. "The archbishop is causing a convergence of realms."

Swithun held his sword higher, shouting, *"Shut your lying hole, traitor!"*

The archbishop spoke calmly. "Inquisitor ... hold thy peace."

Biting back his rage, Swithun slowly lowered his blade but didn't sheath it.

"Alack, the faithless priest doth not deceive," Blastilv, his voice menacingly serene, continued. "Verily, I *am* producing a convergence of realms—an inadvertent occurrence, albeit one that I do hold control over."

"I don't understand, Your Grace," Swithun said. "What does it supposed to mean—*convergence of realms?*"

"Millennia past," Blastilv began in a measured and chilly cadence, "when mankind was little more than two-legged beasts garbed in filth and furs, aimlessly afoot through the lands that lay frozen beneath the frigid grip of everlasting winter; the Faeries didst elect to leave the Natural Realm and make for themselves a new home. They fashioned a parallel sub-plane that mirrored our continent—envision it as a higher level upon Bikia—and christened it as the *Faery Realm.*

Later still, they forsook this newly created land also, building yet another realm above the continent of Klikate Forest. The former, Bikian realm was abandoned to the Chaos-ridden Irefaeries, where within they were imprisoned. In time, these same Irefaeries, led by the dreaded Queen Datura, declared war against mankind to retake their erstwhile native land, Bikia. The specifics are irrelevant: thou mayest surmise who emerged victorious. What matters is that the war weakened the barriers between the Natural Realm and the Irefaery Realm throughout the lands now known as the *Drevite Nation*."

"Begging your pardon, Your Grace," Swithun broke in. "The Chaos crack I saw wasn't in the Drevite Nation. It was in the chapel."

"The archbishop put it there!" the prior shouted. "Admit it."

Blastilv remained stoic. "I deny not that I ordered a rift to be made in the chapel. Hadst thou come to me in courtesy, instead of harsh accusations, we might could have dealt with these matters pleasantly—without the *agony* thou shalt soon endure. That opportunity hath passed. Yet, first, prithee, tell the inquisitor of Ferus the Good."

The prior seemed shaken, either by Blastilv's admission, the mention of the awaiting agony, or by the fact that he was suddenly to tell a story.

"He . . ." the prior began, his voice trembling. "He lived ages after the Irefaery War, in the fiendish Demonic Era— when the Demons controlled the entire continent. Their capital city, Trasilvok, stood where Dayigo stands now."

"Concisely," Blastilv said.

The prior nodded. "Ferus the Good was righteous, yet powerless against such evil. So, he traveled far north, directly north from Trasilvok, to the great circular lake on the massive triangular peninsula."

"Lake Laqyigo," Swithun said.

"Yes. And, as you no doubt know, it was named after the paradise Laqyigo in the Plane of Light. This was because it was once a portal to there. For seven weeks, Ferus fasted and prayed on the shores of Lake Laqyigo until the Gods took favor on him and emerged from the water. God Déagar cast holy fire at the man and burnt away all flesh and bone, leaving only a pure spirit standing on the shore. Titaness Lágeya, Mother of the Gods, then forged him a new body of white marble and placed his soul within. Next, Goddess Larissa—"

"The trivial contributions of Déagar's lesser siblings are inconsequential," Blastilv interrupted. "Skip ahead."

"Yes, Your Grace. Ferus, renamed Fersivolíel, became a mighty stone warrior serving as God Déagar's general on Perdinok. Not only was he given the strength to fight the Demons, but also the power to capture them in stone forms similar to his own. These captured Demons, called the Vatelam, were stripped of their free will and forced to serve God Déagar's will, becoming an army under Fersivolíel.

"When the Demonic forces had been finally weakened enough," the prior continued, "Fersivolíel stood atop Mount Triumph and summoned forth all Demons and their kith, casting them into the abysmal Plane of Chaos."

"And what, pray, became of Fersivolíel?" Blastilv asked.

"The mountain collapsed," the prior replied grimly, "swallowing him up until the Silthex exhumed his body five years ago."

"Not his *body*. What hath become of his *soul*?"

A cold silence settled on the room. The prior was visibly trembling as Blastilv's piercing gaze fell upon him. "The texts are unclear, Your Grace."

A quick knock at the door broke the tension. Swithun jumped in surprise, like a child hearing ghost stories around a bonfire.

"Enter," Blastilv commanded.

A Dayigan soldier dashed into the room. "Your Grace, Commander Beadurinc's ships have returned. They are docking now. It appears to be most of the fleet."

"So soon," Blastilv muttered ominously. "Arrest the faithless priest and throw him into dark seclusion." He turned to the prior. "I shall release thee when I can mold thee into something *obedient*. Inquisitor, accompany me forthwith."

—

Swithun followed Archbishop Blastilv out from the front of the church through the gate that passed through the short stone wall. The church gate clanked shut behind them as they stepped onto the sprawling, dew-soaked plain edged by tangled woods.

Swithun wanted to break away and rush ahead, but he remained behind the archbishop's slow, somber strides. They walked in silence. Blastilv's ancient eyes were narrowed in deep concern, and Swithun could sense a storm brewing.

As they reached the wooden pier, the first of the ships was already docked. Soldiers hoisted up the long wooden ramp onto its deck.

First off the boat was Commander Beadurinc, who raced up to Archbishop Blastilv with terror etched across his face.

His usual smug grin was nowhere to be seen—instead, he seemed shaken. He paused for a moment to gather his thoughts before speaking. "We've failed, Your Grace."

The eyes of Archbishop Blastilv narrowed with disdain. "Continue."

Beadurinc took a deep breath. "We attacked the Drevite's Feah chiefdom as planned. But there was someone—a sorcerer—unlike anything I've ever seen. He seemed to be empowered by..." He glanced at Swithun before resuming in a slightly hushed tone, "...the thing within the chapel."

"The inquisitor is well aware of what lies within the chapel. Continue."

Beadurinc nodded grimly. "I'm told this sorcerer wielded Chaos magic, Your Grace."

"Impossible," Blastilv said. "That energy is wielded by Irefaeries alone. 'Twould drive any mortal man to madness."

"And yet he was indeed a mortal man—a Terovae. My source is valid, Your Grace. He swore—by the Flaming Sword of Déagar—he knew what he witnessed. The fiend rose above the battlefield and summoned a great crimson mist that flooded the shore outside of our fort in the Drevite Nation. Within it, our men fell, in agony, to their knees. Then, unrelenting, the savage fiend thrust out his hands to cast twisted rays of crimson light that tore through our troops, rotting the meat from their bones. Our army had no choice but to retreat, Your Grace. And still, the fiend pursued them to the ships. He slaughtered hundreds of good Déagrian men, and one ship was damaged, presumed lost."

Blastilv boiled with contempt, yet his voice remained steady and cold. "*I want that creature responsible for my men's destruction to be seized, so I might examine what it is.*"

"Yes, Your Grace. It will be done."

"Tell thy soldiers to encamp here so they may rest and regroup. Once they are again fit for battle, your unit shall march back to the Drevite Nation and lay waste to their entire forest—and whosoever dwelleth within. If these savage reprobates desire war with the Holy Dayigan Empire, they shall have their fill of it."

Swithun knocked on the door of the archbishop's apartment and received a muffled response from inside. He opened the door carefully, making sure not to disturb the heavy silence that hung in the room.

The air was thick and hot, despite the rainy autumn morning outside. A blazing fire roared within the fireplace, casting flickering shadows across the green velvet chair where the archbishop sat. Blastilv's eyes remained fixed on the flames, as if he were unaware of Swithun's entrance.

"You summoned me, Your Grace." Swithun stepped farther in.

The archbishop kept his gaze on the fire, his voice low and mournful. "I have not beheld thee in these last few days, Inquisitor," he said. "Pray, wherefore hast thou been absent from my sight?"

Swithun took a step closer, but still Blastilv did not turn to face him. The archbishop seemed drained and hollow as he stared into the crackling flames.

"I . . ." Swithun hesitated, the man's dismal state throwing him off guard. "I've been interrogating the prisoners, Your Grace. I've been trying to figure out what they know about the Chaos sorcerer who killed our men."

Silence hung heavily between them, broken only by the sounds of the fire.

"Initiative," Blastilv finally said, still keeping his gaze. "Thou hast progressed far, Inquisitor. 'Tis thine own fault I am unkind to thee. Thou dost force my wrath by thine unending stupidity."

"Forgive me, Your Grace. I'll try harder."

"See that thou dost. I am only strict with thee because I see thy potential. Dost thou recall the day in Wendian when we captured the Karulent tailor?"

Swithun's blood boiled at the mention of the man from long ago. His fists clenched at his sides. "Of course, Your Grace." His voice lowered with rage, "The fucking savage spread his Blue Sickness through the city, killing most every-one there, including my family."

"He was thy friend?"

"I thought he was."

"I can still recall what thou said unto me in his cell. 'Hurt him.'" The archbishop's eyes remained on the flames, his words cold. "That was when I truly saw thee, Inquisitor. That was when I knew thou comprehended what needed to be done. Those two words—*Hurt him*—spoken with such ardor, have brought thee here today. The man that I have wrought thee into would not need me to hurt him. Now, the wrath of God resides within thine own hands."

Swithun glanced down at his hands, stained with blood beneath his nails and along his fingers. It was as if he could feel a divine power coursing through him. "Thank you, Your Grace."

"Were thine inquisitions fruitful?"

"No, Your Grace." Swithun shook his head sadly. "The Drevites say they hate Chaos magic, and they're claiming their lady priests—what they call druidesses—are working to be rid of it altogether. They say Chaos is wicked." He paused, watching the archbishop, who still watched the flames. "If I can ask a question, Your Grace . . ."

"Why doth a rift spew chaotic energy within our abbey grounds?" Blastilv grinned darkly. "Yes, thou hast earned thine answers. The rift doth emit but a small quantity of

Chaos, which is effortless for me to contain. True, it doth draw the Irefaery Realm closer, but that minor issue shall only be ruinous for the Drevite Nation. We who are righteous shall remain unharmed by what the treacherous priest called the 'convergence of realms.'"

"'Twill affect them 'cause the Drevites got weak walls between them and the Faeries? Because of some old war?"

"Horribly stated. But correct." Blastilv folded his hand across his stomach. "But fear not, though the Chaos-tainted *Irefaery Realm* may converge somewhat, the *Plane of Chaos*, itself, shall not. The gates barring it from us—forged by the True Light—are impossible to breach. We need only worry of a few minor Irefaeries plaguing the indecorous Drevites."

"But . . ." Swithun hesitated before continuing, averting his gaze from Blastilv. "You yourself use Chaos magic, don't you? That's why that thing's there in the chapel?"

He gave a mirthless laugh. "Be thou not a fool, Inquisitor. I am a man of God and use no sorcery, be it of Chaos or otherwise. I wield only the blessed miracles bestowed upon us by God Déagar to aid our holy cause. The treacherous prior was indeed correct: The scriptures are unclear on what became of Fersivolíel's soul. Even the True Light Gods are ashamed of his fate and remain silent on the matter. But God Déagar whispered his ancient secret into Patriarch Krasil's pious ear, and he, in turn, shared it with me. Lo, when Fersivolíel disincarnated and led the Demons into Chaos, the Gods acted swiftly, constructing three powerful gates to seal Perdinok off from the Plane of Chaos. Alas, they had no time to save their faithful warrior."

"You're saying he's stuck there, in Chaos, with all those Demons? All this time?"

The archbishop gave a somber nod, still gazing at the flames. "Fersivolíel did sacrifice himself for the betterment of the world, Inquisitor. And I intend to harness his strength to better it further. The fissure in the chapel grants access to such might, Fersivolíel's might from within his infernal pit. The slight Chaos it emits is but a woeful consequence, not its intention. And, as Fersivolíel's Vatelams purged the darkness from the Demons and made them obedient to Déagar, so shall I do unto our enemies." He slammed his fist onto his armrest and shouted, *"But we must have more Drevites!"*

Stunned by the sudden rage of the usually composed archbishop, Swithun watched, dumbstruck. The wrinkled face contorted with fury, illuminated by the fire in the hearth. Blastilv seemed to be wracked by torment—a suffering unlike anything Swithun had ever seen in him before.

Stepping closer, Swithun positioned himself between Blastilv and the fireplace. "If I may speak my mind, Your Grace, I don't get why we're wasting time on a bunch of tree savages when back home, those Karulents in the Veiled River are attacking good Déagrian men and women."

"The Drevites are *nothing*," Blastilv hissed, casting an icy glare at Swithun for the first time since he had entered. "They are mere objects of study to enhance our weapons against the villainous Karulents. As such, we must conquer all five chiefdoms of the wretched Drevites so that we may use their people as raw materials for our experiments.

"True," Blastilv continued, "we have had a share of triumph in erasing the quarter of our own empire befouled as Karulents. But northward of the river, a myriad of kingdoms remain fraught with those wretched blue enemies of Déagar. There, in the Karulent Alliance, only one out of five bow to our God. If we wish to purify those lands of all others, then we must create better methods than we have. Nevertheless," he paused and turned away, "the Drevite Experiment hath failed."

"Commander Beadurinc will—"

"Commander Beadurinc is dead," Blastilv growled, "burnt at the stake like a vile savage. That *abomination*—the chaos sorcerer or Irefaery, or whatever it may be called—pursued our men to our very doorstep."

"Here?" Swithun drew his sword, his heart racing. "I swear I'll—"

"All outside these abbey walls hath perished," Blastilv said coldly. "The beast descended upon us in the stormy night and slaughtered all in its wake."

"All of them?" Swithun's grip on his weapon loosened as sorrow consumed him like a fog.

Blastilv offered no words in response; his expression said enough.

"But they were supposed to be the new Silthex," Swithun mumbled sadly. "I don't get it. Why do people keep coming after us when we're just trying to make the world better?" Fury boiled within him. "I will find that fucking creature and—"

"No," Blastilv interrupted calmly. "Gather thy belongings and prepare thyself to depart. Already, thou hast thine own quest for justice against she who murdered the Silthex. Thou shalt bring me the Blue Rose—*alive*—so that I may use Fersivolíel's power to transform her into something obedient."

"Of course, Your Grace. The Blue Rose'll pay for what she's done to us."

"Give me thy sword."

Swithun hesitated before handing it over.

"With this blade, *I* shall slay the beast *myself.*" Blastilv inspected the steel. "The Drevite Experiment may take much longer than anticipated, but here alone, I shall continue Beadurinc's research on the few Drevites we have acquired. And, with the fires of God to guide me, I *will* perfect a means to purify the Karulent Alliance of all its *many* transgressions." He grinned. "And, in time, the world."

Born at War

Karvlent
Alliance
D
Aorta Road
Hyvile River
Wendian
Port Haven
Dayigan
port Lytel
W
E
N
S
0   30   60   90
Miles
Mount Triumph

CHAPTER THIRTY-TWO

Efflorel 19, 837: Six Years Later

A salty breeze filled the air as gulls cawed overhead, diving and snatching fish from the wide expanse of the Hyvile River. The sun descended toward the eastern horizon, its pale gold and orange rays spilling across Port Haven, flowing over the wooden ships that swayed gently in the harbor. Their masts were like a forest of spears reaching for the heavens and casting shadows across the sailors and dockers, who shouted to one another, hoisting crates and barrels onto the creaking wooden planks of the docks. From the nearby market drifted the voices of merchants, shouting of all sorts of treasures and curiosities.

Amid this bustling commotion, toiled Verónica. Clad in black trousers and an off-white blouse, her dark hair tightly braided down to her waist, Verónica strained at a thick rope, helping dockworkers lower a massive wooden crate down a ramp toward the pier.

"Ease it down slow," she directed, hands coiled around the frayed rope. "If this heavy bastard slides down too fast, 'twill crash straight through the pier to the river." Sweat beaded on her brow, but her piercing brown eyes stayed focused.

"*Lady Verónica,*" Father Joachim called, voice vexed, as he approached just behind her. His tall, slender figure was draped in a pale gray cassock topped by a sapphire-blue cowl.

"I'm a little busy here, Father Jo," she said, without ceasing her efforts.

His stern eyes remained locked on her from beneath the blue hood. "I'd really rather you wouldn't call me that, my lady. And you should not be straining yourself with such *crude* labor. 'Tis unbecoming of a lady."

"One of the dockworkers is out, tending to his sick child," Verónica replied, eyes remaining on the crate ahead of her. "Would you rather he be here doing this just so I can be off . . . eating pastries?"

"As a matter of fact, I would. You are the *mayor* of Port Haven, not some . . ." Father Joachim paused, eyeing the rough bunch of men working alongside her. He seemed to reconsider whatever he'd meant to say next. He sighed. "There is an important matter that requires your attention."

"This will go faster if you help us," Verónica said, her muscles straining as the crate inched its way down the ramp.

"Don't be absurd, my lady." He gave an upturn of his nose. "A dignitary has arrived and says the matter is rather pressing. I believe it would be best if—"

"See to it that he's given a room and a hot meal, Father," Verónica instructed. "I'll meet with him when I can."

"Karulus help us," he sighed. "Very well, my lady." Clearly unsatisfied with her response, Father Joachim bowed stiffly and walked away, mumbling something under his breath.

At last, the colossal crate touched the docks with a thud, and a low cheer rippled through the surrounding workers.

"Excellent work today, men!" Verónica said with a satisfied smile, extending a hand to pat a few men on their backs. "Take the crate to Duncan's workshop," she told a group of nearby workers, "and I'll meet it there."

"Will do, m'lady," a dockworker said, nodding respectfully. "We'll make sure the heavy bastard gets there safe and sound."

"Róni!" a familiar voice called from the sky. A lithe woman, twenty-one years of age, descended onto the docks and folded her ash-brown wings behind her back. Her short hair, matching the hue of her feathers, was cut in a neat, pixie style.

Verónica greeted Swift with a warm smile. "How fares the town militia today?"

"It fares fair, I guess," Swift said. "My men are doing their normal patrols, but there's been no issues."

"That is always good news. Would you stop by the Great Hall? Father Jo is going on about some damned *visiting dignitaries*, but I need to finish a few things here and then head over to Duncan's to take care of something else."

"Fucking mayor's life, right?"

"Yes." Verónica smiled. "Just see what they want."

Swift shrugged. "Simple enough. Later on, you and me should head over to the tavern."

"Definitely. I could use some drinks after this." Verónica rolled her sore shoulders. "My muscles are aching."

"Maybe you should invite the dignitaries there." Swift smiled. "Or Father Jo."

Verónica laughed. "Can you imagine Father Jo in a tavern full of dockers and sailors—him, standing at the wall, saying, '*Well, I never. Well, I never. Karulus help us all.*'"

"'Twould be worth the invite just to see his flabbergasted face," Swift said with a loud guffaw. "Well, I should better be off to the Great Hall. Good evening to you, m'lady." She gave a nod. "Karulus keep you well." She jumped up from the dock and spread her wings, catching a river wind as she flew away.

—

The moons cast a dim glow amid thick shadows over the worn dirt streets of Port Haven as Verónica neared Duncan's blacksmith shop. The clanging of a hammer on metal rang out, growing louder with each step she took.

She pushed open the door and was met by waves of heat emanating from the blazing forge, the fiery light flickering across the walls and benches and stacked equipment. She watched as Duncan worked tirelessly near the boiling embers and glowing iron, his face glistening with sweat that ran down his grimy body with each strike. A welcomed gust of wind blew through the open door and windows, carrying with it the scent of the river and the distant laughter of dockworkers.

Duncan stabbed the red-hot steel into the bucket, causing plumes of steam to rise into the air. He looked up from his work and grinned warmly.

"Hello, Róni," he said. "Your crate's just arrived, but I ain't opened it yet." He wiped his brow with the back of his grimy arm.

"So I see." She looked toward the heavy wooden container in the corner of the workshop. "I went to a lot of trouble getting that here. And I don't just mean unloading it from the ship."

He neared the crate and ran a calloused hand along its rough surface. "What's inside, then?"

Verónica flashed him a devilish smirk. "Why don't you find out yourself?"

He grabbed a pry bar and stabbed it where its lid met its wall, levering it up with a creak. Inside, swords with snapped blades, shattered shields, and dented helmets were piled haphazardly atop one another, bearing the many scars of battle.

"'Tis a bunch of shit, I know," she said. "But can you fix them?"

He surveyed the contents. "Fix? A few, but most'll need to be melted down and started from scratch. Still, 'tis a lot of metal to work with. I'm guessing you want me to do something that could get us both strung up from the gallows."

She grinned slyly. "There's nothing illegal about a weaponsmith simply making weapons for his mayor, is there?"

He gave her an unconvinced frown. "And I'm sure that mayor ain't planning on sending them weapons to the Resistance like before."

"Me?" She set a hand to her breast. "What *are* you implying, Duncan?" She fluttered her eyelashes in mock innocence.

"Right." He sniffed as he wrenched his face into a crooked grin.

She sighed. "'Tis bullshit that we can't help the Resistance in the Dayigan Empire anymore, just because we're part of the Karulent Alliance. Rubbish treaty. Most of the town, you and me included, fled the Dayigan Empire because they tried to kill us all. And the Resistant Nations are the only ones doing anything about it."

"You're watering the river, Róni," Duncan said, his eyes returning to the damaged pieces. "Least the treaty means them Dayigans can't attack us here."

"I trust a treaty with Dayigans about as much as . . ."

". . . as much as I do," he said, his fingers brushing over a cracked shield. "I'll get right to work on these. Maybe something I smith will even make it to your brother."

She smiled at the thought. "I always like to think so," Verónica murmured, placing a grateful hand on his shoulder. "Thank you, Duncan. You're a good friend."

As they continued examining the contents of the crate, the door to the smith creaked open, and Swift stepped inside. Her eyes seemed to take in everything at once, scanning the room as if she might find a criminal hiding in the shadows.

"Swift," Duncan said with a nod. "Good evening to ya."

"Did you figure out that dignitary business?" Verónica asked.

"I did. He kept saying, 'I can only talk to the mayor. I can only talk to the mayor.'" Swift said, her gaze flicking to the broken armor and weapons, clearly taking note. "So I had to shoot an arrow about an inch past his smug face."

"Swift, you didn't," Verónica laughed. "What if you'd hit the poor bastard?"

"You know I have perfect aim. It worked." Swift pulled a rolled page from a pouch on her belt. "He said it came all the way from the city of Reyigo."

Verónica's mood shifted, anxiety creeping down her spine. "I'm sure 'tis nothing." She took it, staring at the blue wax seal securing the page. "Probably just another sanction on refugee towns because we're being too . . . something they disapprove of."

"The messenger said it came from the *king* of Reyigo," Swift pointed. "That's his official seal there."

A knot formed in the pit of Verónica's stomach, worry gnawing at her insides. Her first thought was that the Karulent Alliance was sending all the refugees back to their oppressors in the Dayigan Empire—a fear that often lingered at the back of her mind. Her second was that her first thought was ridiculous. Her third was—she wasn't sure. She slowly cracked open the wax seal and unrolled the page.

"'Tis addressed to my brother—*Lord Mayor Estéban*," Verónica said, forcing a laugh to disguise her unease. "He's been gone for a year, Your Majesty." Her smile faded as she read the words, her face turning blank and then tightening as a glower.

"Is it bad?" Swift asked.

"There was a counsel of all the kings in the Alliance," Verónica said, still reading. "They've agreed to unite the entire Karulent Alliance . . . into one mighty empire."

"Another empire," Duncan scoffed. "That's too damn many."

Swift waved her hand at him to hush. "Go on," she prompted Verónica.

"He's saying they think that as one nation—with one massive army, no doubt—we'll be in a much better position to defend ourselves from the Dayigans." Verónica glanced up. "Seems they trust that treaty as much as we do."

"But that's a good thing," Swift said, "forming an imperial army so we're stronger. Isn't it?"

Duncan folded his thick arms. "I remember when we thought it was good that the Dayigan Trade Agreement was becoming an empire," he said darkly. "Next thing I know, me mum's smuggling me out of that blasted empire so I wouldn't be murdered."

"I don't think a Karulent empire would be like that," Verónica said, though with little conviction.

"Does it say anything about us?" Swift asked. "Refugees, I mean. The Alliance still considers us Dayigans."

Verónica read on quietly before shaking her head. "No." She flipped the page over as if there might be more on the back. "Not a word. But I can guess. Fucking za. This is an eviction notice. Why else would they come to a refugee town with this?" All the rage and frustration of a lifetime of oppression boiled over her as she began to pace. "A bunch of fat kings in that mountaintop castle in Reyigo have gotten together and decided to give us all the boot."

"Terovaes don't often get fat," Swift said, a slight smile grazing her lips.

"You know what I mean," Verónica said, annoyance simmering, as she re-rolled the page. "Let me go talk to this *dignitary*. Swift, you're with me. Duncan—"

"I'll get me journeymen started on your project," he said, "first thing come morning."

CHAPTER THIRTY-THREE

Verónica's boots thudded against the hard-packed dirt of the streets, a dull rhythm bringing her ever closer to the Great Hall as her anger increased, step by step. The streets of the market were emptying as vendors packed their goods into crates, and shopkeepers shuttered their windows. Verónica took a moment to see them. Most here had nearly died fleeing the Dayigan Empire, nearly all losing loved ones in the process, but they'd managed to carve out a meager life here in Port Haven. Now, some conference of kings had decided to turn all that upside down again. Verónica would not allow it.

At her side, Swift vigilantly scanned their surroundings for any trouble—as was her habit.

"You're not on patrol," Verónica muttered out of the corner of her mouth.

"If a thief jumps us, I'll be sure to tell him that," her companion replied with a smirk. "Sorry, sir, not on patrol right now. Please rob someone else."

Verónica rolled her eyes, though she was thankful for Swift's caution. This port town—with its growth into a bustling international hub—often held many out-of-towners. Most weren't exactly strangers—traders had their routes—and most knew better than to mess with Swift's militia, but there were the occasional idiots who wanted to make trouble.

Verónica stopped outside the imposing oak doors of the Great Hall. The wooden, twenty-foot-tall building would have looked like a nice barn in a different context. Verónica doubted that the awaiting Reyigan saw the Great Hall as anything great, but it was a reminder of all her town had built from nothing.

Verónica stared up at the blue doors.

"He says he won't leave until you talk to him," Swift said.

Verónica smirked. "Oh, I'll be talking to him all right. And giving him an earful. They will not take Port Haven from us. My mother built this town—along with the other townspeople. It might not be much, but . . ." Verónica sighed, ". . . 'tis our home."

Swift rested her hand on Verónica's arm. "Perhaps, *try* letting him talk before you lose your temper. You don't know what he's going to say yet."

Verónica sneered with contempt. "Nobles, royals, they're all alike—full of their own importance and eager to bend others to their will."

"Yes, *my lady*."

Verónica pursed her lips and glanced sideways at Swift. "I haven't been a noble since I was in nappies. I only use the title 'cause 'tis funny."

"Of course, *my lady*. As you say."

"*Swift*," Verónica hissed before she took a deep breath and stood tall. She pushed the doors slowly open.

Shadows bathed the large room, lit only by flickering candles that cast an eerie glow upon the space. This was a church on Sabbathdays, and the sparse décor, along with the pulpit at the front, reflected that. A small room to the right—the prayer room—maintained this purpose seven days a week, and the light from votive candles in blue glass spilled onto the icon of God Karulus—a young man with pale blue skin and golden wings.

A Human man—presumably the Reyigan—stood rigid, arms crossed, as he eyed the icon, but he turned toward

Verónica as she entered. Even if she hadn't expected to find a noble, she would have recognized him as such. His opulent clothing, a blend of blue velvet and other expensive fabrics that she wasn't quite refined enough to name, spoke of wealth and power. His posture exuded confidence and authority. His shoulder-length blond hair was immaculately clean, and his thick beard was perfectly trimmed. Verónica couldn't deny that he was handsome in an arrogant sort of way. But there was something about him that made her skin crawl with annoyance, even before he spoke.

"As I told this boy before he *assaulted* me," he said, his blue eyes narrowing as they swept over Verónica, "I will not leave this hall until I am granted an audience with Lord Estéban."

It took Verónica a moment to realize that by *this boy* he meant Swift, yet the mistake was understandable. Still, Verónica donned a false smile and a mask of calm confidence. "My brother has been gone for a year, my lord. I would have thought *someone* would have told you." Verónica glanced sharply at Swift, who returned a shrug. "He left me as interim mayor, which my people made official once he didn't return. Estéban's in the Dayigan Empire helping to form the Resistant Nations."

He almost seemed to growl the words, "Is he? The Resistant Nations is quite the... *noble* cause. Do you know where he is?"

"He's not allowed to say."

He eyed her down his nose. "And he's left *you* as *mayor?* We were expecting to find someone with more—"

"Bollocks?" Verónica offered with the same forced smile.

"There's no reason to be vulgar, *madam.*" He crossed his arms. "I had actually intended to say *experience.* However, yes, it is quite unorthodox to have a woman—"

"Let us stop a moment, shall we," Verónica interrupted, her bitter smile growing larger, "before you say something that will get you tossed in the river—*my lord*. And let us take one step back in the conversation." She took a literal step backward. "My brother is assisting the Blue Rose. You do know who *she* is, yes. The *woman* who is currently persuading Dayigan king after Dayigan king to pull their kingdoms from their Empire and join her newly formed Resistant Nations. The *woman* who is our only hope to end the empire completely. If *she* can do that, then I'm sure little ol' me can run a little riverside town, can't I? So if we could just skip past the 'oh, she's a woman' bullshit, that would be lovely. My thanks."

The Reyigan only seemed to triple in anger, which he contained, nodding in annoyed agreement. "That still doesn't explain why you are dressed like a pirate."

Verónica huffed. "Why are you in Port Haven, my lord? I read your letter. A Karulent empire. Where does that leave us? Our people will *not* return to the Dayigan Empire."

"I am afraid you've gotten the wrong idea, my lady. I am Lord Onfroi dispatched by His Majesty, King of the Reyigan Kingdom, to share news that your people will find pleasing. If we could speak in private."

Verónica glanced at Swift. "This is the leader of the town's militia. She stays."

"A woman also leads your town militia," Lord Onfroi scoffed. "How . . . *unique*. His Majesty, as well as the majority of the kings within the Karulent Alliance, wishes to acknowledge that the treatment of the Dayigan refugees—"

"We prefer it if you just leave the Dayigan part out," Verónica said.

Onfroi gave a single nod. "Of course. Despite the invitation for the refugees to come to these lands, you and your kind have been treated . . . less than ideal, yes? The kings wish to change that. As such, all the refugees will be granted full citizenship in the newly formed *Reyigan Empire*."

The words melted all of Verónica's defenses, her anger whisked away. "*Reyigan Empire*," she whispered with a smile. Hearing that an empire was to be formed and hearing its name—and that her people would be included—were vastly different. The dramatic change in mood left her feeling as if she might spin with joy. She glanced back at Swift, who grinned ear to ear.

"Thrilling news," Verónica said blissfully, turning back to Onfroi with newfound hope.

"We are pleased that this pleases you, my lady," Onfroi continued solemnly. "In a show of solidarity with the refugees, His Majesty wishes to announce the formation of the Reyigan Empire in the largest refugee town."

Verónica's heart dropped. "Here? You can't be serious? The king himself is coming here?"

Onfroi nodded. "Everyone in the Karulent Alliance who matters at all will be traveling here."

"Fucking za," Verónica said. "Are you mad? Port Haven isn't ready—"

"A staff will arrive shortly to help prepare the town. Under your command. And, extra security will work in tandem with . . ." he motioned to Swift, ". . . your commandress."

"How long do we have?" Verónica asked.

"You have two weeks until the official announcement. I trust you will keep this between us until then."

—

As she entered her bed chamber, Verónica paused, the words of the Reyigan lord still spinning in her head. *"The Reyigan Empire,"* she muttered to herself with a smile. "But all those people, here." She shook her head. Port Haven had grown from a simple port to welcome refugees to the Alliance into a successful shipping hub manned by those same refugees. What it had never become was anything glamorous.

She looked around her room. It had been expanded a few years back, and the floor in the new section was an inch lower than the rest. She'd put an old carpet over the seam, but the slope was still apparent. Her walls were old planks reused from other structures, mostly from ships, with scars from their former lives. Not one of the posts of her four-post bed matched another. Her wardrobe, dresser, and chair had all been very nice—once, a few owners ago.

The whole town was the same, expansions onto expansions onto expansions, all from reclaimed material and stuffed with fifth-hand furniture. The only properly nice things in Port Haven were just visiting—shipped in for resell and then shipped off to grander places.

Verónica sighed. "Where are we going to put royals?"

The floorboards creaked from behind her curtains— repurposed sails dyed dark blue. Verónica drew a knife from her belt and stepped carefully closer.

Once her attention had been drawn to the area, the person behind the curtain was obvious, and she felt like a fool for not having noticed at once. Swift, she knew, would have some cross words on that later.

"How very odd," Verónica spoke up in feigned surprise. "My curtains hang in such a peculiar fashion tonight. Perhaps if I *poke* them with this knife a few times, they'll hang right."

At once, a man vaulted from behind the draperies and dashed for the windowsill, trying to pry open the shutters with frenzied desperation. His efforts gained nothing but a rattling of the wood before Verónica touched the knife to his back.

He stopped his efforts, still facing the shutters. "You no doubt wish to know why I invade your room."

"I had wondered, yes," she said. "Sit in the chair, and keep your hands on the armrests where I can see them."

He looked back, finding the chair, and began toward it. "I intend you no harm."

"I can't make you the same promise, I'm afraid." She grabbed the shutter at the base and lifted it slightly while pulling a cord that hung from the ceiling three times. "There's a trick to it." She slid the shutter to the side, allowing a breeze from the river.

"So I see."

Verónica turned to him, now seated. He was an attractive thief, at least—tall and muscular with short brown hair and dark brown eyes—even if he was clad in a worn cloak over tattered peasant rags.

"Apologies for intruding," he said, voice low yet firm. "I investigate the Dayigans. And that investigation has led me here."

"I'd thank you not to call us Dayigans," Verónica warned.

"You misunderstand me. I speak not of refugees. I investigate the Dayigan Empire. Are you meant to be the mayor?"

"A woman can't be mayor?"

"I know the mayor is a woman," he said. "However, your garb suggests you are a pirate."

"What?" Verónica glanced down at her attire as she adjusted her leather belt. "Why does everyone keep saying that tonight? I'll have you know that I'm quite happy with my clothing choices, thank you."

"Of course." He nodded curtly. "I assume you know by now the Karulent Alliance plans to reform into an empire, and that they plan to announce that reformation here. I am certain the Dayigan Empire plans to attack that announcement."

"Is that so, Investigator . . . ?"

"Adratus."

"And who do you investigate for, Adratus?"

He held her gaze but paused before replying, "The Karulent Alliance."

"*Right.*" Verónica's eyes narrowed in suspicion. "So, you came with the seven lords who arrived in town from Reyigo."

"Indeed."

"There was only one lord." She sighed. "'Tis been a long day, whoever you are, and I don't have patience for—"

The door burst open, and Swift charged in, her bow drawn taut. Two other militiamen, clutching swords, stood behind her in the corridor.

Verónica didn't miss a beat: "Throw him in the prison. I'll sort him out later."

The militiamen rushed in, pulled Adratus to his feet, and yanked his arms behind his back before buckling a leather strap around his wrists.

Adratus didn't resist except to pause as he passed Verónica. "When you wish to speak further," he said, "you know where to find me."

After the intruder was led away and the two women were alone, Verónica muttered, "Cocky bastard. Took you long enough. I pulled that cord ages ago." She motioned to the cord hanging from the ceiling near the window.

"Ages? It was a decent response time, and you know it," Swift grumbled as she thrust her bow into the quiver on her belt.

Verónica looked one last time down the corridor, despite the stranger's absence. She almost told Swift about his claim that the Dayigans would attack. Instead, she said, "Weren't we supposed to go to the tavern? I'm sure some ale would do us both good."

"Definitely."

As they neared the door, Verónica asked, "Do you think I'm dressed like a pirate?"

Swift smiled. "You always dress like a pirate, Róni. You just need a parrot now."

—

Verónica clapped her tankard against those of four drunken sailors, and they chugged from the frothing mugs. A circle of clamorous onlookers cheered them on, with some offering wagers among themselves. The tavern, with its cluttered walls of dark wood paneling, was lit by fiery braziers, with smoky flames spreading flickering light across the crowd that was alive with revelry.

Verónica drained her cup first and promptly held it upside down above her head to prove it was empty. The rowdy crowd exploded with acclaim mixed with some jeering at her opponents who had lost.

"Better luck next time, boys," Verónica said with a laugh as she collected the silver and copper coins from the table and funneled them into a well-worn leather purse. She stood to walk away, but was halted by one of the defeated men who approached her.

He, a tall, dark-skinned Dinikimeran sailor, drew in close, gazing at her with those deep brown eyes she could get lost in.

"How now, Róni?"

"How now to you? Haven't seen you 'round here in a bit."

"Sailor's life, you know." He slid his arm around her waist. "How about you and me head down to that private spot by the river and reconnect?"

"Oh?" Róni smiled slyly. "That was a lovely spot, wasn't it?" She drew closer, pressing herself against him. "A very lovely spot, that was. But ... I can't tonight. Got shit to deal with. Mayor's life, you know."

"I ship out tomorrow morning."

"Next time, yes?"

"Ah, Róni. It's like a dagger in the heart."

"The heart? I'd wager 'tis quite a bit lower than your heart, yes?"

He laughed. "How about you give me a kiss to keep me warm until I return to port?"

Verónica leaned in and kissed his lips.

And then she walked away, a large grin on her face.

Verónica approached Swift, who sat alone at the corner table and took a seat next to her.

"I figured you'd have left with that one," Swift said.

"You can have the lot of them."

"They're not really my type."

"None of them? You're way too picky, Swift. But as for me, I can't stop thinking about that intruder in my room."

"You mean you want to take *him* down by the river?"

Verónica chuckled. "I wouldn't half mind if he asked. Did you see those arms? But no, 'tis what he said." She leaned closer to Swift. "The Dayigans are planning an attack on the announcement festival."

"That explains it."

Verónica gave her a confused look.

"I knew there had to be something going on when I saw how you were acting tonight," Swift said. "You're the life of the party—rowdy Róni—when you're trying not to think of something. Do you plan on canceling the event?"

Verónica sighed heavily. "Maybe. To be honest, I'm not even sure if I believe him, but the fact that he knew about the announcement at all means something. Right? But he lied about who he was. *But*, I can't put the town at risk."

Swift took a sip of her ale and set the tankard back on the table. "This could mean so much for us refugees," she said. "The Alliance hates Dayigans. And as far as the common people are concerned, we *are* Dayigans. 'Go home, go home,' they say. Go where? This is my home. I was born here. And you've been here since you were, what?"

"Three," Verónica said.

Swift nodded. "If the Reyigan king makes his announcement here, it sends a clear message that we are part of this new empire—that we *are* at home. We can't cancel all that because some random man gave some vague warning."

Verónica swept her gaze across the tavern, watching the laughing, joking, singing, drinking men and women, all blissfully unaware that everything would soon change—for either fair or foul. Her people had already suffered so much, yet still they endured.

"Either way," Swift said, "I plan to be prepared for an attack. I was already planning for a Dayigan attack before your mystery man's warning. And I'll keep planning for an attack, even if he turns out to be a madman. And when all's said and done, Port Haven will forever be remembered as the place where the Reyigan Empire was born."

Verónica nodded solemnly. "Or the place where the Reyigan king and his court were slaughtered." She chuckled. "We'll have to change the name. Port Massacre?"

Swift chuckled. "You're horrible, Róni."

"That's it. Swift, you're brilliant. *Port Horrible.*"

"Karulus help us indeed," Swift muttered, shaking her head.

CHAPTER THIRTY-FOUR

The door creaked open, and Verónica stepped into the dimly lit cell, the stench of mold and sweat clinging to the air. Her footsteps echoed against the stone floor until she stopped, staring at Adratus, who sat on a wooden bench and was chained to the wall.

"Enjoying your stay?" Verónica asked.

He looked up at her. "The chains are new," he said flippantly, his voice resonating within the confines of the cell. "So that's a change."

"Yes, they wouldn't let me visit unless you were restrained."

"An acceptable price. I only let myself be arrested so I could speak with you once more."

She raised an eyebrow, skepticism creeping into her tone. "You *let* yourself be arrested?"

"Indeed. What would think of me if I killed your guards? Though I expected you to come sooner. Two days, my lady. What sort of hostess is that?"

"One who's been very busy. The town has much to prepare for."

"Of course," he said solemnly, "you've decided to go along with the announcement celebration?"

"Announcement? Celebration?" Verónica said in feigned confusion. "I don't know what you mean?"

He chuckled with a charming smile.

"If," Verónica continued, "such a thing was a thing, how would you know about it? Surely, such a thing would be a secret."

"As I told you in your quarters, I've investigated the Dayigan Empire for nearly twenty years—off and on."

"Not likely," Verónica scoffed. "You would have been a boy."

"Sixteen," Adratus replied, his voice like steel. He stared at her with dark brown eyes, unyielding and harsh. "Do you want to know what I've discovered?"

She looked away. "How can I trust anything you say? You still haven't told me who you work for."

"No," he said, "I haven't."

"Then why should I bother trusting that you're here to save us?"

Adratus glanced down as his lips pressed together in a grim line. "I never said I was here to save your town. My mission is to observe and report back."

"Well, you're definitely a soldier."

He grinned slightly.

"It wasn't a compliment."

"Now that you have seen me, I will require you to leave me be, so I may do my job unhindered. In return"—the chains around his wrists clanked as he shifted forward in his seat— "I can show you what I found in the same room where you rest your head at night."

A chill crept up Verónica's spine, making her shiver— *What had he found in my room?* She studied him, searching for any hint of deceit or manipulation in his gaze. All she found was determination and conviction, which left no room for doubt.

"If you're lying," she said, "there'll be no mercy for you."

—

The air in the dimly lit corridor hung heavy with unspoken tension as Verónica, sword in hand, followed Adratus to her private chamber. With each step, a mix of doubt and anticipation churned within her—every footfall echoing like a heartbeat against the plank floor. Their hurried pace left no room for conversation, and she found herself grateful for the silence. It allowed her to focus on her thoughts, which were now consumed by the potential implications of whatever item Adratus found.

"Here," Verónica said, motioning to the entrance of her bedroom.

"Yes," he said. "I have been here before."

She opened the door, revealing the familiar sanctuary within. Dusty sunlight shone through the open window, lighting her beat-up furniture better than she liked to see it—*I really should get some new things.* Nothing seemed out of the ordinary.

"You needn't keep your sword drawn," Adratus said. "As I said, if I wished to escape, I would have. If I wished to harm you, I would have. Your weapon does naught but tire your arm."

"I could do with the exercise," Verónica said. "You said there was something here."

"Behind the wardrobe," he replied, moving toward the large, plain piece of furniture.

Verónica's breath caught in her throat as she watched him grab the side with both hands, pulling at it. It screeched against the floor as he slid it from the wall.

"My investigation has led me to a Dayigan commander called Eadwulf," Adratus said, as he reached down, stretching for something on the floor behind it. "Or at least his name. He's a lesser noble who's managed to earn a spot in the inner circle of the Dayigan High King." He reached farther, setting his other hand on the wardrobe. "I believe he plans to lead an attack on Port Haven."

Finally, Adratus stood, and with a triumphant grin, he presented a beautiful wooden box, its lid covered with intricate designs painted blue.

"Here, what are you playing at?" Verónica asked with annoyance. "That's my own box, though I'm not sure how it got back there. My brother gave it to me as a gift."

He set it on the table at the foot of her bed. "You'll find its content is *not* yours. Open it."

Verónica gave him a wary glance before she approached the box and set her sword on the table beside it. She lifted it cautiously, as if something might pop out and bite her. As soon as she cracked open the hinged lid, red light spilled out. She paused and looked at Adratus.

"'Tis all right," he said. "I've neutralized it."

Verónica opened the box to find a golden orb, the size of an orange, covered in strange carvings in green. Four emeralds were spaced evenly around its side. Around it, six rings of red lightning maintained various orbits.

"What is it?" she asked.

Adratus lifted it from the box and held it to hover just above his fingertips. "Some sort of magical device created by the Dayigans. I've yet to determine its function, but the rings of lightning bind it."

"The Dayigans don't practice magic."

"If you believe that, you are a fool."

"Fucking hypocrites," Verónica muttered. "After all they've done to us because *some* of our priests use magic. But you said 'tis neutralized. By *you*. You put the rings around it. That's . . ." Verónica looked at him as her heart began to race.

"That's red magic." She dropped the box to the table and snatched up her sword. "That's Dark Light magic." She held her sword firm with both hands.

"True," Adratus said, his eyes meeting hers.

"I should kill you here and now for—"

"Existing?" he said angrily. "The True light is the only way; all others will perish—I've heard it before, my lady."

Adratus cast his left hand toward her, and from each of his fingertips, a cord of red light erupted. Two bound her wrist. Two bound her ankles. The fifth coiled around her waist. He lifted Verónica from the floor.

"Put me down, you wicked savage, or I'll call for my guards."

"Be you silent," he said calmly.

A warmth grew in her throat, leaving her unable to make a sound other than gasps.

Adratus stepped forward, his hand still outstretched to the cords that restrained her. "You can attempt to throw me into a fire—as your people tend to do to my kind—or you can leave me to determine the function of this orb the Dayigans put in *your room*. The decision is yours."

He lowered her to the floor, and the cords dissipated.

"As I said," he continued, "if I wished to hurt you, I could have. Speak."

The warmth left her throat and her voice returned, but she didn't use it. Instead, Verónica only watched him, not knowing what to think.

He neared the wooden box on the table and set the orb inside.

"This *Lord Eadwulf*, he put this in my room?" Verónica said at last.

"Or someone who works for him."

"You'll tell me what it does?"

"If I can determine what it does, yes."

She thought for a moment. "And you'll do nothing to hurt my town, its people, or the Reyigans visiting for the announcement celebration."

"Announcement? Celebration?" Adratus feigned confusion. "Of what do you speak?"

"Bastard." Verónica grinned. "Vow it."

He closed the lid of the box and turned to face her. "I will harm no one here unless they give me cause, so I vow on the blue cock of Karulus."

She folded her arms. "You keep letting that humor leak out, I might forget you're a wicked savage." She sighed. "A Dark Light sorcerer—Karulus help us."

Verónica set the sword on the floor. "Go to the blacksmith; he's called Duncan. Him and his wife rent out a room and provide two meals a day—nothing fancy but 'twill fill you up. Tell him that I sent you and will cover the rent. Tell him I said not to ask any questions of you. He'll probably think you're something to do with the Resistance. I'll be round soon to confirm things."

"Gratitude."

"Go," Verónica said, her voice barely above a whisper. "Find the answers you need, and return quickly."

He grabbed the box and hurried out of the room. She shouted behind him, "And I want that box back when you're done. It was a gift."

Adratus nodded once before disappearing into the shadows of the corridor, leaving her alone with her thoughts. And as she stood there in the sunlight pouring through the window, her heart heavy with the weight of her decision to release him, Verónica knew that the fate of Port Haven—of all the refugees in the Alliance—rested on her actions.

release him, Verónica knew that the fate of Port Haven—of all the refugees in the Alliance—rested on her actions.

CHAPTER THIRTY-FIVE

Verónica stepped into the smithy, and the familiar smell of smoke and metal greeted her. Duncan sat atop his stool, hunched over and polishing a blade that glinted with a dull sheen in the faint light of a crackling fire.

He raised his head as he looked up at her. "Róni," he nodded. "Just finishing this one up. 'Tis one of yours."

"One of mine?"

"The sword. For the Resistance. We have a dozen finished, plus loads of arrowheads and spearheads."

She gave an absent nod. "Right. Forgive me. This celebration tomorrow has me scattered."

Duncan set aside his work and wiped his brow with a cloth. "'Twill be fine," he said. "The town's looking real nice, more so than I've ever seen it before. Blue flags flying everywhere and streets so clean you can eat off them." His face lit up briefly with pride. "Them Reyigans are bound to be impressed."

Verónica gave him an unconvincing smile. "That's my hope." Turning from him, she glanced at the corner of the workshop, where a wooden staircase led to an upper-level door. "How fares our guest?"

Duncan shrugged his burly shoulders. "Keeps to himself, mostly," he said. "Comes and goes some, but I don't ask questions of him." He leaned forward on his stool. "So, you gonna tell me who he is, then?"

"'Tis better if you don't know," she replied.

He nodded knowingly, as though he expected nothing less from her.

"Is he up there now?"

Duncan nodded once again in confirmation, and Verónica walked toward the stairs. With one final glance at him, she began her ascent.

—

Slowly, as quietly as possible, Verónica opened the door to Adratus's room. A part of her almost wanted to catch him in the act—of what, she wasn't sure. She still didn't trust the Dark Light stranger.

The attic room had a slanted roof with exposed rafters and joists—debarked, unpainted logs—so low that a grown man would certainly need to duck to avoid smacking his head. Sunlight filtered between the planks that sided the gable, this with a small open window.

Verónica passed a small dining table cluttered with a shirt and papers filled with scribbled writing and hasty sketches. Stepping further in, she froze, seeing the bed.

Atop the thin old mattress, Adratus lay on his back, head tilted on a pillow, eyes closed. Neither a thread of clothes nor sheets covered his muscular body.

Breathless, Verónica watched him sleep; the rhythm of his thick chest slowly moving up and down was hypnotic. She grinned naughtily, as her eyes slid down his body, taking in the view.

"Do you not knock?" Adratus asked sleepily, rolling onto his side.

"This from the man I met whilst he hid within my room?"

"Fair." He yawned, clearly unbothered by his state of undress.

"Why are you still sleeping at this hour?" Verónica looked away, eyes wandering the roof, the wall, anywhere but him. "'Tis well past noon, and the celebration is tomorrow. You have to figure out that orb."

"I progressed significantly last night," he said as he sat up and moved to the side of the bed. "I stayed up past sunrise to continue my work. Thus, I slumber now."

She huffed, giving up her pointless attempt to look away. "Were you not planning to put clothes on?"

He grinned wickedly as he stood and approached her slowly, unabashedly. Once again, her gaze traced every solid bulge that comprised his form, his rippling muscles visible beneath a few scars of battle.

"Does my flesh offend you, Karulent?"

"Nothing I haven't seen before." Verónica glanced down. "Though never quite so hairless. Do all Tridulans shave their bodies?"

"Nearly all." He stepped closer. "It separates us from barbarians."

"Is that what we are to you?" Verónica grinned as she set her hand on his solid chest. Her heart raced, and her breathing hastened. Enthralled, she stared into his dark eyes as she unconsciously licked her lips. "And yet, I have heard many tales of the wild and wicked ways of the Tridulans."

He reached out his thick arm, bushing her hip as it passed.

"You are not my type, my lady." He grinned as he grabbed a tunic from the table behind her. He stepped away.

"Not your *type*?" she huffed.

He slipped the tunic over his head. "I believe we were speaking of the orb."

"Right," Verónica said, flustered. "The orbs. Of course." She set her hand on her neck. "It does get rather hot up here, doesn't it?"

"We *are* over a forge." He slapped a belt around his waist. "I had planned to seek you once I awoke. I've had a break-through in my research."

"Yes, you said. You're not doing trousers, then?"

He looked down at his knee-length tunic. "Everything is covered that needs to be. I needn't wear barbaric trousers in private."

"Right. Trousers are barbaric, too," she snickered. "Is that what the Dark Light calls civilization? No body hair and no trousers."

"In part, yes," he grumbled.

"All right, then. Well, I'm not as concerned about a Dayigan invasion as I was before. The Reyigans went above and beyond with security. They've sent a thousand soldiers to team up with our town militia and stationed twice that num-ber in camps forming a perimeter five miles from the town. And look." She motioned to the small window.

Adratus approached and looked. Outside was a massive wall of blue light, part of a dome that enclosed the entire town.

"We must leave," he said, darting to the table to stuff his things into a large black bag. "That is how they attack. They circle the town with green fire and then—"

"Calm down." Verónica set a hand on his shoulder. "That's not green or fire. Look. The Azerent Mages put it there. Seven of their high-ups came straight from their mages' hall in Reyigo."

He set down the bag but stared, shaken, leaning on the table.

"'Tis something the Blue Rose invented," Verónica continued in a consoling tone. "Anyone who goes through will pass right out. No Dayigans are getting in here."

"Apologies," he said. "When I was but sixteen, the Silthex nearly killed me."

"With a wall of green fire?" she asked.

He nodded. "The event yet haunts me."

"'Tis all right. I'm no stranger to nightmares myself. Very few in Port Haven came here by pleasant means."

He breathed, regaining himself. "The Azerent's ward will prove ineffective," he said. "My assumption that Eadwulf would lead an army here was incorrect—or so I now believe." He moved to a chest of drawers and slid out the bottommost. From it, he grabbed the golden orb, still circled by rings of lightning. "This, in itself, *is* the attack."

With her concern rekindled, Verónica stared at the thing. "Will it release the green fire you spoke of to destroy the town?"

Adratus shook his head. "Unlikely. That knowledge seems to have died with the Silthex." He set the orb to hover just above the table. "This is much more complex. The components within it are so rare that they make the gold and emeralds encasing it seem trivial in comparison." He leaned forward to gaze at it, the lightning rings casting an eerie glow of red across his face. "And the amount of time and effort to properly combine those materials—someone's been brewing this for years."

"I'm happy you're impressed. What does it do?"

"I have thoughts, yet I'll need to check you before I can verify them."

"Me?" Verónica shot him an inquisitive look. "What do I have to do with this?"

"That's what I mean to determine," he replied, moving closer until he stood directly in front of her. "Stand still, with your feet together and arms slightly from your sides. You may want to close your eyes."

"I'll keep my eyes open, if 'tis all the same to you," she said, a hint of annoyance in her voice as she assumed the position he described. "What do you plan to do?"

Without answering, Adratus stretched out his arm, his palm toward her feet. "Detect magic."

A spot of light from his palm landed on her boot, reminding her of sunlight reflected by a hand mirror, but red. As he slowly moved his hand, the light moved back and forth and up her body. Finally, she felt the point of warmth move up her neck, chin, and face. It stung as it touched her eyes. She flinched.

"I told you to close your eyes," he said.

At last, it passed the top of her head, and he dispelled it before going quiet.

"And?" Verónica asked.

A grim expression marked his face as he glanced downward. He waved his hand toward her. "Reveal."

Suddenly, dozens of wavering tendrils of green light emanated from various parts of her body, most from her hands. Frightened, she tried to swat them away, only for her hands to pass through.

Adratus waved his hand again, and they were gone.

"You have a dormant hex on you," he said solemnly. "The cords were there before I bound the orb, and they yet remain, though unseen. Apologies for not finding it sooner. The hex was undetectable until I knew what to look for."

Horrified, Verónica stared at her hands, knowing those writhing bonds remained. "What are they?"

"The magical signature is Silthex, combined with something old. Very old. An ancient magic I cannot identify. It appears to connect you to anyone you've had physical contact with since you gained the hex—and everyone they touched, too, and so on. No doubt most of Port Haven is affected."

Frightened, Verónica's voice trembled with rage. "What does it fucking do!"

Adratus's face grew grim. "Mind control," he said. "I cannot confirm its exact purpose, but given tomorrow's event, I would guess the army Eadwulf plans to lead to attack your town and its envoys . . ." He paused, looking away from her. ". . . will be composed of the citizens of Port Haven, themselves. 'Tis only speculation."

"No," Verónica whispered, lightheaded. Her vision swam as she searched for the bed and took a seat. "If my people even attempt an attack, they won't stand a chance against the three thousand Reyigan soldiers here now. Our whole town will be killed, and all refugees throughout the Alliance will be blamed." She looked up imploringly at him. "But you must know how to deactivate it, right?"

"Not yet," Adratus said regretfully. "I will take it to the Black Temple in Vohcktara. There, they—"

"There's no time for that." She jumped up. "The announcement is tomorrow. My people will be *massacred* tomorrow."

He glanced away. "Condolences," he said, "truly. I've given you all the information I have, but I did say I'm not here to save your town. My orders are to gather information and report back."

She slapped his face. "Don't give me that heartless soldier bullshit!" She snatched the orb from the table. "If you won't help, I'll take it to someone who will." She darted to the door and hurried down the stairs into the forge below.

"Verónica," Adratus called from the top of the stairs. "I can stop you, if I must."

She stopped, remembering his cords of light.

Duncan approached. "Is there a problem here?"

Verónica shook her head.

Duncan looked at the orb. He nodded. "I'll be working nearby"—he shot a sidelong glance at Adratus, who was drawing nearer—"not seeing or hearing a thing 'less you call." He departed to a finishing table at the edge of the room, but kept his eyes on Adratus.

"I'm taking this to the Azerent Mages," Verónica said firmly.

"No," Adratus said. "I cannot let you take a device entwined with Dark Light magic to the Azerents. Revealing my powers here, before an event of unrest, would give them cause to believe Tridual is involved. And I will not give the True Light another reason to kill my people."

"Then remove your magic."

"You wish me to remove the spell binding its power? For all we know, it may have already stopped the next phase."

"Then I'll destroy it." She rushed to a blazing furnace and held it close, her gaze trained upon him.

"Do you know what will happen if you melt it?"

She paused. "No."

"Nor do I," he said. "It could destroy its power. Or unleash it. The one certainty is that any knowledge the Black Temple could gain from it, knowledge that could prevent future attacks, would be lost."

She stepped back from the heat of the forge, her gaze hardening and her voice low. "You are not as heartless as you're trying to act. We're talking about the death of my entire town here. I can tell that you want to help us . . . I can see it in your eyes."

Adratus turned his gaze to the grime-covered workshop floor, his tone thick with sorrow. "The last time I attempted to save a Karulent town—to save them from the Silthex—the people there tried to execute *me* instead. They blamed *me*, not the Silthex, for the attack and, by extension, the Tridulan Empire. The Dayigan Empire responded with force and started what is now known as the Disregarded War—named so because the common people of the kingdoms of Light barely know of it and barely care of its ongoing toil on my people. Yet, for nearly two decades, I have fought in this war as the Dayigans pushed our border back a hundred miles. I have lost more friends than this town can even hold. So do not tell me what you see in my eyes, my lady, because I owe *nothing* to the Karulents."

Verónica felt the weight of his words in her heart. She wanted to speak in defense of her people, but she was all too aware that the laws of this kingdom called for his death.

However, her town was her responsibility. Steeling herself, she took a deep breath. "If you can't reveal your magic," Verónica said, her voice hard yet her eyes unable to meet his gaze, "you can't use it in this street-level room with a dozen windows. You can't stop me from leaving with this." She held it up. "Remove your magic from it, or the Azerents will see it. I'm certain whatever this orb is meant to do, it won't do it until tomorrow. The Azerents will have time to bind it with their own magic."

He paused, studying her with those sorrowful eyes for a lingering moment. With a wave of his left hand, the lightning surrounding the orb disappeared.

"I won't have you staying under my friend's roof," Verónica said sadly. "Gather your things and go." With that, she walked away.

"I won't have you staying under my friend's roof," Verónica said sadly. "Gather your things and go." With that, she walked away.

CHAPTER THIRTY-SIX

Dread filled Verónica as she approached the massive blue tent that stood at the edge of town. Beyond it, the vast dome of blue light met the ground. She clutched the orb, its surface slick with her sweat. The sounds of revelry from the celebration behind her grated against her nerves, yet she mustered her courage and continued forward.

Verónica neared the two Reyigan soldiers guarding the entrance to the tent. "I must see the Azerent Mages," she said firmly.

The stoic soldiers wearing their blue tabards emblazoned with Reyigo's crest—a golden rampant gryphon within a triangle of three crossed sevens—stood unmoved.

Undeterred, Verónica raised her voice. "Our town, and everybody in it, is in grave danger."

"Sorry, miss," one soldier replied, barely sparing her a glance, "the Azerents are occupied with maintaining the dome. Their focus cannot be diverted."

"The dome is useless," Verónica shouted, her heart pounding in her ears. "This orb has already enchanted half the town. The threat is *here*, within these walls, not outside."

"Lady Verónica?" Father Joachim emerged from the tent, his eyes scrutinizing her as if she were a wayward child. "What is this about?" he asked sternly. "The Azerents have been assigned their task: safeguarding our borders by sustaining the anesthetizing ward. We cannot risk allowing in any danger by diminishing our defenses."

"This orb is a magical device planted by the Dayigans." Verónica said, fury igniting within her. "The people of Port Haven have been—"

"It is an interesting trinket," Joachim interrupted. "However, everyone knows the Dayigans despise magic. Most likely, one of the visitors in town simply dropped it."

He pulled her aside before continuing. "With the announcement so close and all these unfamiliar things in town, I understand that you might feel overwhelmed." He smiled. "You've always been a headstrong girl, always getting into trouble. Perhaps it would serve you well to focus more on finishing the decorations and leave the defense to those better suited."

"Father Jo . . ." Verónica forced a bitter smile.

"I really would rather you didn't call me that."

"*Father*, I really would rather not punch you in front of Reyigan soldiers."

Joachim's face hardened instantly, and he crossed his arms with displeasure. "I'm currently dealing with the needs of the Azerents, yet . . ." He sighed with annoyance. "I will ask Lord Onfroi to meet with you and address your unwarranted worries."

"Lord Onfroi?" Verónica scoffed, her anger flaring. "What good will he do? This requires magical expertise."

"Please, Lady Verónica," Father Joachim urged, exasperation creeping into his voice, "trust in our judgment. The Reyigans are doing what is best for our town."

"Your judgment is flawed," Verónica said, her eyes narrowing.

"Róni," Swift called from the sky before alighting beside Verónica. "I have a pressing matter that I must discuss with you."

Verónica's gaze, still as steel, remained on Joachim. "Fine, send for your precious Lord Onfroi. But if any harm befalls our people, it will be on your head."

"Understood, my lady." Joachim forced a smile. "May God Karulus keep you well."

As he returned to the tent, Verónica clenched her teeth, frustration churning within her like a storm. She then walked away with Swift, navigating the street crowded with revelers and lined on either side by tall, timber-framed buildings. Small blue flags hung from ropes that crisscrossed overhead, each waving in a gentle breeze that carried the faint smell of cooking meat. Cheery music, different instruments at different distances, filled the area.

"What matter did you need to discuss?" Verónica asked Swift.

"Oh, nothing much, just the fact that the mayor looked like she was about to attack a priest when the town's full of Reyigan soldiers."

Verónica grinned despite all. "It was probably best you intervened. What can you tell me about tomorrow's security?"

"The Reyigans have taken most of the important duties. They have my men looking for pickpockets in the market, controlling drunks, and similar matters."

"I have a more important task for your militia." Verónica grabbed Swift's arm and guided her to the edge of the crowded street. "We may not have the support of the Reyigans, but I won't allow our people to suffer because of their negligence. We must be on high alert."

"I assure you, my lady, we're already on high alert."

"'Tis not enough." Verónica frowned, her voice dropping to a whisper. "An enchantment lies over this town, so powerful that it will turn our own people against the Reyigans. We must prepare for tomorrow's bloodshed."

Swift averted her gaze as the gravity of the words weighed upon her. "So, I assume you and me are both . . ."

"Enchanted." Verónica nodded grimly. "I need you to station guards throughout the town square. Keep your eyes open for any signs of enchantment or danger." Verónica scanned the bustling crowd, the surrounding laughter and revelry seeming so very distant from their grim conversation. "Should anything happen, we must act quickly."

"Understood," Swift confirmed, giving a curt nod. She turned to leave.

"Swift," Verónica murmured. "I thank you. I couldn't do this without you."

"Always by your side, m'lady," Swift replied, her hand resting on Verónica's shoulder before she jumped up from the ground and spread her wings.

As Verónica watched Swift fly away, she forced herself to stand tall, masking her anxiety beneath a veneer of confidence. All around her, the townspeople rejoiced, unaware of the dark cloud hanging over them. It was up to Verónica to protect them all.

Her mind raced with possible strategies, each one more desperate than the last. If only she could reach the Azerents, convince them of the urgency... But Verónica had to work with what she had, and that meant relying on her resourcefulness.

As the night wore on, her eyes never stopped scanning the surroundings for any signs of enchantment. The laughter of children, once a source of joy, now sent shivers down her spine as she imagined them—she tried not to think of it. The flickering torchlight cast sinister shadows against the walls of the town square, each one threatening to reveal some hidden danger.

"My lady," one of the town militiamen said as he approached, snapping her out of her restless vigilance. "Lord Onfroi awaits you in the Great Hall."

"Finally," Verónica replied tersely, her heart pounding in anticipation. "I pray he brings the assistance we need."

"Let's hope so," the guard agreed. "Commander Swift informed us of a potential danger. She also awaits you at the Great Hall."

"May Karulus protect us," Verónica murmured, drawing a deep breath as she prepared herself for whatever fate would bring.

—

The air seemed to grow colder as Verónica approached the Great Hall, and she shivered despite the warmth of the late spring evening. The sounds of celebration and merriment that surrounded her felt far away—distant and muffled. Her heart thudded in her breast like an ever-growing storm, each beat pounding louder and louder in her ears. She kept envisioning everyone around her transformed into fighters for the Dayigan Empire—and fearing she would be among them.

Verónica walked around an empty stage that waited for tomorrow and saw Swift waiting at the door of the Great Hall.

Swift placed a comforting hand on Verónica's shoulder. "He's inside."

"God Karulus, grant me courage," Verónica whispered, her voice tight with tension. "Make him believe me and grant us your mercy."

Swift grinned. "When have you ever been religious? You have a church as your drawing room and never go."

"True. But this . . ." Verónica shook her head. "This is beyond us."

Verónica entered, Swift just behind her, to find Lord Onfroi awaiting, shrouded by shadows in the center of the vast room. Verónica recalled when she first met him here, only two weeks past, yet seemingly so long ago. His noble posture from that first meeting was absent. Instead, the Reyigan slouched his shoulders and appeared worried as he paced.

"Lord Onfroi," Verónica said with a forcefulness that echoed through the chamber.

He hurried forward, relief present on his face. "Lady Verónica," he said as he clutched the large, golden, crossed seven that dangled from his necklace. "Where is this orb of which you spoke?"

Verónica opened up the bag strapped over her shoulder and produced the golden object. "It holds an enchanting power that will cause our people to attack the visiting nobles tomorrow." It reflected candlelight off its surface as she held it up to him.

Lord Onfroi's eyes lit up as he took it in his hands, relief seeming to wash over him.

"'Tis Dayigan magic," Verónica said. "Do you believe me?"

"Yes," he said. "Rumors abound of select Dayigans who engage in the magical arts, believing themselves *above* those forbidden to use it. I am pleased you found it in time. Yet, how do you know this item holds magic?"

Verónica hesitated, yet Swift spoke up. "One of the townspeople reported it to us, my lord. He heard two

Dayigans plotting, but didn't see their faces. What he heard was clear, though."

"Interesting," Onfroi said. "You were right to bring this to me. This orb must certainly go to the Azerents. I assure you," he said, voice firm and steady, "I will personally ensure they receive it and act accordingly."

Relief washed over Verónica. "I thank you."

He placed the orb into a large pocket of his robe. "I trust you will handle this matter with discretion. The fewer people who know, the better. We wouldn't want your townspeople or the esteemed visitors in a panic, would we?"

"Definitely not. Only the town militia knows," Verónica said.

He nodded. "It is imperative that you tell no one else. No one wants our important celebration ruined over something so trivial. The item will be neutralized, and all will go as planned."

"Again, my thanks, my lord," Verónica said, her eyes locking onto his. "Time is of the essence."

"Yes, it is," he replied, his gaze solemn as he lifted the golden seven of his necklace toward her. "Have faith God will protect those who are deserving. I shall make haste."

"May Karulus keep you well," Verónica said.

As he disappeared through the door, she prayed that their actions would be enough, that they could avert disaster and protect those they held dear, yet she found the knot of anxiety still set firm within her core.

"Róni," Swift said softly, her hand squeezing Verónica's shoulder. "We did what we could, and my men will continue to watch for trouble. Now, all we can do is remain vigilant and trust in the Azerents' abilities."

"Trust," Verónica echoed, the word bitter on her tongue. Trusting had never been easy for her, but now, it was all she had left.

CHAPTER THIRTY-SEVEN

Verónica paced at the foot of the large stage erected before the Great Hall. The celebrations surged all around her, merriment filling the air, yet her body was a coil of nerves. She rubbed the shoulders of the long sky-blue linen dress that the Reyigans had selected for her. The shadows grew short, noon approaching, lighting the streets where the townspeople had gathered for the announcement. She shuddered, not from any chill, but from the weight of responsibility bearing down on her.

"Are all the guards in position?" she asked Swift, her voice steady despite the turmoil inside.

Swift nodded. "Yes, my lady. As they were the last time you asked. Any word from Lord Onfroi?"

Verónica stopped pacing and shook her head. "You would think they'd have the courtesy to update us either way."

"The Reyigans have not exactly found the courtesy to give us much information at all," Swift said with annoyance. "The town militia has its tasks, but we aren't in the loop for overall security. As much as I hate to make assumptions, I'd have to assume the celebration would have been canceled if Lord Onfroi had failed."

"Let's hope you're right," Verónica said, scanning the crowd for any signs of danger. Her heart tightened as she thought of those innocent people being transformed into fighters.

"Lady Verónica?" a scrawny teen dressed in a Reyigan soldier's uniform said as he approached her.

"Yes?" Verónica replied.

"I bring word from Lord Onfroi."

"At last," she said, anxiously gripping Swift's hand. "Go on."

The boy nodded. "He says the matter has been resolved. All is well."

Verónica released a breath that seemed to release two weeks of stress from her body. "Praise be to Karulus, spirit of truth, and of compassion." She nodded to the boy, saying, "My thanks."

He hurried away.

"See," Swift began, her voice softening. "All is well, after all. Now, quit your worrying, and go tell the world of our new empire."

Verónica took another deep breath, steadying herself. Swift was right—this wasn't a time for fear. This was a day of celebration. The people deserved to know the good news for which they had waited, and she was excited to tell them.

As Verónica ascended the wooden steps leading to the stage, she felt the weight of countless eyes upon her—some filled with admiration, others with suspicion. She knew too many of the visitors below viewed her as but a Dayigan refugee trespassing in their land. But Verónica held her head high, refusing to let their judgments hinder her.

"Friends and fellow citizens of the great Karulent Alliance!" Verónica called, her words echoing across the square as she tried to stifle the tremble in her voice. "Today, His Majesty, the magnanimous King of the Reyigan Kingdom, has honored me to speak on behalf of all the Dayigan refugees who have been accepted into these lands. Soon, His Majesty will take the stage as we gather to announce our future as *one* people and the unified path that we must take to protect all that we hold dear."

Verónica's gaze swept across the crowd and then stopped suddenly when she saw them—Adratus pushing his way through the crowd as he pursued Lord Onfroi through the sea of people. The golden orb glinted in Onfroi's hand.

"Our resolve must remain unshaken," Verónica said in a steady voice, though her heart thundered with dread. "We must stand united against the Dayigan Empire that seeks our destruction."

As Adratus closed in, his fierce eyes locked on his quarry, Verónica felt a mix of fear and confusion. *Why would Onfroi still hold the orb? Why does Adratus pursue him?* She barely knew either of the men, yet she realized one had betrayed her.

The crowd erupted in mummers as the pause in Verónica's speech drew too long. She'd frozen, knowing she needed to act, to intervene before it was too late.

"Swift!" Verónica called before she leaped from the stage and into the fray, ready to confront whichever man was her enemy.

Red lightning shot through the crowd as Adratus unleashed his magic, surging from his hand to circle Lord Onfroi.

The Reyigan lord called out in pain as he was lifted from the ground. The air crackled with energy, and the townspeople gasped, forgetting their revelry while they gawked at the unsettling display of Dark Light power.

"What have you done, Adratus?" Verónica muttered to herself, her eyes widening at the sight of Onfroi, coiled in lightning, being lifted above the crowd.

Fear gripped the onlookers, and screams rang out. Many began shoving their way to flee, as confusion and horror rippled through them.

"Monster!" someone cried out, hurling a rock at Adratus.

He weaved and ducked as other stones flew. The towns-people kept coming—their screams of hate like thunder. As the fearful mob surged around him, some chose to flee, yet others pressed on with determination, intent on tearing him apart.

Winged soldiers, bows armed, flew in to hover above the maelstrom as they looked for a shot that avoided the towns-people. Human soldiers, swords drawn, pushed their ways through the crowd.

"Stop!" Verónica shouted, her voice cracking with urgen-cy. "He's trying to help us! . . . Maybe?"

But her words were lost in the chaos, drowned out by the cries of the mob. She gritted her teeth, cursing under her breath, as she realized that it was up to her to protect Adratus—if he was even her ally. With determination, Verónica fought her way through the throngs of anger.

Another rock hit Adratus. His magic faltered, and Onfroi, released, fell to the ground. Adratus cast his hand toward the archers overhead—"Disarm!"

Their bow ignited, causing them to cast them away. Still, the Tridulan kept his sword sheathed as the crowd moved in around him. Two townspeople ran at him, and he coiled them in cords of light before setting them further up the street. He moved another three people by the same nonlethal means.

Verónica fought her way through the rabble—finally standing between Adratus and his attackers. She could feel their glowering stares, full of wrath and fear, as she demand-ed they back down. The locals obeyed, but the visitors continued to press forward, goaded by hatred and fear.

Verónica caught sight of Onfroi as he slunk around a small shop, darting into shadows like a snake into its den.

The golden orb was gone, and its loss slapped Verónica across the face.

She turned to Adratus, beaten and battered, yet standing. "Are you all right?"

He nodded, face grim. "I'll live. Do you trust me?" He drew his sword.

"Not really, no."

"Understandable, yet try." He grabbed her from behind, his sword pressed to her neck. "Stay back!" he shouted to the surrounding people.

Reyigan soldiers pushed to the front to circle them but paused, eager to attack.

Verónica could see Swift hovering above them with bow drawn and finger on the string. She met Swift's eyes and shook her head—a silent command for her to stand down.

Swift relaxed her bow and shared hushed words with her men.

A sphere of red light formed atop Adratus's left hand. "If anyone draws near," he shouted, "I will burn the fifty-foot radius around me to ash."

Adratus made a steady path in the direction Onfroi had gone, with Verónica held captive by the blade at her throat. The frightened crowd parted, allowing him a wide berth.

Once he and Verónica reached the edge of the town square, Adratus tossed the sphere upward. It exploded into countless lights, spiraling in all directions like crazed red fireflies.

Panic ensued as people scrambled to flee the points of light.

"Run," Adratus said to Verónica.

She paused, watching the horrified people. "What did you do to them?"

"Nothing. 'Tis but lights, I assure you. Run before they figure that out."

—

Blood dripped from Adratus's split lip, stark against the pallor of his face. Verónica held Adratus firmly as they stumbled along the narrow alleyway. The air was damp and cool, shadowed from the sun, a welcome respite from the chaos they'd just left.

"Where do we go?" Adratus asked, wincing as he stumbled over a loose stone.

"Somewhere safe and hidden," she replied, her voice low. "We need to catch our breath and plan our next move."

The passage ended at a few broken wooden stairs that descended to the riverbank, its rocky shore littered with the remnants of an old rowboat. Verónica inhaled deeply, allowing the scent of salt and sand to fill her lungs and ground herself in reality for a moment. She guided Adratus into a small rickety fishing shack built into a short cliff, its front open to the river. She sat him on a wooden crate.

"Stay here," Verónica instructed, rummaging through the pouch of her belt for a handkerchief before hurrying toward the river. After dunking it in the water, she returned and dabbed at his wounds.

"Gratitude," Adratus murmured. His sad eyes seemed to pull her in, and in that fleeting moment, she felt a fragile trust form between them.

"You revealed your power even though it would place you at this—how did you put it—this event of unrest," Verónica said, her hands steady as she wiped blood from his cheek. "Whatever happens now, they'll blame it on Tridual."

"A foolish act that proved futile."

"A noble act that proved you're not an arsehole. I knew you wouldn't let this happen to our town."

A voice sounded from the shadows. "Not to interrupt this lovely moment . . ."

Adratus jumped up, grabbing his sword.

Swift stepped in front of the shack. ". . . but that orb is still out there."

"I am aware," Adratus said, his voice strained as he sat back down. "I failed to capture the Dayigan."

"Are you certain Lord Onfroi is a Dayigan?" Verónica asked.

"I believe Lord Onfroi is Lord Eadwulf, or at least works for him. I caught him trying to activate the orb."

"At least you stopped him." Verónica turned to Swift. "How did you find us?"

Swift answered with a smirk. "Your brother didn't make me head of the town militia just because of my looks. But no one else followed you, I'm certain. You're safe here."

Verónica nodded curtly. "I need those tracking skills again. Find Onfroi—or whoever he is—but don't engage him. Only use men you trust and avoid involving the Reyigans. Report back to me."

"Yes, my lady." Swift spread her wings.

"Wait," Adratus said. "Take this." He opened a pouch on his belt and produced two necklaces, holding them by their long, thin strips of black leather. The pendants were two-inch hexagonal prisms of smooth black stone. "'Tis tourmaline charged with a protection spell," he said. "'Twill shield you from the influence of the Dayigan hex."

The women took them, both eyeing them.

"Is this Dark Light magic?" Verónica asked.

"Of course."

"Of course," she uttered, pausing before giving Swift a hesitant nod. They put them on.

"If we're giving gifts." Swift removed her sword belt and handed it over to Verónica. "Take this and be safe, my lady." With that, she spread her wings and jumped, flying away.

"I must go as well," Adratus said as he rose from the crate. "We haven't long until the orb recharges and the Dayigan can use it again."

"No," Verónica said. "You can't search for Onfroi with the soldiers searching for you. Let Swift's men do their jobs."

His gaze held hers for a moment before he relented, nodding in acceptance of her words. "You know how to use that?" He motioned to the sword Swift had given her.

"Well, that is the funny thing about being hunted down by soldiers as a little girl—you come to find it rather pressing to learn to fight. But, you gain a strange sense of humor, apparently." Verónica scanned the dilapidated hovel. "Hiding from soldiers—how very . . . *nostalgic*." She grabbed another crate and sat beside Adratus.

"How young were you when you escaped the Dayigans?"

She took a deep breath and released it. "Too young to properly remember. The memories are just flashes that creep into my nightmares. I remember hiding in awful places. I remember not understanding what a Karulent was except that I was one of them—and everyone hated me for it. What I can't remember is my father, who died keeping us alive. He was a count, according to my mother. Evidently, we had some grand house and all that before they kindly asked all the Karulent nobles to die by beheading—you know how

Dayigans get. My mother used to go on about that *lovely house in the lovely kingdom of Fielalaluz* and how *wonderful* it all was. Bla, bla. 'This is all temporary, Verónica,' she would say. 'Someday, we will return home.' My brothers actually believed it—even now, my oldest, Estéban, is in the Dayigan Empire fighting in the Resistance to return things to how they were. But to me"—she sighed—"it was all like some silly Faery story. And just as fake."

"Is your mother here?"

Verónica shook her head. "No. After your warning, I took her to the next town over whilst you were staying at Duncan's." She paused for a moment before she continued. "Do you think the spell will reach her there?"

"Unlikely. I saw the Dayigan when he attempted to activate the orb. He used a golden version of the crossed number seven . . ."

"A Septenar," Verónica provided the name of the True Light symbol.

"Yes. He inserted the Septenar into the top of the orb, like a key, and turned it. Afterwards, an emerald-colored disk of light emerged from the orb and spread outwards. I stopped him before the disk left the room, but it seemed to be an area-of-effect spell. Although I know not how far it would have spread if I hadn't interrupted, I doubt it would have reached your mother in the next town."

Verónica lowered her head with a sigh. "So if I had just evacuated all my people—"

"We knew not how it worked until now. You bear no fault."

Verónica faced the sandy, rocky ground. She gritted her teeth and balled her hands into fists. "They're horrible, the Dayigans. They're like a . . . a storm, twisting through the lands, destroying everything. Moving from target to target. 'We hate these people. Now we hate these people over here. Actually, we hate these people now.'" She looked out over the glistening water of the Hyvile River, stretching miles across, the Dayigan Empire unseen on the distant, opposite shore. "And you *pray so hard* that the storm goes somewhere else, anywhere else, even when you know, on some horrible level, that you're praying for another group of people to be hit." She sighed. "That's why you're here, isn't it?" She looked at him. "To see if that storm might leave Tridual to come here."

Adratus nodded. "We never wanted this to happen to your people, and we did nothing to cause this. But we hoped . . ." He glanced down. "We have fought for so long, Verónica. If war erupted between the Dayigans and the Karulents, perhaps they'd leave us be."

"Reyigans," she corrected softly. "We aren't the Karulent Alliance anymore. We're the Reyigan Empire. And I won't let our new empire blame the Tridulans for what the Dayigans have done. If that means the storm comes here, we'll face it, as one unified nation."

Swift landed at the mouth of the shack. "We found Onfroi."

CHAPTER THIRTY-EIGHT

Breathless and sweat-drenched, Verónica sprinted through the chaotic streets of Port Haven. Adratus by her side, they cut through the panicked crowd like blades. Her heart pounded in her chest as they tracked Onfroi, desperation fueling their determination.

"Verónica, there!" Adratus shouted, pointing to a figure disappearing into a narrow alley. They gave chase, dodging bewildered townspeople along the way.

"How long until the orb is ready to use again?" Verónica called to Adratus as she raised her sword.

"Unknown," he said. "We must assume we have little time."

Verónica and Adratus cornered Lord Onfroi in the alleyway, swords drawn and ready for a fight.

Onfroi smirked, unfazed by his predicament. "My lady, what is the meaning of this?"

Verónica scoffed, eyes locked on his. "Don't try acting like you're just having a nice evening stroll. I know you kept the orb, and I know you plan to use it."

Onfroi chuckled. "Congratulations. You're not a *complete* idiot. However, you can't stop me."

"*Traitor!*" Verónica shouted. "You turned against us when we've done *nothing* to you."

"Do not speak to *me* of betrayal, woman," he thundered back. "You, like all the other so-called *refugees*, are subjects of the Holy Dayigan Empire. It was *your* kind who betrayed our land to join our enemies against us."

"We fled death by your hands."

"You fled conforming to the laws of His Highest Majesty, whom you were born to obey."

Adratus stepped forward, his left hand glowing bright red. "You are not Lord Onfroi—an established member of the Reyigan court. I believe you are the Dayigan Lord Eadwulf. Admit it, so I have a name by which to arrest you."

He snorted mockingly and slowly raised his hands to concede. "I admit it." He lowered his hands. "And what will you do with that confession, Faldénrus? You are far from your jurisdiction. And I doubt that even these vile Karulents will allow you to travel far while dragging a lord bound by Dark Light magic through the streets."

"Adratus, look." Verónica pointed to Eadwulf's neck. "The Septenar he wears as a necklace. 'Tis gone."

"Then he but delays us," Adratus said, scanning the area. "The orb is not here, or we would see its disk of light."

Verónica thrust her sword toward Eadwulf, the blade piercing the wall just inches from his face. "Where is it? I won't let my town be pawns in your game."

He only sneered in response, his smug expression intensifying her urge to draw blood. "*Pawns* do as they are told, as is dictated by their station. They do not run to the opposite side of the board and join the enemy. But soon"—he grinned—"your people will pay for betraying the Dayigan Empire by betraying your *new* home. Fitting, really."

"Verónica, leave him," Adratus called. He peered into a scarlet ball of light atop his palm. "I can track the orb as I did before, yet the process is slow."

"Your demonic tricks will not save you," Eadwulf said. "See for yourself." He motioned.

Verónica turned back to the mouth of the alleyway to see a flat band of green light advancing quickly toward her. Before she could react, it passed through her—prickling like static over her body—and continued through the walls.

"*Now*." Eadwulf grinned as he stepped forward, his eyes glaring. "Kill the Dark Light savage." He pointed his finger at Adratus.

Verónica glanced around to see who Eadwulf commanded.

Adratus leaned her way. "He means you. He thinks you are enchanted."

"Right." Verónica looked at Eadwulf and chuckled. "Well, I wish I'd realized. I could have used that to our advantage."

Eadwulf grew angry. He lifted his hands high. "*Come*," his word echoed unnaturally, "and kill the Dark Light savage and your treacherous mayor."

Townspeople began to enter the alleyway, an army of mindless drones with vacant eyes and blank expressions. The same trap Verónica and Adratus had used to corner Eadwulf had now become their own.

"We can't hurt them!" Verónica called, horrified by the sight of her friends and fellow townspeople transformed. "They're my people." Her voice was barely audible above their shrieks and screams.

"I am aware," Adratus growled. He shook his hand, dispelling the red orb. He then lifted his hand high. A misty cable of red erupted from his palm, latching onto the apex of a roof. "Grab on to me."

The townspeople, like feral beasts, drew closer.

Verónica grabbed Adratus, and he wrapped his arm around her before the cord lifted them, bringing them up to the thatched rooftop.

From her high vantage, Verónica looked over the town of Port Haven. Every way she turned was a brutal battlefield, as her people waged attacks on the visitors while Reyigan soldiers retaliated in force.

"No," she whimpered in horror.

"Focus, Verónica." Adratus grabbed her shoulder, his voice steady despite the pandemonium. "We can end this. But we must retrieve the orb."

"Adratus! Behind you!" Verónica called, as one of her former guards flew at him with a snarl.

Adratus spun round just in time to send a single scarlet cord flying from his hand like a whip, binding the madman tight within its strength.

Raising his hand skyward, Adratus shouted, "Rage!" In response, the cable began to crackle and spark like lightning, sending shocks of torment through every muscle of the poor man's body until, finally, he fell unconscious. Adratus set him on the ground below.

"He'll be fine," Adratus said.

Verónica surveyed the sky, eyes widening. "Yes. But will we?"

Ten Reyigan soldiers in blue leather tabards flew in their direction—not enchanted but just as deadly.

"Fucking za!" Adratus growled. "Why is this town everything at once?"

Verónica cast him a sharp look. "Maybe if your magic wasn't a shining beacon saying, 'Look at me, I'm doing Dark Light magic over here—'"

An arrow flew toward them, but Adratus yanked her from its path.

"Stay close." His eyes blazed with determination. "We must find that orb." He hurried to the edge of the roof, pausing to cast lightning around the nearest soldier.

The Terovae shouted in pain until his body grew limp. The lightning set him over the apex of the roof.

Adratus cast again—"Disarm!"—causing the bows of the other Reyigans to burst into flames. He jumped down to a wooden awning over the door and jumped down onto the street.

Descending into chaos, Verónica and Adratus quickly lost the pursuing Terovaes. Verónica clung to her sword, heart hammering as she watched people she'd known all her life fighting against one another. It felt like a nightmare, one from which she desperately wished to awaken. But she couldn't let it overwhelm her. She knew too much still needed to be done.

"The orb is this way," Adratus motioned ahead.

"You're tracking it?"

"No time," he said. "Yet Eadwulf assumes I am. There."

Up the street of madness, Verónica saw Eadwulf scurrying away in the distance.

"He will lead us." Adratus hurried toward him.

The townspeople began to close in on them from every direction. With their vacant eyes and wild expressions, they looked like mad wolves ready to rip them apart. They wielded weapons with little skill, but swiped with reckless abandon at anything that moved.

Verónica brandished her sword, parrying strikes while trying to avoid wounding any of them.

When one drew too near, Adratus coiled him or her in lightning, delivering the limp body to rest down the street.

Suddenly, a voice called from above: "Róni!" Swift flew overhead and shot four arrows into the legs of four assailants, each howling as they fell to their knees.

She landed beside Verónica and uttered in shock, "My men . . . they're all . . ."

"I know," Verónica said. "Eadwulf is just up the street." She pointed. "Watch him until we reach him."

"Yes, my lady." She jumped back to the sky.

"We'll never reach him at this pace," Verónica shouted to Adratus over the noise.

"Get behind me." He slammed his sword into its scabbard and pressed both hands together before bowing his head in concentration. After a deep breath, he cast his hands forward. "Arc!"

Red lighting shot from his palms, twisting as one to course through the nearest person before jumping from foe to foe until twenty fell unconscious.

Like frightened rats, the remaining feral crowd scattered in terror.

Adratus stumbled back with a groan, his hands cupping his head as a trickle of fresh blood ran down his nose.

Verónica rushed to his side. "Are you all right?"

He nodded slowly before speaking through gritted teeth. "I used too much magic too quickly . . . but I'll be fine," he assured.

"And them?" She motioned to the fallen townspeople.

"They'll be just fine too—it was only a stun spell; not proper lightning." He regained himself and took off in the direction of Eadwulf.

As the two moved through the battle, Verónica forced herself to focus on incapacitating rather than causing permanent harm to the friends and neighbors she'd known all her life. Each strike felt like a betrayal, but she reminded herself that pushing forward was the only way to save these same people from the control that bound them.

Screams tore through the air, punctuated by the clash of steel and desperate cries from the visitors to the town. Verónica's heart pounded in her ears as she and Adratus hurried to Swift, just outside a bakery.

"He's in here," Swift said resolutely, though fear lingered in her eyes.

"Stay near," Verónica commanded, scanning the surrounding madness. "Assure no one enters the bakery."

"Understood." Swift nodded, her voice steady, even as she sidestepped an attacker lunging at her.

—

As Adratus and Verónica stepped into the bakery, the scent of freshly baked bread and pastries clashed with the metallic stench of blood. Once bright and inviting, the shop was now a scene of horror: blood smeared across the floor near the entrance. Verónica thought of the baker and how he'd worked tirelessly to prepare a superlative assortment of fancy cakes, decadent pastries, and honeyed biscuits for today's event. He was thrilled that the king of Reyigo would taste his works. He could never have expected how his efforts would end. She swallowed that thought away, not wanting to think too long about his fate.

Adratus and Verónica advanced cautiously through the shadows, their feet crunching atop crusts of loaves that had spilled out onto the floor. Ovens crackled in the background as they made their way past large baskets of various breads. The ovens' light flickered up eerie shapes on the walls.

Verónica gestured toward a dimly lit doorway leading to a back room. Its door was left ajar, as if someone had retreated through it.

Adratus nodded at her suggestion, and they proceeded silently forward.

The door groaned open, and they entered the large back room. The walls were old brick, flour-strewn prep tables pushed against them. Some tables were overturned. At its center, a dozen townspeople stood in a rigid, motionless formation around Lord Eadwulf, their eyes glazed over as they served as mindless puppets. In his hand, Eadwulf clutched the orb crowned by the crossed seven—the Septenar—its golden surface gleaming in the firelight.

"Ah, Lady Verónica and her filthy Dark Light dog," Eadwulf said disdainfully. "As you can see, you are too late to intervene. These people stand in complete obedience to me."

Rage coursed through Verónica as she stepped forward and met his gaze with defiance. "Release these people. They have no part in your twisted wars."

"On that, you are mistaken," he chided coldly. "They are integral; an attack by refugees on the Reyigan royal court will launch this new empire into civil war and shatter the unity it attempted to forge."

"I won't let that happen," Verónica shot back, her hands twitching with anticipation for her sword.

"Patience, Verónica," Adratus said, his eyes never straying from Eadwulf. He placed his hands together and bowed his head.

"Enough!" Eadwulf roared, raising the orb high above him. "Tear them apart."

The enthralled people advanced with grim determination, circling Verónica and Adratus.

Adratus flung both of his hands forward and shouted, "Arc!"

Red lightning burst from his palms to arc through the bodies of the enslaved, before finally striking Lord Eadwulf with thunderous force, leaving him and all those under his spell senseless on the floor.

Verónica surveyed the fallen before looking at Adratus. She chuckled. "Is that really it? I mean, I was certain it would be a lot harder than that."

Adratus grabbed his forehead as he fell to a knee.

She rushed to him, setting her hand on his shoulder.

"Get the orb," he said, clutching his forehead.

She didn't hesitate, snatching the ominous sphere from Eadwulf's limp fingers.

"Got it," she affirmed, feeling the weight of their victory in her hand. But as she looked around at the unconscious townspeople and the man responsible for their suffering, Verónica couldn't help but feel a deep sense of unease.

"Remove the key," Adratus groaned as he slumped to lie down on the floor.

Verónica grabbed the Septenar at the top of the orb and turned it, pulling it out. Nothing seemed to happen. "Is it over?"

"Listen," Adratus said softly while drawing shallow breaths.

She complied, hearing the sounds of battle continue outside.

Adratus closed his eyes as he whispered, "We yet have much to do."

—

Verónica staggered out of the bakery—Adratus half unconscious and slumped on her shoulders—as they returned to the chaos-filled streets.

Swift descended to their side with a thud of boots and her bow ready to loose an arrow at any moment.

"We have it," Verónica gasped, managing to keep Adratus from falling over as she held up the orb for Swift to see. "But nothing has changed."

"'Tis still something. Right?" Swift asked, her eyes scanning the battle engulfing them. "We must make our way to the Great Hall. The dignitaries have taken shelter there."

Verónica nodded grimly. With a final glance at the carnage that surrounded them, they set off, praying to Karulus that they'd reach safety before the battle consumed them.

CHAPTER THIRTY-NINE

The heavens wept as Verónica and Swift struggled to keep Adratus afoot while they slunk through the shadows of Port Haven. The muddy streets were slick beneath their boots, the blood of innocents washing away in the afternoon rain.

As they neared the heart of the town, they found a brutal mockery of the once-bustling market square. Everywhere Verónica looked were ghastly sights of her people distorted by Eadwulf's cruel spell—familiar faces twisted into masks of hatred and malice. The poor few others who remained unenchanted in the streets fought for their lives against insurmountable odds.

Most of the thralls had converged upon the Great Hall, swarming it, screaming and shouting like creatures from a nightmare, while a ring of affected Terovaes circled above it like vultures. The temporary stage for the announcement had collapsed beneath their weight, as the assailants seemed determined to lay siege to the hall beyond it. Duncan—her dear friend—was among them, his warm smile replaced with a feral glower as he held aloft his blacksmith's hammer and roared.

Here, for the first time, Verónica could truly see the magnitude of Eadwulf's influence—so many people centralized in one area. The sight nearly overwhelmed her, but she kept her focus. "Well, we clearly can't go in the front door," she said. "But I know another way."

"No." Adratus groaned weakly as he stood on his own. "I cannot go to the royal court of Reyigo. They will kill me without question."

Verónica took a deep breath. "I will vouch for you and ensure your safety," she said. "We need a safe place to deactivate the orb, and we *must* tell the king that this is not the refugees' fault." She met his gaze, staring deep into his eyes. "I know you're not here to help us, but I must—"

"I will help you," Adratus said solemnly, his eyes reflecting the darkness that had taken hold of their world. "Lead on."

—

Verónica and Swift, sprinted up the stairs into the Great Hall, their feet pounding against the cold stone, as Adratus limped behind them. When they reached the top, they were met with chaos and despair.

The main entrance door was a cracked ruin, barely holding on against the relentless onslaught of the horde outside. The Reyigan soldiers fought fiercely to keep the pieces in place, but it was only a matter of time before they would be overrun.

The once serene hall was now filled with frightened people seeking refuge, their faces etched with fear that seemed to seep into every corner. In a side alcove, the High King of the Reyigan Empire knelt before the icon of God Karulus, his fervent prayers drowned out by the deafening roar from outside. A small group of nobles huddled around him, guarded by a dozen grim-faced swordsmen.

At the front of the hall, Father Joachim delivered a somber sermon to the few haggard souls who listened, his words echoing bleakly off the high walls.

"Swift," Verónica commanded, her voice cutting through the din. "Join the soldiers at the door. We must hold this room."

With a determined nod, Swift rushed off to join the fray.

Adratus stood by Verónica's side, his eyes taking in the scene with a grim expression. "I can weave a barrier far stronger than that door," he said, his voice low as he leaned nearer to her. "But you will need to convince these soldiers to allow my use of magic."

"No. Your strength is dwindling. Save your magic for de-activating that orb. There's an empty storage room over there." She pointed to a small door in the corner of the hall. "Set up inside and—"

"You want me to hide in some fucking closet while a battle rages? I am a Tridulan legionary."

"Yes, but right now, I need your brains, not your brawn. If you can't stop that orb, then securing this place means nothing. Go."

Adratus hesitated for a moment before nodding. He slammed his sword back into its sheath. "Yes, my lady."

Verónica raised her blade and charged toward the fifty valiant soldiers desperately defending the main door. With a fierce snap and the deafening crack of splintering wood, the barrier collapsed, and the enthralled poured inside.

Panic and screams erupted in the hall as Swift joined Verónica's side, the two fighting fiercely alongside the Reyigan soldiers.

Verónica danced and dodged with expert skill, parrying blows from dockers and merchants, most of whom she knew well, until her fight brought her against the blacksmith, Duncan. She ducked beneath a mighty blow from his hammer.

"Forgive me," she whispered as she delivered a swift kick that sent him crashing to the ground.

"We can't hold them off much longer!" Swift shouted over the clamor of battle, her blade dripping with blood as she fought back to back with Verónica.

"We must," Verónica roared, striking down the enthralled with calculated precision. She couldn't bring herself to kill them, but she delivered deep injuries nonetheless. "We fight them to save them."

Amid the clamor of battle, Verónica's gaze snapped to a new commotion. Townspeople, their faces warped in violent rage, fought toward the royal court. The king's guards, outnumbered and outmatched, were overwhelmed.

"Swift!" Verónica ordered, pointing with her sword. "We must reach the king!"

The archer nodded, drawing an arrow from her quiver before they fought their way through the mob.

Clangs of steel and screams of pain filled the air around them as they hacked and slashed through the enchanted. The floor ran crimson with blood and carnage as twisted townsfolk clashed with ardent soldiers within a surging storm.

Verónica parried and struck with precision, skillfully avoiding lethal blows, while Swift covered their backs with skilled marksmanship. Despite the exhaustion weighing them both, they pressed onward.

"Watch your left!" Swift warned as a dagger flew toward Verónica's throat.

She blocked it, her arm trembling with effort. But she wouldn't falter. Step after step, they pushed forward until, at last, they reached the king's side.

The ruler stood tall amid the raging storm, his face a mask of fury and confusion. But beneath it all lurked something else—fear. Fear he tried to conceal, but couldn't.

"Your Majesty," Verónica said with a tight nod, her voice steady despite all. "We must get you to safety."

"Keep your distance, woman," said the king. "I know you lead these rebellious refugees. I would be safer to flee with a crazed lioness."

Verónica met his gaze without flinching. "Trust me or die."

After a moment of hesitation, the king gave a curt nod.

"Swift, cover our retreat," Verónica commanded, taking point as they weaved through the pandemonium toward the same storage room where she'd sent Adratus.

Swift loosed arrow after arrow, keeping their pursuers at bay while they inched ever closer toward relative safety.

At last, they reached the small door. Verónica darted forward and ushered the king inside, fending off any attackers who tried to follow.

Yanking Swift into the room, Verónica slammed the heavy door on the howling mob outside. Inside, tension hung thick in the air, but for now, they were safe.

"Swift," Verónica panted, her tan face glistening with sweat against dark strands of hair plastered to her forehead. "Barricade the door."

Without hesitation, Swift grabbed a nearby shelving unit and heaved it in front of the entrance.

Meanwhile, Adratus sat cross-legged in the center of the wooden floor, cradling the golden orb in his hands.

Verónica turned to him. "Any progress?"

He exhaled heavily, keeping his eyes on his work. "Some. Your people are under a hex of both obedience and hate.

However, it is temporary—four hours remain on its duration."

"We'll be dead by then," Verónica shouted over the relentless pounding at the door. "Give me something better."

"I require more time," Adratus said, his brow furrowed in concentration.

The king stood at the edge, surveying them all with suspicion and displeasure.

"Your Majesty," Verónica said calmly but firmly. "We will do whatever it takes to protect you."

He scrutinized her for any hint of treachery or duplicity. "Ensure that you do," he warned.

"I may have found a solution," Adratus said. "I've discovered a way to control those affected by using the orb itself." He met Verónica's gaze. "Yet it will take time to execute."

"Do it," Verónica said, turning back to face the now bowing and cracking door. "Our lives depend on it."

—

Verónica paced restlessly in the cramped storage room. Outside, the sounds of battle raged on, the pounding on the door unceasing, threatening to break in at any moment. Inside, everyone was silent, except for a restless tapping from Swift as she fiddled with the quiver on her belt, clearly yearning to draw her bow and rejoin the fight. Yet Swift's eye conveyed worry and grief.

How many of their own people, Verónica wondered, had Swift injured today. Killed? She wanted to say something reassuring, but her mind was too troubled to compose any such comfort. In truth, Verónica knew too well that they still moved toward an even grimmer fate.

The High King of the Reyigan Empire stood rigid, unmoving, and calm. His narrowed gaze remained locked on Adratus, glaring.

Verónica edged closer and whispered, "We'll make it through this, Your Majesty." It was easier to lie to a stranger.

"Your *High* Majesty," he corrected harshly. "Do you take me for an imbecile? That man is clearly harnessing Dark Light magic."

Verónica looked at Adratus. The Tridulan remained seated on the floor. His palms glowed with a sinister red, while between them the orb hovered, surrounded by rings of scarlet lightning.

"Yes," Verónica managed a smirk, "that does seem rather hard to deny. A lot of *red* going on there. But he *is* trying to save us, so maybe we won't set him ablaze just yet."

"Save us from whom?" the king asked with contempt. "Your own people? The Dayigan refugees whom we welcomed into our lands when no one else would have you? The notion that you would betray us so completely when we planned to incorporate your people into our new empire makes my stomach turn. And now this, *Dark Light magic*—in the house of God, no less. We will not abide it."

His words were a slap across Verónica's face, but she held her composure. "My people did not betray you, Your High Majesty. It was Déagrian magic cast by Lord Eadwulf in service of the Dayigans that cursed my people to fight. They don't act by their own will."

"The Dayigans do not practice magic."

A deep thud shook the door, and a fist smashed through, aimlessly grasping for anything within reach.

"Really?" Verónica scoffed. "Well, that certainly is a great relief, isn't it? Swift, please open the door. His Majesty—His *High* Majesty—says the Dayigans don't use magic. We should all just be perfectly fine, then."

"How dare you speak to me with such insolence, girl. I could have you executed for—"

"Be you silent," Adratus said.

The king clutched his throat, glowing red, suddenly unable to speak.

"I have it." Adratus stood, staring at the orb.

With a splintering crash, the door caved inward, slamming against the bookshelf-turned barricade. The frenzied mob clawed their way partway into the room, hands reaching around the door.

Swift and Verónica unsheathed their swords while the king scurried toward the farthest wall.

"Adratus!" Verónica shouted over the clamor. "Whatever you figured out, do it now."

Adratus raised his arm, clutching the orb as he thrust it high. "*Halt!*" he commanded, his voice echoing unnaturally.

The frenzied horde outside instantly ceased their riot.

"Go," Adratus grunted, clinging to the orb as he hunched forward in pain. "Your people are halted, yet now stand helpless. You must tell the soldiers to stand down."

Verónica and Swift shoved aside what little remained of the damaged barricade and dashed into the main hall.

All the enthralled townspeople were frozen in place, their arms limp at their sides, their eyes vacant and empty.

The Reyigan troops, swords ready, cautiously circled the townspeople.

"They're no longer a threat to you!" Verónica shouted urgently. "Please, stand down. And tell your men in the town to do the same."

All heads turned toward what could only be their leader. The commander glared at Verónica before nodding. "Do it." Five soldiers spread their wings and flew from the chamber.

Verónica allowed her body to relax as a wave of relief washed over her; she clutched her chest as she breathed. "Praise be to Karulus."

"Verónica," Adratus groaned, stumbling from the storage room and leaning against its doorframe. "Hours yet remain on the enthrallment." He clutched the orb to his chest. "I cannot break it completely, and I've only barely attuned to the vibrations of its magic. I can force control slightly longer, but I cannot hold the entire town in place until the end of its duration." He winced in pain. "They will resume fighting. Soon."

"Fucking za," Verónica whispered, exhausted. "There has to be a way."

"Apologies, my lady. I hadn't anticipated how much effort this would—" He grunted as his body jolted. "'Tis like lifting a stone with one's fingertips."

Desperate for an answer, Verónica surveyed her surroundings—the petrified townspeople and the terrified visitors. Her duty was to save both groups. She ran her hands through her hair, drawing her long, thick braid in front of her shoulder. Her heart raced as she looked out of the main door into the faces of more of her people—all frozen yet soon to be monsters again.

Beyond them, at the edge of town, she saw the wall of blue light.

"The wall of light!" she exclaimed, pointing out past the broken entrance of the hall. "It was designed by the Blue Rose to knock people out without any lasting harm. Adratus, command them out of town. They'll walk through it."

He nodded weakly and lifted the orb as high as he could manage. "Abandon . . . Port Haven," he commanded with effort, struggling to control its extraordinary might.

As one, the enthralled people turned and marched from the Great Hall, leaving a chilling silence in their wake.

Verónica dashed out of the building to see the same sight in the streets—all the citizens were proceeding toward the outskirts of town. It was eerie to watch them go, advancing like a single mindless entity. Verónica lowered her sword as the adrenaline slowly drained from her veins.

With a large, accomplished smile on her face, Verónica strolled back into the Great Hall. "'Tis done."

The voice of the king rang out, "Arrest that woman!"

Before Verónica could react, Reyigan soldiers grabbed her arms as she struggled.

The king neared and peered down at her with cold eyes. "You stand accused of high treason against the Reyigan Empire," he said. "What say you?"

"I swear to you I had nothing to do with this. It was the Dayigans! How can you not see that?"

"The only Dayigan I see here—is *you*," said the high king, "and the other residents of this vile town who dared to act in murderous rebellion against us, even when we came in peace."

But before Verónica could utter another word, cords of red light circled the king, lifting him from the floor.

"How dare you," Adratus growled as he stepped forward. "How dare you give credit for *my* diabolic works to this Karulent barbarian. She and all these people were but pawns enthralled by the might of God Zeanázel, helpless but to carry out his infernal bidding. And now"—he grinned wickedly—"I have caught the king."

Inside her head, Verónica screamed. *Adratus, don't do this! Your actions will cost your life.* But it was done.

Adratus remained steadfast, shouting, "Now, the Reyigan pseudo-empire shall know destruction on its natal day as it falls, broken, to the wrath of the one *valid* empire, the great *Tridulan Empire!*" Adratus lifted the orb high. "Hail Zeanázel, Lord of Darkness and Defiance, God of Fire and the First Hue of light, he who teaches wisdom, he who teaches might, he who teaches reliance on our selves. Show us the path of reason. Show us the path of will. Show us the path of Night. Hail Zeanázel! Hail to the Dark Light!"

Swift lunged forward and grabbed Adratus from behind, setting her dagger to his neck. "Lower the High King—gently—and unbind him, or I will take your head from your shoulders." Whatever she said next was whispered into his ear.

Adratus paused before allowing the cords of scarlet light to lower and fade away.

"Take the orb," commanded Swift as she gestured toward a Reyigan soldier. "It is where all his power lies. Without it, he's just a normal man, unable to do any magic."

The soldier warily stepped forward and seized the orb.

"Capture him," commanded the king.

They grabbed Adratus, pulling him away.

Verónica dashed toward Adratus, but Swift stopped her, grabbing her arm.

"How could you let them take him?" Verónica demanded. "You know that he's lying."

"Because he *understands*, Róni," Swift said solemnly as she pulled her from the Reyigans. "As do I. Despite all the years of conflicts between the Déagrians and Karulents, the *one* thing the True Light fears most of all—is *the others*. They would not have believed you about the Dayigans, not without proof, but despite all evidence showing that Adratus helped us, they had no trouble believing this was the work of the Tridulans."

Verónica sighed as she found a final glimpse of Adratus before he was led from the room.

"He saved our people," Swift continued. "Now, our people need their mayor."

CHAPTER FORTY

Verónica watched as the soldiers brought the unconscious townspeople into Port Haven. Through the portals in the dome of light, they marched in grim processions, each carrying a limp form draped upon their powerful arms. Every person was placed into a bed—not necessarily their own, but it was a kindness, nonetheless.

However, this act wasn't entirely out of mercy; the soldiers wanted to ensure all townspeople were contained within the dome.

The dome of light, built to protect the town, was now a prison while the authorities began their investigation.

Not allowed to leave or help bring in her people, Verónica aimlessly roamed the streets, first amid soldiers carrying comatose friends and then alone, trying to comprehend what had happened. The dark streets remained eerily vacant, save for a handful of patrols.

For hours, the silence hung over Port Haven until, finally, a piercing shriek rang out. More screams followed—cries of terror and anguish as the sleeping awoke to find loved ones as corpses among rubble.

Verónica's breath left her, as sorrow and rage flooded her heart. She looked at her people, wishing to console them, but no words seemed fitting for the moment. Only desolation seemed to fill the air like an overwhelming fog.

In agony, Verónica could but witness.

CHAPTER FORTY-ONE

The heavy door groaned open, revealing the dimly lit cell where Adratus was held captive. Verónica's heart ached at the sight of him, chained to the damp stone wall, his posture defeated as he sat on the wooden bench.

"We should stop meeting here," he said, his tone flat despite his intended levity.

"I'm so sorry about all this," she said, her eyes downcast. "And sorry that I couldn't come sooner. The town has been under martial law all week, whilst the army did their investigation. Our movements were restricted, and no one was allowed in or out of our own town, except for soldiers and Azerents."

Adratus looked up at her, his eyes still fierce despite the bruises that marred his face. "Your apologies are unneeded, good Verónica. What I did was necessary. Already, your people have suffered enough."

"Then I give you my thanks instead," she said with a slight smile. "It might be some consolation to know that your sacrifice wasn't in vain. The town's been absolved of all wrongdoing, and an hour ago, the Azerents dispelled their wall of light. The soldiers are pulling out of the town even as we speak."

A smile tugged at his lips, but before Adratus could respond, footsteps echoed from the corridor. Three Reyigan soldiers in blue leather tabards stepped into the chamber, their faces stern as they approached the prisoner.

"Adratus," a soldier said with cold authority. "You will come with us."

The other soldiers marched toward him, unchaining him from the wall without a hint of sympathy before yanking him up and shoving him forward.

Confusion marked Adratus's face. His brow furrowed as he rubbed his sore wrists.

"I don't understand," Verónica began. "What is happening here?"

"Additional evidence has come to light," the first explained, his piercing eyes never leaving Adratus. "We have found irrefutable proof that the attack on Port Haven was orchestrated by the Dayigan Empire via Déagrian magic."

"Oh, was it really?" Verónica scoffed. "Who would ever have guessed that?"

"*However*," the soldier resumed, "this man has still been found guilty on multiple counts of Dark Light sorcery—crimes punishable by death by burning at the stake."

"How can you say that?" Verónica objected. "I won't allow it."

The soldier's face remained stern. "My lady, such authority does not rest in your hands. Yet, His Highest Majesty, the High King of the Reyigan Empire, has deigned to generously commute his sentence under the merit that this man saved the lives of multiple people of importance. His reduced punishment shall be banishment—never again to set foot within our lands."

Verónica felt relief course through her veins, yet tempered with sorrow at Adratus's impending fate. Her heart weighed heavily with emotion, though she could find no words.

The soldier continued, "Everyone who has knowledge of this man's presence in Port Haven or who has witnessed the use of Dark Light magic here has been collected and made to take an oath never to speak of it. As far as the world is concerned, this *Tridulan* was never here and never helped in this matter. You two shall both take the same oath."

"He should be honored," Verónica said softly, looking away.

"He is correct," Adratus murmured. "'Tis better if I was never here." He raised his left hand. "I, Adratus, swear upon the flaming bident of God Zeanázel that I will never speak of how I saved the most sacred ass of the High King of the Reyigan pseudo-Empire."

The corner of Verónica's mouth twitched into a smile, despite herself.

The soldier straightened his posture a little stiffer. "I suppose that will do," he said. "You will be transported to the Vohcktaran Kingdom at once."

"And what of Lord Eadwulf?" Verónica asked.

The soldier turned to her, his face grim. "The search for him continues, my lady. However, it appears likely that he traveled south across the river into the Dayigan Empire— well away from our authority." Returning his eyes to Adratus, he continued, "If you would come with us, we can get this underway. I trust chains will be unnecessary."

Adratus nodded. "I happily depart. But my things... Verónica, I have a bag packed and ready in my room at the blacksmith's—since you evicted me. Could you retrieve it for me?"

"Of course," she said.

"You may meet him at the docks," the soldier said. "However, the ship departs soon and will not wait."

"I won't be long." Verónica hurried from the cell.

—

The wind blew against Verónica's face as she ran, a large black bag over her shoulder. She had taken too long, she feared, and she was certain that she had missed Adratus— but she searched for him, nevertheless. The cawing of gulls and the groaning of ships dominated the air, a symphony of harbored chaos that was all too familiar. But even amid the din, there was an oppressive silence that hung heavily over everyone, a sense of loss that marked every face as they somberly performed their tasks.

Verónica stopped running—he was gone, she conceded. She bleakly faced the river.

"Verónica," Adratus called, his voice cutting through the noise. He approached slowly, flanked by the three Reyigan soldiers. "I wished to bid you farewell before my departure."

"Yes," she smiled. "As did I." She looked at the soldiers. "*Alone.*"

The soldiers nodded and stepped away.

Verónica gave Adratus the bag, their eyes meeting in an unspoken bond forged through their shared fights and survival.

"I'm not sure what to say, really," Verónica began. "'Tis like the whole world is sideways. I can't believe that we've all been saved by a . . . Dark Light-tian. Lighter? What are the people of the Dark Light called, anyway?"

"You mean besides *savage?*" He grinned, and Verónica rolled her eyes. "There are many Dark Light paths," he continued, "but the proper catchall would be Diabolite. Yet, we more often identify ourselves by nation."

"And you'll be fine to get back to your nation, then? The Tridulan Empire and the Vohcktaran Kingdom are in opposite directions."

He chuckled. "'Tis not as bad as it seems. There's a—we'll say magical portal—connecting the two capital cities."

"Right. Of course." Verónica laughed. "Of course, there's a magical portal connecting the Diabolite nations. Why wouldn't there be?" She sighed, turning somber. "Magic, magic . . . magic. I've been hunted my whole life because my people condone magic, and it seems like everyone else uses it so much more." She shook her head. "Fucking Dayigans."

He leaned in close, his voice low. "The Dayigans do not hunt you because they despise magic," he said gravely. "Perhaps the commonfolk might look upon its use with disdain, but not those who wield true power over their realm."

"So why, then?" Verónica asked.

He shook his head slowly. "I have yet to determine," he confessed, reluctant to say more. After a moment of hesitation, he continued, "A more pertinent question would be: *What is a Kla?* They rule the Church of Déagar with Krasil as Supreme Patriarch. Ask any Dayigan what Krasil is and they will answer, 'He is a Kla.' Yet ask them *what is a Kla*, and they will say, 'That is what Krasil is.' All I can confirm for certain is this: they are a circle of impossibly old men whose history goes back no further than sixty years. However, decades-old accounts claim that Krasil appeared to be over one hundred years of age even then, and the other Klas were described as considerably older. Now they hold nearly all the highest seats of power in the Church of Déagar. Patriarch Krasil is but one. The College of Ocelli—the highest-ranking Déagrian clergy, second only to their patriarch—is mostly composed of Klas, including their leader, Dean Hidyark. Before their destruction, the Knights Silthex too had a Kla at their helm."

Verónica felt an uneasy chill run up her spine, despite the balmy river breeze. "I don't understand," she said, her voice laced with dread. "What exactly are these Klas? Are they even Human?"

He glanced at the awaiting soldiers before exhaling. "That is a question I have yet to answer. Whatever they are, the hate of your people began when Krasil ascended to Supreme Patriarch during the great plague."

"The Blue Death," Verónica muttered. "I've heard of it, but 'tis from before I was born. They blamed us for it."

"Prisoner!" a soldier barked from up the dock. "Wrap it up. Our ship is leaving soon."

Verónica pressed her hand to her forehead, thoughts racing as her heart pounded in her chest.

"Apologies," Adratus said. "I should not have overburdened you without answers to give."

"Quite all right. I was actually worried that I might run out of things to worry about."

"I'm pleased I could help," he said. "Before I depart, I want you to have something." He crouched to dig through the black bag she had brought him and soon stood, presenting a small wooden box.

Verónica smiled. "The box my brother gave me."

"You did say you wished it returned. Look inside."

She opened the lid to find a gray stone, smooth and flat and the size of her palm.

"'Tis a whisper stone," Adratus explained. "If ever you need my help, place it in a bowl of oil—preferably a copper bowl and olive oil, but any will do. Light the oil on fire and speak my name three times into the flames."

"Prisoner!" the soldier called again with a sharper voice. "Your time is up."

"Afterwards," Adratus continued, "either speak your message directly into the flames or use them to burn a page holding it, and I will receive it—at least I will, once I get another stone."

Verónica kissed Adratus's cheek. "My thanks for all that you have done for us. I won't forget your kindness, and someday, I hope to repay it."

"Unneeded," he said solemnly. "And I fear you have greater concerns. The Dayigan attack on Port Haven nullifies the Dayigan/Reyigan treaty. 'Twould appear your new empire is born at war."

Verónica sighed and nodded, casting her eyes to the waters of the Hyvile as she clutched the box. "Born at war, just like me, hated by the Déagrians from the first moment I cried out in the midwife's arm because my very existence challenged their twisted faith. And also like me, our empire will carry on, keep fighting, and grow strong."

With a somber nod, Adratus muttered, "May God Karulus keep you well." He turned and joined the soldiers at the awaiting ship that would take him far from Port Haven.

Verónica watched in silence as they made their way up the wooden ramp and boarded the vessel.

She couldn't help but feel sorrow. He had risked so much for her town, and while she knew that his departure was necessary, it still left a void within her.

As sails unfurled and the ship slowly began departing from the harbor, Verónica couldn't look away, continuing to watch as the ship grew smaller down the river.

"May the Gods watch over you, Adratus," Verónica murmured, her gaze fixed on the ship. ". . . whichever Gods that may be."

Devoid of Gray

Reyigo
Reyigan Empire
Freloh Lands
Caróg Lands
Allar Lands
Rúcah Lands
Feah Lands
Voho
Hyvile River
Dinikimera
N
W
E
S
0   30   60   90
Miles

CHAPTER FORTY-TWO

Dekiés 30, 839: Two Years Later

Their steady sandals struck the gravel like claps of cadenced thunder. The clinking of their black steel, segmented armor was like metallic rain. Through wilderness ripped in twain by their newly constructed road, this army of darkness, composed of six thousand Human legionaries and support, marched on.

The mighty sound vibrated through Adratus as he rode ahorse before them. It reverberated down into the depths of his soul, like rumbling pulses of supremacy.

Even now, Adratus recalled how it felt to be a boy within those ranks, to feel, for the first time, what it was to be part of such a mighty totality. His blood had coursed with fire. He'd felt secure in ways never known before. And proud. So strong.

But no longer a boy, Adratus rode before this juggernaut and outranked the thousands within, second only to the legion commander.

The legion commander, Legate Maximus, was a stern, dark-skinned man of fifty with a hard face and dark eyes. Like that of Adratus, his breastplate was formed to resemble a muscular man's torso—though his was of black steel over a red tunic, while Adratus's was silver over black. Centered on the metal chest of both was the infernal symbol, the Triébis, formed as three number twos carved with their bases joined as a triangle—the mark of the Dark Light Gods to whom the Demons bowed.

Adratus gazed past Maximus, off into the virgin forest ablaze with leaves of orange and yellow. It had never known the entrance of men until now—at least not civilized men. Did Faeries roam therein, Adratus wondered, within the thick shadows undefeated by the sun?

For hours, he'd listened to the regular thunder of sandals and hooves on gravel as he'd trekked deeper and deeper into the wilds. Same as yesterday. And the day before. Nearly a month had passed since the proper sound of marching on the stone roads of civilization.

The standard-bearers marched before them, and Adratus proudly watched the flag of his homeland flapping in the autumn wind. The red square of cloth displayed the same symbol as on his chest—the Triébis—in black. Two circles around it. Below it, the words "TRASILON ETERNAL" in grave black print.

He grinned.

"Pray, why do you smirk so, mighty Adratus?" Legate Maximus asked. "Have you beheld humor I noticed not? Share it, and alleviate the boredom of this march."

"'Tis not in jest I smile, Legate, but in pride. We are not long from our destination, and soon we will introduce a new people to the dark majesty that is our mighty empire."

"Yes," Maximus said with a sigh. "Alas, I hold not the same joy in our arrival. Between you and me, Brother, I say damn the Drevites. Let the dirty barbarians fight their own fucking war. And leave us to our own."

"If I may differ," Adratus said, "'tis but two fronts of the same war, with the Dayigans the shared foe."

"Ever the loyalist." Maximus chuckled. "But I need no reminding of His Imperial Majesty's words. I beheld the speech alongside you."

"And yet you forget this new campaign is meant as a reward for victories past. 'Twill be great here, Legate. I know it."

Maximus chuckled lightly. "I shall not quell delight if delight you have," he said. He then lifted his hands and raised his voice mockingly, saying, "Let the empire say of me, 'All hail Maximus, lord of the mudmongers!'" He glanced at Adratus. "But I cannot help but fear our reward may be more of vinegar than wine."

"Legate!" An urgent call came from up ahead, from two of the legion's outriders, who approached on galloping horses.

The outrider pulled at his horse's reins, stopping before the leaders. "Apologies, sir," he said, calmer, though not calm. He touched his fist to his chest and bowed his head. "I bear distressing news, Legate."

"Continue."

"'Tis the Drevites, sir. They are in arms against our engineers, hindering the construction of our road."

"What numbers?"

"Barely fifty, sir," said the legionary. "Our advanced forces keep them at bay. Yet we stand uncertain how to engage. You charge us to protect these same people who attack."

"By all that is infernal," Maximus cursed as he clenched his fist to his brow. He turned to Adratus. "As I said, more of vinegar."

"By such words you hexed us, Legate," Adratus quipped, "and the result is quick." He motioned to the sky, where, some few feet above the highest trees, five men approached in flight.

They were Terovaes—the race accounting for nearly all the Drevites. And in traditional Drevite fashion, these here were long haired and naked from the waist up. Below, they wore thick belts and kilts of brown leather. Most of their visible skin, head to toe, was marked with thick tribal designs of dark purple ink.

"Are you the one leading this here army?" bellowed a Terovae warrior, his wings like a falcon's—in brown with touches of white—matching his hair in dreadlocks bound as a sloppy ponytail.

Maximus and Adratus looked up at the source of these words and glanced irritably at one another.

"I'll be asking you again now," yelled the Terovae at the front of the flying wedge, "are you the one—"

"I will not address you," Maximus shouted, "whilst you flutter above me like some *pigeon*. Alight, so we may talk as men and resolve this unfortunate situation."

The Terovaes shared momentary glances. Then three, including the one who'd spoken, descended, and landed in front of Maximus and Adratus.

"You are responsible for the attacks on my men," the legate demanded without wait. "Why?"

"I am . . ." The Terovae stood taller. "I am Lann of the Feah, one of the five tribes that ye be calling the Drevites. This be our land here, handed down from the ancestors to us. The trees. The rivers. The forest and all of it. But ye come around, chopping out your fucking road through our sacred places. We say we don't want ye here. We say, ye best be getting on your way back where ye came from."

Maximus rolled his eyes as he sighed. He then raised his voice with forced diplomacy, saying, "Fear not, native people of these lands, for you are without reason. We are *friends* from the far, far east, from the great *Tridulan Empire*, the paradigm of civilization. The Drevite chief, known as Kaie, called out for aid in your people's conflicts with the Dayigan Empire. Thus, we came. Do you understand? Do you know *Kaie*?"

"We know Kaie, aye, right well." Lann's words were bitter but controlled as he locked eyes with Maximus. "Kaie is chief of the Feah lands. And we know that wicked symbol on your wicked flag there."

"Excellent," Maximus said. "I am glad we have that straightened. 'Twill save some trouble, no doubt."

The barbarian man drew a simple mace, gripping it tightly as his eyes stared with hate and his teeth clenched. "We might have been needing help before when we was desperate, but never from some Dark Light goat fuckers that come here defiling our sacred forest! Get back where ye came from."

The legate sighed. "These people have lost their minds. Adratus, disarm and capture the *Lann* person."

"Yes, Legate." His eyes narrowed as he thrust his left hand toward Lann, and from his fingertips shot five flickering cords of red light.

The first cord encircled the mace, snatching it from the wielder. The others cuffed the man's wrists and ankles.

Lann struggled against the cords, his face flickering and contorted in red light. He spread his large, brown wings and tried to fly away, lifting himself a few feet from the ground, fighting madly. But the scarlet cords were strong, firmly tethering every limb.

Again, Lann cried out, but another sound, equally distressed, came from above. The single word "No!" called out with such concern as to distract Adratus from his doings. He looked up.

Within those Terovaes who hovered above the trees was a male youth, about twenty. His wings and long, dirty hair were both ginger. Adratus knew it must have been him who'd called out, for his eyes still held horror, even as he held an arrow firmly nocked at his drawn bowstring. His eyes, blue and sad, entranced Adratus.

The pale skin of his lean body was not covered in tattoos like those of the others. Only a seven-pointed star marked his bare semi-muscular chest. Even from Adratus's distance, he could see the star moving with quick breaths.

"Adratus!" Maximus interrupted his thoughts. "Your magic falters."

The prefect's eyes snapped from the youth to the man still held within his cords of light. "Apologies, Legate."

"'Tis no matter," he said, bored. "Point is made. Release him."

Adratus complied, and the cords vaporized.

Lann fell to the gravel of the unfinished road and then pushed himself up on his hands and knees. He rubbed his wrists as he panted.

"Now," Maximus began, speaking down to the Drevite. "I will finish my road to my intended destination, build a camp, bathe, and relax until I am ready for sleep. If you wish time to discuss opinions on the Tridulan presence in this region, I suggest you arrange an audience after tomorrow morn. Understood, Lann the Drevite?"

"I do, aye." He panted, still rubbing his wrists.

Adratus stole another glance up at the Terovae who'd intrigued him.

Though he had lowered his bow, the young man looked at the Tridulans as if they were vile.

Adratus blinked downward, ashamed.

"Fly away, Lann the Drevite." Maximus waved him away. "Go tell the men attacking my engineers to retreat. If again they attack, I will crucify every one of them without hesitation."

Lann stood to his feet but only stared blankly forward, not looking up to those atop horses. "Aye." His tone, defeated.

"Legate," Adratus spoke up. "Would it not behoove us to collect collateral? To assure his word is kept."

"Very well." The legate glanced curiously at his second-in-command. "What have you in mind?"

Adratus looked up at the Terovae who had caught his attention. And the Tridulan thrust his left hand forward and cast cords of light, shooting out to surround the Terovae and secure his arms and wings. Though there was no pain in this confinement, the captured youth struggled and called out.

"*Ubaz!*" Lann shouted. "Let him be, you liver-chomping ogre!"

Adratus did not relent. The man had intrigued him, and he could not let him fly away. Thus, Adratus plucked him from the sky and pulled him to himself.

"I suggest you hurry," Maximus said to Lann. "Assuming you wish the boy to continue breathing."

Adratus set the Terovae on the ground beside his horse, and the light hardened, becoming a circle of copper chains around the prisoner's waist, arms, and wings.

Lann's gaze lingered on the younger Terovae, a helpless, apologetic look, before his angered eyes turned to Maximus. "By the Three Mothers, I vow, I'm not done with ye yet, you be sure." He leaped up, spreading his brown wings to fly away.

The other Drevites followed.

Once the Terovaes had flown, Adratus turned to Maximus. "'Twould seem we've been thrust into an extensive clusterfuck, Legate."

"Funny"—the legate chuckled—"I have suddenly begun enjoying myself." He glanced down at the chained Terovae and back to Adratus. "I assume your motives for collecting this barbarian are carnal. Yet, I have another use in mind.

Tell me, Drevite"—with his ebony staff, he harshly tapped the prisoner's shoulder—"know you where to find Chief Kaie?"

The Drevite glared upward, his blue eyes burning with hate. He nodded, once.

"Excellent," Maximus said. "Go, mighty Adratus. Have the boy show you to his chief. I must know if this attack upon us is of isolated rebels or actions representing the majority of the Drevites."

CHAPTER FORTY-THREE

On foot, Adratus and the Drevite trudged through the untamed wilderness. No roads were here, not even paths. A horse would be of little use—he'd left it back with the legion. The air was cold and damp on Adratus's face, but within his heavy steel armor, his skin was slick with sweat. He ignored it and pressed on, circumventing mighty trees—some as thick as two chariots combined. Their incredible heights almost seemed to reach the heavens.

The steel of Adratus's gladius cut through the oppressive underbrush as he moved ever forward. The ancient woods were alive, humming with a chorus of insects and ringing out with the occasional shrieks of startled birds disturbed by their intrusion. Each step Adratus made sent crisp leaves crunching beneath his sandals and echoing loudly in the solitude.

"Have you a name, boy?"

The Drevite said nothing. He'd barely spoken the entire venture save for intermittent mutterings of "turn up here" and "we follow this here stream 'til it curves."

Occasionally, Adratus scanned the twenty-year-old Terovae: the dirty ginger hair that hung straight just past his bare shoulders, the strange, purple, seven-pointed star tattooed on his upper chest. He scanned his body itself. Attractive. Distracting. Copper chains still circled him, keeping his arms and orange wings secure. A thin line of orange hairs centered down his pale stomach, trailing beneath the kilt's low waistline. The sights only added to the heat swelling in Adratus as his mind wandered.

"Very well, hold your tongue if it pleases you," Adratus grumbled after a wait. "I meant the question as naught but conversation. For already, I know what you are called."

"Do you now? And what might that be? Barbarian, like your chief was calling me?"

"Ubaz," Adratus said flatly. "It was the word the other Drevite called when I captured you. I cannot think what it could mean, but your name."

The Terovae said nothing. He walked on.

After a few more paces, Ubaz spoke up, saying, "I see how you're looking at me, lustful like."

Adratus laughed. "You are pleasing to behold. Does it bother you?"

"I'm *bothered* that I'm chained up by you," he responded angrily. "Would you release me? *Please*," Ubaz gritted, his tone maintaining hate. "I give you my word by the Three Mothers, I'll not be attacking you."

"Attacking me?" Adratus scoffed.

"Or running off."

"I know nothing of the Three Mothers," Adratus said dismissively and continued walking.

"The Three True Light Mothers, they're called." Ubaz caught up with him. "Lágeya, mother of the seas and waters that nourish us and connect us all. Larissa, mother of the land, the home, and the hearth. Ashatra, mother of the sky, the breath in us all, and the soul. They're worshiped by my people. I vow to them that I won't be running off. And that I'll carry on leading you to our Chief Kaie. But the village is near now, and I . . ." He looked down.

". . . don't appreciate how fashionable chains are?" Adratus asked with a chuckle. "That is very realistic copper. Perhaps your entire village will be awed and wish for a personal set."

"'Tis nothing to be joking about, you Human cock. 'Twould be a dishonor. Do you even know what that means?"

Adratus paused, a tense, thick silence as he thought. The wind blew chill.

"In the Tréréaldéag," Ubaz began somberly. "That is, in the sacred guidance handed down by the Three Mothers, it says, '*Keep true to oaths, for he whose word is meaningless is meaningless, himself, and cannot be trusted.*' Believe me when I vow to you."

Adratus scanned the bound Terovae. He moved his hand very near the smooth chest, pausing before touching the copper chains. They crumbled and blew away, dissolving as glittered air.

Ubaz spread his amber feathered wings to full span, stretching a moment before he refolded them to his back.

"Better?" Adratus asked.

"Aye. Fecking grand," he said. "I suppose you're wanting me to thank you for taking off the chains you put on me in the first place? Don't hold your breath now."

"Just lead on," Adratus grumbled, despite his moving forward without him.

Ubaz walked on, passing him to enter a dirt path that Adratus soon realized was no path through empty forest. It was the main thoroughfare of a village hidden away in the wilderness. Narrow footpaths meandered off between the trees, while small huts were barely visible among the thick foliage, squeezed into whatever recess involved the least alteration to the woods. The dwellings lacked doors, and some were little more than canopies of logs and sticks.

All the people who Adratus and Ubaz passed were Terovaes. All but the youngest had at least some purple markings on their skins.

A woman caught the Tridulan's attention, and he followed her with his eyes as she flew high, traversing a flock of blackbirds before alighting on the thick bough of a towering orange-canopied tree. She had a hut there within the tree, and Adratus spotted other homes built up high.

Everyone who saw the heavily armored Human paused in whatever he or she was doing to stare. Some peered from the corners of their eyes, while others landed on lower branches, crouching like Faeries in the shadows. Most did not even attempt to hide their curiosity.

To the amusement of Adratus, only two people paid him no attention whatsoever: two men. One was pressed against a tree, while the second was pressed against him, kissing him deeply. Their lustful hands explored each other's sweaty skin.

Adratus chuckled at the sight, saying to Ubaz, "I suppose 'tis true what they say: 'Although Drevite women are fair indeed, the Drevite men prefer each other's flesh.'"

"That's not the case . . . for most. But for some . . ." Ubaz ran his eyes down the legionary's body. "For some, aye, 'tis true. You're one to be talking though, Human. You meant to bugger me in the woods back there."

The words removed the Tridulan's smile. Heat flashed through him as he scanned the nearly naked barbarian. "Is that what you wanted?"

"I—em . . ." Ubaz started as he bit his lip. He then grew angry. "Feck off, you. I'd never bed a wingless, fecking Human. I'd rather be tied up to a tree and eaten alive by mad vultures."

Angered, Adratus jumped in front of him, grabbing him by the shoulders. "You disrespect me without end," he growled into his face. "And I will have no more of it. We are not aggressors in this event. We came here, to the bowels of the wilds, to help the Drevite Nation. Yet you attack us." He shoved the Drevite, causing him to stumble back a few steps. "Your anger is baseless."

Ubaz's eyes burned with rage. "You're a Human," he snarled. "Humans be invading our villages and slaying us 'cause they say we're foul and wicked and don't deserve to be alive. They take our loved ones..." He hung his head in solemn silence, as his blazing fury simmered down into cold ashes of sorrow.

Adratus did not ask who'd been taken. Given the region's history, he assumed it was more than one. Instead, he was quiet. Still. Allowing the sad youth to regain himself.

A Terovae man approached. "This Human bothering you, Ubaz?"

Ubaz looked up and shook his head. "I'm all right. Thank you, though."

Frozen, Adratus looked at Ubaz, so much more vulnerable with his shield of anger lowered. The Human brushed the Terovae's limp hair behind his ear. He then cradled his jaw in his palm, turning Ubaz's head to face him.

"You speak of the Dayigan Empire and their hateful crusades," Adratus said softly, looking deeply into sad eyes. "Not us. I assure you, the Tridulan Empire is not like them."

Ubaz shoved his hand away. "Not like them or us, either." He motioned to the Triébis engraved in black in the center of Adratus's shining steel breastplate.

"It is the symbol of defiance," Adratus began, "the first lesson of the Dark Light Gods—never obey without thought, not even the words of the Gods."

"No," Ubaz said. He crossed his arms. "'Tis a sorrowful symbol that. The symbol of the moment when the entire world of Perdinok fell lost into darkness." He went silent for a moment, eyes darting up and down the Tridulan soldier as if trying to decipher an enigma. "I'm supposed to believe what then?" Ubaz said calmly, though with anger just below the surface. "You'll be our . . . *salvation.*"

"I hope so."

Ubaz scoffed. "Right. That's what the other Humans said last time. Before they massacred our people. You're all alike, you. Fucking Humans." He turned and walked away. "Well, come on then."

He approached a large hill. However, as Adratus neared, he soon realized the hill was not a hill at all but a dome structure, two hundred feet across and thirty feet high, covered in tall grass. A cluster of small trees grew near its apex.

The path ended at its steps, formed of thin slate stacked in such a way as to appear as if a natural part of a hill. They rose three feet to a rectangular opening framed by three massive stones, with a stone-framed transom above it. He and Ubaz entered.

—

Adratus stood in awed silence, his gaze sweeping the mysterious chamber within the ancient hill temple. Guided by Ubaz, they had descended a long, slightly curved ramp from the surface to reach this cavernous hall. The left wall was cloaked in thick vines, adorned with strange magenta flowers that glowed with otherworldly light. Above them, simple chandeliers made of brushed brass hung from the rafters, their flickering candles casting eerie shadows.

But it was the display on Adratus's right that drew his attention. Wooden shelves, standing ten feet tall and set along the curved outer wall, displayed row upon row of skulls.

"Your people have many enemies," Adratus remarked with a smirk.

"No." Ubaz's eyes gleamed for the first time. "These are our most revered ancestors, the bravest and wisest amongst us. We seek their guidance in times of need." His words were passionate, and Adratus couldn't help but be captivated by his fervor. "There is no greater honor than to be granted a place here amongst these hallowed walls.

"Come here to me," Ubaz beckoned, approaching one of the shelves. "See how each skull is intricately carved, a unique work of art lovingly tended to by our druidesses every day. Not a speck of dust can be found on a one of them. I could tell you a thousand tales about these noble and grand people you're standing surrounded by. Like this one down here—" He darted down a few feet to another shelf. "This one is said to be the very first—"

"Apologies," Adratus cut him off. "Another time, perhaps. Now, I must visit your chief."

The young man's excitement melted as he nodded. He then scanned the soldier.

"You . . ." Ubaz's pale cheeks flushed as he averted his gaze from Adratus. "You can't be wearing your—em . . ." He cleared his throat. "You can't wear your armor into the Temple Grove, you know."

Adratus was silent a moment, grin growing wide as he basked in the charming bashfulness that had washed over Ubaz. "Can I not?" he taunted playfully.

Ubaz shook his head. "We'll need to be going in here first," Ubaz said shyly, before heading to a low doorway through the wall of shelves.

They entered a dimly lit room, the air filled with the scent of fresh water. An ornate brass spout poured water into a small basin, while three natural sponges sat on a large rock nearby.

Ubaz approached a wooden shelf and retrieved two folded white linens. "We have special temple garments." He returned with the cloths lying over his arm.

"Very well." Adratus unfastened his black cape and folded it. "Where should I . . ."

Ubaz, his nerves getting the best of him, flung his free hand toward the opposite wall covered in wooden pigeonholes.

"Jumpy?" Adratus teased as he set his cape within the cubby.

"Feck off, Human," Ubaz retorted with a scowl.

Adratus unfastened his breastplate and placed it in one of the pigeonholes on the wall, followed by his other armor, belts, sandals, and weapons.

As he stood before Ubaz in only his unbelted black tunic, he couldn't help but notice the youth's silence and his unbreaking stare. Ubaz stood frozen, his arm still outstretched under the linens like a garment-holding statue. He licked his lips unconsciously, unable to tear his gaze away from Adratus, as he longingly awaited.

Adratus asked, "Do only foreigners need to change?"

The stillness shattered, Ubaz became a flurry of stutters and fumbles. He awkwardly tried to place the linens somewhere, yet he couldn't quite figure out what to do with them as he simultaneously attempted to undo the buckle of his kilt. "I shouldn't have grabbed the garments 'til we were . . ."

"Naked?" Adratus offered with a smirk.

Ubaz nodded as he clutched the cloths to his chest, while he also pulled at his buckle.

With one swift motion, Adratus removed his tunic, revealing his chiseled and shaved body beneath.

Ubaz froze again, his arms dropping at his sides. The sacred linens fell to the stone floor. His eyes lingered, unblinking, on the legionary.

"Now who looks at who?" Adratus smiled as he walked forward.

"You . . ." Ubaz licked his lips, then bit them to stop himself. "You're still wearing a ring there."

"Not where you look."

Ubaz looked up. His eyes were lost in lust. His mouth parted as he breathed slowly and deeply.

"The ring is fused to my finger," Adratus said.

Ubaz nodded stupidly. "Right. Course."

The prefect was certain that he could have given any answer and received the same response.

Adratus touched the buckle of Ubaz's kilt, and the Terovac's body jolted. Nevertheless, Ubaz locked his eyes on the soldier's, pleading eyes above a mouth that begged to be kissed.

The soldier gradually released the buckle, and the leather kilt thumped to Ubaz's ankles, releasing the warrior's prick to spring up, hitting Adratus's wrist with its wet tip peeking from skin.

Mortified, Ubaz recoiled and tried to hide himself with his hands.

Adratus only watched him, thinking him all the more adorable for his bashfulness. Yet, even as he covered himself, there was a primal desire burning in Ubaz's eyes, calling out to Adratus just as fiercely as if it were spoken aloud.

"'Tis all right," Adratus said with a grin as he kissed his own wrist. "I'll turn away."

"No." Ubaz paused as if trying to think. His head lowered, but his bold gaze never wavered from the nude legionary before him. "You..." He swallowed. "You can look at me. If you're wanting to." And with those words, his hands parted slowly, sliding around his legs to hang at his sides. "Not that I'm much to see."

Now, Adratus could take in the full display of Ubaz's stunning body—his handsome face, athletic chest, lean pale stomach centered by a trail of fiery orange hair that led from his navel downward to, Adratus now saw, orange curls from which his rigid manhood stood.

Adratus, too, had grown achingly aroused, this only exacerbated as he gazed. The prefect hurried forward, wrapping his arms around him and pressing their bodies together— swords crossed between them. Ubaz shuddered in response, seeming ready to burst before they'd begun.

But then, without warning, Ubaz began pushing Adratus away. Adratus released him and stepped back.

"Fucking Human," Ubaz spat, his eyes filled with a mix of desire and anger. He approached Adratus, only to shove him.

"What?" Adratus asked.

"You're what, Human. Mixing up my head like that. What was I thinking?"

Adratus glared at Ubaz a moment longer before he snatched the temple garment up from the floor and walked away.

CHAPTER FORTY-FOUR

Silent and seething, Adratus trailed behind Ubaz—both men now wearing only simple white linen skirts—as they entered the large stone-framed entrance of the grand chamber at the heart of the temple.

Despite his simmering irritation toward Ubaz, Adratus couldn't help but feel a surge of blissful energy wash over him as they stepped into the tranquil atmosphere of the inner sanctum. The lush green grass beneath his bare feet soothed his troubled mind, while the sweet melody of a small harp filled the towering walls of the hundred-foot-wide heptagonal room.

At its center stood seven ancient oaks, their branches interwoven above to twist around the black wooden rafters of the dome ceiling. From those branches hung countless orbs of delicate, lavender light.

Ubaz led him into the sacred circle of trees, where twelve maidens dressed in flowing white gowns sat in meditative poses. Their wings, ranging in hues from red to deep brown, were spread wide behind them. Faces serene and eyes closed, they exuded an aura of complete tranquility.

The maidens encircled a thirteen-foot monolith made of rough gray stone, its sides etched with the same symbol that adorned Ubaz's chest—a seven-pointed star surrounding three spirals converging at their shared center. The symbol glimmered with a soft purple glow.

Before the monolith sat a stone altar, resembling a large table adorned with offerings of apples, turnips, small cakes, and a brass bowl filled to the brim with acorns, all laid out on a bed of autumn leaves.

The authoritative voice of a woman echoed through the chamber. "So, you've brought our lost guardian back to us. I give you my thanks."

Adratus looked up to see the woman seated atop the monolith. Directly above her, a circular opening in the dome revealed a clear blue sky. The portal, thirteen feet wide and ten feet thick, was guarded by brushed brass bars forming the shape of a seven-pointed star. This star was set within a brass spiral.

"Elations you are pleased, madam. I *gladly* return him," Adratus replied with a vexed glance at Ubaz. Turning back to the woman, he said, "I am Adratus, Camp Prefect of the Ninth Legion. I seek an audience with Kaie, Chief of the Drevites."

"Chief of the Drevites?" She laughed. "Mothers help us."

With a graceful leap, she descended, spreading her silver wings before landing gently in front of Adratus. Her hair matched her wings in color, though she appeared to be in her late thirties. She was clothed in a long cloak made of luxurious gray and white fur and adorned with elegant bone jewelry.

"I am Kaie, Archdruidess of the Feah Temple of the Three Mothers and Chief Tierna of the Feah lands. And what a sight *you* are." She grinned. "I've seen Humans can get thicker muscles than Terovaes, but you, sir, are like a mighty bear, with river rocks as a stomach." She slapped his core.

Adratus, locking his hands behind his back, stood straight and reported, "As legionaries, we must ever remain combat ready, madam. For the honor of the Empire."

"Is it so?" She grasped his bicep. "And what empire is that then?"

He stood taller. "The only *valid* empire, madam. The great Tridulan Empire."

"Tridulan? By the Mothers, is that not all the way across the whole Dayigan Empire?"

"It is, madam. Beyond the Dayigans and beyond the Gellic Nation, too. As far east as one could travel without falling off the edge of the continent. Yet we possess a . . . let us say 'magical portal,' that allows us to travel from our capital to the capital of your neighboring nation, the Vohcktaran Kingdom. From there, we built a road straight here."

She continued to circle him, scanning him as if he were a piece in a museum. "Don't Human men have . . ." She brushed his cheek with her fingertips. "*Beard?*" She said it like a foreign word, and Adratus realized he'd seen no bearded Terovaes, either in Drevite lands or elsewhere.

"'Tis regulation, madam. Legionaries must keep their hair short and remain sheered, face and below."

"Below?" She grinned slyly as she glanced down him.

"We've come in response to your call for help," he said. "You sent a messenger to Vohcktara, correct? Yet already, your people met our benevolence with attack."

"From Lann, Chief," Ubaz added. "Humans cannot be trusted in our lands."

"Lann?" Kaie repeated, obviously disturbed. "Aye, he's never been quite right since the troubles years back. And I'm guessing that's where you ran off to—helping your uncle with this foolishness?"

"I have, aye, Chief." Ubaz nodded curtly. "The Humans must be stopped, or they'll ruin our woods and strip us of our ways. He hates the Humans, Chief. With rightful cause."

"With misguided cause," Adratus interjected. "As I said, we have come to help."

Kaie looked at him another moment before producing a knowing grin. "You think me a fool, Human? Why have your people come here?"

Adratus studied the chief. "For years, I have overseen an investigation into the Dayigans and have come to the conclusion that they move towards actions that will be detrimental to the entire continent of Bikia—or at least East Bikia. Somehow, the Drevite Nation is key to their plans. Thus, 'twould be advantageous to secure this region before they gain control."

"Secure?"

"Protect your people and assure the Dayigans stay away. I assume this is a goal you and I share."

Chief Kaie crossed her arms, thinking. "And what's all this 'detrimental actions' that you mention?"

"I've yet to determine. Judging by the Dayigans' history, I suspect it will be *unpleasant*. They tend to burn those with whom they disagree."

Kaie nodded solemnly. "You're not wrong there." She turned to Ubaz. "And what're your thoughts on this?"

"They're Humans, plain and simple." He glanced toward Adratus before continuing. "Last we let Humans into Feah lands, we were nearly wiped out by them. We already know all too well from what's happened before that the Humans—"

"*Dayigans*," Adratus growled.

"*Humans*"—Ubaz maintained—"cannot be trusted."

Kaie was silent for a moment, a contemplative silence with a stern face. "Thank ye for coming, but you must realize the whole matter is well complicated. We be good, True Light folk, just like the Dayigans claim to be. But one day, they jumped in their boats, sailed up the Hyvile River, and talked us into some trade post we never needed or wanted here. After that, they got to capturing our people, without warning or provocation. *Our people.* They traveled miles to come to *our* shores because they knew no one would care what happened to the 'savage Drevites.' And lo and behold, they were right. We sent messengers to the surrounding True Light nations." She sighed. "They all sent us away. We aren't quite True Light enough for the True Light, it seems. The raids on our people carried on 'til finally, in desperation, I called upon the Dark Light." She glanced down. "'Twas a mistake, that."

"A mistake?" Adratus asked with an arch of his eyebrow.

"It was, yes." She nodded. "I never dreamt ye'd come so far. I wish I could give you more than an apology, but we're not needing your help anymore. The last attack was eight years back now."

"You think they are finished with you?" Adratus scoffed. "Just like that? Never mind the Drevites? The Dayigans ignore you, and us, because they now focus their troops on the Reyigan Empire."

"The *Reyigan* Empire?" She glanced at Ubaz to receive a shrug.

"Yes, madam. The Karulent Alliance reformed into the Reyigan Empire in response to years of tensions with the Dayigans. Tridual could not send you aid whilst we battled the Dayigans, yet now—with the Dayigan Army refocused— we come."

Kaie shook her head. "Empires, empires," she said. "All these kings these days wanting to prove who has the biggest this and that."

"I assure you, madam," Adratus said firmly, "the Tridulan Empire does, in fact, have the biggest *this and that*. And by order of His Imperial Majesty, the Ninth Legion may remain stationed here indefinitely. The Dayigans will not focus on the Reyigans forever. Would you turn us away and live in fear?"

"Eight years ago," she said, "I would have welcomed ye here with arms open wide. But aye . . . aye, ye have my leave to stay here."

"Feck sakes," Ubaz mumbled.

"Gratitude, Chief. The—"

"However," she cut him off, "when it comes to the desire of the 'Drevite Nation,' there's not one. Because there hasn't been a nation by that name in ages. We're five separate lands here, each with its own chief to govern it. So if you're wanting an alliance, you'll be needing the consent of the other four chief tiernas as well.

"Ubaz," she continued, "since you've already made good friends with these Humans, I'm assigning you as our representative to them."

"Begging your pardon, Chief, but that's bollocks." Ubaz started. "I cannot be looking after a bunch of wingless invaders in our lands."

"Temple guardian . . ." She shot him a stern look.

"Yes, Chief."

Adratus glanced sideways at Ubaz and crossed his arms. "We need no escort."

"The decision's been made," said the chief. "And he's not just your escort. He can advise you well in the ways of our region. Maybe," Kaie sighed as she turned slightly away, "it *is* best for the Five Tribes to come together as one."

And here's the *inside* of my house," Ubaz said, as Adratus ducked through the low doorway of thick, rugged beams. "Sorry, 'tis wrecked. I wasn't planning to have guests over."

Ubaz was in the room a step or two from the doorway.

Adratus had seen from outside that the hut was half submerged, carved into a hill at the base of a gigantic tree. The inside followed what he'd expected. The walls remained natural dirt, with spindly, spidery roots dangling here and there. A few areas were fortified with mud bricks, particularly around the fireplace and the room's upper sections above the hill.

Adratus found himself slouching without genuine cause. The ceiling, though low, was a few inches above his head when he stood upright and was composed of crisscrosses of branches tied together as an uneven frame. Above it, the roof was evidently whatever forest items worked and were available. It was not quite organized enough to be truly called a thatch roof, but Adratus guessed it fit some loose definition. Living vines twisted within it.

"'Tis not much to look at, I know, but it does the job," Ubaz said. "As the temple guardian, I'm allowed a place in the temple, but..." He glanced down. "...there's too many memories in there. Back when the Dayigans attacked, me mam was second-in-command of the Feah under Chief Kaie, and me da was the temple guardian. We all lived there, in the temple. They... Sorry." He took a deep breath. "This place serves me good enough now."

The modest furnishings were plain and worn. Two benches by a small table offered seating. A bookcase held little knickknacks—mostly carved stones with runes or spiral designs—and three books.

Adratus eyed the mound of fur-topped straw at the farthest wall. "Your bed is in the front room?" he asked.

"There's only the one room here. All we Feahs—all the Five Tribes, really—live mostly outside. Inside's only for sleeping and storing a few personal things."

"One room. One bed." Adratus laughed.

"No," Ubaz said rather abruptly, instantly flustered. "I mean—em . . ." He swallowed as his eyes trailed up and down the Tridulan prefect.

"You are maddening when you're confounded."

"Maddening?"

"Enjoyably so," Adratus said. "I will have the floor."

"You won't, no. You're the guest here—whether I'm liking it or not. I'll be fine on the floor."

"Whatever the case," Adratus said, "it seems early for talks of slumber. 'Tis but twilight. Do Drevites sleep so early?"

Now Ubaz laughed, which seemed to relax him. "We do not. And we'll be staying up much later than normal tonight as well. Tonight's a grand celebration, and Chief Kaie wants me to show it to you."

"Ah. You celebrate the arrival of our legion. I wish I'd known to invite the legate."

Ubaz paused for a moment, seemingly attempting to read if Adratus was serious.

"'Tis not to celebrate—" Ubaz began. "I do believe you're a fair bit vain, Prefect. 'Tis the Threshold Fair tonight, ya silly eejit, when the walls between the worlds thin. I've just come home to change into costume. Don't you worry, though; the chief has someone coming 'round to bring you something too. Should be here real shortly now."

Ubaz dashed to the side of the room and grabbed up a log. "And I've come to get this." He bounced it on his palms. "For the fire."

Adratus looked at the hearth. It was not only empty, but also cleaned out as much as something like that could be: black, but a smooth black.

"Not for that one," Ubaz said. "At least not exactly. All throughout the Feah lands, there'll be nine great bonfires tonight—one in each parish. Same in all the Five Tribes and their parishes. And everyone will flock to the nearest one for the fair. When 'tis all finished—well after midnight—everyone'll take a coal from the fire to bring it home to their own hearth. Then everyone will be kept warm and safe with one united fire."

Ubaz glanced out the doorway, where little of the sun remained. "But we've no time to be talking about it. We best hurry."

—

Adratus couldn't tear his eyes away from the mesmerizing sight of Ubaz standing as a dark silhouette against the blazing hilltop bonfire. With a log held high above his head, the Terovae called out ancient prayers to a True Light hearth Goddess, who—he'd explained—protected them from dark Faeries.

Clad only in a scanty green loincloth and crowned with a wreath of autumn leaves, Ubaz's body glistened in the dancing flames and was painted with intricate swirls and spirals of deep purple ash. His wings, spread wide, were adorned with vibrant ribbons that fluttered in the wind. And yet, it was his face that held Adratus captive: handsome and resolute, bathed in the fiery light as he fervently implored for protection.

It was the same ardor marking all the Drevites who came to add their logs to the fire. They, too, had donned various Faery guises, some nothing more than body paint. Yet, by the sacred fire, they were solemn, each in his or her private moment. Each pleading for help.

Adratus felt as if he intruded by watching, yet he could not turn away. There was beauty in their appeals. And the soldier wondered if their calls for protection truly extended well beyond the traditions of warding off Faeries.

Ubaz threw his log into the fire, stirring up swirls of orange embers.

He turned to Adratus and, after a breath, gained a large smile. "Your horn seems to be falling down on you, Prefect," Ubaz said.

Adratus wore tight trousers of spotted deer fur, laced up the side, and set low on his waist. Above the waist, he wore nothing but a leather headband holding two antler points, each set just inside one of his temples.

"If anyone can get it back up," Adratus said with a grin, "you're certainly fit for the task."

Ubaz gave a sly grin. "I'll be ignoring what you meant there, but I'll fix it all the same. Go on. Kneel down." He began around behind the Human.

Adratus complied, taking a knee, and Ubaz untied the headband before pulling it tight.

"Too tight?" Ubaz asked.

"Nearly. But better than them falling. I might have to be a hornless satyr before night's end."

Ubaz tied the headband and circled to his front. "You're a faun, not a satyr. Satyrs are *dark* Faeries, and the whole reason we dress up like proper Faeries is to ward the Dark ones off."

"I'd rather be a satyr," Adratus said with a laugh.

"No shock there, you Dark Light bastard." He smiled and pulled Adratus to his feet. "Course, if you were a satyr, you surely wouldn't have bother with your horn wilting down. Always upstanding, them."

They both laughed, and Adratus cautiously set his hand on Ubaz's shoulder. They looked into each other's eyes. A moment passed.

"I shouldn't've been an arse to you earlier," Ubaz said. "I've been meaning to say."

"No, you shouldn't have. Yet, I find it difficult to remain angry with you."

Ubaz grinned slightly before biting his lip.

Quick pipe music and drums began to play. Ubaz looked away to his fellow Drevites, who danced and frolicked.

Ubaz grabbed Adratus's hand and pulled him toward the others.

Adratus happily followed. Soon, a youthful woman wearing nothing but blue ash to paint her body and ribbons in her hair and wings offered the Human a wooden cup of beer.

"To Adalheidis the Noble," she said.

Despite having no idea who they were toasting, Adratus clapped his cup to hers all the same.

"Adalheidis be one of the Fornir," Ubaz shouted near Adratus's ear. "From ancient times."

But Adratus had no idea what Fornir meant either.

"I should tell you," Ubaz continued, "I don't drink beer and all, because I'm the temple guardian. But don't let that stop you a bit."

And not a moment after Ubaz said this, another Drevite was clapping his mug to Adratus's, toasting that same unknown person.

Thus, long into the night, Ubaz and Adratus danced and laughed within the forest among the crowd of Faery-dressed, merry Drevites, pausing every so often to toast and refill cup after cup of beer.

The area remained charged with music and other sounds of celebration. Many a time, a playful squeal would erupt from a flirty game of chase around a tree.

"I must admit," Adratus began with a smile as they moved to the edge of the festivities, "the Drevites are unlike any other True Light culture I've encountered."

"Any of them?" Ubaz shouted over the noise.

"No. In most of the Kingdoms of Light, half of what's going on here would be punishable by . . ." Adratus stopped and glanced down. "Apologies."

Ubaz sighed as his sad eyes met the Human's. "You're not quite as bad as the last invaders before. When will we be heading to your camp?"

"Tomorrow, I think. After sleeping in. Or the next, if you like. They currently build it."

"Will it be *all* Humans there?" Ubaz said uneasily.

"You'll be fine. I assure you." Adratus set his hand on Ubaz's neck and thumbed his lower jaw, thumb moving closer to his lips.

The soldier leaned to kiss the guardian.

Ubaz turned away and shook his head.

"Apologies, I thought . . ."

"You're all right. Just . . ." Ubaz shook his head.

"Begging your pardon, sir," a man said to their side.

Adratus looked at Ubaz a moment more before he turned to see a Terovae in his mid-thirties dressed, similar to himself, as a faun, though with a cape hiding his wings. *A hunchback faun*, Adratus thought, cracking a drunken grin.

The man continued, "Chief Kaie wishes to see you, if that be all right with you, sir. Won't take long, says she."

"'Twill be about the other tribal chiefs, I'm sure," Ubaz joined. "Go on without me. There's a much more somber part of the Threshold Fair that I must do alone."

—

The sounds of celebration were distant, as Ubaz kneeled and set his lantern on the forest floor. Beside it, he set a small wooden box.

Alone, Ubaz breathed in the ambient power of Nature. He felt the cool night. He heard the songs of insects, frogs, and night birds. He gazed up at the pale blue moon and then at the lavender-tinted smaller moon, greeting them both with a nod.

"Let this be a place of calm and reverence," Ubaz whispered. "Let this be a place of remembrance. Mother Lágeya, she who is Nature, bring peace."

Ubaz cleared away the dead leaves to uncover a small section of the ground. He opened the box and took out a small pouch. From it, he poured a circle of ash. He then took a white taper candle, lit it in the lantern, and pushed it into the ground enough to stand upright within the circle.

He took a deep breath. "Treasa, my honored mother, I remember you."

Ubaz took the other candle, lit it, and stood it beside the first.

"Cal, my honored father, I remember you."

He then folded his hands, closed his eyes, and bowed his head.

There was suddenly a commotion from the sky, like birds fighting.

Ubaz tried to ignore it, instead meditating on his parents, but the sound grew louder, closer.

Finally, Ubaz's eyes shot upward, only to be greeted with a writhing cluster of crows tearing at each other's flesh in mid-air like savage beasts. His heart pounding, he watched as three of them careened toward the ground, exploding into a thousand blackened fragments upon their impact.

Ubaz grabbed the sack of ash and leaped up as the shards began to swirl and writhe around him, coalescing into three ghastly beings with skin so pale that it was nearly translucent—like half-decayed corpses.

The skeletal creatures were naked but for their black tangled hair and black-feathered wings that sprouted from their bony arms. They had no eyes except for glowing red sockets, empty pits of hellfire that seemed to see straight through Ubaz's soul.

Snarling and hissing like rabid animals, they lunged at him from all sides.

Ubaz's eyes dashed about frantically—looking for any escape—but the wall of claws and fangs had encircled him completely. As he prepared himself for death, a flash illuminated the darkness.

A boy stood in the clearing. He looked Human, a few years younger than Ubaz. Fearing for him, Ubaz nearly shouted at him to stay away, but then he saw the boy's black hair was tucked behind pointed ears. Ubaz then saw his eyes—fully black.

In one smooth motion, the boy unsheathed his sword—not metal, but glass with an amber hilt. He charged at one of the beasts and delivered a fierce blow with his blade.

The thing called out as it swirled and reformed into a glowing orb of red.

Ubaz fumbled to open the bag of ash, scooping out a handful. Hoping to the Mothers it would actually work, Ubaz launched it at another one of the creatures.

The creature screeched as it faded into nothingness.

In another flash, the mysterious boy moved to the remaining beast, striking it down to reform into another orb of red.

The boy then turned his empty black eyes toward Ubaz. Still gripping the hilt of his glass sword, he stepped closer.

Friend or foe, Ubaz could not be certain. He braced himself as he scooped another handful of ash.

"Who are you then?" Ubaz asked shakily.

The boy darted away and slashed his sword through the air, cutting the air itself as if it were a fabric. Through the opening, Ubaz could see a dark world of black glass.

The boy jumped through it, and the cut sealed and vanished.

"Ubaz!" the voice of Adratus rang out from a distance.

"I'm here. I'm all right."

Adratus soon sprang from the trees, sword in hand.

"I'm all right," Ubaz said again, as much to Adratus as to himself.

Adratus sheathed his sword and grabbed him, hugging him tightly against himself. The heat of their bare upper bodies pressed together, hearts pounding as they panted together.

"Something attacked me," Ubaz finally said. "I think they were Sluagh."

"Sluagh?" Adratus stepped back, scanning Ubaz up and down for injuries.

"Aye," Ubaz said, shaken, "they're not truly dark Faeries, themselves, but they're part of their realm. They're a kind of Scácasta—souls of people that the dark Faeries have snatched up."

"Whatever they were, they were all over the village, about thirty of them. Your people threw ash at them."

Ubaz nodded. "We make the sacred bonfire to make the sacred ash. Since they're only partly in our realm, it sends them back. But I don't understand it. 'Tis just tradition, that. All the Threshold Fair is just tradition. No Faeries have crossed over here in centuries."

"They're gone now," Adratus said. "Most of your people ran to the safety of the firelight, whilst others fought them off. A few people were clawed, yet nothing serious."

Ubaz nodded and looked down. His candles had been trampled under his own feet. He crouched and picked up a larger section of broken wax, staring at it.

"What is it?" Adratus asked.

"'Twas for my parents. When the Humans attacked eight years ago, my da was killed, and me ma was captured. I'd say she's dead now, as well. That's when the temple took me in. At twelve, I wasn't old enough to live on my own, and . . ." He looked up at Adratus with sad eyes. "It shattered me. And now, fecking Faeries here." He threw down the candle fragment and stood up.

"What did Chief Kaie want with you?" Ubaz asked.

Adratus paused before answering, clearly not wanting to change the topic. "She wants me to write four letters, one to each of the other tribal chiefs. She plans to send them via Ravenshade—whatever that means."

Ubaz nodded absently and glanced down at the broken candles. "I'm ready to be heading home now. I'll take us some coals from the bonfire to light the fire there. 'Twill keep us safe in case those Faeries come back. And I'll bring some coals to your camp, too, when we go, to light your fires there." He looked at Adratus. "You think I'll like it there in a Tridulan camp?"

Adratus paused before replying, again glancing at the broken candles. "We will soon know."

CHAPTER FORTY-SIX

The afternoon sun warmed the newly built fort, competing against the cold autumn breeze for supremacy. Within it, Adratus strolled through the bustle of marching legionaries and intense training exercises, breathing in the scent of freshly cut wood, sweat, and worn leather. A sense of pride swelled within him as he gazed upon the rows of identical wooden barracks that lined the compacted dirt streets, each one built with meticulous care and still bearing the pale yellow hues of fresh timber. The fort's quick construction was a testament to Tridulan efficiency—each man knowing his task and completing his section, taming this untamed wilderness into a small piece of civilization, even in this foreign land.

"Hail, Prefect," said a pair of passing legionaries as each touched his fist to his heart and nodded. Adratus returned the same. They continued on. This repeated every time he passed anyone, although the occasional young munifex would shoot him a terrified look as if he thought the prefect might gut him.

This road Adratus walked spanned the half mile between the sharpened log walls of the camp before continuing straight out for five hundred miles northeast to the city of Vohcktara. And from there, his true home in Tridual was another twenty-six hundred miles farther. Never had Adratus been so far away.

"Adratus," called Maximus from behind him.

"Hail, Legate."

"Have you anything to report on the Drevite chiefs?"

"Nothing new, Legate," Adratus replied with a slight note of disappointment. "Two weeks have passed since the Feah chief dispatched messages to the others, calling for a summit. Yet none have replied."

"None?" Maximus stroked his cleanly shaven chin as he reflected a moment. "If this summit fails, we may have cause for more forceful tactics."

"With respect, Legate, that would be ill-advised. The Drevite lands are vast, scarcely populated, and lack what we'd recognize as infrastructure or centralized authority. 'Twould be difficult to take this region by force."

"A practical answer forged for your legate," Maximus said with a grin, "yet I wonder if it but masks an impractical bias. 'Tis well known you and your barbarian have grown... close."

Adratus chuckled. "The advice is sound, Legate, I assure you. The Drevite Nation could prove to be a valuable ally rather than a mere province. There is something... magnificent about these lands that deserves preservation instead of domination." A fond smile graced his features as he continued, "However, yes, Ubaz and I have indeed grown... close. I seem to favor him more each day."

"I will consider your advice, yet I pray you, take mine." Maximus leaned closer. "Keep your affections out of diplomatic affairs."

Adratus's smile faded, and he clenched his jaw. "Are these words from my legate or friend?"

"They come from a brother who has stood by your side for decades and wishes not to see you harmed."

A squad of ten men passed, each giving his salute to the legate and prefect.

Maximus waited for them to pass before he continued, his voice low. "On any other occasion, I would rejoice at your finding delight. Yet here and now, you open yourself to heartache by consorting with barbarians."

Adratus averted his gaze but did not respond.

"Never have I understood your constant sympathy towards the Kingdoms of Light," Maximus continued. "Time and again, you attempt to save them when they would gladly throw us into fires for existing."

"The Drevites do not burn people."

Maximus shook his head. "Perhaps not. In truth, I have yet to hear the words 'All others will perish,' since our arrival. Nevertheless, the Dayigans *can not* have these lands; thus, we *must* secure them. If your attempts at an alliance fail, we will have no choice but to take the region. What will your barbarian lover do then, when you sit as second-in-command to a governor he rejects? Remember, he fought alongside those who greeted us with arrows upon our arrival."

"It will not come to that, Legate. We *will* forge a proper alliance."

"Let us hope you are correct, good Adratus. However"— Maximus knocked twice on the steel chest of the prefect's armor—"guard your heart, brother. It is a good one, and I wish not to see it injured."

"Yes, Legate," Adratus said sadly.

Maximus took a breath, switching from friend to commander, as his tone hardened. "Keep me advised of your summit, Prefect. Yet recall, every day we delay gives more time for our enemies to strengthen."

With his fist to his chest, Adratus stood tall and replied, "Yes, Legate."

With that, Maximus strode away, leaving Adratus alone with his troubled thoughts, the weight of their mission settling heavily upon his armored shoulders.

—

The dense canopy above sifted the sunlight into a golden mosaic, casting dappled patterns upon the forest floor. Ubaz meandered through the trees as his fingers trailed along the rough bark and soft leaves as he passed. He stopped at a small tree and gently grasped an oval leaf, his thumb rubbing its slick yellow-green top, while his forefinger slid along the leaf's downy underside. It was a goat willow if he remembered correctly from his mother's teachings. As an archdruidess, Treasa had known all the different types of local plants and had tried to teach them to her son.

However, Ubaz had paid little attention and had forgotten most of what he'd learned. He'd had no idea, at the time, how abruptly her lessons would end, never to resume. Now, he wished he'd listened to her more, savored those fleeting moments when she'd been alive. He remembered laughing at an amusing detail she had shared once—goat willows were either boy trees or girl trees. There was a word for that type of division—dio-something. This one here was a male willow and, thus, would later have little pods covered in what would look like goats' fur.

Ubaz sighed through a sad smile—at least he remembered some of what she had taught him.

"Ubaz." A whisper from above drew him from his thoughts.

He looked up into a tree—an ash tree, its leaves ablaze in fiery red—and saw his uncle Lann perched on a lofty bough.

Ubaz spread his wings and leaped up to join him, landing on a nearby branch. "I got your message to come and came," he said, scanning their surroundings warily. "But you shouldn't be here. The Tridulans know you're trying to start an uprising against them now."

"You and me both, last I checked," Lann replied, crossing his arms over his bare chest. "You're still with us, aren't you, lad?"

Ubaz hesitated before nodding slowly, his gaze drifting down to the woodland floor twenty feet below and carpeted with autumn leaves. "But . . . they're not like the other Humans were."

Lann snorted, uncrossing his arms. "So 'tis true then? Weeks now, I been hearing whispers about me own nephew getting rather cozy with a Human on New Year's Eve."

Ubaz's fists clenched at his sides, his jaw tensing. "Chief Kaie ordered me to stay close to him, didn't she now?"

"Close, aye, she did that, but she didn't say to suck his cock."

"I haven't done that," Ubaz spat angrily, the word "yet" nearly escaping his lips. "But . . ." His eyes traced the intricate patterns of the bark on the tree. "I can't deny I might be caring for him some. And him for me as well."

"Fuck's sake, Ubaz."

"You haven't met him properly. He's . . ." Ubaz sighed with a smile. "He's all right, him. And isn't that your proof right there—him dancing at the Threshold Fair? The last Humans we welcomed to one of our fairs insulted my parents, condemned our tribe as wicked, and ended the whole thing with bloodshed and accusations."

"Different or not, they're still Humans, all the same," Lann maintained. "And we can't be forgetting the atrocities they done to our kind. Stop thinking with your bollocks, lad, and open up your eyes." Lann gestured. "Just look."

Ubaz followed Lann's hand to stare out over the nearby Tridulan camp—a square half mile stripped of anything natural and enclosed within wooden walls. The houses within were uniform and made of fresh lumber, while larger structures stood in the center. In the time Ubaz had spent there, he'd barely found a single blade of grass within the whole confines. Never in his life had he seen anything so unnatural. He said nothing as he stared, embarrassed by the sight and without any words to justify its presence.

Lann continued, "The chief says we can't attack it."

Ubaz scoffed and turned back to him. "You'll have more to worry about than herself, if you attack it. There's six thousand well-trained legionaries in that camp. We've only got a disorganized bunch of fifty."

"More than that now, near four times that number. Whilst you've been shacking up with a Human, tensions amongst our people have risen high. Many believe your man to be a dark wizard that summoned the dark Faeries to attack us on New Year's."

"A dark wizard, aye, he is that," Ubaz grumbled. "But I don't think they caused the Faeries to come here. Though, to be honest, I did suspect it a bit, even if it wasn't intentional like."

Lann regarded him with a scrutinizing gaze. "Suspicions won't do a thing for us, lad. You've been in there for weeks. You must have found some proof that they're trouble."

Ubaz shook his head. "Nothing like that. We've been trying to figure out the best way to unite the Five Tribes."

"Find proof. And bring it to Kaie," Lann said. "She won't take action without it. She's accused *us* of being the ones causing trouble and has banished our whole group of us."

"Banished?"

"She has, aye," Lann said grimly. "She's ordered us to leave the Feah lands for the time being. That's why we must convince her that *we* are in the right here and that these Humans must get out of our lands."

Ubaz nodded solemnly and glanced back at the fort. "If there's something to be found, I'll find it, you be sure."

CHAPTER FORTY-SEVEN

Under the cool night, the prefect's pace increased as he turned a right angle onto a footpath. Ubaz was just a little up the way, lying on a large stump set outside the mess hall door between the building and the path. On the wall was a torch just above the Terovae, illuminating him in the flickering light.

Adratus paused to admire the scene. Ubaz was lying on his side, with his wings against his back and his arm beneath his head, his legs pulled up nearly to his chest. Adratus saw a sort of beauty in his sadness, as if he viewed a masterfully crafted melancholic sculpture. It pained him to see, he wanted to intervene, and yet he, too, wished to drink in the sight without destroying it.

Nevertheless, Adratus whispered, "Ubaz? Are you well?"

Ubaz rolled to face Adratus. "I'm not real sure, to be honest," he whispered remorsefully. "I know this tree, Prefect."

"The tree?" Adratus chuckled. "'Tis merely a stump someone left in place because he no doubt thought it would make a fine table. I admit, it is ideally located."

"This place was *ideal*, before you Humans came here to it. You could've left some of nature be when you were building your fort."

The prefect's humor faded with a sigh. "I thought we were past this," he muttered, as a dull hurt throbbed through him. He steeled himself. "Weeks in camp, yet you still mourn trees? We have an entire nation to unite. Come. I need to contact—"

"'Tis more than just a tree," Ubaz persisted as he sat up. "I recognize it, you see, so I recognize this place, this spot exactly." Ubaz scanned the area with heavy eyes; Tridulan soldiers milled along the thin dirt paths between the freshly built wooden structures. "Used to come here, me, for meditating, maybe grab a bite to eat and all. But 'tis all . . . just gone."

He looked up at Adratus with sincere eyes. "This tree, right here, was once mighty tall, higher than the rest. Look at how many rings it has here." He rubbed his entire arm across the rough top of the stump. "At least two hundred years of age, I'd reckon. And there were countless other trees, too, surrounding it, some as old as this one, if not older." His voice grew distant and far away. "And there was a stream just there," he motioned out toward where a barracks block now stood, ". . . just flowing round through the woodland floor and all." His eyes glazed over as he stared at the ground in front of him. "I can't see a trace of it now."

As the Tridulan looked at this place through the Drevite's eyes, the described loss saddened him. With the many camps Adratus had helped build, he'd always thought of them as creating, not destroying. Now he questioned. He was further ashamed to know that the stream Ubaz had mentioned was, in fact, there, covered up as a simple sewer.

"Apologies," Adratus said stiffly. "I know how much the forest means to you. I should not have spoken so callously." He sat down on the stump beside Ubaz and set his arm around his bare, warm shoulders. "Are you not cold?"

Ubaz chuckled. "Try flying a few hundred feet up in a snow cloud. That'll make you cold. This here is nothing to a Terovae." He set his head on Adratus's metal chest and pulled the soldier's arm tighter around himself. "Though I wouldn't half mind thick arms like these keeping me a wee bit warmer." He slid his hand over the swollen bicep, pushing up the short black sleeve. "I bet you swing a sword with the best of 'em, yes?"

Adratus nodded, though he wasn't sure if Ubaz could see. "Legate Maximus has trained me since we were boys, and I owe him my life for the skills he's given me."

"But you're an ambassador now," Ubaz said. "The only way you're gonna get anywhere as a diplomat to my people is to learn and understand our reverence for the One Soul—it flows through everything in nature."

"You speak of the power of Titaness Lágeya, who forsook mankind." He paused. "Apologies, I know she is adored by your people." Adratus began combing his fingers across the soft, amber feathers of the winged youth. "Believe me, fair Ubaz, I want to learn. You make me want to learn."

"I hope you really feel that way, because we need a strong ambassador. There's loads of scared people and angry people in the Five Tribes right now."

"As I am aware," Adratus said darkly. "Your uncle first amongst them. Any word on him? Lann?"

Ubaz paused. He glanced downward and shook his head.

"Fucking coward."

"He's not a coward, Prefect." Ubaz pulled back enough to look him in the eyes. "Best you be remembering that. You don't understand what they did to us."

"I understand he greeted us with arrows, though we came by Chief Kaie's invitation."

Ubaz sighed. "They took control of him," he said, words slow and sad. "The Humans . . . the *Dayigans*, they took control of his mind and made him lead an attack on the Feah temple."

Adratus went silent, his features softening as he listened.

Ubaz continued. "He doesn't talk about it much, but he remembers, every detail of it: everyone he killed under their spell, handing over his own daughter to the Dayigans, never to see her again. And he's not the only one. Most of them in his group have similar memories of things they were made to do under the Dayigans' control."

Adratus absorbed the words. "Apologies, I knew not. I've seen similar tactics employed by the Dayigans in other lands. My investigations led me to suspect the methods were developed here, yet I was uncertain."

"Developed here?"

Adratus nodded. "Perhaps. They call it the Drevite Experiment. But I've yet to determine what exactly it entails or why they chose this area—"

"Because no one cares about the Five Tribes, that's why. They can do what they want to us, and the rest of the world just looks away."

"I care," Adratus said firmly. "You should know the Drevite Experiment did not end. My sources believe it suffered a major setback and needed to be paused and reestablished. I am certain the Dayigans will return, attempt to claim these lands, and try to use them to forge catastrophic weapons to use against all they hate."

"All they hate?" Ubaz said bitterly. "There's a long list there."

"Indeed." Adratus chuckled. "But they won't succeed. We will unite this nation and impede them."

Ubaz drew closer to the soldier, moving his arm across him. "Loads of folks fear you, your kind of magic. What's this ring you always be wearing?"

Adratus held up his left hand so Ubaz could see it. The ring was a thick band of black titanium topped with an emblem engraved in silver: an eye within a triangle. A small garnet was set just above the eye.

"'Twas fused to my finger the day I became a Faldénrus. It focuses my inner gifts as thirteen spells. I've yet learnt them all, but I do well."

"Aye, but how does it work? Where does it draw power from? What effect does it have on the surrounding nature?"

"I'm no scholar," Adratus said. "The ring was issued to me, as it is to all Faldénri." Adratus twirled his fingers to form a red orb that shattered into a hundred sparkles. He then blew them upward into the night sky, and they scattered, each growing larger. Some darted randomly; some flashed manically.

"Proper grand, that is." Ubaz gazed in wonder at the dazzling display above them, his eyes shining with awe.

Adratus placed a comforting hand under his wings, on the small of his back just above his kilt, and began stroking slowly.

Ubaz leaned closer, transfixed by the dancing lights, as he basked in contentment. "Truly fantastic," he murmured as he rubbed Adratus's arm.

"You there," Adratus called out to a passing legionary. "Pray you, fetch a jug of wine and another of water for my ever-sober companion."

"Yes, Prefect." The legionary nodded and touched his fist to his chest. "And may I say, sir, 'tis a fair companion you have." He was away to the mess hall door.

"He is correct." Adratus purred, squeezing him. "You are quite amazing."

"Was it amazing he said, Prefect?"

"And fair."

"And you," Ubaz said. "How is it that the world around us is so altogether twisted up?"

Adratus sighed. "'Tis madness, I know. The Dayigans see only black and white, devoid of gray. And, into this flawed dualism, they drag us as well. Good versus evil. Terovae versus Humans. True Light versus Dark Light. Our peoples are not enemies. Yet, even as the Dayigans are far from here, their hateful shadow lingers, creating discord amongst we who should be united." The prefect withdrew his hand and moved to sit a foot away.

Ubaz kept his eyes even further. "I sometimes feel like I'll never be free of them," he whispered, "even if I never see them again. Everything and everyone I know has scars from them. You, as well."

Adratus nodded sadly.

Ubaz sighed. "We can't be doing this, can we? This thing between you and me?"

Adratus shook his head. "No," he said softly. He sniffed.

Silence followed.

"Prefect?" interrupted the legionary who'd returned with two jugs and two cups. No doubt sensing the change in mood, he carefully set them down on the tree stump with as little interruption as possible.

Adratus poured a cup of water for Ubaz and handed it to him. He poured a cup of wine for himself.

Ubaz drank and stared into the cup. "What's the source of the lights you cast?" he asked. "Are they draining anything from the area? Are they emitting anything?"

"They are but lights. Why does my ring interest you so?"

Ubaz paused, still staring into the cup before shaking his head. "It doesn't matter, really."

Another legionary approached. "If I may interrupt, Prefect."

Adratus kept his eyes on Ubaz a moment longer—the young man seemed weighed by something unspoken. He grudgingly looked up. "Speak."

With a bowed head and a fist to his chest, the legionary said, "Apologies for disturbing you, Prefect, but a courier brought this to the gate." He presented a rolled page of leather. "For you, sir."

Adratus stood and took the letter, unrolling it. "'Tis from the Chief of the Rúcah tribe," Adratus said with growing excitement while reading. "He . . . no, *she* and the other chiefs have discussed our summit. They have decided . . ." He stopped abruptly and rolled the page before letting it sink to his side.

"Well then, come on." Ubaz smiled. "Don't be making a mystery of it."

Adratus looked downward. "The other four Drevite chiefdoms decided 'twould be in everyone's best interest if our legion left the Drevite Nation." Pausing, Adratus looked at Ubaz. The Terovae seemed wilted.

Adratus crushed the page and slammed his fist against his leg.

Ubaz nodded sadly. "As you said, 'tis all black and white with the Dayigans, and somehow they've made us believe it. Us versus the Humans. It was foolish to think we'd overcome it." With that, he began away.

"Ubaz, wait," Adratus said. "We can—"

However, Ubaz spread his wings and jumped into the sky, flying away.

CHAPTER FORTY-EIGHT

Adratus cautiously creaked open the door and peered into the pitch-dark room. "Ubaz?" he whispered, but there was no response. He pushed the door further, casting more light into the small room, which held little more than a bed with a black trunk at its foot.

Ubaz lay on the bed, his orange wings spread out under him, covering the entire mattress as he gazed blankly at the ceiling.

"You've been in here three days," Adratus said, his voice barely above a murmur.

Still, no response.

"Lucerna, illuminate," Adratus said, and the terracotta lamp suspended from the ceiling released a luminous smoke that swirled together to bathe the room in soft light.

Ubaz turned his head to the side as he groaned, setting his arm over his squinting eyes. "Lucerna, disilluminate."

The cloud above the lamp darkened and dispersed.

After a moment, Ubaz sat up and addressed Adratus with a bleak tone. "I was awful nervous to be talking to all five of the chief tiernas at once," he said. "I kept practicing what I was going to say to them, over and over, afraid they wouldn't listen to me. It never crossed my mind that they wouldn't be showing up at all."

"It no longer matters," Adratus said. "Come. I have a gift for you to lift your spirits."

Begrudgingly, Ubaz rose from the bed and followed Adratus through the prefect's quarters to a door at the back of the house.

"Close your eyes," Adratus said through a grin.

Ubaz shot him an irritated glance.

"I assure you, fair Ubaz, it will please you."

Ubaz reluctantly closed his eyes, and Adratus took his hand, leading him through the door and a few steps beyond.

"Now . . ." Adratus released Ubaz's hand and stepped back. ". . . open your eyes."

They stood on a gravel path down the center of a small courtyard. Wooden columns lined the edges as a peristyle, supporting a slight overhang of the roof, with the walls beyond the columns adorned with intricate paintings of the forest. Within the courtyard lay a meticulously landscaped garden blanketed with neatly trimmed grass and filled with small trees and rounded shrubs—everything in careful symmetry.

Ubaz spun slowly, taking in all the sights. "'Tis fantastic," he said in awe. "You did all this?"

Adratus smiled proudly as he looked into Ubaz's eyes. "I did a lot. Yet it helped to have an entire idle legion at my command. Look." He drew Ubaz's attention to the birdbath in the garden's center as they approached. Atop it stood a three-foot statue depicting a woman with the head of a yellow cat. Her long hair pushed back behind her feline ears was painted gold. What little of her skin that showed around her long white gown was covered in yellow fur, and in her hands, she held a golden bowl filled with actual fire.

"Mother Larissa," Ubaz said as he drew nearer, and his smile grew wider.

Adratus grinned. "Forgive its crudeness. The camp's potter is more adept at making jugs than—"

"'Tis perfect. All of it, perfect."

"It is yours. If you wish anything added or changed—"

Ubaz shook his head and pressed his lips to Adratus's in a long-awaited kiss that sent waves of bliss and heat down Adratus's body. When they finally pulled away, both men were breathless and beaming.

"I shouldn't have done that," Ubaz said breathlessly, a hint of a smirk playing on his lips. "But I think I should like to do it again."

Without hesitation, Adratus pulled him close and claimed his lips once more. This time, the kiss was fierce and frantic, as if they were trying to unleash something primal within each other. When they finally broke apart, they stood in silence, gazing at one another with unspoken words hanging heavy between them.

"You make me happy, Ubaz, and I wish to return in kind. Perhaps I do not show it well. I'm not the sort to frolic merrily. In truth, my life has left me with many scars."

"As has mine, as well. Guess 'tis good I found another broken man, so our fractures fit together."

Adratus grinned contentedly as he gazed at Ubaz a moment longer. He wanted to say more, but the words eluded him.

Finally, Ubaz looked away and spoke. "'Twas a kind thing of Chief Kaie to be sending messages for us, but 'tis clear it wasn't enough. We must go ourselves to the chief of the Rúcah lands and have a talk with her directly. And then we should pay a visit to all the other chiefs as well."

"Yes." Adratus took a deep breath and nodded. "I will begin assembling a unit at once. And we will leave tomorrow morn."

But Ubaz stopped him with a gentle touch. "Would you stay a moment longer?" he asked, wrapping his arms around Adratus. "Right now, let us enjoy my wee garden cut off from the rest of the world and all its troubles. Let the flow of Nature wash over us as we bask in its gentle currents, just the two of us."

Adratus nodded and kissed Ubaz's lips. Not like before. A brief peck this time. "We *will* unite the Drevite Nation."

CHAPTER FORTY-NINE

After half a week's toil toward the Rúcah temple village, Adratus was ready to slaughter every tree in sight and pave the whole region with stones. Horses were out of the question in the untamed Drevite forest, as was bringing an entire century of men. It was just Adratus, Ubaz, and two squads of ten soldiers each.

They hacked their way through the thicket with gritted teeth and bared blades as tree limbs whipped around them. Then one struck Adratus square across his jaw with a sharp slap that sent him reeling. A surge of frustrated rage swept over him, and he lashed out at the nearest tree, slicing into its bark.

Ubaz watched beside him and broke out laughing, shaking his head. "You're meant to be learning to flow *with* the forest, Prefect," he said, "not fighting against it like you try. Stop for a moment, will you?"

Adratus shot him a dark glance. "We haven't time for a Drevite, Mother Nature speech."

Ubaz glared back. "Would you be wanting me to punch you square in the face for that instead?"

Adratus looked at him for a moment, brow furrowed. "*Detachment, halt.*"

The soldiers behind them stopped.

Ubaz forced a serious tone, though his grin was barely cloaked. "Take a breath now," he said. "And really look at the nearby woods. You be vexed, for as a Tridulan, you rush through problems and such like some dragon of old, powering your way through obstacles and the like. Your eyes remain fixed on your ultimate aim, as if naught else matters."

"We are short on time, fair Ubaz," Adratus grumbled.

Ubaz rolled his eyes and shook his head. "And ye scarce notice what you're destroying on your undeviating path."

Adratus glanced downward.

"But you're not a dragon now are you, Prefect? And for all of your destroying, there's a wee deer twisting and turning its way up already rutted-out paths, getting to its destination faster than you ever will. Look around and see."

Adratus took a moment truly to see the area. He breathed in mulch-scented air as he looked up. The place was truly beautiful. The canopy had thinned, allowing in the grayish blue above. Many of the leaves had already fallen, but most of the red and orange ornaments clung to their branches. Adratus could feel the tranquility in the chill wind, as if the breeze itself blew calmer here.

"The world's a gentle river, Prefect," Ubaz whispered, "flowing from Lake Laqyigo. You can battle against it or flow with it."

Adratus turned a full circle to survey the hacked-up, broken route his men had cut through in their travels. And Adratus felt ashamed for defiling the wilds.

"Apologies," he said softly to Ubaz, though his words were just as much meant for the surrounding woods.

Ubaz looked where Adratus looked and saw what he saw. "Seeing's the start of a better path."

Adratus turned to face forward and spoke up to his men. "There is a goat path just over there, heading in our direction. We will follow it and see where it leads."

—

The endless days of traveling continued, the earth beneath their feet unforgiving. As each night fell, Adratus and Ubaz huddled together for warmth, their bodies intertwined under a black cape. The night sky glimmered with stars as they lay there, trying to ignore the burning desire that thrummed through their veins.

"What was the world before I met you," Adratus said one night, "but a desolation with no purpose but war?"

But Ubaz remained silent, his eyes closed—asleep or feigning, Adratus did not know.

Adratus pulled him closer, feeling Ubaz's chest rise and fall with each steady breath, a calming rhythm in the midst of chaos.

In time, facing the night, Adratus slept.

—

The next morning, the Tridulans continued northwest, trying to stick to natural paths as much as possible.

Ubaz remained distant, and Adratus watched him from afar.

Late in the day, they hit a stream that wound toward their destination. They resolved to follow the stream as far as they could toward the Rúcah temple.

"You've been silent today," Adratus finally said. "Did I somehow anger you?"

"I'm not angry with ya, no."

They walked at the front of the formation. The two squads, their sandals crunching along the forest floor, walked staggered on either side of the rocky stream.

Ubaz fidgeted uncomfortably. "Nothing's changed, has it? Your people. My people. Us stuck in the middle of it all. 'Tis clear where the path we're traveling leads, and 'tis not one we should be traveling down."

Adratus grinned. "We travel the path to the Rúcah temple."

Ubaz shot him an annoyed stare before a grin crossed his face. "You know full well what I mean, you cheeky bastard. The *path* we're heading down at nighttime." He sighed sadly. "A path I want to continue on, but . . ."

Adratus stepped in front of him and took his hands into his. "Our people are not in conflict. We are but victims of a mad misunderstanding set in motion by villains far from here. And soon, we will resolve that confusion."

Ubaz nodded somberly. "Maybe so, but 'til all the confusion's cleared up, we might do well to be sleeping separate."

The words hurt, but Adratus only nodded. "If that is what you wish."

"I don't know what I wish, to be honest." Ubaz looked up, eyes wanton, at Adratus. "I . . ."

"Prefect!" one of the Tridulan legionaries called out.

Adratus looked back to see the men scrambling to pull their red rectangular shields from their backs and raise them to the skies.

It was suddenly raining arrows. Two Tridulans fell at once. Blood flowed into the stream.

"I told you to leave these lands." Lann flew before a great swarm of hundreds of Terovaes blocking out the sky.

"They're from the Rúcah tribe," said Ubaz, frozen, his eyes wide. "Their kilts are black with a purple stripe down the front."

"Quickly," Adratus ordered him, "grab a shield from a fallen man and stand behind it."

"I can talk to them. The Tréréaldéag says—"

"Do it! Now." Adratus shoved Ubaz back to stumble onto a man bleeding out through a pierced neck. "And put this cloth over your nose and mouth."

Three Terovaes swooped down, snatching a Tridulan before taking the struggling Human high above the group. They dropped him on his brothers in arms.

"Slingers!" Adratus commanded. "Ready sludger!"

On his command, five legionaries drew red pottery eggs, each of them painted with a black line around its length, which they loaded into their handheld sling weapons. The whirring buzz spread across the battleground as they spun their slings.

"Launch!" the prefect shouted.

They complied, launching each sludger at the Rúcah line. Amid air, the pottery shattered, expelling an inky cloud of black dust that engulfed the winged foes and transformed into a sticky sludge, causing their wings to lose lift.

The Terovaes sunk to the ground, even as they struggled to maintain flight.

"Melee, attack!" Adratus ordered and charged forward with his men to meet the fallen Terovaes in combat.

However, the Tridulans found them tougher to kill than planned. The Drevites' skin was unlike skin but more akin to wood, every cut requiring multiple strikes and much effort.

Adratus stabbed his sword at a Rúcah's gut, but the weapon merely scratched across its target's stomach, far from fatal.

A sharp twang came from behind Adratus as an arrow pierced through one of the Rúcah's eyes, killing him instantly.

Adratus looked back to see Ubaz armed with a bow.

"Feck your *'stand behind a shield'* shite," Ubaz said, as he shot another arrow. "I'm the temple guardian."

"Apologies," Adratus shouted back as he continued to fight another Drevite. Like before, his sword could barely cut the skin.

The Tridulans were horribly outnumbered, and the thinning canopy offered little cover against the deadly downpour of arrows. Retreating under fire all the way to their fort, eight days southeast, would be impossible.

The slingers reloaded and launched again. More Terovaes, wings caked in inky goo, glided down.

Adratus locked eyes on Lann in flight and thrust his left hand forward. Five cords of red light shot from his fingertips.

But the cords did not seize Lann as they had at their first meeting. Instead, when they touched him, they dispelled and were gone.

Adratus quickly tried again. Same outcome.

"I weren't ready for your magic before, Human," Lann said. "Never fought against a Dark wizard 'fore now. But me skin still had room on it for a new protection seal." He armed his simple bow and shot it.

Adratus dodged and cast toward Lann. "Disarm!"

The Terovae's weapon became engulfed in fire. Lann shouted in pain and cast away his bow. When it hit the road, the fire vanished, and there was no sign it was ever there.

"I have more than one spell," Adratus scoffed.

Lann stared hate. *"Kill all of them dead!"* he called to his men.

Undaunted, Adratus cast out his cords of light again and successfully snatched one of the soaring enemies—one who was evidently not as well-protected as Lann. The cords took hold, and Adratus flicked his wrist, causing the Rúcah warrior to crash through his comrades like a giant mace on a chain.

"Prefect," called one of the squad leaders, "we are at a disadvantage, depleted of sludger, and can take little more."

"I am aware, Centurion," Adratus said. "Stay on task. Ubaz, you know this area. Are there caves or the like nearby?"

"I don't know it too well, Prefect." He shot an arrow. "This is Rúcah lands here, not ours. But I might know a place. 'Tis not much, though."

"'Twill have to do. *Detachment*," the prefect shouted, "when I give the command, we follow Ubaz at full sprint. First, cover me whilst I cast."

Despite all the surrounding conflict, Adratus took a deep breath and closed his eyes.

He calmed his mind and focused on a point of light.

A single shining point of light in the darkness.

He exhaled.

When he opened his eyes, the point of light was there, a ball of red hovering above his palm. The orb then shattered into a thousand pieces. He blew them toward the Rúcahs.

The pieces, all of them, grew larger as they hurried through the air, some becoming extremely bright, some beginning to flash madly. They surrounded the panicked Rúcah warriors, twisting around them at dizzying speeds.

"What do those do then?" Ubaz asked as he watched.

"Same as before. Only that. 'Twill blind and confuse them. But we have only minutes. *Detachment*, retreat!" A sickening word but necessary.

With a limping sprint in clanking armor, the remaining men followed Ubaz. First down the stream a way, then rushing into woods to twist around trees and dash around undergrowth.

Ubaz stopped within the indistinguishable trees. Perplexed, he turned a full circle, looking around like a frightened deer.

"Why do you stop?" Adratus demanded more harshly than he'd meant. The impatient prefect looked back to see if the Rúcahs were coming.

He saw them in the not-too-distant skies.

"I'm sorry. I'm sorry. I told you I don't really know this place very well." The pressure weighing on him was clear as he seemed near panic.

"You're doing fine," Adratus said with a hand on his shoulder. "I need you. Calm yourself, and think of the destination."

Ubaz nodded, paused a breath, and resumed running.

CHAPTER FIFTY

Bow armed, Ubaz bolted into the small cave, his eyes adapting to the darkness as he searched for beasts.

"Clear," he shouted back and relaxed his bow before shoving it into the quiver strapped to his belt.

Bodies battered and injuries bleeding, the remaining squad members limped into the cave. They clutched their grimy wounds, trying to hold on to the life within their broken bodies as they crutched against one another. The group—originally of twenty-two—was now a haggard bunch of twelve. The dead were left where they'd fallen, feasts for the wolves and vultures.

A nearly dead legionary whom Adratus dragged by the shoulders was in even worse shape than the rest. Ubaz hurried to him and helped the prefect, who was injured and struggling as well.

The other men began crumpling, either propping themselves to sit against parts of the earthen wall or lying flat on the ground.

"They won't chance coming in here," Ubaz said, as he helped Adratus lie down the nearly dead man. "The ceiling's too low, and they'd lose their advantage."

Adratus rushed back to the mouth of the cave and set his hand on the rock. He bowed his head and closed his eyes.

Ubaz watched, perplexed by his actions, until a surge of electric red lit up across the entrance, blocking it in what looked like a spiderweb of lightning.

"I'd rather be certain," Adratus said, returning to Ubaz. He fell to his knees, pausing before falling to his butt. He then bent forward into a slouch as he gripped the gaping wound on his upper arm.

Entranced and saddened, Ubaz watched him for a moment. It was as if he viewed a broken God, leaving him breathless.

"You're seid depleted," Ubaz asked, "aren't you?"

"If you mean magic depleted, nearly. But not enough to be fatal."

Near panic, Ubaz looked at the surrounding nightmare, lit red by the web. The legionaries moaned and winced. Some had already begun ripping apart their tunics to bandage others, even while they bled themselves.

"Are you injured?" Adratus asked of Ubaz.

He shook his head. Ubaz grabbed the prefect's black cape and, with his arrowhead, ripped off a bandage.

Adratus grabbed Ubaz's shoulders and pulled him into an embrace, kissing his lips. "I feared for your safety," he said.

"And I yours," Ubaz said sadly. He pulled away and pressed a wad of cloth against the prefect's bleeding arm.

"No," Adratus said, as he took the cloth himself. "Him." He pointed to the nearly dead man.

Ubaz rushed to the other man, who had now begun to move, coughing deeply. Foamy blood oozed from his mouth and streamed down his cheeks. Ubaz rolled him on his side.

Ubaz could see no injury and had no idea what to do for him.

The man convulsed violently. Blood spewed from his mouth. Blood filtered through the horizontal strips of metal that formed his black segmented armor.

Panicked, Ubaz grabbed his knife and began frantically cutting the leather straps that held his armor at the shoulder.

"Stay with me," Ubaz said. It seemed like the thing to say. This man's life had been thrust into his hands, yet he held it as futilely as sand.

The man began shaking more violently, clawing at Ubaz as he fought to breathe, his eyes wide, terrified of impending death.

Finally, Ubaz was able to throw open the armor, only to reveal horrors.

His ribs were shattered, with slick white bones erupting from a ripped red tunic and mutilated flesh.

Ubaz's stomach seized, but he did not vomit.

They'd dropped the man, Ubaz guessed—one of the ones the militia flew up into the sky before releasing him to crash into the ground.

"What do I do now?" Ubaz shouted.

The dying man's eyes stared in a desperate plea for help, for air. He coughed and choked—horrible sounds, desperate sounds. Ubaz could hear his ribs grinding with the motions of his lungs.

Petrified, though shaking, Ubaz stared at the gory chest as he searched his aching brain for any answer. How does one reassemble a broken ribcage?

"I'm sorry," Ubaz whimpered. "I don't know . . ."

The convulsions stopped. The coughing stopped.

The dying man became the dead man, as Ubaz could but watch helplessly.

"No," Ubaz said. Now, his own breathing quickened. "No." Hyperventilating, he grew lightheaded.

Someone screamed in agony. Ubaz turned to see a legionary holding down a young soldier whose lower leg was tattered meat. A third cranked a stick stabbed through a bandage just above his knee, tightening it with each turn to stop the flow of blood.

Ubaz wiped his bloody hands on his kilt and hurried to another injured legionary. He meant to say something comforting, but no words came out. Instead, Ubaz just found his injured forearm and began cutting a bandage from the soldier's short red sleeve.

Even as Ubaz mended this new man, in his mind, he could see the eyes of the man he'd lost. He could hear his coughs and his grinding ribs. Ubaz kept wanting to look back at him but stopped himself.

Ubaz moved to the new man's second injury, but his focus remained on the dead. He wanted to call out. There was no time. Ubaz worked faster, as if finishing a new task took him farther from the failure.

Ubaz moved on to another injured soldier.

In time, everyone was somewhat stabilized, but very few were in any shape that seemed hopeful.

A fire burned in the center of the cave, not large but enough to heat a sword hot enough to cauterize the worst of the wounds.

Drained, Ubaz sat in front of Adratus and stared, his eyes blank.

"I should have brought a medic," Adratus said absently.

"'Twas a diplomatic mission."

Adratus nodded.

"That was more than just a rebel faction," Ubaz said. "They were wearing Rúcah battle colors. That means they were acting under the sanction of the Rúcah chief, herself."

Adratus was silent for a moment—staring past him to the opposite root-garlanded wall—no doubt taking in the gravity of the words.

Ubaz checked the bandage on Adratus's arm. "My mam was a brilliant healer," he said sadly. "She'd have all this sorted in no time, if she was here." He slowly scanned the area, viewing the agonized legionaries. "She'd be able to fix all this, no problem. I should've paid more attention to her when I had the chance to." He moved to another of Adratus's bandages, checking it.

"I'm fine," Adratus said, shrugging him off. "The diplomatic journey is over. We return to camp."

"Chief Kaie said they can't attack us in Feah lands," Ubaz began, his words a lost whisper. "But we're five days from the border." Though his tone was bleak, with very little in the way of inflection, his mind screamed, *How can we possibly survive in Rúcah lands for five more days after the damage we've already taken here?*

Adratus gave no reply.

After a wait, Ubaz stood. "Those bandages alone won't do them much good for long. I need to pack the wounds with moss. There's a bog just down the way where—"

"You don't plan to go back out there?" Adratus snapped. "The Rúcahs will be searching."

"I have to. Bandages just stop the bleeding. The moss will keep the wounds from turning septic on us."

"There must be moss in this cave. Use *it*."

"Cave moss is not bog moss and won't do a thing good. We can't be dragging half-dead legionaries all the way to the border. Plus, everyone's canteen needs filling up."

Adratus looked down in contemplative silence.

"Would you be wanting yourself and these men to get worse just so I can stay pristine, Prefect?" Ubaz asked. "I didn't think so, no."

Adratus looked at him for a moment. "Ward down," he said, and the lightning web vanished.

CHAPTER FIFTY-ONE

Ubaz crouched within the encroaching darkness. The sun had already begun to sink below the eastern horizon, and he was now cloaked within the lengthening shadows as he listened keenly for any sounds that might betray the Rúcah warriors' positions.

Nothing.

Spreading his wings, he leaped up, keeping his flight low, just high enough to keep his feet from rustling the forest floor, but not so high as to be spotted.

Ubaz landed behind a large oak.

He set his arm across the five metal canteens that hung from long bands around his neck so they wouldn't clank. He set his other hand on the rough bark of the tree and peered in all directions, searching for the slightest motion in the forest's dimming light. Barely breathing, he perked his ears for any sound. Nothing.

Taking flight again, Ubaz moved to another sturdy tree and pressed himself against its girth. This time, he could make out a distant murmur echoing through the woods—an unmistakable exchange of voices.

Acting quickly, Ubaz flew upward with a combination of climbing and flight and perched on a bough where he lay prone.

Ubaz saw them, a dozen Rúcah men, gathered below, Lann among them. Their words were hushed, and Ubaz couldn't make out most of what they were saying. Perhaps he heard something about "back to the house" and "continue in the morning."

Either way, the Rúcah warriors spread their wings and darted above the trees, flying west.

Somewhat relieved, Ubaz jumped from the branch and flew in the opposite direction, toward the bog.

When he landed, Ubaz saw a strange woman kneeling beside a stream.

He froze. Watching. Mesmerized.

She was a wingless woman with long white hair and unnaturally white skin. Her thin, tattered gown was black. There was something horribly sad about her, and though Ubaz could not see her face, he thought that she was weeping.

He set his arm across the canteens and stepped closer, intending to comfort her.

A voice whispered just behind Ubaz, "Keep your distance."

Ubaz jumped, drawing a knife from his belt as he turned toward the voice.

It was the boy he'd seen at the Threshold Fair, the strange yet beautiful boy with black hair pushed behind his pointed ears.

"She washes the garments of the dead," the boy whispered.

Ubaz stepped carefully forward and saw a bloody patchwork of leather and cloth clutched in the woman's hands. She dipped it in the water, scrubbed two parts together, and wrung it out. Repeat. Repeat. All the while, blood ran far down the stream.

"Those who *have* died," the boy continued. "And those who *shall* die."

"Who?" Ubaz asked, turning a little too quickly to clang the clatter of canteens.

The strange woman snapped the bloody patchwork to her breast as her eyes—empty voids of crimson light—snapped to Ubaz. She jumped up and dashed a step down the stream before fading as a crimson mist.

"She was one of the dark Faeries," Ubaz asked, "wasn't she?"

"If you mean an Irefaery, then yes. Yet, it is not Darkness that twists them, but Chaos. Chaos resides in all Fae-kind. The Irefaery have lost themselves to its grasp."

"And you? What are you then?"

"I am the Sword Elf," he said gravely.

Ubaz looked into his eyes, wholly black and glossed like obsidian.

"I may be no expert on Faery folk," Ubaz began, "but I know well enough to know elves don't carry swords. Nor do they have eyes like yourself. Are you a proper Faery or a Dark—that is, an Irefaery?"

"Alas, I know not what I am. Perchance I am neither. But once, I was a Faery." He lowered his head. "Yet that world is now lost."

His demeanor told Ubaz more than any label. The Terovae sheathed his knife and stepped closer.

"I . . ." Ubaz began. "I didn't tell a soul that I saw you at the fair."

"Why?"

Ubaz shrugged his bare shoulders. "Don't know, really. I thought I oughtn't to."

"Why did your kind dress as Faeries that night?"

"To frighten away the Irefaeries who might try to come through to our realm on New Year's Eve. There's these cracks, you see, from ancient times, to the Otherworld. They spread across the skies of the Five Tribes. You can't see them, but they're there."

The Sword Elf looked down sadly. "Your people err. The Irefae hold no fear of the Fae." He looked up at Ubaz. "But the costume suited you well. You are fair enough to be a Faery."

"Am I now?" Ubaz grinned. "And you're too young to be talking like that, lad."

The elf remained solemn. "Again, you err. I am surely older than your great-grandfather. Nevertheless, it was but a compliment. I know where your heart lies. I saw the Human run to you after the attack."

"Is he . . ." Ubaz began. His heart started pounding at the impending question. He could barely speak the words. "Is he the reason the Irefaeries have come back here?"

"No. Neither your love nor his men have weakened the walls that divide your lands from the Bikian Faery Realm."

Ubaz breathed a sigh of relief, now realizing how anxious he had been about the matter. But the elf, he saw, turned more solemn.

"Twenty-five years ago," the Sword Elf recounted, "a wicked man attacked my home. He destroyed my city and my parents, both. You know this same heartache; I watched you light your candles."

Ubaz looked away from him and nodded.

"This same wicked man," the Sword Elf continued, "has come here, to a river island southeast of your people's land. There, he holds captive one of the Fornir—those who are the greatest and wisest of the Fae. And so I have traveled many miles to set her free."

"This 'wicked man' you talk of, he's reopened the cracks in the Faery Realm, then?" Ubaz asked.

"Methinks yes. The villain dabbles in magics far beyond his understanding."

"I see. For such a sweet-looking lad, your words are well grim." Ubaz gave a half smile. "I wish I could speak to you longer, but I must hurry back. Badly injured men await me there." He grabbed the elf's hand and shook it. "I am Ubaz, Guardian of the Feah Temple of the Three Mothers."

"Well met, Guardian Ubaz. I am . . ." He hesitated. "I am Valqyer the Sword Elf."

"Good luck to you on your quest, Valqyer. May the Three Mothers bless you and guide you."

As Ubaz walked away, he reached into the leather pouch on his belt and removed a knife wrapped in thin hide. He unwrapped it to reveal an iron blade in the shape of a crescent moon atop a smooth antler handle.

Seeing a patch of bog moss, Ubaz crouched and set his blade sideways above it.

"I acknowledge the good spirit of Nature, the One Soul, the aspect of Mother Lágeya that connects all things. I ask you to release these gifts to me, though—sorry to say—I've nothing to give in return."

The stream, in the corner of his vision, distracted him. He looked at it, where the blood had run. It was now clear.

Ubaz looked back.

Valqyer watched him.

"Whose clothes was she washing?" Ubaz asked.

"I know not. But there were a great number of patches, and most were yet to come."

—

Ubaz packed the moss tight on Adratus's injured upper arm and rewrapped the bandage.

"You have been quiet since your return," Adratus said.

Ubaz tied a knot in the black cloth. "I saw someone. Out by the bog. An elf."

"Ah. Did you get a wish granted?" Adratus joked.

Ubaz kept a somber tone. "A lot of folks around here are thinking ye Tridulans caused those Irefaeries—that's the dark Faeries, if you didn't know—to come back here. I was thinking it myself before, I'll admit."

"You thought that?"

"I wasn't saying that you did it on purpose, but you be worshiping Dark Gods and dabbling in magic without truly understanding it. But we've gotten to the bottom of it now. This elf says it was some wicked old man who snatched up a Faery maiden and caused all the trouble. He went off to save her."

"With a kiss, no doubt."

"I'm stone serious, Adratus. And the truth needs to be told to the Rúcahs as well. Many joined my uncle's gang thinking your legion was responsible for bringing back the Faeries. I . . ." His gaze dropped to the rough floor. "I have to tell our Lann that it wasn't true."

"No." Adratus crossed his arms and straightened his posture. "I will not allow it. Going off to the marsh is one thing, but—"

"I'm not one of your legionaries, and I'm not asking for permission to go. I just came back to give you the moss and water and let you know where I'd be flying off to. Alone. All of ye need your rest anyways."

Adratus grabbed him tenderly by the back of his neck and pulled his face close.

The prefect's gaze was as steel as he said, "Be safe, brave Ubaz, and return. I will await you."

Adratus then kissed Ubaz's lips, a slow kiss of somber farewell.

CHAPTER FIFTY-TWO

At the edge of a forest clearing, Ubaz landed, taking a few steps as he folded his wings and came to a stop.

He stood before a Rúcah roundhouse—a large circular house with short, stick and mud walls and a thatch roof angling steeply upward.

Ubaz felt strangely intimidated by it—*strangely* because on any normal night, he'd have had no qualms about walking straight up to a Rúcah roundhouse and going straight in.

Instead, he stared, his eyes lingering on the log-framed doorway curtained by bearskin. He could hear the people inside laughing and chatting. A house about this size could comfortably fit about fifty people, and the noise sounded just about right for that number.

For a good five minutes, Ubaz stared at that bearskin curtain. If they were his proper enemies, he would at least know to draw his bow, go in shooting, maybe grab a hostage, or the like. But they were Rúcahs.

Ubaz's whole hesitation seemed silly to himself. The Rúcah was one of the Five Tribes. And the leader of this particular group of Rúcahs was his mother's brother. He was fairly certain that Lann had changed his diapers at some point—not that he could remember, but he recalled Lann joking about it at some point.

Ubaz would go in, he resolved, calmly. Lann would listen to him about the elf, surely.

He wished someone would just come outside, and the matter—for better or worse—would be resolved. The someone would either invite Ubaz in or pull him in by the arm.

Ubaz stepped forward, and like a rock rolling down a gradual hill, the motion propelled him forward. He knew he couldn't stop again, or he'd be outside debating for another five minutes.

Ubaz pulled aside the thick bearskin and stepped in.

A fire burned in the center of the smoky room—one room for the entire house. The bulk of the smoke lingered in the high apex of the conic roof of logs supporting thatch.

The edge of the circular outer wall—too low for standing—held a ring of beds formed of straw covered in pelts.

Further in, men and women sat on wooden benches or on the floor as they clutched cups of ale and told boisterous tales.

Silence seized those closest to the door, and it spread rapidly across the house. The eyes came, too, staring.

A few people drew daggers and stood, bowing up as they faced the newcomer.

Ubaz jerked toward the entrance, ready to bolt, but someone grabbed him.

"'Tis all right. Let him go," Lann spoke up from the farther side of the room. He sat in a wooden chair that seemed to imply authority.

The man who'd grabbed him released him, and Ubaz shrugged him off.

With the return of some courage, the uninvited newcomer stood tall and stepped forward before announcing, "I am Ubaz, Guardian of the Feah Temple of the Three Mothers, here on a diplomatic mission to speak to your chief. Ye rebels—"

"Rebels, is it?" Lann cut him off before laughing. "Well, aren't you right proper, lad? You're sounding like one of your fucking Humans. But, O Guardian of the Feah Temple, you know we're not rebels. You see our colors clear yourself. The chief of the Rúcahs has granted me leave to form an official militia in her name. And I've done just that, so. And we've made it quite clear what we think about your fucking diplomatic fucking mission."

"Feck off, Uncle Lann!" Ubaz shouted back. "You near about killed us. And I'll be having a word with Chief Kaie 'bout that when we return to the temple."

"Right," he scoffed. "I've known Kaie since we was weans," Lann said. "Good heart. Smart. But she's wrong about this with the Tridulans, and you are, as well. We can't invite in Human invaders to protect us from Human invaders."

A woman in the house called out, "Tell that fecking pup, Lann! We're not having it." Others joined in with taunts and jeers.

Ubaz had never stood as a single voice against an entire room. It gave him a sinking feeling, and he wanted to escape. The firelight seemed to grow dimmer, and his lungs grew tight. He clenched his jaw, but not in anger, in sadness. Ubaz felt betrayed by all there, his own uncle grinning among them.

The chatter quickly shifted topics, as if the militia had lost interest in the temple guardian. A few talked about him and the Humans, but many returned to, *as I was saying before.*

Ubaz breathed and continued, louder, "I know you're thinking the Tridulans are responsible for the dark Faeries popping up throughout our lands. But I know, for certain, they're not."

The chatter ceased. The people stared.

Ubaz cleared his throat. "I spoke to an elf."

"A elf?" Lann released a mighty laugh as he slammed his hand against his armrest. "A fucking elf, he says."

The laughter spread quickly throughout the house, and loud conversations followed.

"The elf told me it wasn't the Tridulans," Ubaz shouted over the noise. "We can trust the Tridulans. With them at our side, we can stand strong against the Dayigan Empire."

But Ubaz wasn't winning back the attention. He'd been dismissed, as far as the militia was concerned, and it didn't seem likely that would change.

Lann stood and approached his nephew.

And when he was near, Lann said, "Come on, lad. Let us have words outside."

—

As soon as they were outside, Lann slapped Ubaz hard against the back of his neck.

"By the Mothers, lad," Lann began, "what was you thinking coming here like this? Are you that thick now? You shot and killed some of our fellas just some hours past."

"In self-defense."

"Self-defense, he says? Tell that to the lad in there, your age, whose father got one of your arrows in his skull. I thought, for sure, he'd have a go at you. And believe me, there's more than a few in there who aren't exactly thrilled to see the Prefect of the Ninth's wee bugger-boy."

"I'm not Adratus's bugger-boy, you ogre."

"Well, be glad what you are is me nephew, or what you would be is a corpse thrown out in the woods and waiting for the vultures to come."

"Feck off," Ubaz barked. "You'd have a civil war on with that: a Rúcah militia killing the Feah temple guardian."

"'Tis Kaie that's aiming for a civil war now, if she don't change her ways. Not a one of the other four tribes is agreeing with her alliance with the Humans."

These words silenced Ubaz. The Feahs were alone. It wasn't news, but hearing Lann say it took the steam out of him.

"I think I love him," Ubaz whispered. "I know I trust him," he said more strongly. "What's more, I remember how unprepared we were when the Dayigans attacked us before. We need an ally."

"Don't you be acting like I forgot, boy," Lann snapped. "Whilst you was off hiding, I battled the Humans. And me wife and your da, we was all fighting, side-by-side with the rest of the village. And there they was, right next to me, when Human swords cut 'em both from the world. You think I forgot that? And I remember . . ." He inhaled sharply. "I remember the Humans taking me daughter and me sister— your mam—along with countless others, off with nothing but mysteries surrounding where they'd gone to or what was done to them. And you think you love a *Human* now, do ya? Fuck every one of the bastards."

Intensity lost, Ubaz sadly maintained, "It was the Dayigans, not the Tridulans. And they'll return here."

Lann put his hand on Ubaz's shoulder. "And we'll be ready for them, ourselves. Stay here with us, Ubaz. You was with us before. Join back up with us and help us rid our lands of Humans. If we can take out their second-in-command—"

Ubaz grabbed Lann's hand and flung it off his shoulder. "If you lay as much as a left pinkie on Adratus, I'll have an arrow so deep in your brain that you'll be dreaming of flint in the life to come." Ubaz gave Lann a hard shove, sending him stumbling back a step.

"Right then," Lann said. "All right. But you leave here, and you have my protection no more. You'll be a target, just like the rest of the enemies."

Ubaz glared daggers into Lann's eyes. He didn't feel fear. He didn't feel sadness or anything like before. He felt fire. He felt anger. He felt hate.

"Tell your new chief," Ubaz began, "the Tridulans aren't the cause of the dark Faeries. At least be honest in your reasons. You hate them 'cause you hate them, nothing more."

Ubaz spread his wings and jumped up.

He could hear Lann shout as he flew away. "You best not come back here again, lad, or I'll kill you meself."

—

"You told them of the elf?" Adratus asked.

"I did, aye," Ubaz said, head lowered and shoulders slouched as he entered the cave. "But they didn't listen to a word of it."

"Ward up," Adratus said, and the lightning web reignited.

"I'm shattered." Ubaz tossed his quiver to the dusty ground. "And I think I made things worse now."

Adratus didn't stand. "The people who wanted to kill us still want to kill us," he said flatly. "It doesn't sound like you did much harm."

The prefect dusted a somewhat flat section of the cave floor and lay on his side. He reached up a hand and waved Ubaz forward.

Ubaz unbuckled his belt, tossed it down, and lay in front of him as Adratus wrapped his arms around him.

Ubaz said, "Lann told me if he can kill the camp prefect . . . Well, I don't know the next bit, because that's when I threaten to kill *him*."

"Vowing to protect me?"

"Of course." He smiled.

"The hero Ubaz." Adratus squeezed him tighter for a moment as he kissed the back of Ubaz's neck. "Now turn around, fair hero, as I'm getting a face full of feathers."

Ubaz chuckled lightly as he shifted around, and Adratus rolled onto his back. Ubaz set his head on the prefect's chest.

"But you're a target now," Ubaz said.

"Legate Maximus and I often are. Now, we must sleep."

Ubaz nodded against the grimy black tunic smelling of sweat. He sighed a lengthy breath.

Silence.

Ubaz whispered. "You think we'll be making it back to Feah lands?"

Adratus paused a beat. "We have no other option."

CHAPTER FIFTY-THREE

Deep within the tangled, shadowed forest, Ubaz trailed closely behind Adratus. The stinking, limping legionaries were now nothing more than a wretched sight—their armor bloodied and chinked by arrows, tunics ripped. All but Ubaz had the beginnings of beards. They no longer marched like proud legionaries of the Tridulan Empire; instead, they slunk through the shadows like fleeing rats.

Days had passed since they'd left the cave, yet they knew all too well that they were still hunted.

Two hawks now flew overhead, shrieking when they saw the haggard men.

Adratus flung his left hand upward, releasing cords of red light from his fingertips.

The cords whipped around a hawk, pulling it down toward Adratus as he raised his gladius.

"No," Ubaz called out. "Not the hawk."

Adratus lowered his weapon. "Fucking hawks," he grumbled and dispelled the cords. "Why do they watch us with their *fucking pets*," he yelled, "yet not attack. *I know you hear me, Lann!*"

The hawks flew away, presumably to their unseen masters.

The Tridulan unit barely spoke, hardly at all, their faces perpetually grave. Most were fighting against pain, along with a fear that they could not continue. Yet they crept along, trying to keep the pace set by the prefect.

A boy younger than Ubaz struggled on a makeshift crutch. He had had to have his leg chopped off. Ubaz had been one of those to hold him down as a gladius hacked through flesh and bone. Four chops. Four screams. Four ruptures of living meat. Four splatters of blood.

Yesterday, another man had died. His body had simply shut down.

Most knew the Dark One, who reaped the souls of the dead, followed close behind this group. One could almost feel him and his ravens waiting in the shadows.

Adratus stopped behind a large tree and lifted his hand as a fist—a signal for the unit to halt.

Ubaz watched as the prefect crouched low and peered around the tree.

Had Adratus heard something, Ubaz wondered. *Rúcahs?*

Even less so than the other legionaries, Adratus's armor was not made for cowering. A single plate of steel covered his front, a single plate on his back. They forced posture when he now needed bend. They dug into his hips, rubbing the same spots they'd already rubbed raw.

Nevertheless, Ubaz could see no sign of either that pain or the pain from his injured arm. Adratus had gone cold—a Tridulan camp prefect through and through—as he led his men to safety. And despite all, Ubaz believed that Adratus's strength would in fact deliver them home.

He needed to believe that.

Adratus waved his hand, signaling them to continue forward.

—

The Dark One—Xanorael—came again that night, taking another soul.

The others found the legionary's body at sunrise when they awoke.

There was no mourning—no sound at all.

They all just stood as a somber circle, looking down, their breaths steaming in the cold autumn air.

Twenty-two men struck down to nine.

"We must continue," Adratus said.

—

The nights grew increasingly colder, but the Tridulans could not risk giving away their position with fire. Still, tonight, it was not the chill that kept Adratus awake. He'd endured plenty since joining the army, yet here in this uncultivated land, he felt a fear he hadn't experienced since his youth. His fear for Ubaz's safety kept him restless and sick to his stomach. He feared, too, what would happen to himself if he lost him.

Five days after the attack, Adratus lay sleepless on the ground, his gladius clutched tight against his chest. The survivors of the detachment slumbered nearby, yet Ubaz did not.

Adratus watched as Ubaz perched atop a lofty limb of an immense tree, his silhouette barely visible in the faint moonlight. The Terovae stared out over the land, no doubt searching for Rúcahs.

Adratus cast a small orb of light toward Ubaz.

The self-appointed sentinel flinched, grabbing his bow. He briefly searched the night before spotting Adratus, who waved him to come.

Jumping from the tree, Ubaz spread his orange wings and glided down.

"Get rest," Adratus whispered. "'Tis not your shift to guard."

Ubaz crouched nearer to his level, yet scanned the surrounding forest. "We pass back into Feah lands tomorrow," he whispered. "I doubt the Rúcahs will cross the border, so if they're going to be attacking, they'll be doing it tonight."

"'Twill be fine," Adratus began, "though our numbers are few, I will protect you."

"Will you stop with the protecting me talk? 'Tis not myself I'm fearing for; 'tis you. For some fool reason, I've grown attached to ya, you silly fecker."

Adratus snickered lightly. "And I you, mouthy Ubaz. Try to rest. If you're correct, we'll need our whole detachment alert tomorrow."

Ubaz sat down on the carpet of leaves as Adratus sat up.

"You and the others must be rather used to this sort of thing," Ubaz said. "Sleeping with the enemy about."

"Indeed. Though less so now that the Dayigans have turned their eyes from us to the Reyigans."

"You've been fighting a long while, then?"

Adratus nodded. "Since I was sixteen, fresh to the army. My first station was near the Dayigan border," Adratus recounted, thinking of how young he and Maximus had been back then. He sighed. "So many of my friends have been reduced to bricks in the lamentation labyrinths."

"Not sure what that is."

"No, you wouldn't know it," Adratus sniffed. "When a Tridulan is cremated, the ashes are mixed with other elements—some for ritual purposes, some to give it structure—and formed into a brick. These bricks become walls in intricate mazes that people traverse to remember those who have gone before them."

"'Tis good your people also honor your ancestors," Ubaz began somberly. "'Tis an important thing, that." He was silent a beat, staring out toward the thick woods before he continued, "Do you ever think, why are they the ones gone and not me? I think about it all the fecking time, seeing their faces—the ones I can remember now. Better people than myself are gone. My mam told me to hide when the Dayigans attacked us, but how's that fair to the rest of them?"

"Perhaps it isn't. Perhaps all we can do in exchange is fight for those who no longer can."

Ubaz nodded. "I think the True Light is crumbling apart," he whispered sadly as he drew a seven-pointed star in the dirt.

Adratus said nothing to this. If anyone else, at any other time, had uttered these words, he would have thought it a glorious statement. But to hear it so despondently spoken from the lips of Ubaz pained him.

"When the Dayigans come back for us," Ubaz continued in the same dismal tone, "do you think they'll wipe us out?" He ran his foot across the symbol.

"No." Adratus set his arm around him and rubbed his neck just above his wings. "The Drevite Nation—the Five Tribes—will be under Tridulan protection."

"How that, though?" Ubaz paused in thought. "You can't still be thinking that'll happen. Not now, after what we faced with the Rúcahs? They'll never be agreeing to it."

Adratus withdrew his hand and turned away from him to stare at the ground. "Just trust us."

"Trust what? They'll never agree to it," Ubaz said again with more urgency. "Tell me that what the chiefs decide about ye staying here matters."

Adratus remained silent.

"We never did have a choice, did we?" Ubaz asked.

Adratus continued to look down. "'Tis for your good."

Ubaz shoved him away and jumped up. "I can't believe it." He was shaking.

"Ubaz, lie down. We need sleep."

"Feck's sake, Adratus. Lann was right." He paced like something caged. "I went to the Rúcah militia—putting my own life in danger—and I stood there, I stood there, like a fucking idiot, telling them to trust the Tridulans. To trust you."

Adratus stood and reached out to him. "Ubaz—"

He punched Adratus in the face.

Legionaries sprung up, grabbing their swords.

"Stand down!" Adratus commanded. The punch left no injury to the war-hardened soldier, but it stung on a deeper level. His lungs tightened around shallow breaths, and his throat and eyes ached.

Ubaz just stared at him, eyes narrowed, jaw clenched, fist flexed at his side. "Fucking Humans." A tear fell.

The Terovae flew up from the ground, back to the lofty branch.

"*Ubaz!*" Adratus shouted, but got no response.

—

The Rúcahs did not attack the Tridulan detachment again on their return.

And Ubaz didn't speak to Adratus.

CHAPTER FIFTY-FOUR

Prefect Adratus and Legate Maximus stood silently in near darkness in a small room attached to the hospital in Fort Casdrevite. They watched a man in a long, black robe who stood at a small black altar. It held a triangle of pillar candles—two black, one red—surrounding a silver bowl filled with olive oil. Submerged at the base of the bowl sat a gray stone, smooth and flat, and three inches in diameter.

He tossed a flaming stick into the oil, causing it to ignite.

"Hail Zeanázel, Lord of Darkness and Defiance, God of Fire and the First Hue of light, he who teaches wisdom, he who teaches might, he who teaches reliance on our selves. Show us the path of reason. Show us the path of will. Show us the path of magnificent night. Hail Zeanázel! Hail to the Dark Light!"

Maximus and Adratus echoed him, saying, "Hail Zeanázel! Hail to the Dark Light!"

"Let no one see the words we release here, save for the emperor and those acting on his behalf. Let no one *hear* the words we release here, save for the emperor and those acting on his behalf. Protect our missive, that it may not go astray. Guard. Guide. Guard. Guide."

The whisperer extended his hand toward Maximus, and the legate stepped forward, handing him a folded sheet of paper.

The man laid the letter in the bowl. It ignited. "Take these words to the emperor of the great Tridulan Empire! Hail Zeanázel! Hail to the Dark Light!"

Again, the legate and prefect repeated these last words. "Hail Zeanázel! Hail to the Dark Light!"

—

Closing the black doors behind him, Adratus walked beside Maximus along a moonlit colonnade. To their left, a whitewashed plank wall separated them from the hospital's wards. To their right, evenly spaced wooden posts framed a rectangular courtyard.

Adratus recalled the courtyard he'd made for Ubaz. This one was larger and more elaborate—two of what looked like original trees remained, but the undergrowth had all been cleared away. In its place grew neatly trimmed shrubs and neatly mowed grass. Late autumn had banished all the flowers and turned everything brown. Night, in turn, painted all in blacks and blues. It was nature devoid of the wild. Civilized. Was it better, Adratus wondered, than what was here before?

He turned to Maximus. "How long do you think it will take?"

"Secure messages travel slower," the legate said as he walked, "and His Imperial Majesty does not directly monitor his whisper stone. It will need to be transcribed and presented. He will also need to reflect on the matter and perhaps consult the Senate. Nevertheless, an incident of this gravity warrants a speedy response. I doubt we will wait long."

Adratus nodded. "How do you expect His Imperial Majesty to have us handle the Rúcahs?"

The legate stopped as his dark eyes went cold. "I am certain you know the response already, Brother."

Adratus blinked downward. "Yes." The single word from his own mouth sounded so very grim.

Maximus entered a curtained doorway.

Incense hung strong within the ward as Adratus stepped through the curtain and to Maximus's side.

The injured men lay on thin mattresses on small wooden beds, each evenly spaced along the room. A thin coat of wall paint—red to waist height and white above—was the only attempt at decor.

Adratus watched the medics in their pale gray tunics as they checked wounds—now properly dressed—and helped the injured legionaries drink cups of water or eat flatbread. No longer was there panic or rushing or moans of pain. Yet, even in this calm, seeing his men in this broken state angered Adratus. He felt it behind his eyes and throughout his tensed muscles. And he was further angered for those not here, those they'd needed to abandon, those currently rotting on foreign soil.

Adratus counted the men again, as he had so many times now. Seven men here when he'd brought twenty legionaries. No change.

The physician approached, and Maximus greeted him with the single word, "Status?"

"Optimistic, Legate," the physician began. "We have administered various treatments as appropriate, primarily focusing on mundane methods unless magic is necessary. As we are far from Tridual and our campaign grows increasingly *complex*, I think it wise to ration our supernatural resources."

"Yes," Maximus said. "Quite right. Increasingly complex."

"And yet I," Adratus said, "am healed completely with not as much as a scab. I should be here, alongside them."

"Apologies, Prefect," the physician said, "but you are a senior officer." He gave a perplexed glance at the legate. "I followed standard procedure."

Maximus snickered. "The camp prefect is aware of procedure, yet is out of sorts. Ever the man of the legion is our Adratus. But he understands why we haven't time for him to lie around sucking up opium, yes?"

Adratus nodded.

Maximus turned to the physician. "The men will be well?"

"Yes, Legate. I expect all will make full recoveries. All but the young munifex who lost his leg. He will need a discharge from service."

Without a word to the other two, Adratus walked toward the soldier whom the physician had mentioned.

He lay in the bed, staring up at the ceiling. Like everyone else—including Adratus—he'd been cleaned up and shaved. He looked younger. He was, by Adratus's estimation, about eighteen years of age.

A thin bed-sheet covered him to midway up his slender stomach where he clutched the top of the cloth in his hand. One might barely notice that anything was wrong with him at all. But the sheet went flat halfway down his right leg.

The staring eyes, too, told of injury, told of darkness, and brokenness. Adratus had seen those eyes too many times before, but it never made them easier to face.

"Prefect." The young soldier began to sit up.

"No," Adratus said. "As you were."

"Are we at war, Prefect?"

He paused. "'Tis too soon to say."

"I hope we are," he said angrily. "I just wish I could fight in it. We should kill every fucking Drevite for what they did to us."

"'Twas the Rúcahs, not the Drevites as a whole."

"The fucking *Drevites*, Prefect," the munifex maintained. "Tridual should rip through every barbaric, tree-fucking, half-naked mollusk who would attack us when we came here to protect them."

The days and nights of running through the wilderness, with little hope of returning alive, were too fresh in Adratus's mind to utter anything consoling. He knew he should further press the point of Drevite versus Rúcah, but he hadn't the willpower. The same hate in the young soldier's eye burned behind the prefect's own.

"Adratus," Maximus called. "Come."

"Yes, Legate." Adratus again glanced back at the patient. "*Through hardship, to excellence.*"

"Through hardship to excellence," the boy repeated.

Adratus walked away.

———

Adratus kept a pensive silence as he followed Maximus back into the hospital's central courtyard.

"You fear for your barbarian," Maximus said, as he stopped and turned to face the prefect.

"I'm uncertain, Legate. Should I let the words of one—"

"'Tis more than one," Maximus interrupted. "The anti-Drevite sentiment throughout camp has escalated quickly."

"I see. Do the men not know that Ubaz fought alongside us?"

"They know. They also know thirteen citizens of Tridual were murdered when Drevites ambushed a diplomatic mission. Where is the boy now?"

"In my house. The hospital released him directly when they found he had no injuries."

"*No* injuries?" Maximus raised an eyebrow. "The men will have much to say of that. I'm confining him to your quarters indefinitely, for his safety."

"Understood, Legate."

Maximus paused, a fretful expression on his face as he looked Adratus up and down. "The physician has released you, as well. Go to him."

—

His mind full, Adratus said nothing to anyone along the short distance from the hospital to his home. He did not even acknowledge the familiar "Hail, Prefect," et cetera that came his way.

Adratus entered his house and closed the door. He paused motionlessly. A few brass lamps were already lit—a luminous cloud hovering above them. One of the base cooks was plating supper on the simple wooden table.

"*Ubaz*," Adratus called.

"He has left, Prefect," the cook said. "He wanted me to tell you he returned to the temple. Permanently, sir."

"You let him leave alone, *at night!*"

"'Twas not my place to—"

"Fucking za," Adratus growled. "If he survives, I will crucify him."

Adratus stormed from the house, slamming the door behind him.

To the gate of Fort Casdrevite, he hurried and continued out into the wilds, and in further haste, he continued the hour-long journey to the Feah temple village.

Nevertheless, he saw no sign of Ubaz.

CHAPTER FIFTY-FIVE

Thick fog wafted through the towering trees of the Feah temple village. The wet air was cold against Adratus's face, chilling him even beneath his armor. An eerie silence sat heavily. Something was wrong; he felt it. He idly thumbed the pommel of his sheathed gladius, readying himself for whatever would come.

As he carefully walked the main path, he searched the area. Even now, in the mid of night, a Tridulan town or fort would contain some activity, though slight. Yet, here was none. Yet here he felt watched, threatened.

Adratus slowed his pace to a creep as he gripped the hilt of his sword.

He searched the undulating white haze, searching, too, the sky that divulged just obscured glimpses of the blue and lavender moons.

"You shouldn't've come 'ere." Lann's voice rang out from a direction Adratus could not quite pinpoint.

The prefect stopped, drawing his gladius as he braced for battle.

"I came for Ubaz," Adratus called without direction. "Naught else."

"He'll never be your prize, Tridulan!"

"I wish no prize, you fool."

Adratus saw an image through the haze. Acting quickly, he darted and swung his sword. Cutting through swirling fog, his blade chopped into the side of a wooden pole carved with decorative spirals.

Lann's laughter rang out from above as Adratus rocked his sword free.

The prefect regained his stance, trying to find Lann's direction.

"Stop fluttering about and fight me like a man!"

"Don't be fretting yourself about me fighting, Human." Lann was to the left; Adratus turned. "I'll kill you soon enough, believe me that."

Then from behind the soldier, Lann called, "I warned you we didn't want you in our lands."

"The Dayigans *will* return," Adratus shouted. "You need us if you wish to survive. I've seen what they can do."

"Invaders can't be protecting us from invaders."

The clap of a bowstring sounded.

Adratus dodged as an arrow whooshed past his face.

The prefect followed the arrow's path with his eyes and saw the assailant hovering to his right.

Lann armed another shot as the fog churned to re-envelop him.

Wasting no time, Adratus cast out a cord of red light to wrap around the bow. In turn, Lann flapped his falcon-like wings in a fury as he strained to keep hold of his weapon. Yet Adratus maintained, pulling stronger with the cords.

Finally, Lann relented and hurled his bow aside. He drew a mace barbed with lethal shards of bone and plunged downward through the fog.

Their weapons thundered as they clashed, and the force of Lann's onslaught drove Adratus back. The legionary fought with skill and strength, but Lann's every counter-blow was fueled by more than mere rage—hate pushed against Adratus, shoving him ever further back into the fog.

"Ye Humans killed me wife," Lann shouted as he swung harder. "And sister! And friends! And ye stole me precious daughter!"

Adratus stood firm against him, each strike hard and calculated, putting Lann on the defensive. Soon, the winged warrior's fight began to weaken, while his own grew only stronger. When their weapons locked, they faced each other, mere inches apart.

"I have no wish to kill you," Adratus growled. "I seek only Ubaz."

Lann snarled in reply. "You come for the dead then." He spit into Adratus's eye. "I killed him meself."

Adratus went still in shock—disbelief paralyzing him as sickness overwhelmed him. "Tell me you lie," he demanded.

Lann stepped back, yet held his mace firm. "He's better off with the ancestors than in the arms of a Human."

"I . . . don't believe you," Adratus said, though numbness spread throughout his body.

Lann, seizing the moment, threw himself forward and swung the mace at Adratus's neck, sharpened bones of the weapon piercing through skin and ripping into flesh.

The mighty legionary called out and crashed to his knees as his ruptured jugular burst open with torrents of red.

Lann stayed fixed above him, ready to deliver a final fatal blow.

"Tell me he lives," Adratus said, clasping his neck and groaning as he fell to the other hand.

Lann lowered the weapon. "You're still fearing for Ubaz when you're dying yourself?"

"Yes." He coughed blood and collapsed to the dirt. "Tell me he lives."

Lann stopped, staring at his bloodied mace with shame. He then threw it down as he backed away.

Through his fading hearing, Adratus heard a young man's shout, followed by the word "No!" expelled with absolute heartbreak. Through his fading vision, he saw a blurry form running toward him.

Ubaz threw himself over Adratus and grabbed up the prefect's sword, holding it firm at Lann.

"Get away from him," he shouted.

"What other choice did he leave me with?" Lann said dejectedly. "They'll destroy all we are."

Ubaz dropped the sword and turned Adratus's head limply to face him. He softly kissed his lips.

"He said you were dead," Adratus whispered. "And my world died without you." Blood filtered around his fingers from his neck.

"I'm alive, you silly fecker," Ubaz said, "same as ever before. But I fear . . ." He began panting heavily as he gasped for air and grasped his hand to the soldier's hemorrhaging neck. "Chief!" he yelled back. "Please help!" He inhaled sharply. "Hurry, please."

"Stand back, stand back," the voice of Chief Kaie neared. She paused to see Adratus. "Mothers help us," she murmured. "Ubaz, step aside. I must reach him. Lann be gone with yourself."

Lann stared in horror for a moment longer before flying away.

Ubaz squeezed Adratus's bloody hand and then let go and stood away.

Kaie kneeled beside Adratus and placed her hand near his neck. "With the healing waters of Mother Lágeya," she intoned, "I imbue you." She repeated this, again and again, as her words echoed away into the black void, and Adratus felt himself drift into a deep, dreamless sleep.

CHAPTER FIFTY-SIX

Through the apex of the hill temple, the sun shone down onto the stone monolith, each side carved with a seven-pointed star around three spirals joined at their shared center. A ring of druidesses sat cross-legged on the floor around the obelisk as they sang a slow, tranquil song accompanied by the soft strumming of a hand-held harp.

Beside them, within the circle of ancient oaks that supported the high-up roof, Adratus drifted bit by bit into consciousness, finding himself lying on a bed of soft furs within the Temple Grove. He wore only the white temple garment he'd worn before. The warmth of Ubaz, in the same garment, enveloped him as his legs crossed his and his head lay on the prefect's smooth bare chest.

Adratus smiled at the bliss of it all as he pulled Ubaz tighter against himself.

"Awake are you?" Ubaz cooed. "I feared I'd lose you."

"I feared—" he began, his voice hoarse. He cleared his throat. "I feared I'd already lost you. The bastard Lann claimed he'd killed you."

"Aye, 'twas a wicked thing for my uncle to say."

"I'll kill him for it." Adratus tried to sit up but stopped as a sharp something poked his neck. He slapped his hand to the offending site to discover some type of long leaf wrapping his neck with a moist mass held in place beneath—bog moss, he guessed.

"It can come off now," Ubaz said tenderly. "Here, let me." He leaned in to free him from the unpleasant wrappings.

"'Tis healed?" Adratus asked.

"It is, aye. Altogether. Chief Kaie's quite the healer, herself." Ubaz picked at the long leaf with careful hands, tearing it apart piece by piece. "She had some bother at first. Said you were shielded."

"Yes. I have a spell shield against True Light magic."

"*Had.* She was able to pop your shield and fix you right up."

"It seems I've required much healing as of late," Adratus said with a slight grin as he looked at Ubaz's handsome face.

Long ginger hair framed his pale features. Sunlight streamed through the ceiling to bounce off the amber of his wings and glint across his athletic frame. Adratus couldn't help but adore the beauty of the man he had nearly driven away.

"That moment when I thought you were dead . . ." Adratus shook his head.

"I know," Ubaz whispered. He nodded solemnly before pressing his lips against the prefect's. The two kissed slowly and passionately, lost within a tender embrace.

"You left me," Adratus whispered beside his ear.

"Never mind that now, all right." He kissed the prefect again, their bodies fully together, as they held each other tight.

"And that'll be enough of that now." Chief Kaie chuckled. "Entertaining as it is to watch."

Ubaz jumped back. "Sorry, Chief," he said breathlessly.

The chief, standing just a few feet to the side of the two, scanned them. "Ubaz came back to us, saying that Lann and his lot might be onto something. Is it true that the Tridulan Empire won't be letting us choose whether or not you stay here?"

Adratus glanced downward a breath. "My words were true when I told you why we came—to assure the Dayigans do not claim this region. But as for the methods we were prepared to take to assure that security—apologies for not being as forthcoming."

Kaie nodded. "Why are our lands so important—I mean, I'm rather fond of them myself, but why are they so important to everyone else now?"

"I'm uncertain. I wish I had a better answer."

She gave him a stern look. "Ubaz says you believe the Dayigans are creating a weapon."

Adratus nodded. "Even those very high within the Dayigan army and nobility seem to know little, if anything, of what is called the 'Drevite Experiment.' I've found no records of it. Yet it appears to surround the development of a powerful magical weapon."

"Seems to me that someone's gone to a whole lot of trouble to hide something very important."

"True. I have seen the Dayigans take control of the minds of an entire town and turn them into fighters for their use. And I know you have seen the same."

She glanced downward. "I have, yes."

"From the little information I've uncovered, I believe the Dayigans aim to refine their technique so they may permanently convert all those who deviate from their twisted worldview into mindless things they can control. Then, they intend to forge these converted into an army to conquer the entire continent of Bikia. No more Five Tribes. No more Tridulan Empire. No more anything other than a vastly expanded Dayigan Empire, as they believe is their right and duty under God Déagar."

Kaie took a deep breath and released it. "How long do we have?"

"I have yet to determine," he said gravely. "However, to avoid this, Tridual *will* secure these lands, either as an ally or as a Tridulan province. I prefer the former."

"I trust him, Chief," Ubaz said. "To be honest with you, I was none too sure about him before, but . . ." He looked to Adratus. "I trust that he can forge an alliance that would serve the needs of both our peoples."

"He speaks the truth, Chief," Adratus said as he stood. "I have begun to truly *know* the Five Tribes. And I will do all in my power to ensure control of these lands remains in the hands of the chief druidesses. This, I vow. And *he whose word is meaningless is meaningless, himself.*"

"You quote the Tréréaldéag," Kaie said. "Quite impressive of you. But the other chiefs will be wanting more than the word of a Human to secure this alliance." Chief Kaie took a long, contemplative breath as she scanned the pair of them. "'Twas foolish of you to come here alone in the middle of the night, soldier. What brought you here?"

"Ubaz, Chief. I feared for his safety."

"But why's that?"

"Are you asking why I feared for his safety?"

"Is that what I'm asking?"

The Tridulan gave a confused look as he absorbed her question. He then turned away from the chief to Ubaz at his side. The youth with the sad eyes.

Ubaz's image was fit to be carved in marble and centered in a Tridulan forum. But as wonderful as was his flesh, it was but a frame for a beautiful heart and mind, and a humor that made him laugh. The smitten soldier realized what he, on some level, had known all along.

"You want to know . . ." Adratus said slowly as he stared at Ubaz, and his entire soul was uplifted. ". . . if I care for him?"

"*Care?*" she asked with a smirk. "Is that all it is now? I suppose we should all just go home then."

"You want to know if I *love* him?" Adratus chuckled blithely at saying the word. "Yes, by the diabolic Gods, I love Ubaz."

Kaie stepped toward them and turned to Ubaz. "And you're feeling the same about him, lad?"

"I am, Chief," he beamed. "Beyond a doubt."

The chief smiled softly. "The Mothers teach that 'Love is the third zenith, for only a fool turns his back to it.' I wouldn't want to be a fool, would I now?" She waved them together. "As I said, the other chiefs will be wanting quite a bit more than words. But what a better way to forge a true alliance than by uniting the love of two who'd see it strive."

The men stared confusedly at one another.

"You mean," Adratus began, his heart pounding so ferociously that he could barely hear. "We should be wed?" He stared, uncertain, at Ubaz.

She turned to Ubaz and gave him a sly grin. "He's not exactly quick to the meaning, is he? Are you sure you want this thick bastard?"

Ubaz chuckled. "Someone's got to knock some sense into the poor fellow, don't they now?"

She turned back to Adratus. "Aye, that's exactly what I mean. A union of love to bring together our peoples. But I won't be forcing anything that's not meant to be. Just nudging it along a wee bit."

Adratus couldn't help but smile. "In truth, marriage was not on my agenda for the day. Yet . . ." He met Ubaz's gaze. "Is that what you want?"

Ubaz reached for his hand. "If you'll have me."

"*If I'll have you.*" Adratus laughed. "Of course." He sighed. "Of course. And together, we will build a life. And build a true and lasting unity between the Five Tribes and the Tridulan Empire."

Ubaz further beamed. "Right, then. Kneel before me."

With a tilt of his head and a sly grin, Adratus complied.

Ubaz rested his hand on Adratus's shoulder, stretching out his amber wings from his back.

"In the old times of the first calendar," Chief Kaie spoke firmly and loudly in a voice that rang out through the temple, "Goddess Ashatra, Mother of Magic, lost her divine heart to God Karulus, as did he the same for her. And love was abundant betwixt the two. So, the sapphire God knelt down before the amethyst Goddess, and he implored her to take him as her husband in marriage. Adratus of Tridual, do you ask this same honor from Ubaz of Treasa?"

"With all my heart."

"And do you, Ubaz of Treasa, accept this man into your home and into yourself that he may be forever yours as your husband?"

"I do, aye."

Kaie's lips curved into a smile. "Well, would you believe our luck? I just happen to have all the components for a marriage ceremony, prepared and waiting for ye." She lifted her arms toward the beams of sunlight cascading down through the temple's center. "Away now, lovers, and prepare to be bonded together, soul and body."

The druidesses erupted into cheers as they led Adratus away to the edge of the ring of ancient oaks. Two more of their sisters took Ubaz by the arm and brought him to the opposite side.

As they reached the edge of the circle, another druidess rushed forward, bearing a wooden bowl filled with ashy blue paint. With skilled fingers, they painted intricate designs on Adratus's muscular form, including a triangle of three spirals over his heart and actual triangles on the backs of his hands.

His eyes remained on Ubaz across the circle. Ubaz received the same treatment, Adratus saw, but in deep purple. They drew a spiral in the center of his forehead and a triangle of three spirals over his heart.

Afterward, they led the two men to the stone table set before the monolith, where Chief Kaie awaited. She lifted spans of two ropes—red and purple—side by side. "Join your left hands," she instructed.

The men complied, their faces beaming with joy as they wrapped their hands around each other's.

"See us, rulers of the True Light!" Kaie announced with a clear and joyful voice. "See us, Mother Lágeya!" She wrapped the rope around their joined hands. "See us, Mother Ashatra!" Another wrap of the rope. "See us, Mother Larissa!" The final wrap completed the sacred bond between Adratus and Ubaz. "May this union be blessed in your sight and deemed holy by your divine grace."

Kaie then handed the ends of the rope to the men, who grasped them firmly in their right hands.

"Now," Kaie continued, "step apart, but remain forever joined."

They stepped back, separating their left hands while holding onto the ends of the rope with their right. In a fluid motion, they pulled taut and formed a strong knot.

And from all corners of the Temple Grove, druidesses cheered in unison: "Blessings from the Three Mothers. Blessings from the True Light!"

As silence fell over the area, Kaie lowered her head and clasped her hands at her waist. Ubaz nudged Adratus's arm, silently signaling for them to do the same. Adratus followed suit.

From his periphery, Adratus saw that all but three of the druidesses were leaving the grove. One of the remaining approached him, delicately taking hold of the knotted rope before stepping away with it.

Finally, Kaie spoke again. "Come forward and face me."

The men complied, their heads bowed in reverence.

"In the name of the Three Mothers, your souls have been bound as one. In the name of the Three Mothers, your bodies will be bound as one."

A druidess approached Ubaz, her white gown swishing softly against the grass. She reached out with delicate fingers to his waist and untied the linen that ringed him. It fell to the grass, leaving him bare. Another druidess approached Adratus and did the same.

Adratus's heart raced with both confusion and anticipation as he stole a glance at Ubaz beside him. He watched as Kaie led Ubaz to lie upon the altar, his back pressed against its smooth surface.

Chief Kaie stood over him, by his side. The Septogram glowed with an eerie purple light behind her on the great stone. She stretched out her arms to either side, palms facing upward.

"I call Lágeya and Jerah. Bear witness!" Kaie exclaimed. "I call Ashatra and Karulus. Bear witness! I call Veavia and Déagar. Bear witness! Let the True Light lovers protect this everlasting bond we consummate before you."

With a beckoning hand, Kaie summoned Adratus forward.

The legionary approached the altar where his beloved lay, exposed and ready for this sacred joining.

As a druidess began to play a wild rhythm on her drum, Kaie stepped aside and joined two others in a frenzied dance.

Adratus could see the nervousness in Ubaz's eyes, but too, he could see the desire that was now unhindered. Already, Ubaz had grown rigid from the legionary's approach. Now the prefect softly took the guardian's hand and tenderly kissed his inner wrist before firmly pressing it down onto the stone at Ubaz's side.

A deep groan escaped Ubaz's lips as a cord of red light cuffed him, binding his hand to the stone and securing it in place.

The tempo of the drumbeat grew faster and more fervent, filling the temple with resounding echoes.

Adratus neared his lustful face. "Is it all right?" he whispered.

"It is, yes," Ubaz breathed, his words erupting from deep within him. "But go slow," he whispered. "I haven't done this before."

With a nod, Adratus reached out, and another cord circled Ubaz's other wrist, pulling it down and binding it to the stone.

His hands traveled hungrily over the Terovae's pale flesh, igniting sighs of pleasure as he explored his athletic form. Adratus punched Ubaz's chest, eliciting a primal grunt from the man beneath him.

Ubaz writhed and squirmed under Adratus's heated touches, his mouth open in an animalistic grin. As Adratus kissed down the center of his stomach, Ubaz's muscles flexed, and his breath quickened with anticipation.

Eagerly watching, Ubaz's eyes were mere slits, and his mouth hung open in panting delight.

Adratus descended to the diagonal ridge dividing Ubaz's abdomen and thigh, expertly teasing the sensitive area with his tongue. Ubaz moaned and pushed his head against the stone, arching his entire body as he lifted his butt from the stone.

Chief Kaie danced wildly, her arms raised to the heavens. The drummers beat faster and louder.

Energized by the rhythm, Adratus continued to tongue inwardly down the salty ridge, edging closer to ginger curls.

Kaie began chanting in a rapid and powerful language that Adratus could not comprehend.

Adratus wrapped his fist around Ubaz's throbbing cock and gently tongued the sensitive skin before lapping up the clear nectar from within.

The sound of Ubaz's pleasured moans mingled with the drumbeat and chants, creating a symphony of ecstasy within the sacred space. With delicate precision, Adratus continued, as a misty lavender light enveloped them both. Ubaz's body convulsed in pleasure as he thrust upward, and Adratus eagerly took him deeper into his mouth.

Straining against his bonds, Ubaz was a wild beast caught in the throes of passion. He twisted and turned toward Adratus, thrusting relentlessly.

The spiral on Ubaz's forehead glowed with a vibrant purple light, matching the intensity of his glowing eyes. With a guttural growl and quickened breaths, his body jolted as he neared the peak of pleasure.

Adratus withdrew his mouth and moved back. "Not yet," he said with a grin.

Ubaz appeared lost in a haze of desire, his glowing gaze fixed upon Adratus, as he could do nothing but nod in agreement. Sweat trickled down his brow, dampening his long hair.

The lavender mist flowed all around them, growing thicker and warm, obscuring all but the two while the drums echoed as if from a distant carnal place.

As Adratus moved between Ubaz's legs, the guardian bent his knees and rested his feet on the soldier's solid chest.

The blue triangles on the backs of Adratus's hands glowed, and he felt a heat behind his eyes which made him think they glowed as well. He turned his fists, inverting them, downward-pointing triangles becoming upward-pointing—water symbols becoming fire symbols.

"Gliéska and Zeanázel, *bear witness!*" Adratus shouted. The blue paint on his skin ignited as fiery red. His eyes mirrored the same color as he spread his arms wide and looked toward the heavens. "Let the Dark Light lovers protect this everlasting bond we consummate before you."

Still with Ubaz's cold feet firm against his warm chest, Adratus paused for a moment to relish in the sight of the beautiful, inexperienced man ready before him.

Ubaz gazed back at him and gave a pleading nod. "Take me, Prefect," he whispered.

With a lustful snarl, Adratus pressed himself to the heated crack and pushed gently inward.

CHAPTER FIFTY-SEVEN

Some amount of time passed.

Minutes. Hours. Adratus could not be certain, but it was a time in paradise. He continued to hold the warm, sweaty, spent man in his arms.

And when he opened his eyes, his body pulsated with superlative delight. Dizzy. He remained on the altar with Ubaz atop him.

He could not move. He didn't want to. Adratus only wished to feel the energy they had created, the amazing energy with which they had imbued the entire room. It hung in lavender ribbons, circling within the air.

Another man's voice cut through the bliss, "Marvelous performance."

It took Adratus a moment to think, to recognize the voice of Legate Maximus.

Chief Kaie rushed toward him. "How dare you interrupt the holy marriage ceremony!"

"Stand down, woman," Maximus said, as he entered the circle of oaks around the altar. "I come to collect my man and will soon depart. Besides, from what I witnessed, the marriage was well consummated."

"Twice over." Adratus lazily turned his narrowed eyes to his leader to see Maximus approaching in full armor. He then licked his lips, dry from breathing so heavily. "How now, Brother?" he breathed. "Welcome to my wedding."

"Congratulations, good Adratus. Did you perhaps mention to the recently deflowered that Tridulans cannot marry barbarians and that Tridulan soldiers cannot marry at all?"

"Is it true?" Ubaz tensed in his arms.

"Only in matters of law," Adratus said. "We are married at the heart and soul, my love."

"Nevertheless," Maximus resumed, "we have matters to attend. Come. His Imperial Majesty has answered our communication. We march on the Rúcahs at once."

"The Rúcahs?" Chief Kaie spoke up, while Adratus and Ubaz sat up. "What will you do to them?"

"The Rúcahs," Maximus began, "killed thirteen of my men without provocation. Thus, by order of His Imperial Majesty, the Rúcah tribe will repay their debt tenfold. We shall storm their region and collect one hundred and thirty men for crucifixion along our road."

"Monstrous," Kaie shouted. "I won't stand for it."

"You stand in good favor with the Tridulan Empire, madam," Maximus rebuked. "Unless you wish to aid us, I suggest you maintain your distance from this. Already, a second legion sails here. We would hate to need call more."

Ubaz wrapped his waist in a temple cloth. "You can talk to him, right?" he whispered to Adratus. "We'll have peace, our people and yours. As you vowed to us."

"This is a separate matter," Adratus said, confused, as he backed away from his groom. "You saw what the Rúcahs did to us. Think you such things can occur without retribution?"

"But is one Tridulan life worth ten of ours, though?"

Adratus said nothing.

Lann flew into the chamber and landed some distance from both legionaries. He raised his mace resolutely.

Maximus drew his gladius, and the two men took battle stances as they eyed one another.

The druidesses, save for Kaie, hurried to the farthest wall.

"We'll be having none of that here!" Chief Kaie commanded. "This is a holy place."

"Adratus, fix this," Ubaz implored. "The Tridulans can't be killing a hundred and thirty of my people. You vowed peace."

Adratus felt his heart pounding in his chest. "We *will* have peace," he said. "After."

"Fear not, native people." Maximus raised his voice with forced diplomacy. "There will be no conflict here in your sacred temple. This I vow by God Zeanázel. If the insurrectionist vows the same."

"I'll not be vowing by any Dark Light God," Lann said, "but aye, I vow the same. By the Three Mothers."

The weapons were lowered, yet the tension remained.

"We must go," Adratus said, reaching for Ubaz's hand.

Ubaz stepped away, his eyes saddened. "I can't go off with you to help butcher my own people."

"Come, Adratus," Maximus ordered. "Enough of this."

"We will discuss this later, love," Adratus said to Ubaz. "*At home.* Now, we must hurry."

Ubaz stood, staring and motionless. His eyes watered as he said, "No," so softly that it was more of a motion of the mouth than a sound.

"Ubaz," Lann said, "'tis time to go, lad."

"You must return to camp," Adratus implored. A dull hurt swelled deep within his chest. He forced a smile, though it hid nothing. "I love you. And, at last, we can be together. Surely, you must see we are not villains in this. That *criminal*," he thrust his hand toward Lann, "attacked us without cause, killing men who fought for their lives only feet from our side. They would have killed *you*."

Lann lifted his mace. "Ubaz," he said gently, "your place is with us."

Ubaz remained unmoved, his eyes darting from Lann to Adratus. He made some attempt at speech but failed, leaving his mouth agape. At length, he ran to Lann.

"They were Human, *Tridulan soldiers!*" Adratus shouted. "We *must* avenge them."

"Come, Brother," Maximus said, as he handed his cape to Adratus. "Your fanciful reverie has ended. Condolences. Yet we are here with greater purpose and must act as such."

Adratus tied the cape around his waist as he looked a final moment at Ubaz, standing at the side of the man who had tried to kill him just the previous night.

A tear rolled down Ubaz's cheek. "As the temple guardian," he said with a cracking voice, "I must ask ye to go. Or I'll have to force ye."

Heartbroken, Adratus could say nothing, as he turned to leave with Maximus.

"We will come for you, criminal," Maximus said to Lann. "You and your rebels will learn why you do not *attack* Tridual."

With that, Adratus and Maximus exited the temple.

The Hand of the Blessed

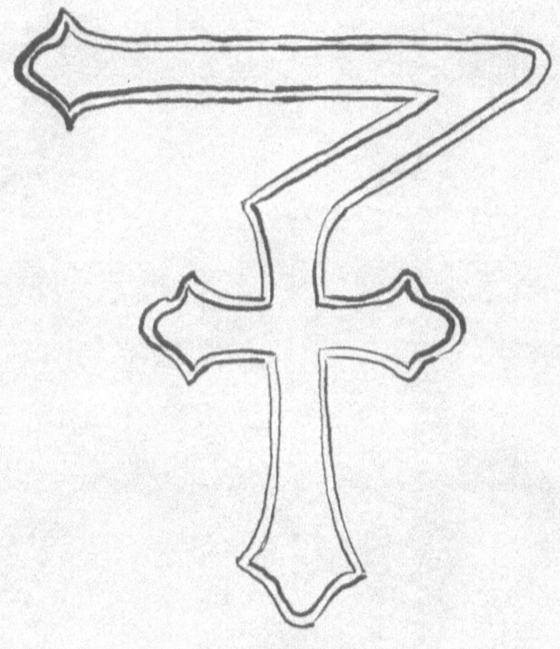

Reyigan Empire
Allar Lands
Feah Lands
Vohcktaran Kingdom
Reyigan Er
Blessed Hand Abbey
Hyvile River
Dayigan Empire
Dinikimera
Kegono
N
W
E
S
0   30   60   90
Miles

CHAPTER FIFTY-EIGHT

Duodeki 15, 839: Seven Days Later

They frightened him. Yet Father Thomas heard them, even now, they who were beyond his thick bedroom door. Morning and noon and late into the evening, he heard the sounds of these strange sick people who were so euphemistically entitled the Blessed.

He heard their footsteps, limping steps with the dragging of feet. Despite their labored gait, the inmates were quite mobile—albeit slow. And evidently, they took some inexplicable delight in their ambulatory abilities, for they, all seventy-two of them, always kept true to their pointless paths, even as it sent them mindlessly shuffling through the aged drab rooms and unadorned halls of this back-country abbey. Even as it sent them, too, through the drafty stark sanctuary of the adjoined Déagrian church.

However, the more maddening of their noises came not from their dirty bare feet, but from their yawning, drooling mouths. For the Blessed muttered incoherent nonsense continuously throughout every moment they were not either eating or sleeping.

It was a wicked thing, Thomas knew, to fear these people, these harmless simple people mandated to his care. Even now, as he stood gazing at the thick wooden beams framed within the simple stone doorway, even now as he hesitated to depart his bed-chamber, he realized completely that he was a wicked man for cloistering himself herein.

Already, he, at a pace that would make a snail seem energetic, had donned his simple, hooded robe of coarse green, meanwhile savoring the precious moments alone. Now he pulled his hood up, covering his head, shaved bald in the center, leaving only a plain, round face. However, one could not wear a hood indoors. He pushed it back again.

He breathed deeply and exhaled. A crossed number seven hung as a wooden pendant from his necklace. He held it in his hand and muttered, "Praise God Déagar, the one and only God, protector from the Dark. You are the Greatest of All. Give me the strength to keep true to the path set before me and to help those who need my help. Astha'will-miabé."

He exited his room, and the noises became instantly louder. Immediately, Thomas was surrounded by the mindless people within the cramped stonework corridor. This place was lit by only two small, arched windows: one nearby at the hall's end and the other within the distant stairwell, where the exits to this place also stood. These windows, too, were the only ventilation.

Enclosed, Thomas could shuffle along no faster than the unfortunate people, who paced with listless tempo. They marched in a disorganized mass up one side of the hall, only to turn at the end and follow the other side back down. They passed, on either edge of the hall, basic wooden doors exactly like the one through which Thomas had just passed, but these doors were opened, revealing small cells dimensionally identical to Thomas's, but devoid of even the simplest decor or furnishing save for two plain cots.

Most of the Blessed were here. They filled this constricted corridor in such a tight mass that Father Thomas felt he could not breathe. Every one of them was dressed the same—in plain, sleeveless, shapeless, off-white tunics hanging loose and unbelted to center calf. Men composed the bulk, with about a third being women. They were almost all Terovaes. Only five of the entire group were Human.

Even as they were all around Thomas, he would not look into their eyes. Their eyes, such horrible recesses of pure emptiness, were insufferable to behold. The eyes themselves exhibited all the normal corporeal features that any normal eye should include: pupil, iris, sclera. But any brief moment the father so much as glimpsed into the vacant eyes of the Blessed overwhelmed him with horrible sensations, a horror that putrefied within his guts while unnerving him head to toe. It was an unnamable horror beyond the limits of the physical senses, a sensation that wrapped around a person, enclosing and crushing him like black chains around the soul.

Thomas was not alone in feeling thus. The nuns who also cared for the inmates also talked of this horror, but the sisters stayed here only in rotations of three months. Thomas, however, had not left these walls in years.

Nevertheless, the priest was not without great sympathy for these unfortunate souls. In the four years Thomas had spent within these hallowed walls, not one day had passed in which he did not pray to God Déagar for their healing. However, whatever malady afflicted the wretched group was beyond his understanding. They, Thomas and the sisters, could do nothing for them but watch over them—those who were already here and those who occasionally joined the flock.

As Thomas drew steadily closer to the stairwell at the end of the hall, a stench suddenly accosted his nostrils. The rancid smell was unmistakably one that originated deep within the lower bowels. His hand darted to cover his nose and mouth, a futile gesture. He scanned the Terovae who toddled before him to see a line of watery brown trickling down the mindless man's inner leg.

Thomas shuddered. He should be accustomed to such sights by now—it was the reason all the Blessed remained diapered—but his stomach and throat seized. Having no other option, Thomas exhaustedly conceded to amble behind this befouled Blessed, while feces dripped in his path.

The father tapped the soiled man on the shoulder. "Go to the bath," he groaned wearily.

Here lay the most bizarre abnormality with the Blessed, the abnormality from which all others spawned. For, despite this reeking man giving no sign whatsoever that he even heard Thomas's instruction, the priest knew, indisputably, that the man was now en route to the very place that he'd been told to go. There, one of the sisters would be waiting. She would not need to change or clean the man herself, but would only need to command him to do it, step by step.

This was because none of the Blessed had a will of his own—not any at all, whatsoever. Their every single action was dictated by the Church, specifically by either Prior Thomas, the archbishop, the sisters, or any visiting clergy.

This man before Thomas shat himself because no one told him to shit elsewhere. Of course, there was no way for the caretakers to know when to tell him this; thus, the diaper instead. Generalized orders—*Do this when this happens*—had been long found to be ineffective.

Something caught Thomas's attention: a closet door up ahead in the stairwell was open—*Strange, it had never been open before*. Only the archbishop had the key, and Thomas had never even glimpsed inside.

He saw two of the Blessed enter and fade away into shadows.

Thomas proceeded straightway to the door, but where he anticipated a closet, he instead found a continuation of the stairwell descending as a spiral into thick darkness. The odd discovery perturbed him—*Had not the archbishop called this a closet?*—but it also heightened his need to retrieve the lost inmates who had entered.

He followed.

—

He saw an emerald light below. It steadily increased as Thomas timidly spiraled downward into unknown places. Habitually, he clasped the wooden seven hanging from his necklace. Soon, he saw the source of the light: a hemispherical geode filled with gleaming crystals of green. Yet this superlative marvel was casually positioned on a small, homely ledge with no more reverence than a common oil lamp.

Thomas continued. Still, he held the wooden pendant. He did not see the strayed Blessed, but he heard their nonsensical ramblings—words muttered at complete random—growing louder. The father's twisted path took him past another geode and finally into a hall.

The thin corridor was eerily familiar. It, in every aspect, matched the hall on which Thomas had lived the last four years of his life. Its only small anomaly was that it lacked exterior windows and that three green-lit geodes hung equidistantly along the hall's ceiling. And the doors, Thomas now saw, the doors had square windows cut into them. And the windows had bars.

The father's heart thumped wildly in his chest. Something about this place felt wrong—tremendously wrong. Whatever this place was, Thomas knew it should not be the foundation on which a holy abbey should sit. He tried to convince himself that it was just another floor of rooms, no more iniquitous than the two matching halls above. Just spare space, he told himself, locked up until what time when more rooms were needed. But he knew better. He felt it.

Thomas stood within the emerald light in silence. Listening.

"Like … tree … ground … against …" the closer Blessed droned in monotone, harsh against silence, "his … then … aye … show …"

But Thomas heard something more—a sound so exceptionally faint that he nearly missed it entirely. A murmured singing, a singing with a melancholic tempo. It was like a gentle breeze from a nearby cell. Thomas stepped carefully nearer, silently nearer, trying not to disrupt the fragile sound. The tenor maintained the high octaves of a woman or child. The voice cracked sadly at every other note. Such a pitiful sound was this. It encapsulated his heart and clutched it tightly.

"Wherefore dost thou come hither, Prior?" spoke a slow, calm voice. A man's voice. It was just behind Thomas. "No place is this for thee."

He recognized the voice immediately as that of the archbishop.

The entire body of the priest constricted as he spun, ever so slowly, to face the intimidating man. Even in the strange emerald light, Thomas could see his ghastly features: his bent spine and his inset eyes. Although Thomas could not begin to speculate an age for this man, he was clearly much older than any person he had ever before witnessed. So extraordinarily aged was Blastilv that his grayed, blotchy skin sagged from his bones in such a nauseating manner that it seemed it might break free and ooze to the floor. His hair was long and brittle white, like that of a long-dead corpse.

The archbishop neared Thomas, growing steadily closer as his eyes stayed locked on the younger clergyman. "I grow wrathful at disobedience, Prior," Blastilv stated harshly.

"F-forgive me, Your Grace," Thomas stammered. "Two of the Blessed wandered into this place, and I followed to retrieve them. See them there, Your Grace."

Blastilv did not look to the Blessed, nor did he reply. His yellowed, murderous eyes remained locked on Thomas. Such icy fury held within. After living such a duration under one roof, the two men should be as kin, yet Thomas scarcely knew this man better than at their first meeting.

Was he violent? Surely not, a man of the cloth.

Thomas suddenly realized how cold he felt. His skin was goose-pimpled with hairs on end.

Blastilv passed by, his long green cloak of fine fabric brushing the prior's skin and stirring up the chill.

"'Tis time thou knowest of this place, Prior," the archbishop said, his words slow and precise. "Fear not. Our deeds are righteous, carried out for God Déagar. *Praise he who is the Greatest of All.* Come, Prior, and witness divinity in force."

Thomas approached as Blastilv unlocked and opened a cell. They stared inside.

The Terovae girl within was an adult, yes, but barely and surely not yet twenty. Her feathered wings and long, tangled hair appeared to have once been shimmering white, but as she lay stripped, curled in filth, they were now filth colored.

There was no song from her now. Pressed into the corner, she stared with silent horror at Blastilv. Her only movement was a quivering of her chin.

"Who is she?" Thomas asked at length.

"An unholy savage, nothing more," the archbishop replied flatly as he stared straight into her eyes. "Before thine arrival hither, the king allotted a unit of soldiers to my abbey. And with them, I was able to rescue many savages from the nearby forest. There, the people live like beasts within the trees and worship a twisted version of the True Light."

"You speak of the Drevite lands, yes?" Thomas asked, knowing the border was only a few days' journey down the Hyvile River.

"Thou art mistaken, Prior. The Drevites are without land. The savages merely occupy a sector of the Dayigan Empire that we have yet to reclaim."

Thomas nodded, though with uncertainty, his eyes darting downward. "You are right, of course, Your Grace."

"Yes," Blastilv said. "Yet the soldiers are now long dead; thus, for eight years, I could not rescue a single savage from his offensive life. This pretty, broken creature here is the last.

"Agaze thou unto this pitiful fiend." Blastilv motioned toward the Terovae girl. "And mourn the wickedness within, for it is utterly dire. Yet know thee, also, the divine mercy of Déagar can wash away such foulness."

He neared the unclothed girl, who huddled in the corner, pressing herself backward as she tried to clench herself into a ball. Her shaking was apparent even from where Thomas stood at the cell door.

"Dost thou wish to be cleansed, savage?" Blastilv asked with pleasure. "Dost thou wish to be *born anew*?"

Her only reply was a succession of slow, deep, terrified breaths.

Blastilv chuckled and returned to the hall.

The Blessed who had wandered into this place were now passing by the cell. The archbishop ordered them to stop.

"Thou art, of course, familiar with my creations, Prior," Blastilv said as he approached the now frozen and silent Terovae men.

"'Twas you? You who made them like . . . *this?*"

"Didst thou not even suspect, Prior? Not in all this time? Interesting. Yea, 'twas I, but 'twas in benefit of these poor souls who refused the path of righteousness. See thou not, O Prior?" Unhurriedly, he circled the motionless Blessed. "Behold, these men who were once sinners are now incapable of sin. This hindered state in which they now exist is for their own benefit. Lo, they will sin no longer." He commanded the two Blessed to seize the girl and stand her up.

Thomas could not move as he watched the sight, like a nightmare enacted before him, a sight so unreal that he could barely accept it. The Blessed harshly snatched up the frightened girl, who weakly struggled and wept. Her quivering flesh, Thomas could not help but witness, was soft and bare and displayed in such a way he'd never seen. Unlike most of the Blessed, her skin was free of the purple symbols called tattoos. Her breasts bounced back and forth as she struggled, her skin so pale. Though Thomas wished to face away, the vision entranced him.

The voice of the archbishop was just behind his ear. "And now the day hath come for this pretty, pretty girl to be blessed. Come, Prior, and I will show thee how to make a true Déagrian, one who is both wholly pure and fully obedient."

CHAPTER FIFTY-NINE

With utmost care not to cross paths with the sisters, they—Thomas and Blastilv—escorted the Terovae girl up to ground level and into the church. Though held firmly by two of the Blessed, she struggled the entire distance, her tangled dirty hair lashing back and forth. Blastilv, however, had taken the precaution of stuffing a length of faded green cloth into her weeping mouth.

Thomas wanted to rescue her, to rush her to the exit and send her running far from this shadowed abbey, but it was not his place to question the archbishop.

A somber, drafty gloom was the church. Within, Blastilv instructed Thomas to secure the thick doors—those through which they had entered and those leading outside. The prior obeyed forthwith and without words. He could not speak, for his mind was so conflicted, so twisted with thoughts.

After setting down the thick beam to cross and impede the door, Thomas breathed. He turned and looked—his body shaking—down the church's center, where the Blessed marched the stripped girl down the aisle. She continued to fight with all of her weakened might, squeaking through the gag. A large part of Thomas wished to save her, but she *was* being saved, he reminded himself. This was for good, for God Déagar. For the betterment of the world.

The aisle was relatively short—here was no cathedral. It was basic for a True Light church with barely twenty feet in its tallest sectors. Across from Thomas, the floor stepped up to a slight stage for sermons. There, centered on its rear wall, was the church's primary ornament: a statue of the powerful and virtuous God Déagar.

With Blastilv to her side, the girl was forced onto the stage before the graven God. Reluctantly, Thomas joined, his heart heavy with guilt. His eyes watered.

In silence, save for the girl's muffled cries, they stood. The clergymen stared reverently at the supreme being.

God Déagar, an ominous figure within a slight alcove, appeared Human. He wore full plate armor with his head, along with his face, fully covered by his helm. A horizontal slit at his eye level offered only a glimpse of the divine face. In his right hand, Déagar held a sword rested downward, its point touching the floor.

"Fear not," Blastilv said to Thomas, "for our actions hither are just and sanctioned by the Almighty."

The girl wept through her gag.

Thomas's eyes remained on his God. This depiction of Déagar was, aside from some minor elements, the standard icon, except that he normally wore a cape. Here, he did not, for this was only the front half of the figure, as if he emerged from the wall. This was done, Thomas assumed, to avoid paying for a full statue. Also, when not depicted with a shield, Déagar held his left hand down and forward, as if directed compassionately to someone at his feet. This was the case with this statue, but here the gauntlet of this hand was, strangely, not stone, but actual plates of gold.

The glove was the only part of the statue's golden armor that wasn't merely painted stone.

Blastilv raised his leathered hands to the heavens and spoke with loud, clear words, saying, "Praise His Divine Infinity, *Déagar*, God of fire and lighting, eldest of the Gods, protector from the Dark. He who is Greatest of All. I bring unto thee this unclean savage who hath denied thy righteous path and who hath lived sinful and uninhibited. I pray thee,

O God, shine thy hallowed blessings upon her and purge her wretched soul of iniquity."

The archbishop faced Thomas, those narrowed, yellowed eyes staring deep into his own, chilling and frightening the younger man. "Take hold of the girl and kneel her beneath the hand of God. Do this so that she may be blessed."

"How?" Thomas uttered.

Yet the archbishop's reply was an impatient glower.

The prior's eyes met hers—the victim, the soon-to-be-saved—as he approached. Her eyes pleaded silently with more fear than he had ever seen in a fellow person.

"It is for your own good," Thomas whispered, his voice cracking even as he forced calm. "You have chosen a path that will lead you to the fiery afterlife in za. We . . . cannot allow that."

Thomas told the Blessed to release her. He grabbed her around her bare stomach. She squirmed within his arms. He held her tight and pulled her toward the statue.

Blastilv shouted out to the lofty ceiling, "In the name of almighty Déagar, I call upon the sacred powers of the True Light. Bless this vile sinner. Her will hath betrayed her. Her will must be purged. *Lyforia, set!*"

The armored hand of God Déagar glowed a faint green.

Though Thomas's heart ached, he forced the panicked girl down to her knees under the divine hand. With all of his might, Thomas held her firmly in place. His arm pressed the back of her head to make her bow. His other arm circled her body. Her face streamed with tears. He tried to ignore. Her sullied wings lashed feebly against him.

"Her will hath betrayed her," Blastilv called again. "Her will must be purged. Let her only deeds hereafter be as directed by thy Church."

The hand began glowing brighter. The girl began screaming through the gag and struggling violently against Thomas. He held her in place, using his arms and knees, though her flesh was hot and slick with sweat.

"Bless this girl!" shouted Blastilv. "Bind her soul that she may sin no longer! *Lyforia, flash!*"

That which could only be described as a bolt of emerald lightning discharged from the gauntleted palm of God Déagar. It struck the eyes of the girl. Her head arched back, and her body quaked as the light entered her, branching out through her skin.

She was then still. No longer did she struggle. No longer did she weep. Those eyes that had, moments ago, pleaded were now vacant. The fear was gone, as well as the life.

They were now the eyes of the Blessed.

Slowly, Thomas released her and fell to his side on the floor next to her. His stomach seized. Vomit trickled from the corner of his mouth. He felt a darkened, hollow pain inside his soul that he could only assume equated to that following a murder. Yet Thomas's victim currently watched him with dead eyes.

Ignoring the prior, Blastilv told one of the male Blessed to go to the bath and told the new female to follow. She stood and obeyed without question.

Thomas remained on the cold floor. Breathing slowly.

The archbishop strode forward, looming over him and peering down. He grinned, revealing a ghastly collection of discolored, decaying teeth. "Thou hast done the work of God, Prior. Be not discouraged."

"'Twas magic we performed, Your Grace," Thomas said flatly. "As it is written in the Word of Déagar: 'Know ye that there shall not be one amongst you who useth divination or sorcery or who calleth out to dark Gods or dead spirits. For the unseen world is the realm of the Gods alone, and any mortal man who intrudeth therein is like a thief within the house of almighty Déagar.' This is why we now war with the magic-using Karulents."

"Thou art mistaken, Prior. There was no magic involved here. This was a holy miracle, bestowed by Déagar himself. And through him, I have made great progress with my work. Initially, the overwhelming power did kill most of those whom I attempted to cleanse. But now, almost half survive. However, the state of incapacitation remains an issue I have yet to overcome."

Thomas looked up at him. "You mean . . ." he began wearily, "you do not intend for them to be helpless?"

"What thinkest thou me, Prior? A monster?" Blastilv chuckled again, the loose flesh of his face vibrating around grayed lips and yellowed teeth. He bowed slightly and fixed his cold eyes on the prior. "My sole desire is that these misguided souls obey the Church unquestionably, like any true Déagrian. Nothing more. And thou wilt aid me in my cause."

CHAPTER SIXTY

Every night after the blessing of the ivory-winged girl, Thomas dreamed of her. Of her screaming through her gag. Of the light fading from her eyes. It had been four days since her transformation, but he could think of nothing else. She had been wicked, Thomas reminded himself. She had needed help. She had been a Drevite savage. But Thomas only recalled her soft song, her face, such fear.

He had barely seen her since her transformation. The sisters said the archbishop was caring for the *new arrival*—this, what they believed her to be—personally in his apartment. It was for the best, Thomas resolved. He did not wish to face her.

Despite the prior's distractions, he continued his daily duties in the abbey, managing the nuns and monitoring the Blessed. Thomas saw the Blessed differently now—the creations of Blastilv.

Praise God Déagar, the one and only God, protector from the Dark. You are the Greatest of All. I praise your name, majestic and holy, without ending. I pray you guide me, my God. Is this truly your will? Should I help the archbishop with this endeavor?

Another day passed, and it was Sabbathday. Thomas was at the pulpit, uncomfortably near the statue of God Déagar. He blankly watched the nuns marching in the Blessed from the door at the back. The sisters maintained a manner betwixt parent and commander. They told them to stop, face forward, stand still, and be quiet.

Thomas tried to begin his sermon, but stopped.

His skin was clammy. His heart hammered out a rhythm of distress. He wrapped his stomach with his arms. He was close to vomiting before the congregation. Surely, he must have been pale.

The eyes of the Blessed, all of them, stayed transfixed on the prior. And Thomas knew that somewhere, behind every dumbstruck set of blank stares, was the memory of what had happened here, in this room, to each one of them.

No longer able to face the countless eyes, Thomas shielded his face with his arm and shrieked like a madman.

The sound echoed away.

Overwrought, Thomas began to flee this place, but another noise distracted him. He stopped at the rostrum steps, panting, and watched, agape, the curious sight.

The large door at the opposite end of the sanctuary had opened. But it was not the door, in itself, that garnered Thomas's attention, but who entered.

The Terovae with the ivory wings toddled with a deliberate, albeit stiff, gait up the center aisle—the same aisle up which she'd been dragged, screaming, only days before. She continued, passing inches by Thomas until she came before the statue of God Déagar. She kneeled rigidly, her arms raised to the heavens.

"Praise God Déagar," she said in a monotone, "the one and only God, protector from the Dark, you are the Greatest of All. I praise your name, majestic and holy, without ending, for I am your faithful servant, Mercy, for through your divine mercy, I have been saved. Astha'will-miabé."

Thomas stared at *Mercy* without words, without breath, without blinking. Yet his relief at her well-being was strangled within thorns of dread. *What would this witness report? Would her telltale tongue cry out accusations here and now before the sisters amassed?*

With prayer complete, the Terovae girl slowly, stiffly stood and approached Thomas, her movements, for a moment, reminding the prior of the marionettes the city churches used in their morality plays.

He stood frozen on the stage, frozen save for his heart, which had tripled its normal pace.

Then Thomas saw her eyes. Her eyes were the empty, grotesque eyes of the Blessed. She was one of them. But so different.

She spoke without feeling, saying, "His Grace commands a cancellation of mass because there are more important matters to attend to. Go to His Grace now. He awaits you in the cloister."

—

Nestled within the looming desolate walls of the colorless abbey, a square of cloistered walkways bordered a shadowed courtyard. In the warmer months, this place was serene, but not now. The gnarled trees and thorny shrubs seemed to claw at each other as frigid winds whipped through. A small pool centered on the mangled garden held an undulating layer of soggy flaccid leaves, emitting a musty stench.

Blastilv, adorned in lavish green and gold robes with a matching miter atop brittle hair, gazed at the filthy pool. Beside him stood the Terovae girl, her body unnaturally rigid, like a corpse propped to stand erect.

"You summoned me, Your Grace?" Thomas's voice trembled as he stood in the shadows of the walkway.

"Come thou hither, Prior," the archbishop said without diverting his gaze from the murky water. "Thou hast no reason to linger on the edge, for thou art now a part of these holy matters."

Thomas reluctantly pulled up his green hood over his bald head and cautiously approached. He tried his best to ignore the unsettling presence of the Terovae girl. As frightening as the other Blessed were, he would gladly choose their revolting company over this motionless, soundless abomination.

Blastilv motioned to her with eerie pride, marked by a rotten grin. "Wast thou not amazed when she came unto thee in mass, Prior? Such progress I have made with her."

"Yes, Your Grace. She is unlike any of the others."

"Very true, Prior. More unlike them than thou understandest. Here, within this reborn savage, is the future of salvation."

"Your Grace," Thomas said with trembling lips, mustering his courage, "I believe we should inform Patriarch Krasil of your . . . *work* with the Blessed."

Blastilv let out a soft chuckle. "Be not a fool, Prior," he sneered. "His Holiness doth know already of mine endeavors. As doth His Majesty, the High King." He approached a ten-foot-tall rectangular mirror made of gold—both in its elaborate frame and polished reflective pane—standing upright in the outer walkway. "Behold, a visitor approacheth."

In a sudden burst of blinding light, the gold mirror, where before it had reflected the courtyard, revealed a large, bright room of white marble. In the room's center stood a low round wall that resembled a fountain, but in place of water, a great fire burned.

A Human man in his early thirties appeared from beyond the mirror and strode confidently into the courtyard through the pane. His long blond hair hung to his broad shoulders, and a thick beard framed his rugged features, adding to his intimidating presence. Clad in the uniform of a Dayigan soldier, he bore the golden emblem of their nation upon his chest.

Overwhelmed by this supernatural manifestation before him, Thomas dropped to his knees in fear. Clutching the wooden Septenar of his necklace, he cried out, "Praise God Déagar, the one and only God, protector from the Dark. You are the Greatest of All."

But Blastilv and the soldier shared a laugh at Thomas's expense, as the man confidently stepped forward.

"I may be many things, Father," said the soldier, amusement fading from his tone, "but I am no God. Surely you recognize a Corridor Mirror."

His words were so self-assured that Thomas felt foolish for not knowing. However, he admitted that he had never heard of it before.

"Truly?" asked the soldier, appearing shocked and annoyed. He looked at Blastilv as if seeking an explanation.

"Never mind the prior," Blastilv said. "He hath been cloistered for too long. I trust thou art well, Thy Lordship."

"Truth be told, I am haggard, Your Grace. This war against magic has dragged on for decades now, but in the two years since we declared war on the Reyigans, it has become particularly brutal."

Thomas stood up, brushing off his coarse robe at the knees. "You have all fought bravely for so very long. Let us pray that they will soon come to their senses and allow our soldiers to return home."

The soldier scoffed, his gaze piercing through Thomas like a sword. "I do not quite think you understand who I am, priest. I am *they*. I am Lord High Constable *Eadwulf*, Lord of Warfare of the Dayigan Army. The decision to defend ourselves against the treacherous Reyigan Empire—of which you speak so flippantly—was a painstaking one, made by His Highest Majesty, His Holiness, and myself in a grueling conference. And let me assure you, we were well within our senses. Let us not forget the thirty million lives lost to the Blue Sickness inflicted upon us by the Karulents and the countless refugees they harbor within their borders."

Thomas opened his mouth to respond, but his words failed him.

"Prithee, forgivest the prior, Thy Lordship. As I spake before, he hath been cloistered far too long. His only idle company consisting of women and fools, leaving him devoid of intelligent discourse. Lo, thou wast wise to take the war to the Reyigan Empire, for they are wicked beyond measure."

"Yes . . ." The lord gave a cordial nod. "Which brings us to the matter at hand. You are on shaky ground with our empire, Archbishop Blastilv. Your past failures have made the High King wary to place his trust in you again."

"How darest thou speak to me in such a manner!"

"I am not one of your knights," Eadwulf rebuked, "as is evident by my continued heartbeat. Understandably, His High Majesty is hesitant to trust you after your repeated failures. His Holiness may have vouched for you, but our king requires tangible proof that your latest venture will bear fruit."

Blastilv's smug grin returned. "'Twas was for this very reason I summoned thee hither. Thy 'tangible proof' standeth just here." He motioned toward Mercy. "She, Thy Lordship, is the paradigm of what is to come."

Lord Eadwulf approached the girl and stroked her arm before lifting her hand and letting it drop limply back to her side. "An attractive paradigm, indeed. But not nearly as impressive as the army of warriors from the Faery lands you promised our empire twenty-five years ago. Or the mighty stone warrior you swore to present thirteen years ago."

Blastilv's yellowed eyes narrowed in anger before he regained his composure and continued in a cordial tone. "Thou art mistaken, Thy Lordship. I do assure thee, she begins a force far greater than any I have pledged before."

"And *completely* obedient, you wrote?" Eadwulf asked with a grin. "'Tis a pity the Blessed only obey clergy. I would have you bless my wife."

The two shared a chuckle while Thomas shifted uncomfortably and looked away.

Eadwulf paused for a moment, his gaze intensifying as he stared at Mercy. Suddenly, he struck her across the face with the back of his hand.

"Impressive," Eadwulf remarked clinically, as he inspected her unmoving form. "She does not even attempt to retaliate."

A trickle of blood flowed from her nose to outline her upper lip, but Mercy remained unmoving and silent. A single tear fell from her eye.

"Very nice." Eadwulf grinned. "What is your name, girl?"

"Answer him," commanded Blastilv.

"His Grace has named me Mercy," she said emotionlessly, "for by the divine mercy of God Déagar, I have been saved from wickedness."

"Do you not remember who you were?" Lord Eadwulf persisted. "You were a Drevite, yes? A pervert living in trees. A savage whore. What sinful, base things have you done? Do you even recall?"

She remained still, her vacant eyes fixed upon the soldier, as if his words were beyond her comprehension.

"May I interpose, Thy Lordship," Blastilv interjected. "Mercy doth stand far above her fellow Blessed, 'tis true, yet to her, conversation remaineth an enigma. But I assure thee: Her past life is no more."

"You are certain?" Eadwulf asked. "If I am to unleash these things onto battlefields, I will not risk them reverting to their savage ways."

"Thou mayest envision her heathen soul as torn from her flesh and chained deep within, where it can do no more sin and will never again. She retaineth skills from her past life, yes, and can be trained further, but little else of her former self doth remain. She is naught but an automaton; her sole purpose, governed by the Church, is to carry out the divine work of God."

Lord Eadwulf paused, stroking his beard as he absorbed the words. "She is still in there?" he asked, locking eyes with the unnerving gaze. "Her true self? Imprisoned in her own flesh. Is she aware of what is happening?"

"Presumably so, Thy Lordship. I believe she both sees and feels all that doth occur."

"Magnificent," Eadwulf smirked. "The ultimate penance." He leaned in close to her face, yelling, "If you can hear me, savage, thank us for granting you the chance to atone for your sins now, rather than in the fiery depths of za's eternal damnation." Stepping back, he turned to Blastilv. "Duration?"

"Forever, Thy Lordship."

"And can control of her be stolen by, say, a Dark Light sorcerer?"

"Impossible, Thy Lordship. The golden orb used on the Reyigan refugee town before—though born of the same power—was but a mere bauble in comparison to the glorious conversion I have mastered in Mercy. And yet, there are no more Drevites to convert. If only I had soldiers at my disposal . . ."

"Every man under your command has died."

"Died in service to God, Thy Lordship, with their souls ascending to Laqyigo."

"Nevertheless, dead, all the same," Eadwulf maintained. "And when we require troops for the war effort."

"My Blessed shall serve as the soldiers thou dost require."

"Perhaps. Whilst your words intrigue me, they remain just that: words, substantiated by a paradigm that seems better fit for a brothel than a battlefield. However, your pretty monster pleases me. In good faith, I have assembled your great *Knights Silthex* in Fidelumair Palace to help in your task." Eadwulf turned toward the mirror. "Come, O illustrious army of God!"

A single man in the uniform of the Dayigan Army stepped through the mirror and stood beside Lord Eadwulf.

"I believe you are acquainted with Grand Inquisitor Swithun, yes?" Eadwulf asked with a chuckle.

Blastilv narrowed his yellowed eyes as he glared. "I am. However, one man shall not suffice for my needs."

"And yet, only one man survived your command." Eadwulf turned to the newcomer. "Inquisitor Swithun," he continued, "you were tasked with locating and capturing the elusive Blue Rose. What is your progress?"

Swithun hung his head in shame. "I found her, sir, but she got away from me."

"More than simply got away," Eadwulf hissed, his anger simmering beneath the surface. "She has since managed to persuade multiple kingdoms to secede from the Dayigan Empire and form the so-called Resistant Nations, which grows stronger by the day."

"I know where she is now, sir," Swithun said. "I can go for her, right now, but the army won't let me."

"No, we won't," Eadwulf snapped. "The witch is in the Kingdom of Freoldreor, which, by your incompetence, is no longer part of the Dayigan Empire."

"Fret not over the insignificant Blue Rose," Blastilv interjected with a respectful nod. "Let the witch draw our enemies out and gather them together. Their so-called victories shall avail not. Both the Reyigan Empire and the Resistant Nations shall be crushed beneath the feet of the Blessed."

Lord Eadwulf drew closer to the ancient archbishop, his voice dripping with menace. "Do not fail us again. Rebellion festers within our borders as those who defy our rightful rule run rampant. Our empire crumbles into chaos, and if you allow that to happen, the High King will hold you *personally* responsible."

But Blastilv merely grinned, unaffected by the threats. "The fires of God will guide us to victory, Thy Lordship."

Eadwulf's gaze lingered on him for a moment longer. "Inquisitor, how many men were assigned to you to capture the Blue Rose?"

"Two hundred, sir."

"And how many remain?"

"Most of them, sir," Swithun replied with a hint of pride. "And my unit's been replenished to two hundred strong."

"'Twould seem you fare much better than your master," Eadwulf said. "Gather your men and report to this abbey for permanent reassignment. Once here, you will march into the Drevite Nation and collect more savages for transformation." He turned to Blastilv. "Prove that your monsters can wield swords, Your Grace, and perhaps we can restore some of your former power."

Blastilv grinned his gray lips. "Thou art too kind, Thy Lordship. The Drevite Experiment will, at long last, come to fruition."

CHAPTER SIXTY-ONE

As the night dragged on, Thomas lay restless in his meager bed, unable to escape the grip of his troubled thoughts. Finally, conceding to sleeplessness, he was compelled to leave his chamber and seek solace in the church, where the statue of God Déagar loomed in the darkness. The cold air and eerie stillness sent shivers down Thomas's spine as he kneeled before the imposing figure of the soldier God—He who is Greatest of All.

With trembling words, Thomas beseeched Déagar for guidance. "If the Blessed are condoned by the Supreme Patriarch and the High King," he whispered, "and are created by your divine power, their creation must be righteous. Yes? Who am I to think otherwise? Why does my heart, to its beating core, still cry out that this is wicked?"

Tired and bewildered, Thomas set his face against the armored hand of Déagar, the cold gold plates against his cheek sapping the heat from his flesh. "Help me, my God."

Suddenly, the gauntlet shifted downward, causing Thomas to lose his balance and strike his head against the gold. Mortified, he reached out to grasp at the revered glove, but it broke free and slipped from his trembling fingers, crashing to the floor with a resounding clatter.

His breath caught in his throat as he saw what he'd uncovered. A white marble hand remained where the gauntlet had been. But it was nothing Human, nothing holy. It was a demonic hand, bestial and clawed.

Before he could comprehend this terrible sight, he heard footsteps approaching. With a sense of urgency, Thomas shoved the gauntlet back onto the marble hand and hid himself among the pillars at the edge of the room.

Soon, a light entered—a lantern that dangled from the shriveled fingers of Blastilv. The archbishop headed straight toward the statue.

Fearful that Blastilv may discover the disturbed gauntlet, Thomas watched in terror, but soon the prior realized the archbishop's aim was not the graven God itself, but a point on the wall just beside it.

A section of the wall opened, and Blastilv entered.

Fearing for his life but needing answers, Thomas cautiously approached the small door, now illuminated from within by the flickering light. He inched his way inside while dragging a thousand pounds of fear behind.

Before Thomas had fully entered, a sickening draft of putrefaction and other caustic aromas—some too obscene to possess decent names—assaulted him. The room into which he peered was small and filled almost entirely by a filthy stone chair with a slight recline.

His hand flew to his mouth to prevent himself from crying out once he saw the chair's inhabitant. Or, more accurately, his hand reacted when he realized that the thing in the chair was a living creature. Perhaps—though it would be too horrible to believe—even a living person.

The thing had pale green skin with a texture not unlike a Human's. Its skull remained fairly intact, though it appeared as if sections were missing, this most apparent at the apex, where the skin drooped inward like fleshy cheesecloth over a bowl. Below the frail neck, the entire skeletal system appeared almost absent, although there were a few lumpy clusters of disgusting mass within the empty skin. These masses—clumped, sparse, and uneven throughout—were like gathered cotton in a haggard, scant pillow of flesh. The organs, too, were evidently gone. Nevertheless, Thomas could see a slight movement from the chest, extremely slow and extremely shallow, hinting, he assumed, at some remnant of respiration. It had breasts, Thomas realized, or at least the empty, shriveled skin sacks that had once been such. *A woman?*

Her wounds where she, the hollowed-out pelt, was nailed to the chair, were bleeding, this from large spikes driven through her shoulders. Her thin blood trickled down years of black scab extending down her body then as disgusting stalactites from chair to floor. Contented flies circled merrily, with plump maggots below.

The woman's right hand was gone—blood trickling down in a larger black crusty column—and the green skin of this forearm was stretched out and nailed around a thick stone shoved up her wrist.

This stone to which her arm was connected was carved to resemble an arm. A demonic arm of stone extended to the wall and, no doubt, through to the demonic hand within the gauntlet.

"Thou hast been quite the investigator of late, Prior," said Blastilv, though he faced away, toward a dusty ledge running the back wall as a table.

Thomas said nothing. He couldn't speak.

Blastilv retrieved a glass bottle and spoon and neared the woman. "Open thy mouth, *Lyforia*," he said, as he removed the bottle's cork.

She complied in such a feeble, gradual manner that it seemed more that the jaw happened to hinge open at that moment rather than by any living effort to do so.

The archbishop fed her two spoonfuls of the liquid before commanding her to swallow. "Thou art perplexed as to thy findings hither."

The prior could make no sound but an assortment of staggered breaths. His lips quivered. His unblinking eyes watered down his face.

"Fret not, Prior. What thou seeth here is no person. This creature is naught but a Faery savage that I control by the power of her name. Alack, the Fae are greatly vulnerable to emotions, and thus aiding me these many years hath, quite literally, eaten away at her insides. Fortuitously, I can prevent her from transforming into something useless through steady doses of an opium tincture known as laudanum."

"You . . ." Thomas whispered, "are a monster."

Blastilv stared his cold, yellowed eyes into the younger man. "Hold thy tongue, Prior, for it wags in ignorance."

"No, Archbishop, I speak *truth!*" he shouted. "I saw the hand within the gauntlet. You lied to me and the king and Patriarch Krasil. The Blessed are *nothing* to do with God Déagar. You cursed those people using wicked magic through a tortured Faery nailed to the arm of a Demon."

"Calm thyself, Prior, or thou wilt know well what monster I can be."

Thomas froze at these words and swallowed. His throat constricted. His courage drained as the blood left his face.

Blastilv chuckled. "Pitiful Prior, thou hast the convictions of a lion and the will of a lamb. I should beat thee in the yard for thy disrespect. But fear not, for my deeds are done for Déagar and by his divine power. Art thou familiar with the stone warriors that fought the Demons in the time before our current calendar?"

"The Vatelams? Yes," Thomas said absently. "The Word of Déagar mentions them briefly."

"Their king was a stone warrior called Fersivolíel. After a tedious and long-seeking search, I found his body thirteen years past, yet a vile witch destroyed it. But lo, his hallowed hand doth remain. I need this Faery to revitalize the stone—an unfortunate requirement, yes, but for the betterment of the world. With it, I shall create a glorious army under God Déagar."

Thomas scanned the atrocities within the small room but remained silent.

"Worry not of sinners and savages and Faeries, Prior, for the True Light is the only way; all others will perish."

"Yes, Your Grace," Thomas mumbled blankly, staring at the Faery. "Forgive me."

"Thou art forgiven, my child." He approached the younger man and set a frigid hand on his shoulder. "Verily, 'twould pain me to watch thee stumble into darkness, Prior. Thy predecessor did, in fact, fall from grace and needed to be *cleansed*. Thou hast seen him many times, I am certain. Father Lewis is one of the few Human Blessed. Thus, never again will he transgress or disobey. But I need not use such measures with thee, need I?"

"N-no, Your Grace."

Blastilv paused, lingering his sight on Thomas. Whether the archbishop was letting his words sink in or examining the prior for signs of betrayal, Thomas was uncertain.

At length, Blastilv grinned. "Away with thee to bed, Prior. Tomorrow, we have much to do."

CHAPTER SIXTY-TWO

In his nightmares, Thomas saw the pulped, green Faery whom Blastilv had called Lyforia. And within these hazy apparitions, Lyforia stared up at him and groaned out a desperate plea for compassion and help. But there was a bottle in his hand in this dream. And a spoon. And Thomas screamed as he shoveled laudanum down the gullet of the Faery.

Thomas, in a cold sweat, sprung up, crying out as he sat upright in bed. With his blanket flung off, the biting chill of the room circled his body. Dressed in nothing but a thin chemise, the chill pierced to the marrow of his bones. Yet, he remained still as remnants of vile visions throbbed and twirled within his aching skull.

His eyes adjusted to reality. The single window in his room was lit, though barely, revealing that Jerah had begun his daily ascension from the western horizon, thus bringing in the dawn.

"Praise God Déagar," Thomas whispered into hands folded around the wooden Septenar, "the one and only God, protector from the Dark. You are the Greatest of All. I praise your name, majestic and holy, without ending. I thank you for this new day, and I pray I will honor you in all that I do. Astha'will-miabé."

A woman's voice then startled Thomas, causing him to shout as he faced the sound. In the shadowed corner of the room was a figure that, with some adjustment of the eyes, Thomas realized was Mercy, sitting in a simple wooden chair.

She restarted, saying, "His Grace has sent me to help you once you wake. You are to exorcize and bless all the salt in the abbey so it can be used to create holy water."

"What? But why?"

She stood and approached stiffly. "His Grace has commanded it so. We need no other reason."

Thomas sighed and wiped his drowsy eyes. "Very well. Go to the storehouse, and I will meet you there once I am dressed."

"I cannot do that, Prior. His Grace has—"

"*Cannot?* But you are Blessed, incapable of refusing. Obey me forthwith."

"My orders come from His Grace, who has more authority than you."

"You . . . understand hierarchy?"

"Aye, Prior. His Grace has commanded me to watch you at all times, and you are not to talk to any of the nuns."

The words, so emotionlessly stated, became a downpour of fear and sorrow that washed over Thomas's entire body like freezing rain, leaving him tense and breathless. Blastilv no longer trusted him to be alone.

When Thomas dressed, he did it quickly while facing away, embarrassed that he should be in only a chemise before the watchful eyes of a woman. But modesty was second in his mind. His worries dwelt on Blastilv.

Once Thomas had donned his simple green robe, he, while assuring that Mercy did not see, pocketed a dagger.

—

With Mercy, Thomas ambled within the line of shuffling Blessed that filled the hall outside his room. He kept his hand within the large front pocket of his robe. What else, Thomas wondered, had Blastilv instructed Mercy to do? *Have I reason to clutch this dagger?* She was behind him. And Thomas feared she would stab him in the back for his knowledge of the imprisoned Faery.

When they reached the stairwell, the prior did not begin the path to the storehouse. Instead, he made his way toward Blastilv's quarters.

Mercy hurried in front of him, impeding his path. "His Grace has commanded you to exorcize and bless all the salt in the abbey, so it can be used to create holy water."

"'Tis imperative I speak to the archbishop at once. I must set a terrible misunderstanding right."

"His Grace does not wish to see you. His Grace has commanded you to exorcize and bless—"

"Get out of my way, savage!" Thomas shoved her aside with such force as to knock her to the wall.

"Seize the prior," Mercy stated, even now not diverting from her monotone. And three of the Blessed from the stairwell hurried to Thomas and, grappling brutishly at his arms and legs, snatched him up.

"That is impossible," Thomas spit furiously. "Blessed cannot command Blessed. Release me at once."

Those holding him did not comply, and Mercy was soon beside him.

"Take the prior to the storehouse," she said.

And the abductors carried him away.

Two Blessed men set a twenty-five-pound sack of salt on a wooden table in front of Thomas. One of them was Human, Thomas noted, as he watched him for a moment.

Of the entire group of Blessed, only three were Human men; thus, this drone could very likely be the one of whom Blastilv had spoken: the previous prior. Thomas couldn't help but wonder what misdeeds had brought him to this mindless state. Had Thomas himself committed such sins, or worse? A creeping fear engulfed him, a strangling dread that these moments were the final of his life.

The two Blessed men moved away, though not far. They were part of a group of seven, including Mercy, who assisted, nay, guarded Thomas in the storehouse. They watched the prior's every action, no longer heeding his commands. And when a nun attempted to enter, Mercy declared it off limits and sent another Blessed to fetch what the sister required.

Weary and tense with anxiety, Thomas faced yet another sack of salt. This was the sixth one he had encountered, with six more awaiting. The endless repetition of this ritual had drained him entirely.

Slamming his hands on the table, Thomas shouted, "This is ridiculous! There is no possible way His Grace needs this much blessed salt. Already, we have enough to sanctify a small lake." Immediately, he recoiled, as fear of what repercussions his outbreak might bring rattled through his bones and caused his hands to tremble. His eyes grew wide and turned to the floor.

With a shivering breath, Thomas meekly said, "You have gotten his instructions wrong."

"His Grace has commanded you to exorcize and bless all the salt in the abbey so it can be used to create holy water."

Thomas nodded stiffly. "I beg you, at least tell His Grace I wish to speak with him."

She said nothing, standing slumped and lifeless, her gaze vacant and haunting.

Defeated, Thomas returned to the salt. With no other recourse, he began reciting prayers over the bag.

As he was finishing the ninth bag of salt, something caught his eye in the dim corner of the storehouse. He turned to see the archbishop making his way inside. But instead of approaching Thomas, the twisted figure clad in regal garments made his way toward Mercy, where they engaged in a hushed conversation.

"Your Grace!" Thomas called out, as he approached hastily.

Mercy charged Thomas.

"Let him pass," said Blastilv.

"You have wronged me, Your Grace, leaving me to the authority of the Blessed."

"'Twas not by *their* authority, Prior, but mine own. As Mercy hath no doubt explained, I require a vast amount of blessed salt."

"A lot, yes, but surely not a dozen large—"

"Hark, Prior," Blastilv cut him off, "and thine uncertainty shall be sated. The Church wishes every filthy savage on the entire continent to be blessed. An unreasonable request. Yet I, through what can only be deemed *divine inspiration*, have solved the quandary. Wherefore should every savage come hither when salvation could, more easily, go hence to the wicked?"

"Holy water," Thomas whispered, sickened as he realized the magnitude of the idea.

"Precisely. The hand of Fersivolíel will bless barrels upon barrels of water infused with your blessed salt, and I will send them out to special encampments, wherein clergymen will bless countless souls into ultimate dedication to the Church of Déagar. 'Twill be spectacular, Prior. Envision armies upon armies of Blessed besieging the same lands whence we saved them. And all whilst sending others back to be blessed and trained before joining with the armies as well."

The words of the archbishop, so emphatically spoken, made Thomas sick. He touched his stomach as he faced the floor. And when the words concluded, silence fell over the storehouse.

"What say thou, Prior? Or hath thy tongue abandoned thee."

"I—" Thomas began hoarsely with a pain in the pit of his stomach growing. "I have sinned, Your Grace." He crossed his other arm across his core. "Since my discovery of what exactly the Blessed are and how they came to be, I have wavered in opinions trying to determine wrong from right. Yet now I know." He slid a hand into his pocket. "The Word of Déagar teaches us: 'He who alloweth sin is a sinner himself.' Consequently, this wickedness must end now."

Thomas drew his dagger and unskillfully lunged it forward toward the vile archbishop.

Yet the Blessed Human grabbed his forearm, stopping the knife's point inches from the wizened folds of the ancient neck.

The prior struggled madly against the heightened strength of the Blessed. With strained effort, Thomas managed to switch his dagger to his free, left hand.

He swiped again, this time carving his meager blade across the gut of the Blessed who held him.

He released Thomas, and Thomas stumbled back from him. The prior watched, horrified, as crimson torrents splattered in gory downpours from the wound traversing the man's stomach. The prior's throat clenched as he gagged. Yet, more so than the sight of the blood, it was the sight of the man that overwhelmed Thomas, sending his entire body into rigid shakes.

Even as his blood puddled around his feet, the Blessed Human seemed to take no notice. Instead, he stood no differently than at any other moment in his wretched pseudo-life.

And still, he kept his horrifying eyes dead upon the prior.

Thomas mouthed the silent word "no" as he stared in shock and horror.

"Didst thou think they were so easily slain?" Blastilv, along with Mercy, had gained some distance within the protection of five Blessed. "These are divine creations."

"No," Thomas cried, knife gripped futilely in his bloody hand, while he desperately backed against a storage shelf. "These are accursed spawns from the infernal shores of Trasilon." He whimpered madly as his wide eyes scanned the area. "I see no Light within this place. By Déagar, how did I not see before?"

The Blessed who was bleeding out, volumes now a trickle, had turned pale like the dead. Yet, he stood. Yet, he stared.

"This," Thomas continued, "is the wicked magic of the fiery devil, Zeanázel."

"Thine actions *disappoint* me, Prior. Verily." There was a weariness, almost sadness, in his voice that Thomas did not expect to hear. "I had hoped to make thee a Silthex chaplain when our order was restored."

Thomas lowered his weapon.

"My actions were wrong," Thomas said, though he shook. "F-forgive me. I let fear take hold of me. True, you have done monstrous things, Your Gra—Blastilv. But I wholeheartedly believe that everyone has the capacity to change."

Thomas controlled his fear and cautiously stepped forward. "God Déagar, despite your attaching his name to atrocities, is truly a forgiving God, imbued by his divine mother with infinite grace. I pray you, put your abominations down to rest in peace, and let me help you return to the *True* Light. Even you can be forgiven, Blastilv."

The ancient man gave the younger a curious look as silence lingered.

Thomas again stepped forward and reached out his shaking hand.

Blastilv's eyes narrowed as he chuckled wickedly. "Pitiful, idealistic, idiotic Prior. Thou wilt find *I* am not so forgiving. Secure the reprobate," he commanded of the Blessed, and Mercy with the Human male—the oozing gash across his stomach, yawning as he walked—complied.

"Please, Blastilv—"

"Hold thy tongue, Human. For thou hast heard not the last detail of my proposal to wipe out all who disobey the Church. Behold," he said as he produced, from his inner robe, a silver flask enhanced with gold filigree surrounding a centered emerald. "Besides the barrels of blessed water within conversion camps, I expect field clergymen will carry portable supplies, as I have likewise prepared."

"Your Grace," Thomas said earnestly as tears streamed his face, "It is not too late to return to the Light. Please, you have no reason—"

"Of course, I know not if one can even carry out the blessing of the stone warrior via water. I shall need to test it before reporting to the capital. *And there are no more Drevites, Prior.*"

Words lost, as well as dignity, Thomas collapsed to his knees, weeping before Blastilv.

The archbishop grinned wickedly as he removed the cap from the flask. "'Tis thine own fault, Prior. Thou knowest I cannot suffer the unfaithful. Yet fear not," he said, as his old yellowed eyes lit up, "for thou wilt soon be cleansed of disobedience. Hold him."

The Blessed grabbed the prior.

Thomas felt faint. He knew too well the futility of struggle. If he was somehow to escape the grip of the two Blessed, five more awaited in the storehouse. He prayed softly to Déagar.

But Blastilv's prayers were louder. "In the almighty name of Déagar, I call upon the sacred powers. Bless this vile sinner! His will hath betrayed him. His will must be purged. Let his only deeds hereafter be as directed by thy Church. Bind his soul that he may sin no longer!"

The archbishop overturned the flask onto his finger, splashing water over his wrinkled digit before returning it aright.

Mercy held Thomas's head firmly as Blastilv drew, with his wet finger, a crossed number seven on the prior's forehead. And the water burned into his flesh.

"So thou shalt be blessed."

Agony ripped through his every particle, burning everywhere at once. And Thomas no longer felt his flesh as he sunk away into darkness. And his own eyes seemed a hundred miles away, as he viewed the world as if through a tunnel. Thomas could hear the muffled voice of Blastilv commanding him to stand.

"Yes, Your Grace," he heard his own voice say, and he felt his own body obey.

"I name thee *Second*," Blastilv's voice was an echoing distance, "for you will be second to Mercy, second of my creations, and live with a second chance to serve me and the Church."

And within his prison of void, deep within his own mind, Thomas screamed.

Yet his body showed no emotion, and his eyes were the eyes of the Blessed.

Within the Shadow of Hate

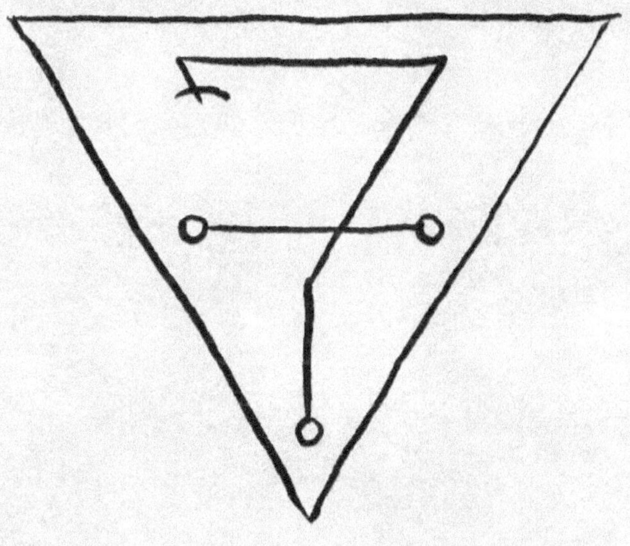

Teréyi Sea
Aklet'rah
Reyigan Empire
Reyigo
Frelon Lands
Caróg Lands
Allar Lands
Rúcah Lands
Feah Lands
Vohcktar
Day
e Dead Lands
Hyvile River
Dinikimera
0 30 60 90 120
Miles

CHAPTER SIXTY-FOUR

Genesary 30, 840: Twenty-Nine Days Later

Under the dwindling rays of the evening sun, Adratus marched, stone-faced and silent, two other legionaries following at his sides. They passed rows of plain wooden barracks, each standing in perfect uniformity and perfect alignment, much like the soldiers themselves.

Along with his usual armor—a steel muscle cuirass, black tunic and cape, and an apron of studded strips of black leather—Adratus had donned a menacing steel helmet with hinged cheekplates framing his face. Two sharp blades, like curved battle axes, formed parallel arches over the center of his head, from front to back, adding to his intimidating presence.

However, beneath this facade of discipline and strength, Adratus was utterly broken. Pain weighed on his soul as he passed fellow soldiers honing their combat skills and preparing for war. Men drilled in formations and sharpened their gladii, while others waxed their shields. For Adratus, it was all a peripheral blur, his body going through the motions. Numb. He walked tall, maintaining the posture the army had taught him and maintaining the steps the army had taught him. He continued moving forward as the army had taught him.

An insectoid woman landed at his side. Folding her veiny, opaque wings behind her thin frame, she bowed her head and slammed her upper right fist to her chest.

"Camp Prefect, a word," her voice buzzed angrily—at least it sounded angry to Adratus, but to him, everything they said sounded, in part, indignant. He'd once heard a Zezovae issue a "good afternoon" like a death threat.

"Speak, Cohort Commander," Adratus responded, addressing her by her title as leader of the newly arrived airborne division.

"My troops have secured prisoners from the Rúcah, sir," she said.

Adratus paused as he regarded the Zezovae, unnerved by the cold alienness that was true of all her kind. Her head was, in every way, like a wasp's save for its holding dimensions similar to a Human's. Her obsidian eyes—watching him— were devoid of anything he understood as emotions. Her neck—impossibly thin—was but a spike atop her shoulders. Her black and yellow torso was roughly humanoid—a wide masculine chest and extremely thin stomach—but in place of skin, she had what they called an *exoskeleton*, which was stronger than plate metal. Wings protruded from her back, and four thin arms each ended at four, long, jointed spikes as fingers. Larger spikes along her forearms told that she was a woman—not that Zezovae men were allowed to be soldiers— and could be used as weapons. Likewise, a scorpion-like tail writhed behind her, ending with a venomous stinger.

In general, Zezovaes disdained the use of any armor, clothes, or weapons—tools of the weak, they said—but this axillary commander wore a black leather armband that told her rank.

Yet, despite Adratus's general unease toward Zezovaes, it was her words, not her appearance, that froze him—*secured prisoners from the Rúcah.*

"Camp Prefect?" she tried again. "They informed me you wished to know of prisoners."

"Apologies," he said with a respectful nod. "You are correct." Adratus had opposed sending in Zezovaes against a Drevite tribe, but the emperor thought that they'd be useful against another flying race. "You bring honor to Tridual," Adratus said, "and to your nation of Maligros." Zezovaes were known to eat their enemies.

"They are but the first of the many we will claim for the glory of Tridual, sir," she buzzed.

Had she already eaten any Drevites? Adratus wondered, as he kept his body from shuddering. "What numbers?"

"Five, Camp Prefect."

"Very well. I will go to them. Dismissed." He continued forward.

With battle looming, the prefect's paramount duty was to motivate his men and lead by example. Accordingly, not even a hint of his pain showed outwardly. He kept it, relentless as it was, buried deep within his uniform. Nevertheless, the heart of mighty Adratus was a masticated pulp, like meat ripped apart by the teeth of wolves.

Adratus loved Ubaz. The fact was undeniable now. He felt it throughout every aching fiber of his body. And likewise, he felt the pain of loss. His love was gone, gone for two months now. But even injured, a Tridulan soldier must press on. It was his duty—to Emperor and Empire.

Ignoring hurt, Adratus stopped before the thick wooden gates of a section of the fort walled off from the rest. The guards stationed on either side snapped to attention, their fists pressed against their chests in salute, their heads bowed in respect.

"Stand down," Adratus commanded, an unintentional tinge of anger in his tone. "I received word we secured five Rúcah prisoners. Take me to them."

"Yes, Prefect."

The sounds of hammering and sawing grew louder as Adratus entered the area comprising four simple houses clad in fresh planks of wood. They were set tight together, the paths between them narrow. Soldiers atop the structures laid thick boards across the spaces in between, forming a slatted roof above the path.

Striped shadows fell over Adratus as he walked. The houses had yet to receive doors; thus, he could see inside when passing. Inside, a single empty room filled the entire interior, and simple square columns supported a low ceiling.

"Are they adequately sized?" Adratus asked, as he paused. "Each must hold thirty-two people."

"They are to specifications, Prefect. I remind you, the prisoners will not stay long."

"True," Adratus said darkly, as a slight chill washed over him.

They continued.

The house to which they ultimately came was in the back corner of the stockade and had "1 OF 4" carved starkly above the doorway. It had received its door: a grate formed of flat strips of woven metal.

The guard unlocked it. The legionaries entered.

Within the murky space, Adratus looked coldly over the captives. They grouped not too far from the door, near one of the wooden columns. Two appeared injured as they lay flat on the floor, while others knelt over them.

They were Rúcahs, not Feahs, Adratus reminded himself, but the difference was slight. The Rúcahs, he reminded himself, prompted this upcoming retaliation. The Rúcahs, he reminded himself, were responsible for this that was happening, not the Tridulans.

"You three," Adratus commanded. "Those uninjured, come forward."

As one of the three turned, his face caught the light of the door, an adorable face framed with limp ginger hair. A single vertical bar of purple now descended from the hairline, crossing the left eye and down the face. Ubaz. Adratus's love. The keeper of his heart. Here, imprisoned by Adratus's men.

Adratus looked away, clenching his eyes as he breathed heavily through gritted teeth. The mighty prefect felt ill. Such an unexpected pain was this when, already, he hurt.

He regained himself, flooding rage over grief. He cast his hand toward the guard who had led him here.

Cords of red light erupted from his fingertips, seizing the Tridulan guard up from the floor and smashing his back against a wall.

"Apologies, Prefect," the guard cried out through pain. "The Zezovaes knew not your boy. He fought alongside insurrectionists. See, Prefect, his kilt . . ." he groaned, "his kilt is black and edged in purple like—"

"Be you silent!" Adratus ordered, and the man's throat glowed red as he was rendered speechless. He dispelled the cords, letting the guard fall to the floor. Again, the Tridulan prefect stared coldly at the captives. "You, and you," he motioned to Ubaz and another Drevite man, "come with us."

"These people are injured," Ubaz spoke up, "and need aid. We cannot leave them here."

Adratus raised the back of his fist toward the young man, his eyes inflamed with hate. But he did not strike. "My orders," Adratus growled, "are not to be questioned by a barbarian dog. Any favor you think you earned with me, boy, died when you fled for enemy arms." He turned away from him, facing nothing but wall.

This was the Rúcahs' fault, Adratus reminded himself. Not his own. He regained his bearings.

"If you want to be a foe," Adratus said, facing away, "then foe you will be."

The Tridulan Empire could not be weak, he told himself.

"Bind their wings and arms," Adratus commanded, his voice in his ears sounding distant as he spoke. His entire body throbbed. "And have a medic summoned to the injured. We cannot crucify the dead."

CHAPTER SIXTY-FIVE

The legionaries led the two captives from the stockades and down the principal road toward the center of the fort. It was a walk from a nightmare, Adratus's head throbbing. His soul, seemingly dislodged from his body, watched his own actions distantly from far behind his own eyes. He kept glancing back to the man he loved: a bound prisoner.

The winter wind grabbed the prefect's black cape as he marched, causing it to whip behind him. It was so very cold now.

This fort was not the original constructed a league from the Feah temple village. This new fort—Fort Castrarúcah—had been built deep in Rúcah lands, where the lengthened Tridulan road crossed directly east of the enemy's temple village before turning north across miles of the Drevite Nation to the sea. This fort, too, was twice as large to hold twice as many.

"Three days past, a second legion arrived along with its auxiliary cohort," Adratus said, facing forward, his voice strong and clear as he addressed the prisoners behind him. "They sailed up from Tridual to the Arctic Ocean and down the Teréyi Sea to Drevite shores. Finally, they marched here. With their arrival, we number twelve thousand combat-ready legionaries and auxiliaries upholding order in the Drevite Nation. The Rúcah territory, we estimate, holds a population of not quite ten thousand. Do you understand?" He turned back to view the captives. "We have more soldiers than you have people. If the Rúcahs seek to fight us, they shall fall before us, their fate sealed by the superior might of Tridual."

The Drevites said nothing. And Ubaz held such hate in his eyes that Adratus could not even look at him.

"Kneel before me, barbarians," said the Tridulan prefect. He paused for compliance, and when he got none, he nodded to the soldiers who guarded them.

The legionaries forced the Drevites down to their knees. Adratus, flooding with anger, watched how roughly his men handled his husband. A part of him wanted to rip the men apart for their audacity.

Instead, Adratus looked away, toward a towering spire of black marble. "I brought you here with purpose," he said in a low rumble. "Behold." The eight sides of the monolith were polished to a dark sheen, rising sixty feet to an octagonal, silver-plated pyramid as its summit. The tower sat atop a massive iron cart, with more thick wheels than could be counted.

"'Tis called an *octolisk*," Adratus said. "We move mobile ones like this throughout our outer empire and have two stationary on the Viyae Peninsula—the heart of the Tridulan Empire. Others sit in the capitals of the Vohcktaran Kingdom, Maligros, and Ojron. Centuries ago, God Zeanázel and his wife, Goddess Gliéska, fused fire and stone to forge these towers, connecting them as gateways to the others. Thus, with this octolisk here, we can travel instantly to any other. And just as instantly, the two legions here can become four. Or eight. Or the entire Tridulan Army could rain down in full force onto the Drevite Nation. This, in a matter of just hours, if we wish. *Do you understand me!*" Adratus shouted.

The guards shoved the prisoners' shoulders.

"Aye," they responded.

"I have the title of *prefect*. Use it."

"Aye, Prefect." *Fear*, Adratus could hear it in his husband's voice. How he wished to comfort him, even as it was he who did the discomforting.

"Do you understand why you do not fucking *attack* the greatest army on Perdinok?"

"Aye, Prefect."

"You will take a message to the Rúcah's Chief Druidess." Adratus snatched a rolled page from his belt and thrust it at the other Drevite.

The Drevite shakily took it. "Aye, Prefect."

"It says," Adratus resumed, "'For crimes against Tridual, we demand one hundred and thirty souls so we might nail them to crosses along our road. There they will hang until they fall *as dust*, all the while reminding the Drevites why you do not revolt against Tridual. Your people have twelve days to present the tribute. When the sun rises on the thirteenth, if we have not received what is rightfully ours, we will come and take it by force."

He stepped forward to stand over the prisoners, his words slow and stern. "*And any lives lost in the claiming of our tribute, no matter how numerous, will not count as part of the one hundred and thirty.*"

Ubaz spit at Adratus. "You're a fucking dragon, you are," he growled, though his chin trembled and his eyes glossed. "A dragon in our lands, and you'll be slain as such."

"The entire Drevite Nation, combined," Adratus said through teeth, "hasn't the resources to *slay* us." He stared fully into Ubaz's eyes for the first time since their departing from each other at their ill-ending wedding. And hate consumed the Tridulan. Hate that this man would hurt him so utterly and to the core. Hate that this foreigner would not understand why certain things needed to be done.

Ubaz was silent. Dispirited. It was clear in his eyes that he understood the truth in Adratus's words. His light faded out, and with it, Adratus's hate smoldered into unfathomable sorrow. Even more so, the prefect wanted to console him. The soldier's arms ached to envelop him. He could not.

Mighty Adratus felt he would be sick.

The prefect cleared his burning throat. "Take this one to the edge of camp," he said wearily to a legionary, as he half-heartedly waved toward the other Drevite man. "Release him there, so he may return to the Rúcahs as a messenger."

The prefect waited a moment in silence as the legionary stood the Terovae man up and led him away.

Adratus stared, having experienced every unpleasant emotion known to man in the last five minutes and now entirely spent.

"How quick and painful has this descent been," he muttered in the general direction of Ubaz. "It seems like only moments past everything was right between us. As if love and joy were abundant. And now . . . winter is here. And I am cold without you."

Ubaz—a belt around his chest to bind his arms and amber wings, on his knees and facing dirt—said nothing. But a tear ran down his dirty face.

"There are requirements to maintaining the supremacy of an empire," Adratus said softly. "Someday, my love, I hope you understand. But I know 'twill not be today."

The prefect turned to the soldier at his side, saying, "Assemble a unit of men to escort this man back to the Feah temple. I want him under twenty-four-hour surveillance. You will personally assure he returns not to this zone of conflict."

"To the Feahs, Prefect?" The man gave Adratus a perplexed look. Suddenly, he turned sharply, pounding a fist against his chest and bowing his head. "Hail, Legate!"

Adratus turned to see Legate Maximus approaching from behind.

"I think I heard orders given, Centurion," Maximus said. "Take this barbarian home forthwith."

"Yes, Legate." The centurion yanked Ubaz to his feet and dragged him away.

"*Please*, Adratus . . . husband," Ubaz called, voice cracking. "Please stop this massacre from happening."

"Tridual cannot be soft," Adratus said vacantly—whether or not Ubaz heard, he was unsure. The crestfallen legionary stared out into nothing, glancing up in time to see the keeper of his heart dragged around the corner of a barracks block.

"The men will judge you for that action," Maximus said from behind Adratus. "'Tis clear you awarded special treatment to your lover. Even after he betrayed us by joining the enemy."

"Let them judge me. Verdicts are correct, for he has broken me, thoroughly. I had love beyond what most will ever know. Something about which poets write and bards sing. And that love . . . is destroyed."

Maximus chuckled. "O mighty Adratus, do you forget the first rule of serving in the wilds: you fuck barbarians only, yet love them not."

Adratus flared up. "Speak not so of my husband!" With his fist clenched and arm flexed, he gained a threatening posture. He stopped, though his eyes burned with fury.

"Apologies, good brother," Maximus said. "They were callous words."

"Who am I to judge?" Adratus took a deep breath and exhaled sharply. "What am I to do, Maximus? I feel his absence in my heart. What I had with Ubaz..." He shook his head. "Sadly, I am old enough to know the rarity of such bliss, and as I have never known it before, I know, fully well, I shall never know it again."

Maximus glanced downward as he placed a hand on his friend's shoulder. "Such emotions belong not in streets. Come, I say we adjourn indoors."

Adratus nodded, and the two moved to the house of Maximus set in the center of the camp near the octolisk.

—

The front room of the command quarters was more of a war room than a sitting room. The walls were made of rough-hewn boards, unadorned and unpainted. In its center stood a large plain table holding a map of the Rúcah region, this weighted by scrolls and codices on strategy. On the wall behind it hung the Tridulan flag bearing a red background with a symbol in black—three twos joined to form a triangle, with a spear emerging from the crest of each number. The Triébis was surrounded by two circles, and below it read "TRASILON ETERNAL."

With pride, Adratus acknowledged the splendid flag as he bowed his head and touched his fist to his chest.

Maximus shut the door behind them. "Never have I seen you thus," said the legate. "Not in all the years I've known you."

"Never have I been thus." He turned to face him. "I suppose you'll try to tell me there are other fish at sea."

Maximus smiled sadly. "No, my friend. I would never utter such nonsense. If you truly love him, as you say, then I fear you will suffer greatly and for quite some time." He let out a weary sigh. "Do you recall our first mission together as boys? Locked in that Silthex cage and facing death? I vowed to protect you."

Adratus nodded solemnly. "And you have, many times since."

"And yet now," Maximus said with a hint of sadness, "I see such hurt in my little brother's eyes. And I wish—by all the diabolic Gods—I could shield you from it. But, alas, I can do naught to alleviate."

Adratus took a seat on a trunk at the side of the room. "He will never forgive us for attacking his people. Neither will the Drevites at large. We told them to be one nation. Now we say, 'But ignore this group we strike.'"

"Such things cannot be helped," Maximus said, his voice heavy with resignation. "These crucifixions are a mercy, recall. Had Tridual deemed the attacks against us as a cause for war, much more than one hundred and thirty Drevites would die."

"I am aware." Adratus looked at the floor. "But the Drevites will never see it as such. We may subdue them, yes, but never will they welcome us. We will be as wardens to these people, not allies. And whenever our watchful eyes turn away, they will speak of revulsion and rebellion."

"Perhaps." Maximus set his hands on the table and stared at the map. "But if we must rule the Drevites with an iron fist, then so we must."

"We must not *rule* them at all. Stop this, Maximus."

"'Twas your investigation into the Dayigans that led us here. Do you yet believe they will return and create weapons to threaten the world?"

"Yes, Legate."

"Then this is necessary." Maximus nodded. "You and I have both witnessed what the Light does to those they see as *others*. Without Tridual's protection, the Drevites will become naught but fields of ash stirring in a frigid wind."

"We are the lesser evil."

"We are the ones who will protect these lands," Maximus said as he approached Adratus, "not only for the Drevites' sake but also for the welfare of the entire continent of Bikia." He set his hand on the prefect's shoulder. "I need you on task, Adratus. You have thirteen days to clear your head of perplexities. Afterwards, you must be whole and ready to fight by my side. Understood?"

"Understood, Legate," Adratus said sadly. "Through hardship, to excellence."

Maximus let out a heavy sigh, worry clear in his eyes, as he gazed down at his little brother seated on a crate. "Through hardship, to excellence."

CHAPTER SIXTY-SIX

The relaxing strums of a small harp tinkled through the inner sanctum of the Feah temple. The merry druidesses sat on the grassy floor and wove small bunches of holly—red berries plump between the dark green leaves—to long braids of dried grapevine. The murmur of light conversation occasionally peaked in delighted squeals and dulcet laughter.

Chief Kaie approached a druidess, setting her hand on her shoulder. "Would you do us a kindness, lass," she asked, "and go fetch more sprigs of hazel? We want our garlands particularly strong against Faeries."

"Yes, Chief." The young woman smiled and hastened toward the large stone-framed entrance of the chamber.

However, her steps suddenly halted as she shrieked. A boy bounded limply toward her, grabbing at her as he collapsed to the floor. His hand, coated in blood and reaching out, slid down her ivory gown, staining the sacred fabric.

Chief Kaie rushed to the boy's side and kneeled beside him. Multiple deep gashes marked his flesh, smeared in blood, grime, and soot.

"Forgive me, Chief," he began weakly, "for not changin' into the temple garment."

"Don't be thick, lad. What has happened to you?"

"We're under attack, Chief." On hands and knees, he panted toward the grass. "Many o' the outer villages are already lost. Burnt up, Chief. The folks there, slain or snatched away. It was so fast, Chief."

Kaie felt as if she sank. Her hands shook—fear and anger twisting together. She clasped them into fists. "Who?" she asked the boy with strained calm. "The Tridulans? The Rúcahs?"

He grunted through trembling lips. "The *Dayigans*, Chief. They've returned here."

"Ancestors preserve us," Kaie whispered.

"I tried to come quick as I could, Chief," the boy cried. "I did try to go so fast, but I were hurt, Chief."

Muffled screams of terror sounded just outside of the temple. Kaie looked toward the sounds as her face paled.

"I'm sorry, Chief," the boy sobbed. "I tried to get here fast. But I couldn't. And they be right outside the temple now."

Kaie stood. Blank. "See to this lad's injuries," she said to the druidess by the door.

"*Women*," Kaie shouted across the Temple Grove. "Prepare yourselves."

Kaie jumped up and flew to the farthest edge of the chamber. She threw open a heavy wooden cupboard. Inside, an array of natural staves hung vertically, each one a unique work of knobby twisted wood. Kaie passed one to each of the queued druidesses before they flew toward the door.

Finally, Kaie took the center staff for herself. "The rest of you," Kaie called as she rushed away, "prepare the infirmary for any wounded."

—

Outside the Feah temple, the evening was lit by raging fires. Black smoke spewed from burning homes and engulfed the high-up canopy of trees.

Kaie could see the Humans fighting their way into the village. They were definitely Dayigans—Kaie could see the emerald green tabards over suits of chain mail. Swords raised high, they fought the Terovaes who'd been driven to the ground, unable to fly up into suffocating smoke.

Other Dayigans launched flaming arrows at everything in sight, setting fires to homes and trees alike. The sound of metal upon maces filled the air as they fought their way deeper into the village.

In teams of two, soldiers manned large wooden machines, each roughly a man's height and armspan. It looked like two massive crossbows connected atop each other at a forty-five-degree angle and armed with four harpoons. The thick bowstrings were tightened by an iron crank at the lower part of the structure, mounted on two large wheels.

Kaie could hear the quick clicking as the two soldiers wound up the device. Then, a loud snap sounded as it launched the harpoons, each at the corners of a net.

She'd seen a net-ballista before, when the Humans came before. But the current invaders had a dozen, shooting net after net into the sky, trapping Terovae men, women, and children, and sending them crashing to the ground.

A group of three villagers, ensnared in a net, cried out as they slammed into the ground. They reached out bloody hands through the restricting bonds, with desperate pleas for help.

Soldiers charged forward to claim their broken bounty, but Kaie rushed forward, too. With her staff pointed at the ground in front of the assailants, her will was made manifest.

Thorny vines erupted from crackling dirt and whipped around the soldiers' lower bodies, entangling them as they thickened and hardened. Thorns pierced into their legs, drawing blood.

Kaie passed the trapped soldiers and hurried to her people within the net. They were screaming and bleeding from severe impact wounds. Two had broken bones. Snatching a dagger from her belt, Kaie quickly cut them free.

The chief druidess touched one's shoulder and whispered, "With the healing waters of Mother Lágeya, I imbue you." The injuries vanished.

She did the same to the rest.

"The effect is short," Kaie said. "Quickly now, to the temple. Fast as you can."

"Thank you, Chief. Mothers be praised."

A soldier roared as he swung his sword toward Kaie, yet she reacted at once, holding her staff with two hands to block.

"Hurry on with yourselves!" Kaie commanded again to those she'd saved. She strained against the sword as she stared into the soldier's eyes.

"Fear me," Kaie hissed in echoing words. "Fear me." She roared like a bear, the sound nearly exact, though unearthly, uncanny. The roar enveloped him.

"*No!*" the attacker screamed in fright. He backed away, head jerking as his eyes darted all around in horror. "Get away from me!"

Using the moment, Kaie swung her staff, striking him hard against his skull.

He fell.

All around her, people scrambled and screamed as Feah villagers were dragged away by their oppressors. Kaie focused on a group of three net-ballistas and slammed the base of her staff into the ground.

"Lágeya, Mother of Nature, hear me," Kaie shouted as she raised her hand to the night. "I call upon the stinging insects; lend me their wrath!"

Buzzing sounded from all directions as wasps, hornets, bees, and many related others rushed in and coalesced into one collective swarm.

Kaie angrily stabbed her finger toward the Dayigans who manned the net-ballistas. The swarm rushed toward the targets.

A soldier tried to attack Kaie from behind, but she swung around her staff, striking him down. Another soldier was soon behind her. She jabbed him in the stomach before delivering a crushing blow to his head.

Fires burned all around Kaie. Her people fought and bled and screamed and fled.

Kaie spotted a dozen Feahs—ropes around their wings, arms, and stomach—bound to a horse-drawn cart. Though they struggled against their bonds, they had no choice but to follow. A woman fell and was dragged.

Staff outstretched, Chief Kaie shouted, "By the Mothers, I command you, stop!"

And the horse, though far off, complied.

"You will go no farther," Kaie whispered.

The horse lay down.

She grabbed a passing Feah warrior. "Free them," she commanded.

"Aye, Chief." He hurried to them.

Kaie heard the clicking of another ballista winding up to launch. She pointed her staff, and the swarm moved upon the new target.

Pain lanced through her skull, and Kaie's hand snapped to her forehead. "There's too much of it all."

A massive flaming limb crashed down through a towering tree before slamming into the ground with an explosion of soot and embers.

"Mothers help us," Kaie pleaded to the sky.

Two Dayigans rushed her.

She aimed her staff toward the ground. Thorny vines erupted and grabbed them by the legs.

"Seize the witch!" a Dayigan ordered as he pointed his bloody sword at her.

Twenty soldiers rushed toward her, circling her.

Kaie slammed her staff down. "Mother Ashatra, encircle me and smite down those who would do harm to me."

A hawk, composed of purple light, flew in rapid circles, clawing and pecking every soldier in its hurried path, moving with such speed that it became a blur of violet light.

The soldiers fell. The hawk vanished.

Kaie fell to her knees, yelling in pain as she clutched her head with both hands.

A druidess came running toward her, grabbing her shoulders and trying to drag her to safety. "Chief, you've used too much magic too quickly. You've near seid depleted yourself. Please, Chief, we must get you back to the temple."

"I must keep going on," Kaie groaned through pain. "Our people . . ."

"Chief, if you deplete yourself, you'll die."

Kaie's eyes settled on a small Feah child, screaming and fighting desperately to free himself from a net. She saw a Dayigan charge toward him with his sword raised high.

With a deep breath, Kaie raised her shaking hand, pointing her finger.

The stinging swarm of insects moved to the Dayigan, enveloping him.

The boy—Kaie saw—freed himself and flew away.

Kaie smiled.

Agony stabbed through Kaie's head as if from an iron spike, her body searing with a thousand white-hot needles. Her vision darkened. She felt herself fall. She felt herself impact the ground with a muffled thud.

Kaie could only watch through heavy-lidded eyes as a Dayigan soldier strode into the center of the gruesome battleground. He raised a small golden orb high above his head.

A disk of emerald light erupted from the orb, spreading horizontally in all directions. Nearly all the Feahs it touched were overcome by its mesmerizing influence, dropping their weapons and succumbing to a trance-like state.

Kaie fought against the heaviness in her limbs, willing herself to stand and defend her people.

But exhaustion won out.

Her eyelids slid shut.

Alone, at a long table just outside the mess hall, Adratus sat, forlorn, in the stillness of pre-dawn. A lone figure beneath skies of countless pinpricks of light, illuminated by the two distant moons: the pale blue Kiyes and the lavender-tinted Dar. He had little appetite for the salted bread that served as his banal breakfast and took mindless bites, half melancholic, half absent. Ubaz, he recalled, liked to look at the stars.

"Imagine it," Ubaz had said, months ago, "if I could fly as high as up there. I'd immerse myself in perfect darkness, surrounded by countless sparkling eyes. We're so tiny below them all."

The nights, Adratus mused, had seemed brighter with Ubaz by his side.

Soon, with the arrival of brilliant Jerah, the day would begin. *The* day, in which the time allotted to the Rúcah tribe would end.

Not a single person had arrived to stand as a tribute for the crime against the Tridulan Empire. Force would be necessary.

Adratus slid his gladius halfway from its scabbard and ran his left hand along the blade. The pain was intense as blood flowed. He clenched the fist and held it above his tin cup of watered-down wine. Crimson dripped within the burgundy depths.

Adratus spoke with slow, concentrated words:

"Under the eternal vastness of night, I appeal to the dark prince. Hail God Zeanázel, he who teaches wisdom and will above all. Enlighten me. Vengeance is rightfully ours, but should it come at such a cost? Yet should we be made as fools in the wilds by showing weakness against those who attacked us? Pray you, grant me wisdom."

He drank the wine.

An inexplicable rush flooded over his body, taking away his breath as reality itself ripped open around him. Everything took on shades of red, as the other nearby legionaries froze. Sound silenced. Adratus blinked a blink that lasted far longer than any such action should last.

When he reopened his eyes, he saw a brilliant red star in the sky.

Enchanted, Adratus stood and gazed at the single point of light as all the rest of the world unraveled and fell away. Even the other stars blotted out until he was alone in a void with the scarlet star.

The star grew brighter, consuming his vision. It faded, and suddenly, Adratus found himself within a dark cavern. Therein, he saw the silhouette of a woman, ten feet tall with wings of a bat and cloven hooves. She pointed toward the rocky wall, where, written in red and orange embers, were the words:

"Hate fractures the Light, and through its many cracks, the Darkness rises."

A sudden surge of anguish came flooding from the woman as she screamed in agony. An unseen force pulled Adratus to his knees; he could feel her suffering coursing through every fiber of his being.

"Prefect?" A hand was on his shoulder. He jumped.

Adratus found himself beneath a blue sky. Again, he sat at the table outside the mess hall. He looked around. The source of the hand was a centurion standing beside him.

"Are you well, sir?" asked the centurion.

Adratus looked back at the sky where the star had been. But now there was only blue with puffs of white.

"You were still as stone, sir. Staring like a corpse. Your hand bleeds."

"I'll be fine," he began, though drained and pale. "'Twas magic beyond what I meant to conjure." He glared at the centurion. "What do you want?"

"A Rúcah warrior awaits at the southern gate, sir. He requested to see you, personally."

"Very well. I go straightway." Adratus stood, yet wavered, dizzy from the event. Again, he looked back to where the star had been, confused. He shook it off.

—

Adratus, en route to the southern gate, made his way through Fort Castrarúcah. He was certain this single warrior at the gate marked the beginning of an unclear path. A feeling he somehow obtained from the strange vision of the woman.

Soon, his hastened march to the gate was joined by Legate Maximus.

"Know you what he wants?" the legate asked. "Or who he is?"

"I know neither, Legate. Only that he asked to see me."

"Then we will discover together."

"Legate." Adratus took a solemn tone as he stopped, his voice low. "I believe I had a vision. Of Slinönaka."

"The Archdemoness of Lust?" Maximus chuckled.

"Of lust, yes, but also of love and of the agony left behind by its loss"—he glanced down—"the state in which I linger now. I barely saw her, yet I knew it was her. With arms of profound loss, she summoned me, Maximus. And I felt her dying."

"There I know you err. The Demons cannot die and cannot summon, for they are, every one, imprisoned in the Plane of Chaos. 'Twas, no doubt, your own pain that conjured dreams of she who could commiserate." He set his hand on the prefect's shoulder. "I worry for you, Brother."

"I am well," Adratus said, though his mind puzzled. "We near a crossroads, Maximus, I know it, one far more vital than we realize."

Maximus paused, giving him a once-over with his eyes. "We shall see."

The legate and prefect approached the wooden gate, open wide, the single warrior not deemed significant enough to bother with its closing. They passed through the gathered men, then beyond the threshold, half-buried by dirt and gravel.

Adratus and Maximus made their stance a few feet beyond the log walls.

Waiting was a single warrior, yes, but no Rúcah.

Lann took a knee. "I come in surrender. I'm your tribute."

Adratus hadn't expected the words to make him feel so monstrous, so very sick in the pit of his stomach. He had faced countless men in battle, sliced open foes while their fresh blood splashed his face. But to meet this, a sheep yielding to slaughter, was so very different.

What was it Ubaz had called Adratus, he recalled—*a dragon*? But dragons were noble and mighty, the rulers of the black continent of Volagrok. No, Adratus felt more akin to a hyena, picking off the weak like a craven.

The prefect sheathed his sword and looked down in shame. "This feels wrong, Brother," he whispered to Maximus. "Extremely."

"This is not the time, Prefect," he said. Maximus then spoke up to Lann, saying, "You are late. Your time expired at sunrise. And, as you can see, the sun has, in fact, risen."

Lann's eyes narrowed. "Aye, it took a little longer than I expected it to. But I'm here, amn't I?"

"Yes," Maximus said, searching the surrounding area as if he might locate a hundred more people in the winter-bare trees. "But where hides the remainder of the tribute? I see only you."

The observation caused Lann to bow his head low. "Aye, Legate. 'Tis only meself here, true. And why shouldn't it be? 'Tis my so-called crime you're punishing, right? Nobody else needs to dangle from your crosses for the likes of me."

Lann's words, his humbled stance, disarmed the prefect.

"Legate," Adratus said with a hand on his shoulder and mouth near his ear, "we *must* stop."

"Enough, Camp Prefect," Legate Maximus said, softly but vexed, before jerking away.

"Maximus." Adratus locked his sad eyes on the dark eyes of his legate. "Apologies, yet as a Dark Light legionary, I cannot mindlessly follow a path I know to be wrong. Thus, I must officially declare *defiance*, as is the first lesson of the Gods."

Maximus clenched his jaw as his eyes narrowed. "You are not religious, Adratus. Do not feign to be."

"Yet it is in my rights as a Tridulan citizen."

"Against direct orders from the emperor?"

Adratus gained a rigid posture, arms to his sides and shoulders back. "Yes, Legate. And I ask you to do the same.

End this. Please. This is not you. Or the emperor. If I may better explain the situation to him—"

"Enough." Maximus went silent. Clearly, the gravity of the decision weighed the legate's armored shoulders. His next words could send Adratus to trial and send thousands of legionaries throughout the Rúcah lands, killing countless people along with any chance of real peace in the region.

There was a sudden shout to their side. Then another: "*Legate!*"

Adratus turned to see a Tridulan legionary approaching rapidly on horseback. He did not come from within the fort, but from the surrounding forest.

When he drew closer, Adratus recognized him as the same centurion he'd commanded to take Ubaz to the Feah.

"Legate," the centurion said again, weak and out of breath. He tried to dismount, but crumbled to the ground with a painful thud and wafting dust.

His leg was poorly wrapped in gore-soaked cloth, his body bloody. He looked up and feebly touched his fist to his chest before it slid down to the dirt at his side.

"Medic!" the legate called back toward the fort.

"What has happened?" Adratus demanded, crouching to his side.

"When my squad reached the Feah town, we found them besieged, Prefect. 'Tis Dayigan soldiers. Here in the Drevite Nation. Far too many to count."

"Dayigans?" Adratus asked. "Here?" His eyes widened as his heart felt clutched. "What of Ubaz?"

"Apologies, sir. There was naught I could do. We'd already bound your boy. When the Dayigans attacked, they stole him away. I ordered a retreat, sir, but we were pursued, and all, save I, were killed or captured."

The news weighed the prefect like a net of stone. "You . . . surely did your best, Centurion." He set his hand to his own forehead. His aching eyes stared out, though the world seemed to darken. "Fret not on the matter." Sounds around him became muffled.

"Fuck!" Adratus punched the ground. Cords of lightning shot up, whipping aimlessly before dissipating.

"Ye have to go to them, Legate." It was Lann who spoke, though his words sounded distant to Adratus. He continued, saying, "I'm begging you, please. 'Tis one thing to declare war on the Rúcah. But to battle the Rúcah and leave the Feah behind? The Five Clans would never forgive ye."

"He is correct, Legate," Adratus said vacantly, facing dirt.

Two soldiers came for the injured centurion and set him on a litter to carry him away.

Maximus breathed. "By all that is infernal," he muttered. He looked at Adratus and then Lann. "The matter with the Rúcah is yet undecided. This event does not save them. However, I will postpone the ruling until we return. Adratus, prepare the Ninth Legion and half of the Thirty-second Legion. We move for the Feah within an hour. *Someone arrest this rebel barbarian.*" He waved halfheartedly at Lann. "I will deal with him later."

"Let me come with ye, Legate, please," Lann said. "The Feah is me home, you know that. I must help defend it. Let it be me last request, if you like. Do remember, it was me came here to you. And if I be betraying ye, I risk the lives of a lot of the Rúcahs in doing so."

"Very well. But only if Adratus will accept you as a ward."

Adratus nodded, absently. His eyes stared as he stood. He could only think of Ubaz being snatched away by the

Dayigans. His fist clenched. What were his last words to him, he tried to recall, surely something horrible.

Maximus put a hand on Adratus's shoulder. "This news of the attack on the Feah is a week old, Brother, and 'twill take yet another week to reach them. Prepare yourself for what tragedy has most likely already occurred."

Adratus nodded.

CHAPTER SIXTY-EIGHT

Adratus looked out into the foggy wilderness before him. The forest was an amalgamation of lifeless things. Cheerless gray towers of cold wood vainly reached up, straining to touch the dim evening sky. They split off into twisted branches and then again to twigs, all bare of green. Their leaves scattered the ground in heaps of damp decay. The bushes, too, were bare—nothing more than naked puffs of distorted prickles.

In the direction he faced, two more days east, was the village where Adratus had sent his love. And reason told him Ubaz was just as dead as the forest separating them.

"Never will you be replaced," Adratus whispered, throwing words into the void, for there were no ears to hear. "I pray you will somehow forgive me."

He returned to his tent.

As the camp prefect, he was granted a tent larger than most, and it stood at the center of the camp next to the slightly larger one belonging to Maximus. Usually, it was the prefect's alone, but for this campaign, he was required to share with another.

With a swift entrance, Adratus secured the flap behind him, taking extra care to lock out the growing winds.

His gaze flicked briefly toward his unwanted tentmate. In the back of the goatskin room was an iron cage resembling a large birdcage, but relatively thinner. The bird locked within: Lann.

"Did they feed you?"

"Aye."

"Good."

Adratus grabbed one of three books atop a footlocker and moved to a cot set beside a brass floor lamp. He settled onto it, hoping that fiction would provide some respite from the bleak reality surrounding him. But as he opened the book and stared at the handwritten words, all he could think about was loss. He'd only gotten the book for Ubaz.

"You don't have to keep me locked up in here like this," Lann said again.

Adratus ignored him at first, but after a moment's pause, he rose and neared the captive.

"I require you to take a message," Adratus said, placing a hand on one of the iron bars. "To Ubaz."

"A message to Ubaz?"

"Yes, to deliver after we execute you."

"Right. So you're that certain he's left the world of the living, then?"

"I am practical." Adratus thumbed the iron bars. "Ubaz was taken by Dayigans twelve days ago, and they do not allow non-Déagrians to live. I know you are well aware."

Lann nodded sadly. "I am, yes."

"And I assume you and he will end together in whatever afterlife awaits."

"There's no reason to be thinking anything like that's happened to our poor Ubaz. Not yet. I'll listen to your message for the other side when I have a reason to, but not now. Don't be losing hope, Prefect. 'Tis all we have now."

—

The legion divided near the Feah village. Maximus led the majority up their road to their former fort to secure their kit and prepare for whatever this area might bring.

Adratus was on reconnaissance. He, Lann, and a squad of legionaries were to go straight on to the Feah temple village and collect information on the state therein.

The prefect gathered the detachment and removed his helmet. "Split into three columns moving parallel towards the village," Adratus instructed, keeping his voice low. "The Dayigans can be anywhere, in any number. We must move *with* the forest, not against it, so keep to natural paths as much as viable. Stay alert, stay quiet, and keep your eyes on me. Move out."

Adratus and Lann stayed at the front of the middle column, which remained slightly advanced. Lead from the front—it was the Tridulan way.

The prefect crouched as he walked slowly and carefully. He looked around and listened.

His own words were correct: the Dayigans could be anywhere. They were very near the temple village now, and it had no proper border—no gate for the invading soldiers to guard, no wall to be beyond. Instead, every one of the massive trees the legionaries passed could have had soldiers standing on the other side.

Adratus heard something. He lifted his hand as a fist, signaling the group to halt. He looked to the first and third lines, assuring they, too, had complied.

Perking his ears, Adratus listened as keenly as Human ears could perceive. His breathing paused. He could not quite understand what he heard.

A strange, high-pitched chattering preceded shrill hissing and growling and groans. The noises layered over one another as the sounds of many creatures combined.

Adratus looked to Lann at his side. The Drevite warrior clearly heard the noises, too, but it was not perplexity on his face but sadness.

"Vultures," Lann whispered. "Loads of 'em."

The word struck Adratus to the core, as he remembered the genuine horror they faced was not in finding the Dayigans–but in finding the Feah. He'd barely noticed the putrid scent in the air. Now, it was all he smelled.

The prefect waved the unit to advance. And as they continued, the sour stench grew stronger, and the horrible noises grew louder: the chattering and hissing and squawking. There was a competition ahead as greedy birds fought over shreds of dead flesh. And from the growing sounds of numerous birds, Adratus inferred they would soon be upon a feast of carrion.

Anticipation became actuality as the soldiers were soon upon the first eviscerated corpse circled by fat black vultures rooting through horrors.

Adratus had seen the likes before–people reduced to meat for the stomach of birds. Such sights from the battlefield stuck in the brain like none other.

The Tridulans could do nothing but continue toward the village.

Turning to Lann, Adratus whispered, "When we have the full legion, we will return for them. So I vow."

"I thank you, but there's no need to," Lann said sadly. "My people practice exposure. We leave the dead to be purified by the scavengers of the forest, usually high up in the sacred Tree of Silence, out by itself. But this place here can also serve as a charnel ground, if it must do. *And in death, to nature thou shalt return.*"

Adratus was appalled. "Fucking disgusting," he said with a grimace. "You are sick in the head. These people deserve proper cremations, as does my love. We *will* return for them."

Lann winced at the words but remained silent.

There were more dead Terovaes. And more. The unit navigated gradually around them as the sour stench suffocated. Adratus—hand cupping the end of his cape over his nose and mouth—wanted to ignore them, to turn his eyes from revulsions and repulsions. Instead, he made himself look at every bloated, ripped-open, half-eaten man and woman flanked by happy birds. He had to, for he had to see if his love lay among them.

This place is where I sent my love. The thought was so horrible that Adratus nearly laughed madly as it scratched through his brain.

The prefect heard vomiting to his rear. And at least two other legionaries followed suit.

The unit seemed to be snaking around the last of the dead. In all, Adratus had seen about forty. No Ubaz. Still, he could not help but fear how many other dumping grounds lay around the village.

With so many emotions coursing through the prefect's blood, that is when he spotted them.

They froze. Adratus froze. The squad behind him froze.

It took the prefect's exasperated mind a moment to comprehend what he saw.

Two men. Humans. Each armored in mail covered by a green tabard. Across their fronts, amber threads stitched out the crest of the Dayigan Empire.

These soldiers held a Terovae corpse: one holding the arms, one holding the ankles, and the body sagging in between. After a moment of fixed tension, while glancing around at the Tridulans, they threw down the body and ran back toward the village.

Adratus took off in pursuit at full pace but not only for matters of vengeance. There were surely other Dayigan soldiers nearby, and the prefect knew that if these two alerted their comrades, it would mean death to the entire reconnaissance unit.

Adratus cast his hand forward, sending out cords of red light, but the targeted soldiers evaded. The cords scratched only at trees.

His helmet rattled against his ears as he ran. His breastplate thumped against his chest. Adratus kept a good pace despite the uneven forest floor and the many obstacles. His sandals pounded the mulch and crushed sticks as he gained ground.

Again, Adratus cast out his left hand, expelling cords of light. This time, he caught one of the Dayigan soldiers. He snatched the struggling soldier backward toward himself.

"Praise God Déagar," prayed the frightened soldier, "the one and only God, protector from the Dark."

Shouting, Adratus yanked the soldier's mail cowl from his head and threw it aside.

"You are the Greatest of All."

Adratus stabbed his sword straight down through the neck into the chest, aiming for the heart. Anger pounded through the prefect as blood spurted upward.

"Your blood flows for those in the vulture field," Adratus spat. "Let your deeds weigh your soul when you stand before the Lavender Lady."

He yanked up his sword, creating a fountain before kicking the man to the dirt.

Adratus rejoined the chase. The other Tridulans had now passed him, but he was quickly at their heels.

Soon, the forest floor made way to the village's main path, and as the prefect's sandals struck the dirt, his horrified eyes roamed the area.

"Fucking za," Adratus said, gobsmacked by the sight.

The destruction was far more than needed for attack or capture or even pillaging. The homes, built of forest items and tucked into natural alcoves, were now black and gray pits of ash and charcoal—apparently natural fire but cataclysmic, nevertheless. The soldiers had sawed through many of the massive trees containing homes. Now the towers, charred black, lay fallen.

Even knowing of the True Light's ways, Adratus hadn't been ready to see the Feah village so thoroughly ravaged.

The Dayigan soldier was now shouting, "We're under attack! We're under attack! Soldiers of Darkness are upon us!"

"Detachment," Adratus called, "fall back."

It was too late. The one Dayigan soldier had pulled others, and they now dashed from the trees.

"Disregard," Adratus growled with vexation, his breath heavy from running. His eyes remained locked on the advancing Dayigans. "We stay and fight."

"Seven of us," Lann said, "against five times that of them. I sure hope you Tridulans are as good as you like to say."

"Shut your cock hole, Lann, and begin an aerial assault."

"Aye, Prefect." He spread his falcon-like wings and leaped from the ground.

CHAPTER SIXTY-NINE

Adratus stood as mighty God Zeanázel, poised for battle as he firmly gripped his gladius. His helm crowned with blades glinted in the dim morning light, as did his steel cuirass. His black cape flowed behind him. To his sides, the other legionaries in their black segmented armor and scarlet capes braced for the charging Dayigans.

The two forces collided with a thunderous clang of metal against metal that echoed throughout the woods. And blood flowed forthwith.

To Adratus, combat was the ultimate antithesis of sex, but just as intimate. With steel against steel and piercing eyes locked onto his adversary's, he could feel the warmth of the Dayigan's breath against his frigid face, as well as smell the sweat dripping from his enemy's pores. Evaluating body language and movements, Adratus observed strength and weakness in equal measure. The Dayigan before him was strong, yet seemed to be less experienced in such confrontations.

Adratus thrust hard and managed to strike a blow against the soldier's arm, barely slicing through mail armor, but it was enough for blood to ooze between the tiny steel rings.

"Damn you, savage," the Dayigan growled. "I'll run you through for that. And your soul'll rot in za 'longside them tree-fucking savages what lived here before."

A scowl etched across Adratus's face. "Wrong fucking words," he snarled, as his blade swung and struck away the soldier's sword. Lunging forward with fierce anger, Adratus thrust his gladius hilt deep into the man's midsection while he met the man's eyes with his own.

Those blue eyes Adratus had known so briefly widened in agony as the Tridulan twisted the blade a yank. He kicked him off.

The victory was brief before two other Dayigans were on him.

"A threesome, is it?" Adratus smirked as he pressed his sword against both others, the muscles of his arms burning beneath his skin.

Men on either side fell dead as Tridulan gladii—all uniform—struck the various Dayigan swords.

In the end, only five survived: Adratus, Lann, two other Tridulans, and one Dayigan. But the remaining Dayigan was not long for breath, as he stood on his knees with a legionary's blade to his neck.

"Keep him alive," Adratus commanded. He then clapped his hands, and copper chains formed around the Dayigan's torso, securing his arms to his sides.

Adratus neared the captive. "I . . ." He began, his eyes focusing on the man before him. "I know you."

The man was older, with graying hair and an aged face, most likely near sixty, but remained fit and held himself with dignity amid his captors.

"Your name is Swithun, yes?" Adratus asked, maintaining his composure despite facing this man who'd nearly killed him as a boy, this figure who'd come to plague his nightmares.

"That I am," Swithun replied without emotion. "And who might you be?"

It stung that he was unremembered, but Adratus continued. "I will be your death if you do not cooperate."

Swithun said nothing, keeping his eyes forward and back straight—a soldier's posture, even on his knees and bound by chains.

"Prefect," a legionary interjected, as he presented a golden orb about the size of an orange and etched with green symbols. "We found this on him."

Adratus took it and examined it. It was not exactly like the one he'd seen in the Reyigan town of Port Haven—for one, it lacked the emeralds around its sides—but it was close enough to make Adratus suspect it held a similar purpose.

"You're that boy, aren't you?" Swithun spoke up at last. "The one from the Blue Zone all them years ago? 'Tis only right then that you'd be the one to end me." His words were tinged with regret and resignation. "I'm ready for it."

"I will *end you* when and if I choose to, not before." Adratus handed the orb back to the legionary. "Are there other True Light soldiers in the Drevite Nation?"

"Hundreds of them," he said defiantly. "Just north of here, too, in that abandoned fort. With or without me, my men'll hunt down all those filthy savages in these . . ."

Adratus couldn't help but chuckle, a welcome relief to tension. "In the abandoned fort, you said?"

"I don't know what you're laughing at, you unholy fuck. They'll be after you soon enough."

"Lann," Adratus said casually, "*hundreds* of True Light soldiers are in Fort Casdrevite. How would you guess their status?"

"Well, to be honest, Prefect, being as thousands of—"

"Nine thousand," Adratus expounded.

"Being as *nine thousand* Tridulan legionaries went to the very same place, I reckon 'tis not looking too good for the

Dayigans. If I was to guess, I'd say you'd have a hard time finding one of 'em still with a beating heart in his chest."

"Fucking savage," Swithun growled as he fought against the chain. "I'll kill you. You're evil, the whole lot of you." He jumped up and ran at Adratus.

Adratus cast cords of light to encircle the soldier, holding him in place. "Evil? Perhaps," Adratus said with a menacing grin. "And evil as I am, you best be troubled, soldier, for you took someone *very* important to me. Why do you capture Drevites?"

"I'm not telling you nothing, savage."

Adratus yanked the cords, throwing Swithun against the charred ground.

"Speak," Adratus commanded.

"You're too wicked to understand the tasks God gives us."

"Rage!" Adratus shouted. The cords of light circling the soldier turned to scarlet lightning.

Swithun cried out but said nothing.

The lightning grew brighter; its electrical buzz, increasingly louder as Adratus stepped forward, his eyes lit up with fury.

"Kill me if you're going to," Swithun managed through pain.

Adratus pulled the cord to set the man back on his knees. The lighting dispelled, leaving only the copper chain.

Swithun lowered his head to face the blackened ground. "You might know my name, savage," he began sadly, "but you only know a bit of what I've done. Proper nasty things, me. Things that God needed me to do, true. But"—he sighed— "I'm old and weary now. Just end it."

Adratus slammed his fist into Swithun's face. "I care not of the pitiful self-loathing of a mass murderer. Where have you taken the Drevites?"

The old soldier grinned through bloody teeth. "The archbishop is blessing them."

"Blessing them?" Adratus asked.

"That's right," Swithun said, maintaining the smile. "Freeing them all from their wicked ways. Once they're blessed, they'll have no choice but to obey the Church. I told you you couldn't understand it. The archbishop can even save you, too, if you let him."

Lann exploded with rage, lunging toward the Dayigan, but Adratus grabbed Lann by the arms, holding him back while he thrashed forward.

"That's why they took us!" Lann shouted as he struggled to break free. "All this fucking time? Me daughter and sister, that's what happened to them all? Fucking blessed?"

Swithun kept quiet and faced forward.

Lann relaxed some, and Adratus stepped away, passing him to the grip of the legionaries. He neared Swithun. "Is that what your people call the Drevite Experiment?"

Swithun paused. "That black boy you was with years back . . ."

"Maximus."

"He said he kept me alive, so I could see what the True Light would become. I seen it. I seen it, and I can't unsee it. Monsters, straight from a nightmare. Those horrible eyes just staring right through you, like a corpse watching you."

"Tell me what you know," Adratus said gently, "and I vow we will help end it."

Swithun shook his head. "I can't betray them. Don't you see, they're all I have now. And now, I'm old and tired. You said you was gonna kill me. I'm not telling you nothing, so best be getting on with it, then. I can trust a Dark Light savage to give me what I have coming."

Adratus clenched his fist around the grip of his gladius, pausing as his heart raced.

"Do it!" Swithun shouted. "What's wrong with you?" He began panting, as if in some sort of panic that shifted into breathy laughter. He cast his eyes to the ground. "She let me live, too—the fucking Blue Rose. You and her are supposed to be the wicked ones. But you're useless, the pair of you."

Adratus turned away without another word and returned to his men, signaling for them to gather near.

"If a chance remains that my sweet Ubaz lives," Adratus said, "I must find him. Yet, I cannot order Tridulan legionaries to attack an unauthorized target within the Dayigan Empire. We would need a sanction from the emperor."

"I'm with you, Prefect," a legionary said, as he placed his fist to his heart and bowed his head. "Orders or no."

"Same here," the other said.

"Gratitude, but your place is with the legion. Lann and I will go alone. You two, report back to the legate and arrange to retrieve our fallen brothers."

"What about the Drevite dead, sir?"

Adratus glanced at Lann. He was silent a moment before saying, "Leave them where they lay. To Nature they will return. 'Tis the way of the Five Tribes. And take this Dayigan into custody."

"Alive, Prefect?"

"Yes, alive." Adratus scanned the ruined area. "Xanorael has reaped enough souls today."

CHAPTER SEVENTY

Where do you go?" Adratus demanded to Lann's back, though his destination was clear: Lann rushed toward the hill-like Feah temple. "We have no time for delay."

Lann stopped and turned back to Adratus. His face was stern. "You might only be worried about the one Feah, yourself, Tridulan, but I'll have you be remembering this is me home. I knew everybody here. Everybody. And I need a fucking moment. All right with you?"

Adratus paused, taking in the words. "Proceed."

—

The desecrated temple was draped in agonizing silence, the stench of death hanging thickly in the air. From a distance, Adratus watched Lann as he kneeled amid the rubble of the sacred skulls that had once adorned the many shelves—revered ancestors whose remains had withstood the test of time yet now laid scattered and broken.

With trembling hands, Lann picked up a shard of bone and gazed at it with profound sadness before dropping it to the dust. Adratus said nothing. He knew there was no solace to be offered for this tragedy. The damage was throughout, as was the bloodshed.

When Lann was ready, they continued further in, stepping around corpses until, at last, they entered the Temple Grove.

The monolith rose within a ring of charred oaks with deep gouges opening up their rough bark to the yellow flesh within.

Lann cried out and started running.

Adratus soon understood the alarm when he saw the chief of the Feah tied to the thick center stone, her body stripped and beaten.

She was barely conscious as Lann frantically cut the ropes binding her. "Chief Kaie," Lann said, holding her up, "can you hear me, dove?"

Adratus could tell what the Dayigan soldiers had done to her. There were multiple signs of brutal violations. He unfastened the black cape from his armor and handed it to her.

"Thank you," she managed hoarsely, as she wrapped the cape around her slouched body. She limped forward on bruised, shaky legs before sitting on the grass. After a silent moment of staring downward, she looked up at Adratus and Lann.

"Well, isn't this an unlikely pair now?" She flashed a slight smile, which faded. "But only one thing would bring the two of ye together. One *who*." She took a deep breath before exhaling slowly. "I thought I saw him here, but I prayed it wasn't true. The village was lost by then. And from what we know now, in the far reaches of the Feah lands, the soldiers were taking folks away weeks before"—she coughed—"weeks before they got to us."

"You need not speak if you're unable, Chief," Adratus assured.

"Nonsense." She waved him off. "Lann, do us a kindness, please, and fetch me a cup of water."

"Aye, Chief." He hurried away.

"By the time we knew what was happening," she continued to Adratus, "it was already too late for our village. People from all over the Feah lands started coming to help us, but there was nothing they could do." She blinked downward. Her face seemed so much older than before, so worn. "Our people just stopped fighting—some sort of spell cast on them. Their faces went blank, they dropped their weapons, and they left with the invaders. Those of us who weren't affected tried to stop them from leaving, but . . ." she trailed off with a sorrowful sigh and shook her head in resignation.

"Did they take Ubaz?" Adratus asked.

Lann handed her a cup, and she drank. "There's just no way to know," she said. "'Twas confusion."

Adratus faced the grassy floor. "I'm familiar with the mind-controlling power used by the Dayigans on your people."

"Aye, us as well," Lann grumbled.

"The spell has two components," Adratus continued, "a dormant hex found within the target and an activation spell originating from this." He unfastened a bag on his belt and drew out the gold sphere encircled by red lightning. "I know how to find the hex within a person. If I can inspect you . . ."

"I was near that thing when the Dayigan used it," Kaie said. "Seems the curse wasn't strong enough to pierce my protective spells, and I doubt your magic would be either. Best to check Lann."

Adratus looked at Lann. "It seems unlikely that he would be affected. He has been in Rúcah lands for—"

"Adratus," she stopped him. "Are you seeing a third choice here, dear?"

In reflex, Adratus scanned the massive room, looking beyond the circle of desecrated oaks. There were other Feahs nearby, true, yet they were all violently dead upon the grass.

Adratus drew closer to Lann. "Stand still with your feet together, arms slightly from your sides, and eyes closed."

Lann stumbled backward in unease. "I'm not having some wicked sorcerer examining me."

"'Tis important, Lann," Kaie replied firmly. "You know that it is."

Nodding somberly, Lann assumed the position described by Adratus.

"Detect magic." Adratus extended his hand, palm outstretched toward Lann's forehead. Eyes closed tight in concentration, he whispered, "I see it. 'Tis similar to what I saw in the Reyigan town but far less complex with a much longer duration. Yet . . . this is very old." He opened his eyes, turning them to Kaie. "Lann has had this hex dormant in him for nearly a decade."

Kaie shook her head in disbelief. "That's impossible. We destroyed that curse the Dayigans put on us years ago now."

"Condolences, Chief, but 'twould seem you were mistaken," Adratus said, "and it has been spreading through your people ever since." He waved his hand toward Lann. "Reveal."

Emerald tendrils of light flowed from Lann. A handful pointed off in arbitrary paths. However, countless cords, up and down Lann's body, flowed off in a single direction.

"Those are the affected people," Adratus said. "Presumably, all of those together represent the people who have been captured. I'm receiving a number close to . . ." He looked at her. ". . . seven thousand." He breathed. "Condolences."

Chief Kaie set her shaking hand to her forehead.

"That cannot be right, though," Lann said as he looked at the green cords writhing off his body. "With that many, it would mean that all nine parishes in the Feah lands would be near empty." His eyes widened with dread. "I mean, it can't be right, can it, though? Not near everyone—"

"Lann," Kaie whispered through grief. "That's enough of that." She closed her eyes, and a tear ran down her cheek.

Adratus waved his hand toward Lann, and the cords disappeared. "The cords from Lann should guide me to your people, Chief. We—Lann and I—will find them and bring them home."

Kaie took a deep breath, gathering herself. "I'll do what I can to help you."

CHAPTER SEVENTY-ONE

Beside the towering monolith, Adratus stood tall and still, stripped of all armor and clothing. However, he was not naked. Not anymore. Chief Kaie had soaked thin sheets of birch bark in water and was nearly finished covering every inch of his skin.

"You vowed protection, yet you immobilize," Adratus griped, unable to move as the bark hardened as an itchy cast around his body. "We haven't time for this nonsense."

"Nonsense?" Lann snapped back as he sharpened arrowheads nearby. "The fucking nerve of him. This is sacred magic, here. No one outside the Five Clans has ever been allowed to even see it before, much less take part in it. You should—"

"Lann," Kaie said calmly. "Leave it be." She added another dripping strip of bark around Adratus's neck. "The prefect here is married into the Feah, don't you forget?" She smoothed the piece in place. "There. Finished." She stepped back and began examining her work.

The hardened bark now covered Adratus, except for his face and the solid mound of his right chest. When Kaie was evidently satisfied with her work, she nodded to Lann, who begrudgingly grabbed a simple drum beside him.

He began a measured beat with his hands.

The steady rhythm guided Kaie as she began a graceful curving dance, though her feet remained rooted in place. Her arms stretched toward the sky as she called out:

"Praise be to Mother Lágeya, she who is Nature and birthed all life—the birds, the trees, the grass, the ants. To them, she gave an aspect of her spirit. To them, she gave the One Soul that flows through all nature as a living river."

As Kaie's dance intensified, a gust of wind swept through the temple. And lavender light flowed downward through her hands and cascaded around her body, encircling her as misty ribbons.

"Praises to Lágeya, who is the One Soul!" Kaie's voice echoed through the temple walls. "Praises to the One Soul, who is Nature! I honor you. I honor you. Bless this man with the strength of the birch. Protect him with skin of bark. Blessings from the Three Mothers. Blessings from the True Light!"

She paused, looking at Adratus as if she meant for him to repeat this, but he remained silent and rolled his eyes downward.

Kaie nodded understandingly and was still, but the drumming increased. She held out her hands, conjuring a large lavender orb that hovered just above her palm.

"Do you know it?" she asked Adratus.

It hurt him to see, but immobile in bark, he could not look away. The orb was bliss beyond bliss, yet he was so very sad to see it. Joy and loss intertwined and enveloped in hurt. Tears streamed down his face as he gazed upon it with wonder and longing.

"'Tis the energy of your love," Kaie said. "The grand energy that you and Ubaz threw into this chamber when ye sealed your love for one another. 'Tis so very powerful. And it will protect you."

She moved her left hand back, along with the orb, as her right moved forward toward the stationary soldier. And as the orb absorbed into her one hand, bolts of violet lightning shot from her fingertips of the right, hitting the section of Adratus's chest left unbarked.

He called out with echoing screams as the bolts ripped and burned into the flesh of his chest. The pain was agonizing, unrelenting, all-consuming. His sight faded to black as he became momentarily numb.

Soon, Adratus found himself hunched over with his hands on his knees. The last of the ache throbbed away and felt pleasurable as it tingled through his flesh. His head spun while he grinned.

Regaining himself, he realized that the bark was gone, leaving him bare. He looked at his chest. A symbol was there: the symbol of the triple two, with their bases together as a triangle. Here, the Triébis was red, and in the fashion of the Tridulan Empire, twice circled.

"A red tattoo, Chief?" Adratus asked as he stood upright.

"We had no time for a tattoo," Kaie said. "The red you see is your blood. I carved the symbol into your flesh."

"It feels like it." He grimaced as he rolled his shoulder.

"'Tis not a sigil I'd normally be using, mind you, but it has meaning to yourself." She approached with another piece of bark and placed it over his upper chest, covering the Triébis. "'Twill make a lovely scar for you there."

The bark dissolved into his skin.

Lann handed Kaie a leather kilt, and she began to wrap it around Adratus.

"I cannot wear that." He stepped back. "I'll appear—"

"Like a barbarian?" She glared into his eyes. She slapped him. "You say *barbarian* like the Dayigans say *savage*."

"'Tis different how we say it."

"Different, is it? It doesn't feel any different." She threw the kilt to his feet. "The soldiers all called me savage when they came to me, one after the other, whilst I was tied to the monolith."

"Apologies, Chief," he said. "But you mistake me. I can neither appear to be Feah nor Tridulan."

Her eyes remained narrowed, and her lips pursed.

Adratus continued, "The Dayigans tube their individual legs in *trousers*. And wear a unique style of tunic. I will need to scavenge the Dayigan soldiers to find these items. I would suggest the same for Lann, yet his face is inked."

Adratus ran his fingers up the ridges of his own stomach. "My skin feels normal. You are certain this armor functions?"

"You know well how our armor works," Lann said bitterly, sitting behind the now quiet drum. "You've tested it yourself."

Adratus recalled his failed attempt to stab a Drevite's gut. The warrior's skin was akin to wood, and the prefect's weapon had deflected sideways, scratching its point across the stomach, its bloody mark shallow and far from fatal.

"Like the mighty birch," Kaie began as she approached Adratus, "your skin is tough. But everything will still feel the same." She ran her nails, slow and hard, down his upper arm to demonstrate. "And 'twill still hurt when you get cut, that you can be sure of. But injuries won't go deep enough for much harm to yourself. And you've got nothing weighing you down and nothing hindering your movements."

"Gratitude, Chief. I will use your gift for the glory of the Five Tribes."

"Send your thanks to Nature." She left him and began gathering her equipment. "We are good to Nature and are rewarded with strength."

"'*Respect the land and forest and all of Nature*,'" Adratus quoted, "'*Unto thee, Nature will give life and unto thy children, life too . . .*'"

She looked up from her gathering. "Again, you quote the words of the Mothers as written in the Tréréaldéag—you've become well learned."

"I had the privilege of loving a clever man." Adratus smiled sadly. "One I should have listened to more when I had the chance."

"But you quote only half a verse. Do you know the rest?"

"No, Chief."

"You needn't say the whole thing, but you must *know* and understand the whole verse before quoting any of it."

"Apologies, Chief."

"None needed." She picked up a rolled page of leather and approached Adratus. "It is a copy of the Tréréaldéag. *'Knowledge is the first zenith, for he who is wise is great, and he who is foolish bears no favor with the Light. Only with wisdom is reason sound.'*"

She placed it in his hand. "Take it, and remember that not all of the True Light is what the Déagrians have become." She smiled thinly. "Now go. Your love's awaiting you. May the Mothers guide you."

CHAPTER SEVENTY-TWO

For days on end, Adratus and Lann braved the treacherous waters of the Hyvile River. Their small Feah boat, fashioned from wicker covered by sturdy skins, held up surprisingly well, but it was not built for speed. Adratus cursed its sluggishness as they rowed east toward the empire of their shared enemy. Amid the perilous journey, Adratus revealed occasional glimpses of the emerald tendrils reaching out from Lann—guiding them toward an unknown destination filled with unknown peril. Only Adratus's assumption told them that the captured Feahs would be there at all.

After what felt like a lifetime, they finally reached the shores of a foreign island amid the mighty river. As Lann set off to scout their surroundings, Adratus sat upon the sandy beach, his eyes fixed on the winter-bare woods in the direction of Ubaz—*hopefully*. The sky above was bleak and foreboding, heavy clouds pregnant with snow looming overhead. The frigid winds whipped at Adratus's cloak—a green Dayigan garment he had taken to blend in on their mission. It covered his stolen attire of an off-white tunic with a laced V-neck, black trousers, a brown leather belt, and sturdy brown boots.

Alone on that wooded island, Adratus's thoughts turned to his love—memories both joyous and heartbreaking flooding his mind. Above all else, he feared for his sweet Ubaz, now in the clutches of the Light. *Freeing them all from their wicked ways,* that is what Swithun had said, whatever it meant. He pictured his love scared before a screaming priest, imprisoned and alone. He imagined Ubaz unaware of how deeply he was loved. He envisioned his love as despondent with no hope of rescue.

"Stay strong," Adratus whispered to the wind as he sat on the shore. "I will come for you, even if I must slay armies en route."

"You really love me nephew, don't you now?" Lann said from a short distance, his arms wrapping a stack of sticks.

"I knew not you were there."

"Aye, 'cause 'tis some grand secret, sure: the mighty Adratus has a heart deep in there." He dropped the bundle to clatter on the shore. "I seen it with me own two eyes afore I near killed you outside the temple." He began arranging the wood. "That's why you're breathing now."

"You were wrong for telling me Ubaz was dead. I haven't forgotten."

"Aye, 'twas a wicked thing to do, that be true. But," he wagged a stick toward him, "you're no blameless babe yourself." He threw it in the pile and returned to stacking. "I never seen him like he was that night after you said you'd attack the Rúcahs. The state of him when we left the temple, broke me heart just to look at him, truly it did. He still loves ya though. Even now."

"I have no reason to discuss such things with *you*. You nearly killed him when you attacked us in the Rúcah lands."

"*He* were never in no real danger. But yourself? You were very much so. But he saved your life back there, you know. He said for us to tell the Rúcah chief that it weren't you bringing the Faeries down. I did that, and then she said we couldn't be attacking ye again if ye kept heading eastwards. Maybe she was right there. To be honest, I still haven't made up me mind 'bout you, Prefect. 'Tis right and good that you see Ubaz as a person, but I know how the rest of us look to ye—Barbarian! Barbarian! Barbarian!"

"'Tis a two-way road. You've seen us as nothing but imperial invaders since the moment we arrived."

"Aye. Cause ye are imperial invaders, you bastard."

Adratus sighed. "We're not," he said somberly, "but we should have striven harder to show your people we're not. When I traveled with Ubaz before, hacking through the thick forest, I turned back and saw how much destruction our journey had caused. I see that same destruction behind me now—with the Five Tribes." Adratus looked at the ground and raked the sand with his fingers. "'Seeing is the start of a better path,' Ubaz told me. But is it enough now?"

"A start." Lann laid another stick on the pile. "We're not your enemies, you know."

"I know. Nor are we yours. Yet, your people must be protected, and the Dayigans must be stopped." He looked into Lann's face, at his eyes. There was a hint of Ubaz around the eyes—Adratus had never noticed before. He sighed. "However, we have hacked through the Feah lands without true regard for your people."

Lann took a seat on the shore next to Adratus and stared out at the dark waters of the Hyvile. "You don't need to tell *us* the Dayigans need stopping." His words were somber as he said, "That dormant hex you found on me from years back, it weren't always dormant."

Adratus nodded. "Ubaz said they made you fight for them."

Lann looked down. "They did, aye. Led an attack on our temple. I fought against friends and family, killing some. I just wish the bastards had let me forget it all. I gave away me very own . . ." He took a deep breath. "I know what you're going to be saying: 'twas the Dayigans, not the Tridulans. But even so, ye still need to realize that ye can't just march into our lands, proclaiming ye'll be saving us when we've heard it all before. And it didn't end too well for us then."

"Apologies. Sincerely. I know the single word does little, but I will work to see my people do better."

"And forgive us and all. Now, come on. Let's stop this idle chattering and get a fire going here." He pulled his cloak of pelts around his shoulders. "Night's coming in and 'twould be a long night to spend out here frozen stiff." Lann stood up, looking around. "Right then, light it up."

"Light it?"

"Aye, with your . . . em," Lann waggled his fingers at the pile of sticks and twigs, as if casting a spell.

Adratus chuckled. "I am a confinest, not a conjurer of fire."

"But you set me bow ablaze before."

"A disarm illusion, naught else."

"It burnt me hands, like."

"Did it, or did it *feel* like it did? 'Tis a powerful illusion. Do you think I can truly make copper chains, too? I'd melt them, sell them, and have a fortune."

"Fuck sake, Human." Lann let out a resigned sigh and grumbled, "You worship a fire God and can't get a fire going? Mothers help us all. I'm off to the boat to fetch some flint for it then."

—

With the fall of night came the fall of snow. The temperature dropped significantly. Both Adratus and Lann sat near the fire. Suspended on a spit over the flames was a skinned rabbit, courtesy of Lann's bow, its aroma teasing the taste buds of the weary travelers.

"Wine?" Adratus offered, as he lifted a bladder toward Lann.

"'Tis like beer, right?"

"Much better."

"And you take it along into conflict?"

Adratus chuckled. "Tridulans are never far from wine. Although, truly, this is posca, which is heavily diluted wine sweetened with honey and flavored with herbs. 'Twill not intoxicate unless gorged."

Lann reached for the bladder, and Adratus handed it to him.

He took a gulp. "'Tis all right, that." He passed it back.

Adratus drank again and looked at the flakes of frigid white falling all around. "It never snows on the Viyae Peninsula—that is the heart of our empire. I have, of course, seen snow. Much of it. I've spent most of my adult life off the Viyae. But as a child there, never, not once, saw I snow. All year round, warm winds constantly wash over the peninsula from the Bay of Deception."

"That's a name there." Lann gestured for the wine. "What makes them call the bay a name like that for?"

"It is said that the first lie ever told was spoken on its shore," Adratus said, as he handed Lann the wine bladder. "Thus, a great snake, named Deception, was born and slithered into the waters. Even now, he dwells within its lowest depths, in a cave of fire, which is why the bay is ever warm.

"'Tis an awe-inspiring sight to behold," Adratus continued dreamily, "miles and miles of glimmering waves lapping against a black sand shore. And there, by the bay, is the dark, eternal city of Tridual, my home—one of the first cities in the world. It was founded when Vampires ruled the world of Perdinok and forged as one of their mighty capitals."

Adratus smiled, envisioning his home. "Now, it stands as a monumental city of black marble buildings and colossal statues celebrating ancient heroes and Dark Gods. There are great amphitheaters and vast forums filled with temples and baths. By all that is infernal, I miss it." He looked at Lann and cleared the smile, regaining himself. "Apologies for my distraction. But no, never any snow."

"Right." Lann laughed. "Ye Dark Light folks be a queer bunch. Ye talk of Vampires, beastly serpents, and devil Gods like they be . . ."

"Magnificent?" Adratus offered.

"If you say so. There must be some good about it. A great mate of mine lives in the other Dark Light city east of us—Vohcktara."

"Also a great city."

"He's the one you be talking about who took Chief Kaie's message asking for help—Ubaz's uncle on his daddy's side. He fell in love with a bloke he'd known since they were wee lads, and the two of them ran off there together. I reckon they liked it and stayed."

Adratus grinned. "Happily ever after."

"Hope so. He's a grand lad, Finn," he said wistfully. "They say there's a tower of black stone in your fort that transports folks to Dark Light capitals, Vohcktara included. Is it true?"

"An octolisk, yes. They connect the major cities of the Autumnal Federation, and we also send them to areas of conflict, so we can quickly deploy more troops at will."

"Areas in conflict?" Lann asked. "Like our lands."

Adratus fell silent and looked down.

"Pardon me," Lann said. "A shite subject to be bringing up. Your home, though, it sounds nice—in a Dark Light sort of way."

"I will show it to you once we rescue Ubaz. You could hone your skills in Nerageat—the place where we forge new legionaries. I think you would do well in the auxiliary."

"You mean, if I'm not crucified and left to rot alongside a road?"

"Yes," Adratus said, as his eyes drifted to the fire. "Barring that."

There was silence afterward, only the popping and crackling of the twisting flames.

The abbey stood stoically amid the peaceful snow. Unlike the grandiose Tridulan temples, with their towering columns and smooth marble, it exuded a humble charm. A cluster of stout brick buildings clustered together within its walls, the largest being a church adorned with powdered gargoyles perched upon its sharp green roof. A slushy stream flowed toward a watermill, adding to the serene atmosphere.

It seemed ridiculous to Adratus that this should be the site of the horrors he'd envisioned. Of course, he wasn't sure if Ubaz was truly here at all or lying dead outside the Feah temple village, a meal for scavenging birds.

As they approached the abbey, Adratus recited a passage from the sacred Feah text: "'Valor is the fourth zenith,'" he said solemnly, his eyes fixed on the structure, "'for thou must defend truth, family, and home. Yet only if they are challenged, for thy will extends no further than another's. Mind thy sphere.'"

Lann placed a reassuring hand on Adratus' shoulder. "You've been reading the Tréréaldéag," he said, impressed. "May wisdom guide us."

They made their way toward the abbey, nearing a short wall that seemed more for keeping out wild animals than intruders. Their destination was the small gate that led to the main doors of the church.

Adratus turned to Lann as they approached. "You will need to leave your bow and quiver behind," he said.

Lann nodded and tossed his gear outside the wall. "You're sure you can be acting like a Dayigan now?" he asked with a crooked smile.

"I've investigated them for years and have needed to play the part more than once," Adratus replied confidently. "Yet, I worry more of your ability to play the role of a slave. The lip on you is rather less than subservient." Adratus placed his hand on the gate and added with a hint of amusement, "Call me master, and feel the weight of the word on your tongue."

Lann reached under his kilt and grabbed himself. "How 'bout you feel the weight of that on *your* tongue?"

Adratus scoffed. "I doubt 'twould be much weight at all."

The Tridulan opened the gate and stepped onto hallowed ground. But as soon as his feet touched the snow-covered gravel, Adratus was struck with unimaginable pain. He fell forward and writhed in agony while Lann rushed to his side. Muscles taut and fighting against each other, Adratus could only groan in breathless torment.

"What's happened to you?" Lann asked urgently.

Unable to form words, Adratus lay limp on his back. Though still struggling to breathe, he had seemingly returned from wherever the pain had taken him.

"Consecrated ground," he panted, his eyes fixed on nothingness. "Stronger than anything I've ever encountered. It has drained my magic completely. I feel its absence like a void." He weakly reached out his hand but could only produce a feeble flicker of diminished red energy. Again, he tried: nothing at all.

"Get up, Adratus," Lann demanded, "before we're seen here." He pulled the weakened legionary to his feet.

Still struggling to regain his strength, Adratus looked down at his now impotent left hand, clenching and stretching his fingers in disbelief. "Forgive my brief weakness. I am fine." He straightened himself up, determined not to show any vulnerability. "What of our armor? Is it equally affected?"

Lann thought before answering. "Your confinement magic comes from a devil God of the Dark Light—they'd surely have protected against that. But our armor combines the knowledge of the Three Mothers with the power of Nature. That, they might've missed. Maybe."

"I'd rather be certain." Adratus drew his sword and, with gritting teeth, ran his forearm across the blade. Despite the pain, the cut was shallow compared to what it should have been and barely bled. Too, when he removed the blade, the incision sealed shut.

"Would you look at that?" Lann said with amazement. "It healed. That really is some powerful armor you have there."

"Not surprising. I am protected by the love between Ubaz and myself. It is extremely powerful, indeed."

Adratus passed Lann as they trekked up the snowy path toward the church. The sounds of their footsteps crunched in the silence, and the chill of winter bit at their skin.

Adratus pounded his fist against the massive green door and waited. There was no response from within. Frustrated, he banged once more, but still no answer came. "Heed!" he called out, his voice ringing in the cold air. "I seek shelter from this freezing wind."

With a sigh, Adratus turned to Lann, and they began devising another entrance.

Just as they were about to leave, the doors creaked open, revealing a figure silhouetted against the darkness inside.

"Salutations," Adratus said. "I seek shelter—"

The man walked between Adratus and Lann, as if they were fixtures on the lawn. At first, Adratus thought him ill-mannered, but then he saw the man's eyes—vacant as death—and his face was listless with an open mouth.

"That man," Adratus said after a thought. He followed after him.

Walking backward in front of him, Adratus examined the inert face and realized beyond a doubt that the man was part of the unit that he'd sent to escort Ubaz home. Even now, this man wore the same red tunic once worn under Tridulan armor. However, the man wore trousers underneath, and a downward-pointing, green triangular badge had been added to the left chest. The badge was embroidered in black with a crossed number seven.

"Look at me, legionary," he commanded. "Do you not recognize me? I am your camp prefect."

But the man continued on, as if he couldn't hear or see anyone around him. He walked until he reached a woodpile and began gathering an armful of logs.

Adratus watched in grim unease as the man dutifully carried out his task, like a corpse controlled by ropes.

"Apologies," Adratus whispered. "I know 'twas I who ordered you to this fate."

Lann placed a comforting hand on Adratus's shoulder, drawing his attention to the open door of the church. Adratus nodded, and the two rushed through into the hallowed hall.

The same hex that had befallen the legionary outside had taken hold of countless others within the vast sanctuary. It was a crowded madhouse from the doors where Adratus and Lann stood to the raised altar at the front. Its dwellers all had the same dead faces and the same dead eyes. All had the same stiff, unnatural movements.

"What dismal shore of za have we stumbled upon?" Adratus whispered.

They were almost all Feahs. Many still wore their leather kilts. However, a scattering of the inmates wore long, dirty white tunics.

Unlike the wood gatherer, who'd been given a task, these individuals seemed to wander aimlessly, muttering to themselves in idle lunacy while navigating around the rest.

Many knelt before a statue of the armored God Déagar at the front of the church, their limp arms raising and lowering in a never-ending cycle.

Others stood unnaturally still.

Nearby, a Drevite woman sat rocking back and forth and back and forth on the floor as she dispassionately recited empty prayers, "...protector from the Dark. Praise God Déagar, the one and only God, protector from the Dark. Praise God Déagar..." so on, she continued.

Speechless, Adratus turned to Lann and couldn't help but wonder how many of these dismal people the Drevite warrior recognized, how many were close friends or even family. Even the Tridulan prefect recognized some: Was that not a temple druidess he now saw, raising her limp arms and muttering stale praises to God Déagar? She had surely once been a friend to Ubaz.

As they stood frozen at the threshold, Adratus's stomach twisted with dread.

Nevertheless, the Prefect of the Ninth composed himself and neared the rear of the former druidess. He lifted his hand toward her. "Detect magic," he whispered somberly.

As she continued her empty prayers, a red glow landed on the back of her head and trailed slowly downward until it lingered behind her heart.

"The make-up of this hex is similar to the one used to compel your people here," Adratus said, "but it is different from any I have yet seen. Much, *much* stronger. It is safe to assume that the other mind control spells I've encountered thus far were but rungs in a vile ladder climbing to *this*, the appalling goal of the Drevite Experiment."

"Can you undo all this?" Lann asked.

The glow faded and Adratus lowered his arm. "We will find a way. And we will also save my sweet Ubaz."

CHAPTER SEVENTY-FOUR

A door at the side of the nave opened to a corridor lined with small chambers carpeted in thick layers of straw. There, within the rooms, Terovaes lay still as death across the floor, side by side by side, spanning its entire surface. Some slumbered, while others remained wide-eyed and unmoving, their empty gazes fixed on some distant point above. Every room, as far as Adratus and Lann could find, held the same.

Silent with dread, the two men navigated the grim abbey until they emerged onto a snowy courtyard surrounded by low walls. There, more melancholic figures roamed. These captives were more organized than the ones inside the abbey, but they still bore the same haunting gaze and lethargic postures. Each wore a belted tunic of coarse wool and dark trousers. Adorning their chests were green triangular badges with a crossed number seven in black.

A wheelbarrow-pushing man wearing this badge brushed past Adratus and Lann without so much as a glance, heading toward the kitchen, where badged cooks mindlessly prepared unremarkable meals. At the corner of the yard, men patched with green triangles sharpened swords with whetstones. Others shoveled snow.

As Lann and Adratus made their way around the kitchen walls, a chilling sight met them. Rows of armed Drevite soldiers stood in formation, all dressed in the same white tunic as the others. At their helm was a young woman with white hair and wings who spoke drill commands in monotone.

The whole unit complied—their movements, slouched and limp—in perfect unison. She had them draw out their swords, take a battle stance, and then return their weapons to their sheath. Never had Adratus witnessed such uniform movement except from the best-trained centuries of Tridual.

"It can't be," Lann said in amazement. "Mothers be praised. 'Tis herself." He was near tears. "I'd lost all hope, but there . . . 'Tis me daughter, me one and only, gone so many years now." He dashed toward her, but Adratus grabbed him, holding him back.

"You must stop. They've ignored us thus far, yet—"

"Lannah!" Lann cried out to her.

Adratus turned to her, knowing she definitely heard, for they were not far apart. But she continued to command the formation without a glimpse in Lann's direction.

Her badge, Adratus noticed, had a green bar above it—a rank, he guessed.

"Calm down, Lann," the prefect said softly. "You act unreasonably."

Lann paused, broken. His eyes were red and wet from tears—his face, anguished.

"Go," Adratus breathed with a heavy heart, "be unreasonable. For no reason resides within this madhouse."

Adratus followed behind as Lann ran to her. He watched the father embrace the unresponsive daughter, who obviously did not know him. Lann shook her as if trying to wake her. He cried out her name, pleading for her to remember.

Adratus felt his heart break at the sight. The Drevites had suffered so immensely. And he knew the Tridulans had only exacerbated the hardship.

A man's voice then came from behind Adratus. Calmly yet sternly, he asked, "Who art thou to trespass in the house of God?"

Adratus turned to see a man, apparently Human but so extraordinarily old that the sight of him momentarily distracted from the gravity of being caught. He was not merely wrinkled; his blotchy leathered skin drooped from his bones as if half melted. His hair was long and brittle white. Even bent as he was, his regal robes of emerald green helped him maintain an air of might.

Lann shouted, "What've you done to her, you shite-eating ogre!" He charged the man.

Without emotion, the daughter stated, "Secure the reprobates."

The formation moved at once, closing in on the trespassers.

Both Adratus and Lann struggled but were seized and firmly held.

"You fucking bastard!" Lann cried. "I'll have you dead for this, you be sure."

The ancient man chuckled, a low rumble from his loose-fitting throat. "Cease thine idle threats, savage, for they are but the feeble weapons of he who hath no other. Lo, thou art *nothing* before the power of almighty Déagar. And within this very hour, thou shalt be blessed. Thus, all thine actions thereafter shall be for *his* glorification, as dictated by the Church."

The priest looked at the daughter. "Pray," he said, "come thou hither."

"Yes, Your Grace." She approached and stood before him.

He placed a shriveled hand on her shoulder. "What name wert thou called by this savage?"

"Lannah, Your Grace."

"And is this truly thy name?"

"It is not, Your Grace."

"Speak thy true name, I pray thee."

"Mercy," she said coldly, "for by the divine mercy of God Déagar I have been saved from wickedness."

"Fucking bastard!" Lann struggled against those who held him. More hands grabbed him, lifting him from the ground.

The priest combed his fingers through Mercy's hair. "How very wretched it must be to dwell outside the Light. Such anger."

Adratus, also held in the grip of thralls, kept his calm. "You are a Kla, yes?"

"That is the name some have come to call my kind as of late."

"I would guess you are the one who once led the Knight Silthex. Blastilv?"

"Thou art well-informed, savage. Pray, who art thou?"

"Never mind him, you goat-fucking troll," Lann shouted. "That's me daughter you have there, me one and only child, her."

Blastilv grinned as he turned his yellowed eyes to Lann. "Then be thou a contented father, for in my quest to perfect the Blessed, Mercy was my first success after many failures. And with her as a template, all these new Blessed thou seest here were created to serve God Déagar."

Adratus scoffed. "Shall the kingdom of God Déagar be filled with mindless fools?"

Blastilv chuckled. "All of thy questions shall be answered, utterly. For soon, thou shalt see the fate of the Blessed from behind thine own eyes." He scanned the prefect. "Yes, thou art strong and shalt make an excellent addition to mine army. Thy pitiful disguise conceals naught. I know thou art Tridulan. I have discovered others amongst the Drevites. They now belong to God Déagar." He drew closer to Adratus's face, so close that his putrid breath was hot upon his skin.

"Indeed, thine eyes have seen much combat. And thy demeanor suggests an elevated rank. Thou wilt possess great knowledge of battle, I presume."

Blastilv took a step back. "'Tis time for thee to be blessed and purified of sin."

Adratus writhed in vain against the vice-like grip of the many hands that held him, their fingers constricting his flesh. More unyielding hands restrained his head, forcing him to face Blastilv.

From within his inner robe, the old man produced a silver flask adorned with intricate gold filigree and an emerald at its center. "With this blessed water, I shall wash away thy wickedness, and so thou shalt be fully obedient to the Church." He uncapped the flask.

Adratus continued to struggle against the relentless hands, though it proved futile. He could not move, not even to look away.

"Thy ring, what is it?" Blastilv demanded, as he paused. He recapped the flask and placed it back into his robe. Moving closer to the prefect's hand—secured within the grasp of others—he examined the ring on Adratus's left ring finger.

"Thou art a Faldénrus." Blastilv grinned. "Yes, thou art very valuable indeed. Thou shalt be another commander and train mine armies alongside Mercy. But I shall not leave thy blessing to a mere touch of holy water, no. No, thou wilt require a more potent ritual.

"Mercy," Blastilv said as he began to move away, "have these men taken to the dungeon and locked therein. There will be no more blessings today, as I must gather my strength."

"Yes, Your Grace."

CHAPTER SEVENTY-FIVE

The Blessed led Adratus and Lann down a dark, winding staircase lit by eerie green geodes set on tiny shelves along the rounded wall.

"More magic," Adratus said to Lann, pointing out one of the geodes. "For those who wage war against it," he called back up the stairs, *"they certainly use it in abundance."*

At the bottom of the stairs, Mercy unlocked another door. Adratus and Lann were thrust inside before the door slammed shut behind them.

They found themselves in a hallway lined with cells, reminiscent of the one above it, but illuminated only by dim, ghostly glows emanating from emerald geodes affixed to the ceiling.

There were people here, more Drevites, and for a moment, Adratus thought more Blessed. But no. These captives, he discovered as he moved farther in, were, save for being downcast and haggard, normal. There were at least three hundred here—some in cells, some out. All the doors were wide open. Lann wasted no time in engaging them in somber conversations and comforting embraces.

"Ubaz!" Adratus called out desperately. "Are you here?"

From one of the open cells, he caught a glimpse of an amber wingtip, followed by a pale arm and shoulder. Then, he saw limp ginger hair framing the side of a beautiful face with a thick purple line crossing down the left. The young man peeked timidly around the corner of the cell door.

Speechless, Adratus looked at him, and a large smile of overwhelming bliss crossed the prefect's face. His heart seemed to glow within his chest, and his entire body relaxed.

Ubaz was alive, something Adratus could not believe until he saw him with his eyes.

"Hail Ubaz, my love," Adratus finally said, stepping toward him. "Eons have passed without you."

But instead of running into his arms, Ubaz retreated into the shadows of the cell.

Confused and heartbroken, Adratus followed inside to find Ubaz sitting against a mound of straw in the shadowed back corner of the room. He appeared to be consumed by sadness.

"I . . . have come to rescue you," Adratus said.

Ubaz's eyes remained fixed on the cold stone wall, his tone grim and defeated. "My hopes of rescue died over a week ago. And seeing you here, locked up same as me, doesn't do a thing to restore it."

"At least be pleased to see me."

But Ubaz remained silent, unmoved by Adratus's words.

"Ubaz," Lann said softly from the doorway. "Listen, I know there was loads of tension before. But your Adratus has come a long way. In his head, like. Well, and by boat and on foot, too. He understands, and me as well, that there was mistakes made on both sides."

"He speaks truth," Adratus said. "I am prepared to be a true ambassador between our peoples. This, I make as an oath. 'Keep true to oaths, for he whose word is meaningless is—'"

"The Tréréaldéag means nothing to you," Ubaz interrupted. Still unmoved, he continued to stare as a heavy silence fell.

Adratus reached out to touch his shoulder, but Ubaz grabbed the hand and threw it away from him.

"'Tis too late," Ubaz hissed. "You want peace with my people? The Feah tribe? Take a good look around, Adratus, because this abbey holds most of them here, now twisted into the mindless creatures they call the Blessed. And soon enough, we'll be just like them."

"We will find a way to reverse it," Adratus insisted.

But Ubaz only laughed—a harsh and bitter sound. "There's no fucking reversal." With wild eyes, he continued, "Even the priest who cast the spell couldn't reverse it to fix his own failed attempts. He had to kill the old ones off."

Ubaz's gaze flicked down to the ground before snapping back up to meet Adratus's in grief. "When we were being dragged in, we saw them all in the garden," Ubaz said. "The old priest watched on as the former Blessed gathered at the edge of a great big hole. With no emotion at all, the first one stabbed himself in the heart. Blood spurted everywhere, but he didn't give a shite about it. He just passed the blade on to the next one before dropping down dead. One by one, they all followed suit and fell into the pit."

Sorrow filled Ubaz's expression as he looked away from Adratus. "Soon enough, my whole tribe will either be dead or turned into puppets of the Church of Déagar." His hands trembled with anger and despair as Ubaz placed them against his forehead.

"Is this truly the True Light?" Ubaz whispered bitterly. "Is this what I devoted my whole life to, as a man and a temple guardian? Where's the love of Mother Lágeya in this nightmare of an abbey?" He shouted in frustration, *"Where is it!"* His voice dropped to whisper, "The True Light has been consumed by hate, and my people are lost in its shadows."

Adratus tried to approach him, but Ubaz pushed him away with rage in his eyes.

"No. Don't you dare come near me, Camp Prefect of the Ninth!" he spat, anger dripping from every word. "Now, *I hate*—them and both of ye. With all your fucking bickering, ye left the Feah undefended. And I hate both of ye for it."

Adratus suddenly grunted in physical pain, clutching his forearm as blood gushed through his fingers. A long, deep gash had formed.

Lann rushed to his side. "Give us your tunic, quick, so I can bandage you up."

Adratus complied, pulling it over his head.

"What's wrong with him?" Ubaz asked, leaning closer though keeping distant.

Lann began ripping up the stolen Dayigan shirt. "He's got Feah armor, and like a fecking fool, he almost chopped off his arm to see if it was working proper. And it did, 'til now." He handed a wad of the cloth to Adratus. "Hold that there, mate."

"Feah armor?" Ubaz asked.

"Aye, Chief Kaie gave it to him. 'Twas powered by the love between ye two. But I suppose that's all done now, it seems."

"But that shouldn't have dispelled his armor."

"Well, it has now, hasn't it? As you can see." He helped Adratus stand up. "Come on. I'll get you sorted out."

Ubaz's eyes followed the departing two, his heart heavy with regret and despair. He collapsed against the cold stone wall, a guttural sob escaping from deep within him. A tear traced a path down his grimy cheek as he grieved for the loss of everything—past and present—all at once, while facing only horrors for the future.

CHAPTER SEVENTY-SIX

Time had lost all meaning for Ubaz. The concept of day and night had become irrelevant, as he'd drifted through a perpetual limbo of waking and sleeping. This place, this dismal pit beneath a church of horrors, had trapped him for what felt like an eternity—longer than any weeks he'd ever known. And in all that time, not once did the sun or moons grace his sight.

The passing of days had been marked by the arrival of the Blessed, who would bring food and claim a new group of prisoners—twice a day, like clockwork. Each passing day had brought Ubaz closer to his fate. Every day, he knew, could have easily been his final.

Hope, too, had become abstract.

He slept and woke again. Another day in this dim, fearful existence. He didn't seek Adratus or Lann, and they no longer sought him, either. It was for the best, Ubaz decided.

He knew he'd hurt the prefect, deeper than any gash on the arm, but seeing him here hurt Ubaz as well, too much to face him. After losing so many others, Ubaz couldn't bear the weight of another death. Nevertheless, he knew that much more death lay on the horizon.

He remembered the old Irefaery woman washing the clothes of the dead in the blood-filled stream. And the elf boy's words echoed in his mind: "... almost all were yet to come."

There was now a commotion in the hall. Some prisoners rushed to see what was happening, but Ubaz stayed back, peeking from the door of his cell.

Four of the Blessed entered with their swords drawn, their soulless voices chanting, "...back...back...back..." as their weapons poked forward with each rhythmic word.

Once the area around the door was sufficiently cleared, Blastilv strode into the chamber, his nose upturned in disgust as he surveyed the captives. With a disdainful sneer, he called out, "Faldénrus, come forth, or thou wilt be sought."

Ubaz's eyes stayed fixed on Adratus. Like the mighty soldier of the darkness his lover was, he stood as solid as ever. His arm was now neatly bandaged in the remnants of his shirt. The symbol of the Triébis was branded proudly on his chest. Even as he faced the end of his free will, the Camp Prefect of the Ninth Legion showed no signs of fear toward the sanctimonious Déagrian.

Adratus stepped forward with an insolent smirk. "You honor me," he said, his words taking a flippant tone. "The favored whore of Déagar himself comes to the underworld for me."

Blastilv scoffed. "Be thou not enflattered, savage. I come solely out of necessity. My Blessed discern only amongst each other and amongst men of the cloth. They would not have known thee to apprehend thee. 'Tis a skill I strive to instill in Mercy, so she may educate the others. But, of course, thou shalt aid her in her instructions, for thou wilt also be trainer class. Come, and be thou readied."

"Wait," Ubaz called out as he ran toward Adratus. He wrapped his arms around his muscular form and rested his head on his bare chest.

Ubaz felt the prefect's finger brush below his eye. "No tears, sweet Ubaz. We are both warriors, you and I."

Ubaz looked up at him, their gazes locking.

"Revolting," came the infuriated voice of Blastilv. "Secure the reprobates, both of them."

Ignoring the priest, Ubaz leaned in for a kiss. But before their lips could meet, they were torn apart by the Blessed.

Blastilv chuckled through a grin of rotten teeth. "Lo," he taunted Adratus as he drew near, his withered face mere inches away, "thy first act of penance unto Déagar shall be to slay the object of thy vile lust. With an excruciatingly slow purpose, thou shalt tear him apart, bit by agonizing bit. All the while, thou shalt watch thine own actions from deep behind thine eyes." He stepped back. "Will you savages never learn: The True Light is the only way; all others will perish. Bring them," he commanded.

"Ubaz!" Lann shouted, reaching out to his nephew before being restrained by the Blessed.

"And bring that one as well," Blastilv added, with a sinister smirk. "He shall be made a slave to my Mercy and witness, through lifeless eyes, as his daughter submits entirely to me."

—

The dark, vacant nave of the abbey's church echoed with the heavy footsteps of the group that entered. Blastilv, like a vulture in lavish green robes, took the lead. His three captives—Adratus, Ubaz, and Lann—followed, each flanked by two disturbing thralls.

Blastilv marched them down the center of the expansive granite floor, to the raised apse where a stone statue of Déagar stood recessed into a niche's wall. The God's form was encased in armor from head to toe, sword at the ready. But it was his left hand that drew Ubaz's gaze—a gold gauntlet protruding from the wall.

On the stage, the players took their places as a triangle: Ubaz and his guards at stage right, Adratus and his guards facing Blastilv up center before the statue, and Lann with his guards to the left.

The show began abruptly, as two Blessed forced Adratus to his knees before the golden gauntlet. He fought against the unyielding grip, but was held firmly in place.

Ubaz watched helplessly as the twisted show unfolded right before him. The iron grip of his own captors was beyond that of a normal man and remained constant, even as they waited.

Blastilv raised his hands and spoke with loud, clear words, saying, "Praise His Divine Majesty, Déagar, God of fire and lightning, eldest of the Gods, protector from the Dark. He who is Greatest of All." He then turned his gaze to Adratus and declared, "I present unto thee this reprobate who hath strayed from thy righteous path. This unclean creature who hath lived a life of sin and debauchery. I humbly beseech thee, O God, to bestow thy holy blessings upon him and cleanse his wretched soul of iniquity."

Ubaz's heart raced as he stole glances at the Blessed to his left—a slightly older man whom he'd known well growing up. He was a cousin, second or third, though they'd never been sure of the exact relation.

"Do you remember me?" Ubaz whispered. "We used to play and all, you and I, when we were lads. Remember that? Our mams were grand friends, as well. Please, let me go. I have to save him."

No response.

Blastilv shouted out, "In the name of almighty Déagar, I call upon the sacred powers of the True Light. Bless this vile sinner. His will hath betrayed him. His will must be purged. Lyforia, set!"

A faint green glow emanated from the armored hand of God Déagar.

With a growl of hate, Adratus tore his right arm free and elbowed the Blessed who'd held it.

"Secure him," Blastilv commanded calmly.

One of the men holding Ubaz released him and rushed to help subdue Adratus. The Tridulan soldier fought against them, punching and kicking, but was soon overpowered and constrained.

Undaunted, Blastilv continued, shouting, "His will hath betrayed him. His will must be purged. Let his only deeds hereafter be for thy divine glory, as directed by thy Church."

The hand of Déagar glowed brighter.

Ubaz's entranced cousin still clutched him, but now stood alone. Ubaz eyed a sword on the cousin's hip. Heart pounding with fear, he twisted and seized it from its sheath, gripping it tightly.

"Sorry, truly I am," Ubaz said. Cringing, he drove the blade deep into the cousin's heart. "But you're already gone, and I gotta save my husband."

"Bless this man!" Blastilv bellowed. "Bind his soul that he may sin no longer! Lyforia, flash!"

Ubaz charged toward the glowing glove and swung the sword with all his might, hitting it with the clank of steel on gold.

But a bolt of emerald lightning discharged, striking the eyes of Adratus.

"Stop him!" Blastilv ordered, his bony finger aimed at Ubaz.

Adratus, on his knees, convulsed and trembled as the light surged through his body, branching out along his face, neck, and bare chest.

Even as three of the Blessed restrained him, Ubaz could not help but revel in the sight of the gauntlet breaking free from the wall and crashing to the ground with a heavy, metallic thud. Happy for his actions, Ubaz grinned triumphantly.

But then his gaze fell upon his love.

Adratus had crumbled to his side, limp on the floor. Motionless.

"Adratus!"

The prefect's eyes now held that unmistakable empty stare of the Blessed.

"No," Ubaz cried.

"Thou art too late," Blastilv gloated. "Behold, the object of thy perversion belongeth now to God Déagar. Arise, my new Blessed, and be thou strong in thy new path of Light."

But Adratus remained still, unresponsive to Blastilv's commands.

Enraged, Blastilv turned his fury toward Ubaz. "Curse thy evil soul to rot in za," he snarled as he approached the young man held captive by his thralls. "Look unto thy deed and grieve. Thou hast *slain* the trainer of mine army." He struck Ubaz with the back of his hand, cutting him with the large triangular emerald on his ring.

"Leave him be, you liver-chomping ogre!" Lann shouted, fighting against the two who held him. "Can you not see you've hurt him as much as you're able to?"

Even as blood trickled down his face, Ubaz's gaze remained fixed on Adratus–the once mighty Prefect of the Ninth now lay still as a corpse, his eyes vacant and staring.

"Thou shalt pay for thine action, boy," Blastilv said, as he drew near to Ubaz's face. "I shall ponder thy punishment with great care and take years upon years to carry it out. So *excruciatingly* slow and ghastly shall be thy torture that thou shalt live on in the grim tales of men long after thy corpse hath crumbled to dust."

But Ubaz only met Blastilv's threat with a stony stare. "You might do better with your time training your so-called Blessed to disarm prisoners." With a swift movement, he plunged his sword deep into Blastilv's gut, unflinching as the priest's hand grabbed for him in a feeble attempt at revenge.

The Blessed tried to intervene, but it was too late. Ubaz watched with satisfaction as Blastilv's yellowed eyes widened in shock and pain before finally closing.

"May the Dark One drag you down into the rotten bowels of za," Ubaz said and spit on his face.

The Blessed held onto Ubaz as he angled the blade downward and watched Blastilv slide off, hitting the ground with a thud to lie as a pitiful heap.

CHAPTER SEVENTY-SEVEN

The ancient man remained motionless in a pool of his blood, staining the holy granite floor. The Blessed, each frozen like eerie statues of flesh, maintained their grip on Ubaz and Lann.

"Right, listen up, Blessed," Ubaz shouted, his voice resonating within the church. "Your master's dead, and there's no one else here who can give orders to ye. Ye have no reason not to stand down."

A moment passed with no sign they'd heard, until they began to move with jerky, unnatural movements. They fell to their knees, heads bowed in submission. Their hands clasped together over their chests, and thus, they remained—eerie statues again.

"Mothers be praised," Lann breathed in perplexed awe. "Brilliant job, you. But," his voice turned grave, "we must slay them, you know."

Ubaz shook his head in disbelief. "No. We can't be killing our own tribesmen."

"'Tis a mercy; you know it to be true." Lann drew a sword from an enemy's belt. He held it to the back of an enemy's neck. "They're not them no more."

Ubaz sighed sadly. "Through the heart," he conceded. "'Tis the way the former Blessed killed themselves before."

Lann nodded solemnly and moved the blade to the target's chest. He thrust with force.

With a heavy heart, Ubaz followed suit. All the while, he felt sick, turning from his actions but still hearing the gruesome sounds. And together, Lann and Finn ended the suffering of the five Blessed in the vast room.

Afterward, Ubaz's gaze fell upon Adratus, and there they froze.

Lann was soon beside Ubaz with his hand on his shoulder. "Sorry, lad," he whispered. "Adratus too. It must be done."

"I know." Ubaz nodded, his words catching in his aching throat.

Lann stepped forward and lifted his sword. "Look away now, lad."

"No," Ubaz called out. His voice cracked. "No, I'll do it meself. Just . . . give me a moment. Him and me need to be alone for a bit."

"I understand." Lann sighed as he stepped back. "I'll head down and free the other Feahs locked up there. The Blessed shouldn't be bothering us no more."

Ubaz barely listened and only nodded vacantly. In the corner of his vision, he saw his uncle search Blastilv for a key. He departed.

"No tears, Ubaz," he whispered to himself. But the words were futile.

He neared his love and rolled him onto his back. Shivering, Ubaz kneeled beside him and held his hand, the warmth of it already departing.

Ubaz took a deep, staggered breath and sniffed. "What do I say to you, husband, my first and only genuine love? I'd've loved you forever, I know it. And I–I still will, even with us parted now. How do I say goodbye, to you? Don't even know if I can, really. I saw so much future for us, and now . . ." He sniffed and wiped his eyes with his arm. "Now, 'tis just all gone, isn't it? Gone. Just like that."

Ubaz looked into those eyes, the horrible soulless eyes of the Blessed. With trembling fingers, he closed them and whispered, "I love you, Adratus. And always will."

He leaned in and kissed Adratus's cold lips, softly and slowly, as he thought of every other time he'd ever kissed them before.

The lips became warm beneath the kiss, becoming animate and returning the same affection.

Frightened, Ubaz leaped back and made some distance. He grappled for the sword, grabbing it up before clutching the hilt. He watched, rigid with dread.

The eyes of Adratus sprung open, and a brilliant red light shone out, filling the sockets. And the Triébis, scarred on his chest, likewise shone.

"Ubaz," Adratus groaned, his veins glowing scarlet, "I love you too."

Tears streaming down his face, Ubaz rushed back to him, and their lips met once again in a deeper, more passionate kiss. Adratus wrapped his arms tightly around him.

"I will never leave you again," Adratus whispered.

"Aye, you won't." He sniffed and wiped his eyes while gaining a brilliant smile. "I'll never let you, you silly fecker."

But their reunion was cut short as Lann burst into the room. "Ubaz!" he called out.

"'Tis all right," Ubaz said as he looked back to his uncle. "He wasn't fully changed, and . . . And he's returned."

Lann hastily slammed the heavy oak doors shut, pressing his shoulder against them as he anxiously barred them with a heavy beam. He then stumbled and collapsed against the doors, clutching at a gruesome wound in his stomach.

Both Ubaz and Adratus rushed toward him, the injury pouring blood, only seeming to worsen as they neared.

"Adratus," Lann's voice was weak and strained, "you're looking well, mate."

"Yet you are not, friend. What has happened?"

A loud banging sounded from the doors, causing them to bow inward under a great pressure.

"The Blessed happened, the rotten bastards," Lann groaned. "The old priest weren't quite as dead as we reckoned." He motioned weakly to where Blastilv had been.

The archbishop was gone, but for a stain of blood.

"I managed to get the other prisoners out," Lann continued, gritting his teeth against the pain. "But the Blessed woke up. I was the only one they saw as a threat—guess they're learning—so I had to leave the others." He grunted as his body jolted. "They're heading to the shore to build boats and escape. Ye both need to get there fast."

"All three of us will be going," Ubaz said. "Together."

"No." Lann weakly shook his head, his face distorted in agony. "I won't be coming with ye."

"But your armor," Adratus said. "It should have protected you."

Lann let out a pained laugh. "I've no had armor since we stepped through that gate. I suspected it, but didn't know for sure 'til your arm split open."

"Right. I was too distracted to see it," Ubaz said with a heavy sigh, placing his hand on Adratus's forearm. "Our love was the *only* thing holding your armor together. The chapel blocked all other forms of magic, including the other components in your armor. With our love lost, you were left unprotected."

Lann smiled weakly, his eyes growing heavy. "And I see ye found it in time to keep him from turning altogether." He leaned against the doors, looking more frail and exhausted than ever before. "I'm happy for that, true I am." His head fell against the wood. "Love's the only force hate can't conquer."

Ubaz turned to Adratus. "You must do something."

But Lann spoke instead in a fading voice, "There's nothing ... But I'll soon be joining me own love. You remember your Aunt Moyra?"

Ubaz nodded, fighting back tears.

"She waiting for me ..." His breaths grew slower and more struggled. "... with all the others who went to the ancestors before. I'll tell your mam and da how ... how brilliant you've got." Lann's body seemed to grow heavier as he pressed himself against the door to keep from falling. "Go on ... before the Blessed break through." He took a slow breath. "Fight now. Mourn later."

Adratus kneeled before Lann, his expression solemn and determined. "To you, Lann of the Feah, I give my solemn vow—as a Tridulan, a Faldénrus, and a Feah by marriage—I will forge true unity between our people."

"You better. Fucking Human," Lann attempted a weak laugh but succumbed to a fit of coughing, blood dribbling down his chin. "Moyra's calling for me now."

With a final exhalation, his eyes closed, and he breathed no more.

Ubaz stared sadly at the fallen warrior before taking a deep breath. "Lann," he whispered, his voice heavy with sorrow, "I honor you and release you." Then, overcome with emotion, Ubaz collapsed onto Adratus's chest, sobbing quietly. But the soldier remained stoic, his gaze fixed on the lifeless body.

CHAPTER SEVENTY-EIGHT

Adratus numbly watched the heavy oak doors bow inward against the thick beam that secured them. The corpse of Lann, slumped against them, swayed back and forth before finally falling to the floor. Despite their initial difficulties, Lann had become a friend, and it pained Adratus to see him slain.

"The last of my family," Ubaz finally said, as he wiped his eyes. "We must go. The rescued prisoners will be waiting for us by the shore."

Adratus nodded, his throat tight with grief. "Can they not just fly away?"

"We're not birds, Adratus," Ubaz snapped. "We can't just fly across the Hyvile River. Especially not in their state."

"Apologies, I meant no insult."

"No. No, I'm sorry myself. This is all just too . . . too much for me. I can't believe he's . . ." Ubaz breathed. "They'll be building boats and waiting on us."

"We cannot leave without destroying that cursed hand first."

Together, the mournful pair crossed the nave of the church and approached the statue of God Déagar. The stone hand had fallen separate from the golden glove. It was the clawed hand of a beast and the forearm too, roughly two feet more than what stuck out from the wall.

"How's that?" Ubaz began, kneeling over it. "It looks more Dark Light than True." He examined the thing without touching. "I don't understand."

Adratus bent down for a closer look. "I suspect it is related to gargoyles—that's True Light magic, or at least it was. But only the Black Temple can tell us for certain." Carefully, Adratus picked up the hand and marveled at its smooth white marble surface.

Adratus seized in pain, grabbing his forehead as a vivid image flashed in his mind—a beautiful woman with pale green skin and four dragonfly wings projecting from her back. Her ethereal form was unclothed, revealing slender legs and toned thighs, curved hips, and full breasts. Her vibrant orange hair cascaded down her back, and her sad eyes glowed a haunting, iridescent white. She reached out for him.

Adratus flinched away from the image, throwing down his hand to tumble across the stage.

"What's wrong with you?" Ubaz asked.

"I remember something." Adratus rubbed his forehead. "Something from when the priest tried to bless me. I saw a woman calling out for help." He stared at the hole left at the forearm of Déagar's statue. "She's in there, beyond the wall," he murmured. "Pray, fetch me a light, Ubaz."

"We must leave," he urged, glancing back at the barricaded doors that held back the many who tried to force entry.

"I felt her pain, Ubaz. Whoever she is, I must help her."

Ubaz nodded understandingly. "Course. Forgive me." He spread his amber wings and took flight.

Determined to reach the mysterious woman, Adratus pulled at the hole in the wall with all his might. "I will save you," he called through.

Returning from the chandelier, Ubaz brought a large white candle and held it close.

"I see a room." Adratus strained as he pulled harder at the wall.

A click sounded.

A nearby section of the wall cracked open, revealing a hidden door.

Adratus stopped and looked at Ubaz.

—

The stench of death and decay hit Adratus like a physical blow as he stepped through the portal. He had seen his fair share of carnage, but even walking among bloated corpses and feasting vultures could not prepare him for this.

In the small room, a reclined stone chair dominated the space, and on it lay the putrefied skin of some poor creature. Ubaz approached with a flickering candle, casting shadows across the grotesque scene.

Other than its pale green color, the empty skin looked Human—a woman, apparently. The skull, though caved, was within, though the rest of the body was pulped.

"I think this is her," Adratus whispered, unable to tear his eyes away from the horror before him. "The woman from my vision. Yet she was not like this. What has he done to you?"

Four large spikes pierced her shoulders, pinning her to the chair. The wounds oozed blood and had evidently done so for years, judging by the thick black that had hardened like scabby candle wax trickling to the floor. There, maggots squirmed within the gore. Her missing right hand similarly bled.

The dried lips of the woman began to quiver. They split apart and croaked out slow words: "With every anguish and lament and gruesome demise, know that I am the one who hath betrayed you."

"You live?" Adratus asked, scarcely believing it possible.

She fell silent once more.

"Can you hear me?" Adratus leaned over her. "What is your name?"

"I . . . am laudanum," came her weak reply. "For naught else remaineth."

"Fear not, Laudanum," Adratus said with determination. "We will free you from this place."

Adratus grabbed a heavy candlestick from the counter behind him and began hitting a spike side-on to dislodge it.

She whispered, "With every anguish and lament and gruesome demise, know that I am the one who hath betrayed you."

"No," Adratus said, as he wiggled a spike free. "You are not at fault. Filthy Blastilv has forced your actions, somehow, I know. I felt the overwhelming remorse you feel for your deeds."

"Prithee," Laudanum whispered, "canst thou forgive me?"

"There is nothing to forgive." He pulled the last spike free and threw it aside. "Actions were not your own."

"I pray thee," she groaned, "canst thou?"

Adratus stopped and looked into the shriveled white orbs of her eyes. "I forgive you."

"I thank thee, Absolver." She took a deep breath, so deep that it partially inflated her body. Then, a second breath and a third with gaining effect. She was no longer an empty skin, but she was far from the woman of Adratus's vision.

Her once luscious hair now resembled a tangled spider web of gray. Her pale green skin hung thin and brittle on her bones—tight on her skull, draping over the collarbone and sinking in between every rib. Her pelvis protruded sharply above bony legs, while one hand was missing and the other was skeletal.

"The Blessed will be here soon," Ubaz said, glancing at the large chamber.

"True," Adratus replied, as he carefully helped Laudanum to her feet. "We must hurry." It seemed mad to speak such words to someone in her condition, but she slowly nodded, her frail neck struggling to support her emaciated head.

"The elf," Laudanum groaned, "prithee, get me to the Sword Elf."

"The Sword Elf?" Ubaz whispered, as if he understood.

"I know not what you mean," Adratus said.

But she only repeated, "The Sword Elf. Prithee."

Once they were out of the room, Adratus grabbed up the stone hand. "We must destroy it."

"No," Laudanum said, using Ubaz as a crutch. "It is not within thy power to destroy the Hand of Fersivolíel. Nor is it within mine. But thou must take it far from Blastilv."

"I will," Adratus said firmly. He ripped a green velvet cloth from the wall and fashioned a crude pouch around the hand, securing it to his belt. "Let us now depart this church of horrors."

CHAPTER SEVENTY-NINE

The doors leading further into the abbey creaked as they were battered by those trying to break through. The sturdy wooden beams holding them shut began to crack and give way.

Adratus, Ubaz, and Laudanum stood at the larger doors that led outside. There was no force pushing against these—for now.

"Just because no one attempts to breach these doors," Adratus began, "is no reason to assume them unwatched. When I unlatch them, hurry and prepare for anything. Laudanum, I will carry you."

"Nay, thou shalt *not*, Human."

"Very well. Then be on guard." With that, Adratus unbarred the doors and swung them open with force. "Ubaz, fly quickly to the gate. Lann left his bow there. Use it."

"Aye, Prefect." Ubaz spread his amber wings and soared out into the chilly winter air.

Without delay, Adratus and Laudanum took off across the snowy yard. However, Laudanum's limp slowed her, one hand gripping her bony thigh.

A command echoed from behind them—Blastilv's voice: "Let not the reprobates flee. They shall either bow down to Church authority or fall down to their demise."

Adratus risked a glance back and saw countless Blessed followers leaping out of windows and pouring out through doors, swarming like locusts.

Undaunted, Adratus remained resolute, sprinting toward the small gate in the surrounding wall.

But before he could reach it, four Terovaes—armed with deadly swords—descended upon him from above. Adratus swung his sword high at the flying fighters, but they evaded.

Struggling but unyielding, Adratus caught a glimpse of Blastilv—his stomach wrapped in bloody bandages—peering down at him from a balcony.

"Your puppet troops are sloppy, priest," Adratus taunted with a bitter laugh. "They will *never* be an army. Abandon this madness."

The Blessed continued their relentless assault, closing in on Adratus. He unleashed another furious swing, cleaving off a foot. But even as blood spattered onto the snow-covered ground, the dismembered foe showed no signs of pain or hesitation.

Before he could catch his breath, a mindless fighter lunged from behind, the sword aimed for Adratus's exposed back. But the blade failed to pierce his skin, leaving behind only a shallow cut that trickled with crimson. Enraged, Adratus whirled around and struck with precision—slicing his attacker across the gut.

Intestines spilled forth in a gush of blood, swinging like grotesque sausages from the gaping wound. But still, the Blessed soldier fought on without faltering, maintaining his unnerving stare.

Amid the chaos of battle, more Blessed warriors descended upon Adratus. Their attacks were savage and fierce, more akin to feral birds than men, as they clawed and pecked at him with their swords.

With his sword uncomfortably high, Adratus spun in a desperate attempt to defend himself from all sides at once. The prefect's skillful strikes kept his attackers at bay, but he was soon surrounded and trapped as the trampled snow beneath him grew increasingly red.

One of the Blessed managed to score Adratus's flesh, causing him to cry out in pain. But with his unseen armor protecting him, the injury was minor and quickly healed.

Suddenly, an arrow shot through the heart of one of his attackers. And another. Both fell dead. Adratus looked up to see Ubaz wielding a beautifully carved ebony bow and taking out their foes with deadly accuracy. More fell dead.

With this brief respite, Adratus made a break for the wall surrounding the consecrated ground. As soon as he crossed over to the other side, the Tridulan Faldénrus breathed in the dark energy of Night, his veins pulsing with infernal magic.

Invigorated, Adratus spun back around to see that the Blessed had swarmed Laudanum. With a wave of his hand, he unleashed cords of red energy that bound the skeletal woman and gently brought her to the ground at his side.

Ubaz, shooting into the multitude of Blessed, descended to only a few feet above Adratus. "You all right, Prefect?"

Adratus nodded gratefully. "Thanks to you, love. You fight well. Yet, that is not Lann's bow."

"I know. 'Tis his quiver." He slapped the pouch on his belt. "But this bow was mostly buried. It called out to me, like."

Adratus gave a puzzled look, but had no time for questions. He cast more red cords and snatched a Blessed from the sky, bringing him to his sword and impaling him through the heart.

Again and again, he repeated this feat with lightning speed—cords of light yanking targets from the sky, his sword piercing hearts. And so he continued, his actions too fast to maintain his inner magic, but required to keep up with the threat. A sharp pain increased in the front of his skull, while weakness spread throughout him.

"I'm running low on arrows," called Ubaz.

"And I run low on magic." Dizziness washed over Adratus as he wiped blood from his brow and cast once more.

The swarm surrounded them, their numbers still exceeding thirty against the two weary warriors. Their attempts to dive down at Adratus and Ubaz were unhindered and increasing.

The prefect tried to cast again, but a searing pain tore through his skull. He clutched his head and collapsed onto the gruesome snow beneath him.

Five Blessed took the opportunity to dive toward the weakened legionary, but even as he saw their approach, Adratus could do nothing to retaliate.

But then, a streak of movement caught Adratus's eye. Someone passed by him in a blur of speed, leaping from the ground to the wall and up toward the advancing fighters.

For a moment, Adratus saw him: a boy a few years younger than Ubaz. But there was nothing childlike about him. Wholly black eyes glared fiercely from a black bar painted across them, while pointed ears marked him as something otherworldly. In one swift motion, the boy swung his glass blade, slicing a Blessed cleanly in two at the chest. He continued on to bisect the next four with rapid strike after strike, until all five fell as ten to the ground.

He landed on the wall and glanced back at Adratus.

"Are you the Sword Elf?" Adratus asked. "Lady Laudanum asked for you."

"She is safe," came the reply, before the elf boy turned toward the abbey and shouted, "Withdraw your minions, foul Blastilv." He leaped into action once again, his movements blending seamlessly into a dance of death as he cut through rows of Blessed with ease.

Somewhat recovered, Adratus cast more cords of light, pulling another Terovae down onto his blade. And then another. But his second wind was short, and pain hit him again.

The elf returned to the wall. "You waste your creations for naught," he yelled up to Blastilv on the balcony. "Withdraw them forthwith, or I will destroy them, each and every one."

But the ancient priest remained unyielding. "Relinquish and avaunt, Valqyer," he commanded.

"Futile words, for you know my name no longer has control over me," retorted the elf, his obsidian eyes glaring. "Your fight, too, is futile. Behold, Lyforia has fled by me into the former Faery Realm."

Adratus looked back to where Laudanum had been, only to confirm her absence.

"Nevertheless," Valqyer continued, "if it pleases you to persist in this pointless attack, send your acolytes down in prodigious force. The Faldénrus and I shall *delight* in slaying every one of your repugnant creations. And when the true battles begin—those for which your armies were trained— you will find yourself a fool with empty ranks."

A tense silence filled the air before Blastilv spoke up with a wicked grin. "Imprudent elf, thou viewest my soldiers as mere people, yet they are *far* superior. They are an interconnected swarm; thus, every death, every swing of the sword, every mistake and triumph made by those slain before thee in the yard was known to my trainers as it occurred. Even as ye fought, Mercy and Second trained a unit to err not as those ye did slay." He raised his hands to the heavens. "And that unit is prepared."

A thick cloud of Terovaes rose from the abbey, darkening the skies.

"Relinquish the Hand of the Blessed, Faldénrus," Blastilv shouted, "and I shall consider granting freedom to thee and thy Drevite."

Drained, Adratus collapsed onto the icy ground. "Fucking za," he muttered.

Ubaz landed beside him, taking his hand.

Valqyer crouched atop the wall above them. "Of what does he speak?" he asked Ubaz.

"A stone hand we discovered," Ubaz said, panting. "He used it to create those monsters. Laudanum—the green Faery—said we must get it as far from that priest as possible."

"Thou hast mere seconds, Faldénrus," Blastilv called. "Surrender the hand, or we will take it by force."

Ubaz looked up at Valqyer with urgency in his eyes. "Can you really defeat the Blessed?"

Valqyer shook his head bleakly. "No. 'Twas naught but forceful lies. Like your beloved, I, too, am nearly seid depleted. The slightest flash step will have me collapsing to the ground as well."

"We cannot let him have the hand," Adratus groaned.

Valqyer's gaze fell to the snowy woods some distance from the wall. Two trees stood together in a V. "There is but one option," Valqyer said with a heavy heart. "But there could be dire consequences." Valqyer raised his sword and aimed between the two trees, and a portal into darkness opened up between them. "Fate, be kind to me."

"No!" Blastilv shouted in alarm. "Secure the reprobates!"

Exhausted, Valqyer collapsed from the wall to splash into red snow. "We must get to the Realm," he uttered weakly.

The entire cloud of Terovaes began to move at once.

"Go, Ubaz!" Adratus commanded. "And aid the elf. I am fine on my own."

As the Blessed swarmed toward them, the three haggard warriors pushed on with all their final strength, struggling toward the portal.

Just before they passed between the trees, Valqyer whispered:

"There is no other option. Fate, be kind to me."

At the Crossroads of Swords

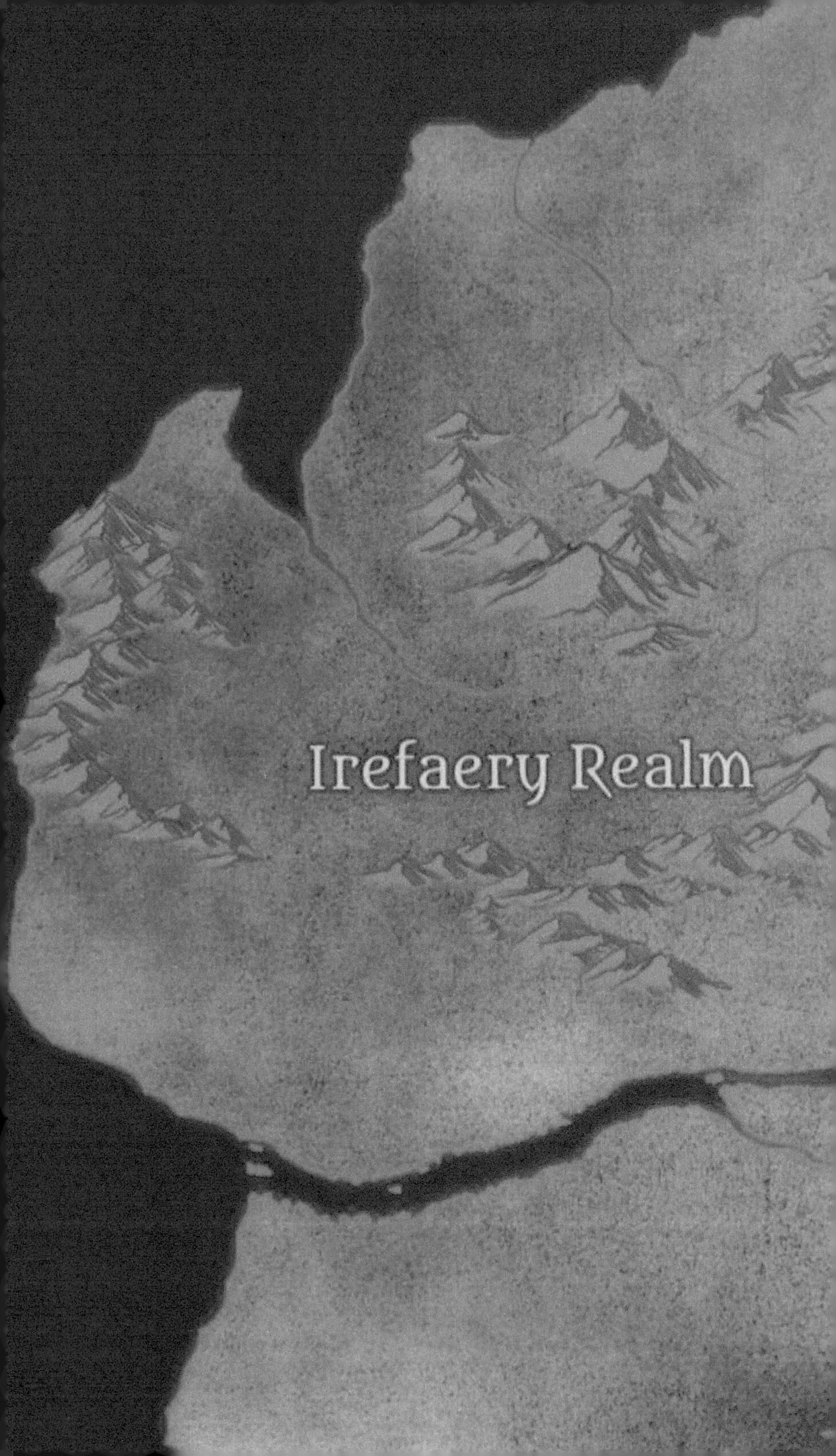

Irefaery Realm

CHAPTER EIGHTY

Immediately After

Cold.

Or, more accurately, a lack of warmth.

An empty feeling slightly beneath tepid.

It was not anything quite enough to produce a shiver, but was just enough to cause a vexing discomfort while providing no real sensation whatsoever.

A hollow feeling. Unnerving. Apathy made climate.

The landscape was black on black on black and smelled of nothing.

This bleak place where Ubaz now found himself was a dark forest bisected by a road of rusted iron. The road's surface angled slightly downward from its center and reminded him of a massive blade. The trees were black glass—some cracked, some shattered, some fallen completely to the slick black ground.

Two such trees stood together as a V, and between them, a portal stood open to snowy Reality.

There, through this twisting portal, countless Terovaes in flight rushed toward the opening. It was through this ethereal rift that Ubaz, with his love and the elf boy, had just entered this ominous place.

With a wave of his hand, Valqyer closed it. And the lone connection to Reality faded away.

Valqyer then crumbled to the rusted road. Adratus, also exhausted from battle, fell near him. Both slept but breathed.

Lost, alone, Ubaz stood in a place more foreign than any destination he'd ever known.

"The Otherworld?" he muttered as he walked cautiously, lifting his ebony bow and nocking an arrow.

Even the sky was bizarre: blackness lit dimly as dusk, but with neither sun nor moons nor stars. Instead, streaky crimson clouds, faintly glowing, offered little light. They twisted around one another in quick shifting currents covering the sky's entirety.

The place frightened Ubaz in a way that he could not understand, and he felt it thoroughly throughout his body—a child's fright—nothing he should feel for a place that had offered him no reason. Yet, knowing that the fear was irrational did nothing to quell it.

He walked on.

No wind was here, no temperature, no sound. He wanted to cry out at the absence of things he'd barely noticed all his life.

Half a dozen orbs of crimson light darted past him, leaving trails—fear and anger and melancholia—in their wake.

Ubaz followed their darting flight, albeit briefly, until he arrived at a point where the rusted road connected with two others, each leading off diagonally to his left and right. There, at the triangular intersection, stood what appeared to be a Terovae woman in her early forties, her skin as pale as snow and her hair and wings as black as a raven's feather, matching the velvet of her dress. Around her slender neck, she wore a thick ring of silver; its ends, at her throat, were fashioned as the heads of fierce birds with a large black gem held between their two beaks.

She remained well-postured and unnaturally still, her eyes closed. Her arms were crossed over her breasts. Her hands, at her shoulders, each held a rusted longsword angled upward.

Mesmerized, Ubaz gripped his bow and drew hesitantly nearer, stopping ten feet away. Mesmerized, he stared.

"Would you use my own bow against me?" Even as she spoke, she did not move, save for a minor motion of her crimson lips.

He lowered the bow, sliding it into his quiver, and stepped forward.

Her whispered words seem to surround him. "I can feel your sadness," she said. "The loss of the Feah agonizes me, as well."

Ubaz jolted at the words as he released a whimper from deep within his aching core. The acknowledgment from the strange being, though slight, caused all that he had hidden and suppressed to well up quickly, overwhelming him. He fell to his knees before her and grabbed his head with both arms.

She maintained her unmoving posture of strength, swords still held high.

"Sorry," he said at length, sniffing and wiping his eyes. "Sorry." His voice cracked as he said, "I've lost the last of me family now. And most of me tribe, too. Seems the whole fecking world's falling apart."

"You are correct," she said, still not moving, still not showing any emotion whatsoever. "It is. The end of the world—perhaps." Her black wings gradually expanded from her back until they reached their full span, and then her voice echoed around him as a powerful force, pressing against his chest: "You stand at the Crossroads of Swords."

On his knees, his body throbbing, he stared up at her, watching as her hands slowly lowered, the swords within them descending to point at the roads on either side of her. "The path you choose shall dictate the fate of the entire world of Perdinok."

"No." Ubaz stood. "Sorry, your words are probably meant for my husband, a Tridulan prefect, or the elf boy who brought us here. Not me. I'm nothing, me."

"My warning is for all within the Perdinokian Realm, which hastens to destruction."

"Right." He nodded solemnly. "'Tis probably for the best, then—that the warning's not for me, directly. There's not much left of me." He looked at her a moment longer, observing her perfect stillness. "Right, then." He began to walk away, shoulders slumped and wings loose behind him.

"Hide there in the shadows, outcast, for the Light has banished you," she whispered. "Mourn your solitude. Mourn your loss. Or open your eyes and see that they have banished more than they have kept. The shadows are filled with many outcasts. And your solitude is an illusion. Divided, all Others will perish. United, all Others will prevail. An army lies within the shadows."

Ubaz turned back to her and shouted, "You didn't see what I saw! They have an army of mindless, fully obedient people who will not stop until we are destroyed. And it will only grow stronger." He huffed. "There's no *prevailing*. The Dayigans have already won."

"Then you have chosen your path." In a swirling crimson mist, she faded away.

He looked toward the glossy black ground and sighed. "Leave, then. Because you know I'm right."

The black landscape cracked and broke open around him. He spread his wings and hovered above, as fissures grew larger.

Rain began to fall, but it was like an illusion. It fell, this rain, through the black trees, touching nothing, wetting nothing. It passed through him as well, yet he felt nothing.

And when the countless droplets reached the glassy ground, they did not puddle or splash, but continued through.

Sadness. It hit Ubaz with an intensity so strong that he could barely maintain flight or breathe. His uncle was dead. Nearly all of his people were dead. His home was destroyed. Every day in the dungeon beneath the abbey, Ubaz had feared it would be the last.

Overwhelmed, he landed at the edge of the cracked ground, only a foot from where it fell away. He took a knee as he began weeping, with cries heaving up from his core. He grabbed his ginger hair within his fingers and shouted until his throat burned.

Torrents of illusory rain fell. Torrents of tragic memories washed over him. Not just the new, but the old, just as potent. The death of his father. The abduction of his mother. Lann holding his hand as he led him through all the other children orphaned in a day.

All Ubaz could feel was a void within his soul, an emptiness though heavy, weighing him so unbearably that he felt he would fall.

Fall: The thought rippled through him as he looked to where the ground stopped. Nothing was there. Nothing. Never had he truly seen nothing. When one says he sees nothing, he invariably sees something. Not now. Now, Ubaz saw overwhelming nothing in the gaps within the broken ground.

Ubaz neared a gap.

It seemed to pull him, to welcome him.

He could hear nothing, not even the rain.

The loss within him was so intense. A million images of a million tragedies. There was so much hurt and emptiness, so much weight pulling him down.

More of the ground cracked around him.

But there was no hurt in nothingness. Ubaz neared it. On his hands and knees, he stared into the paradise of the abyss.

The rain continued to fall.

Losing his family and friends, none of that mattered in the dark nothing.

"Escape," Ubaz whispered.

How long would I fall before I no longer felt anything?

"Ubaz!"

The ground broke beneath his hand and crumbled downward, spiraling into black beyond black.

He was ready to go with it.

The rain fell harder.

"Ubaz, please, come back to me."

He did not look back to the voice of Adratus, nor did he even blink from the abyss. What would he find there, he wondered: Laqyigo, za, oblivion?

Now, Valqyer's voice called out, too, "Your sorrow is rending the ground. You must control it."

"No," he breathed, panting.

"Come to me," Adratus said. "I cannot go any farther, or my weight as a Human will shatter the ground."

"The True Light has taken *everything*," Ubaz said blankly to the gap. His eyes streamed, and he could barely hold himself up. "My world is gone."

"I understand your anguish." It was Valqyer's again. "Once, I was an artist, which is all I wished to be, yet Blastilv ripped my world apart. Now, I must take up arms, though it pains me. But we *must* persevere."

"Why?" Ubaz watched more ground fall away into dark infinity.

"Because we must," Adratus said firmly. "Because no one else will. Help me form a *real* alliance between our peoples. I vowed that unity to Lann, but I need you, Ubaz. For I cannot do it alone."

The ground crumbled from beneath Ubaz. But he spread his wings and rose above.

He cast a final glance into the void before flying to Adratus.

"The army in the shadows," Ubaz said, as he landed in front of him. "The unity of all that the Dayigans tried to destroy. Do you think it could be enough to stop them?"

"I'm uncertain. The Dayigans hate any who differ from them, so their numbers are great. Yet those they despise share no other commonalities. Unifying them seems unlikely."

Ubaz took Adratus's hands. "But we must try."

Adratus nodded in agreement.

Their lips met in a prolonged and tender kiss, and the rain vanished, as if it had never been.

Ubaz rested his head against Adratus's bare chest, finding solace in his warmth amid this comfortless place as the prefect wrapped his mighty arms around him. "Where have you brought us, Valqyer?" Ubaz asked. "Is this the Otherworld?"

"That is the name bestowed upon it by your people." Valqyer stepped forward, scanning the black landscape. "This land of utter darkness is what remains of the first Faery Realm, that which was created over your continent of Bikia. Millennia ago, the People drove my kind away through what is called the Sorrow Passage, and the Old Realm was left to the Irefaeries. And the malevolent Irefaeries drew in twisted energies from the Plane of Chaos causing this realm to blacken and decay. Now, this is the Irefaery Realm, and most Faeries cannot venture here."

"I think I saw an Irefaery," Ubaz said. "But she didn't seem *malevolent*. She *spoke* to me. She said the bow I found is hers."

Valqyer glanced at the ebony bow in Ubaz's quiver. "Forgive me. I had meant to protect you from them, but the battle drained me more than I had anticipated."

"You need not apologize," Adratus said. "You have saved us by bringing us here."

"I saved not *you*." Valqyer turned his black eyes away. "I saved the hand, whatever it may be. And I shall face grave consequences for my actions."

The elven boy surveyed their surroundings. "Methinks the Irefaery you encountered is but one who watches. *Am I correct?*" Valqyer's words rang out into the sky. "Why do you watch us like a panther lurking in the shade? Pray you, reveal yourself."

"Thou hast brought *People* into *my* realm," a male voice echoed from all directions.

Scanning the strange skies, Ubaz moved slightly from Adratus and drew his bow.

"I had no choice, Your Majesty," Valqyer called back.

"There is always a choice."

In a blur of speed and a flash of light, a male Faery stood tall upon the rusty road. He was without clothes and appeared nearly Human. Muscular though lean. His skin was inky purple, and his eyes were iridescent white. His ears drew to points, with his long blue hair brushed behind them. Grown from his head, two great antlers, like those of a mighty buck, crowned him.

Valqyer bowed his head. "Forgive me, O Night Faery, Keeper of the Bikian Realm."

The Night Faery turned his glowing white eyes directly on the people, and Ubaz felt his throat close as sweat glistened on his brow.

Adratus again pulled him into his arms, a warmth so welcomed in this dismal place.

"Hearken, elf," said the Night Faery, "though I know thou art already aware. No People, save for Gels, are permitted in my Realm. And their allowance is granted by an ancient agreement predating even myself."

Valqyer remained silent but hung his head.

"I could perchance, overlook the transgression of bringing mortals into the Realm," continued the Night Faery, "hadst thou not done so during a fierce attack. What if thou had not been able to close the door thou didst open? What if all the horrors of that dreadful abbey had spilt forth here like a swarm of nightmares? Thou knowest well the dangers Blastilv could bring with access to the Realm."

"I saw to it that the Realm was locked to Blastilv. And to Lyforia, who he controlled."

"And yet, thou didst open it again upon his doorstep."

The commanding voice of a woman sounded from the black, crystalline trees. "Prithee, be calm, O Night Faery." And from this murky forest emerged a woman of noble bearing and regal stature, clad only in shimmering, leaf-green skin. Her right forearm and hand were noticeably absent. Her eyes shined as iridescent white light, and her lustrous orange hair billowed behind her, as if she moved through water. "The actions of the Sword Elf were just."

"'Tis her," Adratus whispered behind Ubaz's ear, "Lady Laudanum. Yet as I first saw her, in my vision. Though . . . she had insectoid wings before."

"Alas, dear Absolver," Laudanum began, "I am no longer as I once was and shall never be so again. And these changes run far deeper than the mere loss of wings. Yet, thou hast shown me love whilst I was hidden in a mask of sorrow. And revealed thyself." She turned to face the Night Faery. "These People and this elf are heroes. I will not allow any harm to befall them."

"Laws have been broken," the Night Faery maintained. "Penalties must be paid. The actions of the Sword Elf this day have only proven what hath long been true: he is no longer one of us. Therefore, I rescind his access to the Realm."

"No!" Valqyer shouted desperately. "I beseech you, O great Night Faery, whither shall I go? No place have I amongst the People."

"That is not my concern." Thunder rumbled as he pointed his hand at the elf.

With a scream, Valqyer vanished.

Adratus tightened his arms around Ubaz, yet Ubaz felt small and vulnerable before these powerful beings.

Laudanum stood solemn and silent, though her face tensed and her eyes narrowed.

The Night Faery turned to the Human and the Terovae. "As for you, fear not, for your arrival here was not your own wrongdoing. But now I shall remove you from my Realm at once."

"But first," Laudanum said calmly as she approached Adratus and Ubaz. "Listen well: it is imperative that ye find a way to destroy the Hand of Fersivolíel. The fate of the world now rests in your hands."

"The gap where your realm cracked open," Ubaz spoke up. "Throw it there into nothing."

Adratus began to untie it from his belt.

"That will not be sufficient," Laudanum said. "Yet thou must find a way."

"How?" Adratus asked.

She turned away, toward the turbulent sky wherein streaks of crimson sped in twisted frenzies within the black. "Thou must find a way."

Thunder sounded as the Night Faery cast his hand toward the People.

In an instant, Adratus and Ubaz found themselves in another horrible place—a natural forest, though ravaged by fire and smelling of death. Many of the massive trees had fallen as charred corpses across the blackened ground.

"No," Ubaz whispered as he realized: "This is my home." Captured in the frenzy, he hadn't seen the aftermath. Now, he fell to his knees on soot.

"I choose the path," he whispered. "I choose the path that stops this from happening to anybody else. I will unite the army in the shadows."

An eerie silence lingered as he shook.

The Encroaching Chaos

SERIES

The tales will continue...

Visit

jeremiahcain.com

to find these and future books.

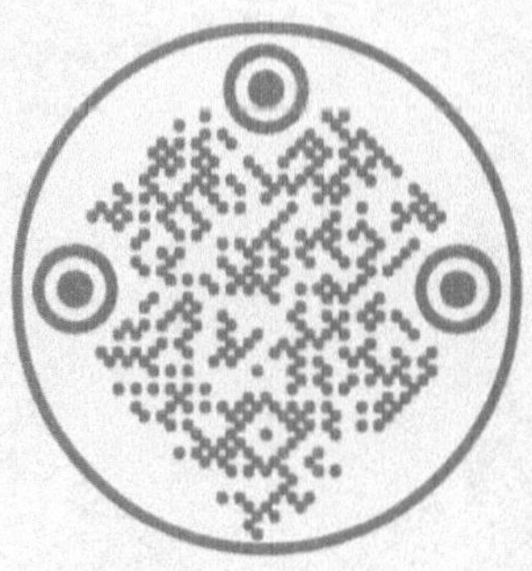